They stood facing each other, inches apart, on her front porch. Jewel's heart thumped. "I'm glad I went."

"Are you?" His brows tightened as he took a step closer, forcing her to look up.

Her throat worked frantically. "Very."

"That's good to know because I want to do it again."

Jewel swallowed. "Lunch?"

"Dinner...and then breakfast."

The implication was clear. Heat flashed through her limbs.

"How does that sound?"

Her head swam. "It sounds..."

Before she could form the words, he'd slid his arm around her waist and pulled her flush against the hard lines of his body, and then the world disappeared as his head came down and those lips that she had fantasized kissing covered hers. The kiss was electric, slow and sweet. She couldn't think over the hum that vibrated deep in his throat as he deepened their kiss, teasing her mouth with a swipe of his tongue. Her entire body vibrated and felt weak all at once. Her fingers held on to the tight ropes of his arms, and all she could piece together in her head was that she didn't want it to end.

Dear Reader,

Whether you are a returning or newly inducted fan of The Lawsons of Louisiana series, let me introduce you to another member of the family—Craig Lawson. With all of my Lawson family members, I want to bring my readers not only a great love story but also a story that touches readers, with characters that you will grow to love and root for as I have.

Freed from the reins of his powerful father, Craig Lawson has built his own legacy, but it has left him with a hole in his heart. A hole that is filled by artist Jewel Fontaine. Although she has her own demons to deal with, Craig offers her a new beginning. Of course, their journey won't be an easy one.

At the center of all of the Lawson tales is the importance and resilience of family. I hope that you will welcome the newest members into your family of characters that help you believe in the power of love and its limitless possibilities.

I want to thank each and every one of my readers for your continued love and support throughout my years of writing.

Sit back, relax and enjoy!

Until next time,

Donna Hill

FOR THE
LOVE OF
You

DONNA
HILL

HARLEQUIN® KIMANI™ ROMANCE

Recycling programs
for this product may
not exist in your area.

ISBN-13: 978-0-373-86457-7

For the Love of You

For questions and comments about the quality of this book please contact us at CustomerService@Harlequin.com.

H HARLEQUIN®

™ www.Harlequin.com

Printed in U.S.A.

Donna Hill began writing novels in 1990. Since that time she has had more than forty titles published, which include full-length novels and novellas. Two of her novels and one novella were adapted for television. She has won numerous awards for her body of work. She is also the editor of five novels, two of which were nominated for awards. She easily moves from romance to erotica, horror, comedy and women's fiction. She was the first recipient of the *RT Book Reviews* Trailblazer Award, won the *RT Book Reviews* Career Achievement Award and currently teaches writing at the Frederick Douglass Creative Arts Center.

Donna lives in Brooklyn with her family. Visit her website at donnahill.com.

Books by Donna Hill
Harlequin Kimani Romance

Love Becomes Her
If I Were Your Woman
After Dark
Sex and Lies
Seduction and Lies
Temptation and Lies
Longing and Lies
Private Lessons
Spend My Life with You
Secret Attraction
Sultry Nights
Everything Is You
Mistletoe, Baby
The Way You Love Me
My Love at Last
For the Love of You

Visit the Author Profile page
at Harlequin.com for more titles.

This novel is lovingly dedicated to my dearest friend and mentor, Gwynne Forster. I miss you, my friend.

Acknowledgments

I wish to thank my ever patient editor, Glenda Howard, for never giving up on me.

Chapter 1

The ten-hour flight from London Heathrow Airport landed in New Orleans, Louisiana, on time, to the delight of the weary passengers, Craig Lawson among them. His return home after more than ten years came with a mixture of regret and anticipation. Regret that for all those years he'd never felt compelled to return to the place where he'd grown up, and anticipation for the reason why he'd finally come home.

After breezing through customs and collecting his luggage, he and his business partner and lifelong buddy, Anthony Maxwell, headed for the pickup area and the car that awaited them. They passed a newsstand, and Anthony tapped Craig's arm and lifted his head in the direction of the magazines, where Craig's face graced the covers of *Entertainment Weekly*, *Variety* and *Black Enterprise*.

"If I didn't know you better, I'd think you were important," Anthony teased.

Craig chuckled. "As long as the importance translates into success at the box office," he said. He took a last glance at the magazines and shook his head. When he'd broken ties with his family—his father, specifically—and headed to Los Angeles to pursue his dream as a screenwriter, it had been one of the most difficult things he'd had to do. To a Lawson, family was everything. Yet as hard as it was, looking back, he would not have done anything differently. As much as his father would like to believe that what he did for a living was nothing more than pandering, the real reason for his distaste for his son's profession went much deeper. Craig grew weary of fighting that ghost. So he left and never looked back. Now he was one of the most successful and celebrated screenwriters and movie directors on the East and the West Coasts. He had an Oscar, a Golden Globe and an NAACP Image Award under his belt. Behind closed doors he was called the golden boy. To his face he was Mr. Lawson.

As the duo exited baggage claim, they walked by the rows of drivers holding up signs with the names of their passengers. Craig's driver spotted him first and stepped out of the line.

"Mr. Lawson," the female driver greeted him with a tip of her head. "I'll get a cart for your bags."

Craig's right brow lifted in question, and he quickly assessed the stunning young woman in front of him. Even in her stark uniform of black slacks and jacket and a starched white shirt she was a work of art. The corner of his mouth curved ever so slightly as he watched her retrieve a luggage cart and return to them. Although he knew it was her job, the Southern gentleman in him wouldn't allow her to do it.

"Let me get the bags on the cart. We'll meet you at the car."

"I can take care of the bags, Mr. Lawson," she mildly protested.

"I'm sure that you can." He easily hoisted the over-size bags onto the cart. "But I'd rather that you didn't. My mama didn't raise me that way."

The young woman flushed, pressed her polished lips together and murmured a thank-you. "The car is this way." She started off toward the ground transportation area.

"Don't distract her from her driving," Anthony teased under his breath as they dutifully followed her to the exit.

"Not my intention. But I will say, it's a pleasure following her lead."

Truth be told, the last thing on his mind was getting with a woman. Although he had a reputation as a ladies' man, especially his leading ladies, it was all smoke and mirrors. The women who drifted in and out of his life were just that—transient. He found none that could excite his mind as well as his body, so he kept his relationships short, practical and amicable. For all of his numerous dalliances, there wasn't one woman who could say she had not been treated like a lady while she'd spent time with him.

"How does it feel to be back?" Anthony asked as they settled into the air-conditioned comfort of the town car.

Craig drew in a breath and glanced out the window as the Louisiana landscape unfolded in front of them. "Still trying to process it. Feels strange. I mean, things kind of look the same but different—smaller." He chuckled.

"You plan to see the family?"

Craig's jaw flexed. He leaned his elbow on the armrest and braced his chin on his fist. "I don't know. I'm sure they've heard that I'm back. Guess it wouldn't be right not to check in on my sister and brother and my cousins." He paused. "And I know that's not what you meant." He flashed his friend a look of censure. "I'm not going to see him."

Anthony held up his hands. "Hey, just asking a question, man."

Craig went back to staring out the window. The rift between father and son wasn't some simple spat that could be rectified with an adult conversation. His father made himself perfectly clear years ago that if Craig were to pursue "this trashy movie thing," he was cut off from the family and he didn't want him to set foot back in his house. His father, Jake Lawson, ran his family the way he ran his international land development enterprise—with an unbending hand. He couldn't—or rather wouldn't—see beyond his own narrow lens to be able to accept that his dreams and goals were not everyone else's. He kept Craig's sister, Alyse, and brother, Myles, on a short leash, but he never could control Craig. And Craig knew that his father's disillusionment with the Hollywood life ran deep, and his mother was at the root of it. But he wasn't his mother.

He pulled his cell phone out of his pocket and speed-dialed his location scout Paul Frazier.

"Yeah, Paul, we landed about an hour ago. In the car now, headed to the hotel. Look, I want you to be ready to take us over to the location when I arrive at the hotel. Yeah, I know I said tomorrow. I want to see it today. Cool. See you in a few." He disconnected the call.

"You don't want to chill for a while before going over there?" Anthony asked.

"Naw. I've seen pictures, and that's about it. I know Paul is good at what he does, but if I'm going to sink my money and a helluva lot of time and people's talent in this film, I want everything to be perfect. I'd rather find out sooner than later."

Jewel Fontaine took her cup of chamomile tea out to the back veranda of her sprawling pre–Civil War home. The house on Prytania Street, which was once a plantation, sat on five acres of land with a creek that ran the length of the property into the wooded area beyond. One of the former slave shacks still stood on the property, but it had been converted into an art studio when Jewel's career took off. Every time Jewel surveyed her home, she was infused with the spirits of her ancestors who'd toiled on this land and served in those rooms. As an artist she firmly believed in the sanctity of preserving the past for future generations. The constant work that had to be done for the upkeep of the Fontaine home and the cost of maintenance had all but drained her accumulated wealth from her art career, compounded with the care of her ailing father—she was on the precipice of being broke.

The idea that she might lose her home kept her up at night and dogged her steps during the day. She hadn't worked or sold a piece of art or sculpture in several years. She'd become disillusioned following her last poorly reviewed show nearly five years earlier, and then the decline of her father's health had turned her away from her passion. She refocused her energies on taking care of the man who had sacrificed everything for her. But in the past six months, she'd realized she couldn't do it alone, and she'd had to hire a live-in nurse. The cost was astronomical.

Then the call came, and like a miracle, her financial problems would be solved. CL Productions wanted to rent her home for the next six to eight weeks to shoot a film and was willing to pay an exorbitant amount of money for the privilege. She'd nearly leaped through the phone at the chance to lift the financial burden off her chest. The influx of cash would give her some breathing room and a chance to find other sources of revenue.

Jewel took a sip of her tea and gazed out onto the midafternoon glory. The tight churning in her stomach had finally begun to ease.

"Ms. Fontaine!"

Jewel spilled her tea down the front of her floral sundress as she jumped up at the frantic call of her name, which could only mean one thing—*Daddy*. She ran across the main level and up the winding staircase. The sound of something crashing and shattering quickened her steps. She reached her father's bedroom door, and her heart stood still.

Craig didn't waste much time at the hotel. Now that he'd arrived in Louisiana, the adrenaline of his upcoming project pumped through his veins, making him more brusque and antsy than usual. He began spouting orders to his team the minute he walked into the suite. Within moments everyone was scurrying around like their jobs depended on it.

Less than a half hour after arriving, Craig, Anthony, Paul and his assistant, along with the photographer and driver, were heading to the Fontaine mansion.

"Why the rush?" Anthony asked again. "You generally don't get involved at this level."

Craig adjusted his shades on the bridge of his nose. "I have a bigger investment this time. I want everything to be on point and run like clockwork. No screwups. We don't have the usual wiggle room on time and cost overruns."

Anthony nodded his head. "Agreed." He clapped Craig on the shoulder. "You've done this countless times, bro," he said, lowering his voice. "This is going to be your best project yet. We got your back on this."

"'Preciate that." He returned his attention to the script and line notes. The film chronicled a poor black family that rose from sharecropping to command the upper echelons of finance, real estate and politics, with great sex scenes and plenty of family drama and scandal thrown in. He wondered if his family would recognize themselves in the characters. Of course, he'd changed names and some professions to suit the storyline.

The driver turned the black Suburban onto a winding road that led to the Fontaine mansion. According to his location scouts' notes, the home had once been a plantation and one of the shacks that had housed former slaves on the expansive land still remained.

When the home appeared and spread out in front of him, it was like being thrown back into time to the days of *Gone With the Wind*. The only thing missing was the Confederate flag. The SUV came to a stop.

Craig got out and fully took in the setting, already beginning to visualize the scenes and where they would take place. It was better than any description or photograph could capture. This was exactly the setting he wanted. What he needed to do now was meet the owner and set up the official working arrangement. Generally this was something that Paul handled, but this project was his dream movie. It was his first time at bat as writer, director *and* executive producer. He had a lot riding on this and knew that there were plenty who wished him well and an equal amount that couldn't wait to see him fail.

"Anthony and Paul, come with me. You guys can wait here," he said to the photographer and Paul's assistant. He flipped a page on his clipboard. *Jewel Fontaine.* It sounded like the name of someone that would live in a house like this. He strode down the pathway that led to the palatial entrance. The front was framed by six white columns, three on each side of the double front door. It was two levels with a wraparound terrace on the second floor and paneled windows.

Craig led his small entourage up the three steps to the front door. He rang the bell and made a mental note to have a temporary door knocker installed for the film.

Moments later the door opened and a woman dressed in what appeared to be a nurse's uniform stood in front of them.

"Can I help you?"

"Craig Lawson. Ms. Fontaine?"

"No. I'm… Ms. Fontaine is busy right now. It may be best if you come back."

"No. I don't think that would be best. I'd appreciate it if you could get Ms. Fontaine. Please let her know that Craig Lawson is here to talk with her about the film."

The woman in white huffed and rolled her eyes. "If you go round back, I'll ask Ms. Fontaine to meet you there."

"Thank you," Craig said, his tone softening to match the smile on his lips.

"I'll get Ms. Fontaine," she said, her tone decidedly changed.

Craig turned and got a quick *I told you so* look from Anthony. He ignored it.

The trio rounded the building and found themselves in a mini paradise.

"You did good, Paul," Craig said, slapping him heartily on the back.

"Thanks, boss. Ron was the one that actually found it," Paul said of his assistant.

Craig pressed his lips together and nodded. What he appreciated about his staff was that they never hesitated to spread their support and share the credit. He set the clipboard down on a circular white metal table that was shaded by a huge umbrella. There was a half cup of tea on the table and a newspaper that had fallen to the ground. He reached down, picked it up and placed it back on the table. He turned at the sound of a door opening behind him.

The woman didn't simply walk through the door. She swept in like a character from a novel. Every nerve in Craig's body vibrated. Like the filmmaker that he was, he cataloged every inch of her, from the riotous swirl of cinnamon curls that seemed to want to break free from the knot on the top of her head to the high cheeks, wide expressive honey-toned eyes, sleek arching brows and full pouty lips all set on a flawless canvas of nut brown. The loosely flowing sundress that bared her shoulder and reached her ankles did nothing to camouflage the curves beneath.

Jewel stopped in front of him. "Mr. Lawson?"

"Yes. And you must be Ms. Fontaine." He extended his hand.

Jewel placed her hand in his, and Craig felt the heat of their contact race straight to his groin. He shifted his stance slightly and cleared his throat to give himself a moment to recover.

"Thanks for seeing me."

"You didn't give me much choice, Mr. Lawson."

"You're right. I realize you were expecting me—us—tomorrow, but I wanted to see the estate for myself and meet you as soon as possible. I hope we can talk for a few minutes, go over the details and work out the schedule."

Jewel lifted her chin ever so slightly, a move that Craig had seen his sister use whenever she was ready to do battle. He reflexively clenched his jaw. Craig glanced over his shoulder and angled his body. "Ms. Fontaine, this is my business partner and a producer of the film, Anthony Maxwell."

Anthony stepped in between the standoff and extended his hand. "Pleasure to meet you, Ms. Fontaine. Your home is better than any pictures."

She offered up a hint of a smile. "Thank you." She

turned her attention to Craig, and he felt her stare right in his center. "We need to talk, Mr. Lawson."

His radar went on full alert, and every instinct told him that this was not going to go well. "Of course."

Jewel stepped down off the back porch and walked toward the brook that ran behind the house. Craig fell in step next to her and wondered what that incredible scent was that floated around her.

"Mr. Lawson—" She stopped and turned to him, and he was hit in the chest again by the depth of her eyes. "I don't know how to say this, but—" She paused, looked at the water and then at him. "I'm going to have to back out of this arrangement."

He'd expected a discussion about more money, no Mondays or eating in the kitchen, or whatever other quirky thing homeowners wanted when they rented out their property, but not this.

Craig bent his head toward her in an almost combative move. "Excuse me?"

"I've changed my mind. This may be a great opportunity, but it will be too disruptive and... I can't allow this." She folded her arms beneath the swell of her breasts. "I'm sorry," she said softly.

Craig was totally thrown. It took him a minute to process what she was saying. Months of work would go down the drain; the time it would take to find a new location would cost thousands and set the production schedule back by any number of days, possibly weeks. As the scenario played in his head, his level of pissed off rose. He'd never been one to take no for an answer, and now wasn't the time to get started.

"Listen—" He reached out to touch her, and the instant his fingertips touched her bare arm he knew it was a major mistake. What felt like electricity brushed across his skin. "I, uh, totally get it that having a film crew in your home is a pretty big imposition." He gave her his best Oscar-winning smile, coated with Nawlins drawl. He held up his hands. "I promise you we will totally respect your home. Whatever rules you set down…that's what it will be."

He watched the pink tip of her tongue peek out and stroke her bottom lip. He swallowed.

"It's much more complicated than that, Mr. Lawson," she said softly, the hard stance that she'd taken earlier seeming to ease somewhat. "I deeply apologize for any inconvenience—"

"If it's about money, we can work that out. It's a big imposition, and you should be compensated accordingly."

"What makes you think I need or want your money!" Her hands dropped to her sides, and her fingers curled into her palms.

The 360 in her tone and body was so sudden, Craig actually took a step back. "I wasn't trying to imply that you did," he said, keeping his voice low and even in the hope of rescuing this rapidly sinking ship. "I'd really like to talk this out. I'm sure we can do whatever it is that you need to be comfortable."

Jewel slowly shook her head. Her lids fluttered rapidly, and her nostrils flared even as she turned her lips inward and tightened them.

Craig took a cautious step closer. There were two things he was really good at: finding movieworthy material and noting the warning signs in a woman's face. *This* woman was on the verge of tears, and he was pretty sure that it had nothing to do with the film, at least not directly.

"I'm sorry," she managed and stuck out her hand.

Craig's gaze ran over her face, but she wouldn't look directly at him. He took her hand and slowly let his fingers envelop hers. "Thank you, Ms. Fontaine. I'm sorry that things didn't work out. If you change your mind, you have the number."

She bobbed her head, and he released her hand, turned and headed back to where he'd left Anthony.

"Let's go," he snapped, storming past Anthony.

Anthony double-timed it to catch up. "Yo, what happened?"

Craig slid on his shades. "We'll talk back at the hotel and Paul can start looking for a new job."

By the time the crew returned—very subdued—to the hotel, Craig's ire had diminished by a fraction. At least he'd stopped cussing and tossing death stares at his crew.

"Look," Anthony said, pulling Craig off to the side once they'd entered the suite, "go easy. We've been in tighter situations. We have some alternate locations on tap. We'll find the right venue and keep it moving. Every one of us has screwed up at some point," he added with a knowing look.

Craig grunted. "Yeah. I know. It's just when you feel something in your gut…" He let his words drift away and wondered if he meant the location or Jewel Fontaine. He clapped Anthony on the arm. "You're right. We'll work it out." He slung his hands into his pants pockets and turned to the crew, whose gazes were glued to the floor.

"Okay, look…it appears that we're not going to be able to use the Fontaine location for the shoot. For whatever reason, the lady of the house has changed her mind." He tossed a look in Paul's direction.

Paul shifted his weight and looked appropriately contrite.

"Mr. Lawson..."

Craig turned his attention toward Diane Fisher, one of the assistant location scouts. "Yes?"

She cleared her throat, glanced briefly at Paul then focused on Craig. She lifted her dimpled chin. "It wasn't Paul's fault. He gave me my first assignment. I should have had her sign the contract." She swallowed. "I didn't. I guess I was a little starstruck when I realized who she was. I'm sorry. But this isn't Paul's fault."

Craig held back a smile. He admired loyalty among his friends and his working crew. It was clear to him, however, that there was just a little something more than work between Paul and Diane, which was cool as long as it didn't interfere with the job. He'd give them both a pass on this one.

"Thank you for telling me that, Diane. You'll know for next time."

The wave of relief in the room was palpable. There would be a next time instead of a goodbye.

"In the meantime I want Paul and Diane to get busy with the secondary locations. We can't afford to have this project fall behind schedule." He paused. "Thanks, y'all." He tugged in a breath and exhaled. "I know how hard you work, and you're some of the best in the business. I don't say it much, but I appreciate each of you." He turned and walked into his adjoining room, totally missing the look of outright shock on the faces of his crew.

* * *

Craig closed the door to his room and crossed the plush carpeted floor to the minibar. He poured himself a shot of bourbon on the rocks. He took a deep, satisfying swallow and allowed the smooth liquor to seep into his veins, warming them before he went to stand in front of the floor-to-ceiling window. His eyes cinched at the corners while he rocked his jaw from side to side and looked out on the city that he'd once called home. Had anyone asked him a year ago if he would ever return, he would have said, "Hell, no." But here he was, back home, doing the very thing that had sent him away in the first place. He snorted a laugh at the irony of it all. The prodigal son had returned. By now his father would know that he was back. Why did it still matter?

He turned away from the past, crossed back to the bar and refilled his shot glass. Jake Lawson had been very clear when Craig announced that he was uninterested in learning about, participating in or ultimately running his father's global real estate firm. As far as Jake Lawson was concerned, Craig was on his own, cut off from the family.

It had been ten years, and though he would never admit it, even with all the success he'd attained since he'd left, what he missed was his father and his blessing on all that he'd accomplished. What hurt him the most was not understanding his father's near irrational disdain for Craig's chosen profession. Growing up, Jake had instilled in each of his children the belief that they could achieve anything that they wanted in this world—apparently as long as it was what Jake Lawson wanted his children to achieve.

Wallowing in self-pity and reflection was never Craig's MO, and he didn't plan to start now. What he needed to concentrate on was getting his movie filmed and produced. His work was what was important. It was his validation. Nothing else mattered.

His thoughts shifted to his meeting with Jewel Fontaine. She'd flat-out told him no. *No* was a word that never sat well with him. If he didn't take it from his father, he wouldn't take it from her, either. Everyone could be persuaded. Everyone had a button that could be pushed. He simply had to discover what her yes button was.

He tossed back the rest of his drink, a plan formulating in his head. He smiled. Tomorrow was another day. He might have lost the first battle, but the fight was far from over.

The house was blissfully quiet. Jewel walked out onto the back veranda and sat on a cushioned lounge chair. She placed her cup of tea on the table beside her and tucked her feet beneath her. The sound of cicadas peppered the night, and the scent of lavender from her garden helped to soothe her unsettled soul. Her nerves were still on edge, a combination of the unannounced visit by Craig Lawson and her father's latest episode. It was hard to distinguish which event had the greater effect on her. Meeting Craig Lawson had had a visceral impact. She felt as if every sense, every nerve was suddenly jolted awake when they met eye to eye and he took her hand. It still seemed to tingle. But that was silly. It was no more than her overwrought emotions at work.

Then there was her father. Her heart ached as if

it had been pounded and abused then shoved back into her chest. Watching the man that she loved, admired and worshipped slowly disappear was, on some days, more than she could manage. Today was one of those days.

Jewel got up from the lounge chair and walked over to the railing that embraced the veranda. She gazed out on the star-filled night. If only she could cast a wish upon a star. She would wish that she had her career back. She would wish that she had her father back, and she would wish that Craig Lawson had never entered her life to remind her of what she'd left behind.

The choices and sacrifices she'd had to make over the past few years had begun to pile upon her soul, weighing it down, an anchor determined to tug her into the depths of no return.

Her stomach twisted with resentment and the guilt of it. She had no right to feel those emotions. But she did. She begrudged the world that had turned its back on her. She cursed fate that had leveled its will upon her father and locked them both in a spinning cycle of decline.

She sighed heavily and searched out the heavens for a star. If only it were that easy. In another six months, she would lose the home she'd grown up in. She'd lose the ability to take care of her father. Opportunity had knocked today—literally—and yet she couldn't let it in. What was she going to do?

Chapter 2

Jewel had spent a sleepless night tossing and turning as dozens of unattainable scenarios played in a loop inside her head. Finally giving up on sleep, she rose with the sun, checked on her father to find him comfortably sleeping, and then puttered around in the kitchen, determined to find a solution to her untenable situation.

Making something always seemed to help clear her thoughts. Had it been at an earlier phase of her life, she would have been found in her studio, sculpting her next piece of art or creating her next abstract on canvas. She couldn't remember when she'd last molded a piece of clay or chiseled granite or stroked vibrant colors with a paintbrush. Instead her hands and her mind realigned themselves and found a new purpose in baking. The same artistry that she'd used in her work transferred itself to create unique and sumptuous cakes, pies, cookies and muffins. She sold some of her confections to a local baker from time to time and had even prepared one-of-a-kind wedding cakes. Minerva, her father's home attendant and Jewel's pseudoconfidante, had for the past year been encouraging her to pursue her baking—take it to the next level, build a business, she'd said. But Jewel couldn't. She was an artist—at one time a renowned artist who traveled the world and held standing-room-only launches in galleries here in the States and abroad. Baking was a poor second cousin, an outlet for her idle hands and nothing more.

Today felt like a blueberry muffin day, she reasoned, and while the house remained under the blanket of slumber, Jewel created her other brand of magic.

By the time the sun was in full bloom, Jewel's kitchen was filled with the warmth and aroma of a high-end bakery. She eased the tray from the oven and placed it on the counter to cool then prepared a pot of chamomile tea. With her cup of tea, she took and a plate with a muffin and homemade jam to the veranda and picked up the newspaper en route.

Nestled in her favorite spot, she opened the paper and was hit in the center of her being by the virile image of Craig Lawson, whose face graced the cover with the caption New Orleans Prodigal Son Returns.

The two-page article went on to talk about his meteoric rise in the movie industry and of course the iconic Lawson family, of which he was a part. It hinted at a rift between father and son, but the details were sketchy, giving way to more questions than answers. The one steady theme was that his return and the ensuing project would bring business to the city, as the article indicated that Lawson was a staunch supporter of employing local talent for his projects.

"A regular saint," Jewel murmured around a mouthful of muffin. She washed it down with a healthy swallow of tea.

She gazed off into the distance. *Craig Lawson.* He was like many of the stars that peppered his films—larger than life. There was a magnetic pull about him, a swagger and self-assurance that was nearly impossible to resist. She'd felt it when they faced each other, when he clasped her hand in his. She'd felt herself become trapped in the undertow of his dark eyes, and it had taken all that she had to pull herself free. But at what cost?

"There you are."

Jewel glanced up and over her shoulder and smiled. "Good morning."

"I see you've been busy." Minerva stepped fully onto the veranda.

"A little." She laughed, but then her expression turned somber. "How's Dad?"

"Resting. I'm going to get him his breakfast shortly. I know he'll be happy to get one of your famous muffins to go with it."

"Hmm." She lowered her gaze.

Minerva sat down next to Jewel and placed a comforting hand on her knee. "There are going to be bad days," she said softly. "You can't let it overwhelm you. And...as hard as it is for us to accept, there will be more bad days than good."

Jewel dragged in a breath. "I know," she whispered. She turned to Minerva. "I'm scared, Minny."

"Of course you are. But it's going to be all right. It will. What you have to do is remember that and be the strong woman that he raised you to be. That's what he needs now."

Jewel slowly shook her head. "I don't know if I can. We're going broke, and fast. How will I take care of him, this house—you?"

Minerva frowned. "I thought you were going to let them do the film. They were willing to pay a pretty big sum, from what I remember you telling me."

"I turned them down."

"Why on earth would you do that?"

"After yesterday's episode with Dad, I realized that it would be too much for him, too much disturbance. I couldn't risk that."

Minerva was pensive for a moment. "It that the real reason?"

"What do you mean? Of course it is. What other reason could I have?"

"Maybe it's because *you* aren't ready to reconnect with the world or forgot how. Your father has withdrawn—and not by choice. You, on the other hand, decided to live this life."

"He's my father! What choice did I have?"

"Taking care of your father is one thing—not living your own life is quite another." She pushed up from her spot and looked down at Jewel. "It's your decision. Make sure you come to it for the right reason. Your father is going to go through what he will go through whether you let them film here or not." She patted Jewel's stiff shoulder and walked back inside the house.

Jewel glanced at the confident face of Craig Lawson staring up at her from the newspaper, almost as if he was challenging her. Was Minerva right? Was it her father that she was trying to protect—or herself from the soul-stirring attraction she felt for Craig Lawson?

While his team scrambled to get the project back on track and into his good graces, Craig headed out. He was unaccustomed to not getting what he wanted when he wanted it. He never allowed anything or anyone to stop him cold—Jewel Fontaine would not become the exception. Everyone had a price, something that could be bargained for. All he needed to do was find out what Jewel's something was. He fastened his seat belt, put the Suburban in gear and pulled out of the hotel garage.

As he cruised along the streets of New Orleans, the landscape of his youth unfolded in front of him. A great deal had changed since he was last here. Signs of gentrification were evident everywhere that he looked, from the small neighborhood shops that had transformed into internet cafés and outdoor eateries to the once debilitated homes that were in the throes of restoration. He was sure it was great for business—but whose business, and where did the people that once owned and lived here go? That was the story that he wanted to tell, the real history of his home and the people who made it.

His dashboard lit with an incoming call. He pressed the phone icon, and Anthony's voice came through the speakers.

"Yeah, Tony, what's up?"

"Where did you go off to?"

"I'll tell you about it when I get back."

"Paul and Diane are out scouting the alternate locations. I should have some news this afternoon."

"All right. Stay on it. I'll be back to the hotel in a couple of hours."

"You're going to see Ms. Fontaine, aren't you?"

Craig bit back a smile. He never could hide much from Anthony. "I'll talk to you later."

"Why are you so dead set on this place? I know it fits the specs, but there are plenty of places to choose from without having to twist the owner's arm to do it. So I know there has to be another reason."

"I don't like being told no. Reason enough?"

"If you say so. Just know that I know you, and I know better. Good luck."

He snorted a laugh. "'Preciate it." He disconnected the call.

Anthony was right. It wasn't as cut-and-dried as being told no, even though that was a big part of it. If he would allow himself a moment of honesty, he would admit that the real reason was that he wanted to see her again. See if on the morning after, she still managed to seep into his pores and flow through his veins. Best way to do that was face-to-face. He took a quick glance at the folder on the passenger seat. The documents inside, once signed, would give him access to the mansion *and* Jewel Fontaine for the next two months. He had no plans to return to the hotel empty-handed again.

The ride over to the Garden District, where Jewel lived, was about a twenty-minute ride from the center of town. Her home was on the edge of the district, set back and away from the street in a cul-de-sac that separated it from view of other homes in the area, which was ideal for the project.

He made his approach to the Garden District. This historic location was home to the some of the most iconic mansions in the state, all of which had been plantations during slavery. Anne Rice, of vampire fame, had a house there, along with the likes of football giant Peyton Manning, who grew up in the district.

Craig turned onto Prytania Street, which was lined with homes in the Gothic style. He reached the end of the lane and turned down the winding path that led to the Fontaine home. An unexpected knot of anxiety suddenly twisted in his gut when the mansion came into view. Or was it anticipation?

He took the path slowly and came to a stop at the top of the line of trees that umbrellaed the grounds. He turned off the ignition. For a few moments, he sat in the car, staring at the old-world majesty of the home and imagining the rich history that slept behind the walls and wafted among the rafters. What did the beautiful and difficult Jewel Fontaine add to that picture?

Craig snatched the folder from the passenger seat, got out and strode purposefully toward the sweeping entrance. Just as he put his booted foot on the first step of the landing, the double front door opened.

Jewel stood framed in the doorway, a mixture of past grandeur and present-day class.

Craig didn't realize that he'd actually frozen midstep until she spoke his name.

"Mr. Lawson. I wasn't expecting you."

He couldn't tell from her even tone if her words

were a reprimand or ones of pleasant surprise. He climbed the three steps until he was inches in front of her. Something soft and inviting spun around her in the morning breeze—her scent combined with the aroma of fresh baking that drifted to him from the interior of the house.

Craig cleared his throat, suddenly unsure of what he wanted to say. "Um, good morning, Ms. Fontaine. I apologize for not calling."

She didn't budge, a sentinel protecting her domain.

"What can I do for you? I thought we concluded our business yesterday."

"I was hoping that we could talk."

"About?"

He ran his tongue lightly across his dry lips. "The house."

Her lids lowered ever so slightly over her deep brown eyes, then she looked directly at him. She tipped her head slightly to the side. Her right brow rose. "Have you had breakfast?"

For a moment he was thrown. It was the last thing he'd expected her to say. "Actually, no. I haven't."

She drew in a short breath, opened the door farther and stepped to the side. "Come in."

Craig walked past her. Her scent clouded his thoughts.

Jewel shut the door. "This way." She led him through the large foyer that was appointed with an antique hall table upon which sat an oversize glass vase filled with lilies. On the walls hung several oil paintings that he recognized as her work. The highly polished wood-plank floors gleamed with their reflections and echoed their footsteps. She made a short right turn, and the space opened onto a kitchen that rivaled any master chef's.

Every size pot and pan hung from black iron ceiling hooks over a polished-cement island counter that boasted a sink and a six-burner stove with cabinetry beneath. The far end of the island was for seating. The double oven and restaurant-size stainless steel refrigerator were in sharp contrast to the perfectly restored potbellied stove that sat like a Buddha at the far end of the kitchen.

"Coffee or tea?"

Craig blinked. "Coffee. Please."

"Have a seat." She went to the overhead cabinets and took out a bag of imported Turkish coffee and prepared it. Within moments the scent of fresh-brewed coffee mixed with the tempting aroma of the blueberry muffins that sat in a cloth-lined basket, waiting to be devoured. She took out a plate and retrieved jam and whipped apple butter from the fridge and placed them both on the table.

"You have an incredible home."

"Thank you." She poured his coffee and brought it to the table. "Cream, milk, sugar?"

"I take it black. Thanks."

Jewel took a seat opposite him. "Help yourself to a muffin if you want. They're fresh."

His eyes narrowed. "You didn't make these?"

"Actually, I did."

The corner of his mouth lifted in a grin. "A woman of many talents." He reached for a muffin and put it on his plate. "I noticed your artwork out there. Stunning." He cut the muffin in half and slathered it with apple butter. He glanced up when she didn't comment.

He took a thoughtful bite and experienced heaven. His eyes closed in appreciation. "Wow, this is incredible." That brought a smile to those luscious lips of hers.

"I learned to bake from my grandmother, right here in this kitchen. It slowly became a passion of mine over the years."

"So you grew up here?"

"The house has been in the family for almost four generations, dating back to the emancipation. I lived here with my grandmother and my father until I graduated high school."

Where was her mother in the scenario? He didn't recall reading anything about her. "You attended the Sorbonne."

Her eyes flashed. A curious smile curved her mouth. "Have you been reading up on me? I thought it was the house you were interested in."

Both, he wanted to say but didn't. "Any time I'm in negotiations with anyone I want to know as much as possible about them."

"I see." Her lips narrowed.

"If I remember correctly, the original owner, Charles Biggs, was one of the few owners of these homes that didn't own slaves."

"True. My great-great-grandparents worked here and earned a wage. They were free blacks. They lived in the house in the back. When the owner died, he left the house, the land, everything to my great-great-grandparents." She huffed. "It didn't sit well with the neighbors." Her gaze drifted off. "My granddad told me stories about how my greats fought off threats both physical and emotional from the landowners around here. Nothing worked, and eventually they came to respect my family."

"Lot of history here," he said respectfully and struggled to contain his surprise and excitement about the eerie similarities of their ancestors.

"Yes, there is." She stared into her cup of tea. "So why are you here, Mr. Lawson?" She leveled her gaze on him, and something warm simmered in his belly.

"I believe that if you hear me out, you'll change your mind about renting out your home."

Jewel seemed to study him for a moment, as if the weight of her reality pressed against her shoulders, and with a breath of apparent acceptance she said, "Let's talk out back." She led the way to the veranda.

"Please, have a seat," Jewel said, extending her hand toward one of the cushioned chairs.

"Thanks." Craig sat and placed his plate and cup on the circular white wrought-iron table.

Jewel sat opposite him, adjusted her long skirt and leaned back. She folded her slender fingers across her lap. "So… I'm listening."

Craig cleared his throat, focusing on Jewel, and for a moment talking about the project was the last thing on his mind. He shifted his weight in the chair. "I believe as an artist you can fully appreciate a project of passion." Her nostrils flared ever so slightly as if bracing for attack. "That's what this project is for me. Everything that I've done and everything that I have accomplished has led me here—now." He pushed out a breath. "It's the story of my family, the Lawsons."

Her lashes fluttered, but her features remained unreadable.

"Of course, I've changed the names, to protect the guilty," he said, not in jest. "The story of a family that came from nothing, with a history of rising up from slavery, starting a business in a shack and building a legacy that led all the way to the seats of power in Washington." He leaned forward, held her with his gaze.

"More important," he continued, his voice taking on an urgency, "is that *now* is the time. With all that is going on in the world, with all that is happening to black lives, this is a story not only of history but of hope. It's about resiliency, about who we are as a people and all that we can be." He took a breath. "From what you told me about your family, we—" he flipped his hand back and forth between them "—have a helluva lot in common. This house, this land and the history of it is the ultimate backdrop for the telling of this story. It won't only be my family story, but your family story as well."

Jewel pushed up from her seat and walked over to the railing to gaze out at the rolling slopes. "I know about your work. I've read the reviews and the write-ups." She turned to face him. "They all say good things—that you are brilliant." She smiled faintly. "And that in an industry that is utterly jaded, you still keep your integrity intact and you never work on a project for the money but for the passion."

Craig took the comments in stride. He got up and stood beside her. He felt her stiffen. "I've read all about you, too." Her eyes widened for an instant. "You're one of the most influential artists of your generation. But suddenly you all but vanish from the public eye. Don't you miss it? Do you still paint, sculpt?"

"In answer to all of your questions, no, I don't," she practically whispered.

He watched her throat work as if she would reveal more, but she didn't. If he knew nothing else about artists of any medium, they weren't fulfilled if they didn't do what they were born to do. But instead of saying what he thought, he said, "If it's about the money, we are more than willing to pay twice what we offered, and I—"

Jewel spun her body toward him so quickly that it forced him to take a step back. Her eyes narrowed in fury.

"You think because I'm not in the limelight that I'm some kind of charity case and that I *need* your money!"

He reached out and gently placed his hand on her arm. "I'm sorry. That's not what I meant. All I'm saying is that I understand that it is an imposition, that strangers would interfere with your regular routine for weeks and you should be duly compensated, not to mention that your home would be the centerpiece of an amazing film. That's all worth something, and for me, having this film made at this location is more valuable than you could imagine." A slow, endearing smile curved his mouth while his eyes danced across her face.

Jewel, by degrees, seemed to relax her body. She lowered her head for a moment then looked directly at him, and the connection was so intense that he felt as if he'd been hit in the gut.

"Okay," she finally said. "You can shoot your film here."

A smile like hallelujah broke out on his face. He

totally kicked protocol to the curb, grabbed her around the waist and spun her in a circle. She laughed like a kid at Christmas, and it was pure music.

He finally set her on her feet, and they were but a breath apart. He saw the flecks of cinnamon in the irises of her eyes, felt the warmth of her body, the beat of her heart. He wanted to know what her lips felt like, to taste her...just a little.

"Sorry," he said.

Jewel gazed at him while the shadow of a smile hovered around her mouth.

"Thank you," he said, "and I swear we'll make this as painless for you as possible."

"I'm going to hold you to that, Mr. Lawson."

"I think maybe you can call me Craig."

The tip of her tongue brushed across her bottom lip. "Jewel."

"I'll have some new paperwork drawn up and sent over first thing tomorrow," Craig said as they walked to the front door.

They stood side by side on the landing.

"Fine. Can I ask you something?"

"You can ask me anything," he said, still euphoric over the positive turn of events.

"If this place and your family's legacy are so important to you, why did you stay away for ten years?"

The question seemed to take him off guard. For a moment he didn't respond, but he quickly regained his composure. "How about this... I promise to tell you all about it if you agree to have dinner with me, to thank you."

Jewel swallowed and took a small step aside. "I don't think so."

"Lunch?" He covered the step she'd given up. He faced her. "Starbucks on the corner of wherever," he joked.

Jewel laughed. "Fine. Lunch," she conceded.

"Tomorrow. One o'clock. I'll come and get you." He jogged down the three steps. "Enjoy your day," he said over his shoulder.

Jewel stood on the porch landing until the Suburban was long out of sight. Why had she agreed to have lunch with him? Why had she agreed to have his film crew in her home? Why was her heart racing as if she'd run a marathon, and why did she feel as if the lights had suddenly come on after much too long in the darkness? She turned and walked back inside. Craig Lawson was the answer to all of her questions.

Chapter 3

Craig was light on his feet as he crossed the threshold to the suite reserved for the crew. Since their arrival his team had transformed the lush two-bedroom suite into a functioning production space with a splash of elegance. His spirits soared even higher when he saw that everyone was already up and at it.

Anthony glanced up from the computer screen when Craig walked in. "Hey, man." He gave him a questioning look.

Craig gave him a thumbs-up and a satisfied grin. "It's a go."

Anthony slowly shook his head in amazement. "I want details."

Craig nodded then focused his attention on the team. "I have some good news. We got the Fontaine mansion for the shoot. So everything is a go. Paul,

I need to get with you a bit later to make a few enhancements to the agreement and then get it over to legal for a quick look."

"Sure thing, boss."

"Diane, I want to get some location shots set up and put on the schedule. When are Stacey and Norm getting in?"

"They should be landing as we speak. They took the red-eye from LA. A car is waiting for them at the airport," Diane said of the unit manager and technical director.

"Good." Craig checked his watch. "Let's all meet when Norm and Stacey arrive," he said. His glance spanned to include everyone. He turned to Anthony, clapped him on the shoulder and with a toss of his head indicated that he wanted to talk out of earshot. He led the way out and across the hall to his room.

Anthony shut the door behind them. "Lemme hear it. How did you get her to change her mind? I'm almost afraid to ask."

Craig tossed him a withering look from over his shoulder. "Yo, what are you trying to say, man?"

"I'm not *trying* to say anything. I'm saying you sometimes maneuver women into that horizontal position that magically gets them to do what you want."

"One time," he corrected, holding up his index finger as pseudoproof.

"Twice."

"All right, all right. Twice. But it was mutual. I never have a woman do anything they don't truly want to do. I'm not that guy."

"Yeah, yeah, I know, man. I'm just pulling your chain." He crossed the carpeted floor to the counter, fixed himself a cup of coffee then took a seat in a club chair by the window. "So, what's the deal?"

Craig sat on the lounge chair and stretched his long legs out in front of him, crossing his feet at the ankles. He linked his fingers across his hard belly. "I made her an offer she couldn't refuse," he said in a pretty good imitation of Marlon Brando's Vito Corleone.

"Yeah, what kind of offer?"

"Well, I was honest…or at least as honest as I can be. I told her exactly how important this film is to me and why. We talked." His gaze drifted away as an image of Jewel filled his line of sight. A grin curved his mouth.

"She must have said something pretty powerful to put that look on your face."

Craig blinked, gave a quick shake of his head and returned his attention to Anthony. "I don't know what it was, to be honest." He leaned forward and rested his arms on his thighs. "There's…something about her. Can't put my finger on it." He looked Anthony right in the eyes. "Getting her to agree to let us use her home for the shoot is a major coup, no doubt, but having lunch with her tomorrow is the icing on the cake." He grinned.

"You dog," Anthony teased, wagging a finger at him.

"It's not like that," Craig said, chuckling. "I swear."

"Not yet."

"Look, I asked her to dinner, and she flat-out said no. I bumped it down to lunch with the caveat that if she agreed I would tell her why I haven't been back for ten years."

Anthony's dark eyes widened in surprise. "Say what?"

"She wanted to know…and that was the only thing I could offer to get her to agree to lunch."

"The offer she couldn't refuse," Anthony said.

"Yeah, something like that."

"Let me get this straight. You meet this woman. You want something from her. She tells you no— something you aren't used to hearing, by the way— and you offer to reveal to her something *I* only got out of you after years of friendship and a bottle of bourbon? Is that about right?"

"Maybe if you'd had her body, those eyes and that mouth I would have told you sooner," he joked.

Anthony burst out laughing, sputtering coffee. He grabbed a napkin and wiped his mouth then leveled his gaze at his friend. "Hey, it's cool, whatever you want to do. I'm just saying be clearheaded—that's all. In another three months, we'll be back in London for the next film. Long distance has never been your thing."

Craig pressed his lips together and slowly nodded his head. "Yeah, I know. It's all good."

"Now for the practical question, how much more is this going to cost us?"

"Another ten grand."

"What? Craig, man, we have a budget, remember? You're adding ten K to the budget and we haven't even started shooting yet."

"I got this. Don't worry." He stood.

"It's my job to worry. It's what I do. I know you have deep pockets, but don't bust a hole in them." His cell phone chirped. He pulled it out of his shirt pocket. "It's Diane. Norm and Stacey just arrived," he said.

"Cool. Give them an hour to get settled and we'll

all meet over lunch. Have room service bring up what- ever everyone wants."

Anthony pushed up from his seat and set his cof- fee cup down on the table. He turned to Craig, slung his hands into his pockets and pushed out a breath. "I know you have a lot riding on this project," he said in a low voice. "I only want to make sure that you make it to the finish line."

"I hear you, brother." He gripped Anthony's upper arm. "I've come too far to screw this up, especially over a woman. No worries. Okay?"

Anthony studied him for a moment. "See you at lunch." He turned and walked out.

Craig faced the window that offered a panorama of the place he'd once called home. He knew that Anthony was only doing his job. When he put on his other hat as first assistant director it was his responsi- bility to keep everything on point, including keeping an eye on the budget. But Craig also knew that wasn't Anthony's main concern. His concern rose out of their decades-long friendship. Anthony knew him, knew the demons that he dealt with—the string of relation- ships to fight the bouts of depression, the outbursts of anger and the weeks of isolation. The chasm between him and his father was at the center of it all, that and his very publicly failed engagement to international model and up-and-coming film star Anastasia Du- mont, the daughter of Alexander Dumont, the London financier. Although the disaster of their engagement had ended three years earlier and it happened across the pond, it still stung. His and Anastasia's faces and every detail of their relationship—at least what the tabloids could piece together—became cover copy for every pop magazine here and abroad for months. At least until the next personal scandal took center stage.

He'd almost waited by the phone for a call from his father telling him, "I told you so." Craig wasn't sure what stung more, the fact that the call never came or that his father didn't even care enough to say, "I told you so."

Anthony was right. He had to keep his head on straight and not get distracted by a beautiful woman who clearly had major issues of her own. The last thing he needed was to haul around someone else's baggage. He'd tell her just enough to tamp down her curiosity, and that was it. He was as good at masking what rested behind his emotional armor as he was a writer and director—and he had the awards to prove it. Whatever he didn't want Ms. Jewel Fontaine to know she would never know.

"I'm going to take your father on a stroll around the grounds," Minerva said as she walked into the sitting room off the veranda.

Jewel placed the newspaper that she was reading down on the table. "I think I'll go with you. I could use some exercise myself." She pushed up from the chair.

"I saw a car pull off earlier. Was that the film people?"

Jewel tugged on her bottom lip with her teeth before answering. "Yes. It was Mr. Lawson."

"Oh." Her voice rose in a note of surprise. "And?" she added when Jewel offered nothing further.

"He came to ask me to reconsider."

"And?"

"And I agreed." She held onto her smile.

Minerva clapped her hands together in delighted relief. "Amen! I am so happy that you came to your senses."

"I'm glad you approve."

"What made you change your mind?"

"I thought about what you said." Craig Lawson immediately came to mind. "It's for the best."

Minerva squeezed Jewel's arm. "This will lift a big burden off your shoulders and give you some room to breathe." She hesitated a moment. "I know I've said it a dozen times, but if you're set against going back to your art, you could have a whole other career in baking. It wouldn't bring in the same level of money as your paintings and such, but…you love it and your customers love the magic you make."

Jewel drew in a long breath and slowly released it. "One thing at a time, Minny, okay?" A faint smile of indulgence curved her mouth. "Let's go take Dad for his walk. Then I actually do need to get into the kitchen. I have an order for three dozen red velvet cupcakes for Ms. Hatfield's daughter's sweet sixteen party."

"See, they love you," Minerva said with a grin.

Jewel slowly shook her head, tucked in her smile and followed Minerva to her father's room.

He'd been out with more women than he could count or remember. There was rarely a time in his life when a woman was not somewhere in the shadows. He adored women, loved the look of them, the way they made him feel about himself. He'd experienced the gamut of emotions for the women he'd been with, but fear was never one of them. But if he were tortured and had to confess, he would admit that he was scared as all hell about this lunch thing with Jewel Fontaine.

He didn't have a damned thing to prove to her. He wasn't trying to win her over and get her into bed. This was business. So there was no reason for the churning in his gut or the galloping of his heart.

Craig made the last turn on the road toward Jewel's home and realized as he gripped the wheel that his palms were damp. What the hell? He maneuvered the Suburban slowly down the narrow dirt lane and came to a stop at the end of it. He cut the engine. Too many scenarios of what came next raced around in his head. He pushed out a breath, opened the door and got out. No point in delaying the inevitable.

He strode toward the front door and up the three steps to the landing. He rang the bell. Moments later the nurse came to the door.

"Good afternoon, Mr. Lawson," she greeted him with a wide grin. "Ms. Fontaine is expecting you. Please come in."

All very Southern, Craig mused. "Thank you." He stepped inside and was once again taken aback by the sweeping grandeur of the home. Tastefully elegant in every detail.

"You can have a seat in the parlor." She indicated the room to her right with a tilt of her hand. "I'll let Ms. Fontaine know that you're here. Can I get you anything?" she asked before turning away.

"No, thank you, ma'am. I'm fine."

Minerva hurried off.

Craig took a slow turn in the well-appointed room. Old-world charm seeped from every corner. The oak beams, padded antique chairs, heavy glass and wood tables and gleaming hardwood floors with strategically placed area carpeting all added to the flavor of what once was and still existed. He could envision the cigar smoke drifting into the air while men of power sat around making decisions and sipping shots of whiskey.

"Sorry to keep you waiting."

Craig turned toward the sound of Jewel's voice and was hit once again with the impact of seeing her. He swallowed. His lips parted for a moment before a response could form.

"Not a problem," he finally said. He took a step toward her. Her eyes widened, and her bottom lip quivered ever so slightly. What was she thinking? If only he could let her know how hard it was for him to rein in the overwhelming desire to kick the door closed, press her body against the wall and kiss away the shimmering gloss she had on those lush lips. He shoved his hands into his pockets to hide the rise that pulsed and to keep from touching her. That would be a mistake. He tipped his head slightly to the side. "Ready?"

"Yes." She spun away and led the way out, giving Craig ample time to pull himself together—although looking at her from the rear wasn't much help, either.

They stepped out into the balmy early afternoon. The sky was crystal clear, the sun high and strong with a breeze off the surrounding brooks and streams cooling the air and carrying the scent of the spring blooms that sprouted from the ground and hung from the trees.

"Did you have someplace in mind?" Jewel asked

while Craig held the passenger door for her and helped her in.

"Um, not really," he drawled. He shut the door and rounded the vehicle then slid in behind the wheel. He turned to look at her. "I was hoping you would suggest your favorite place," he tossed out as a Hail Mary.

Jewel grinned. "To be honest, it's been a minute since I've been out. Can't really say I have a favorite place."

Craig turned the key in the ignition. "Then we'll find a favorite place together. Sound like a plan?"

Jewel fastened her seat belt. "Sure. Let's go."

"I'm working off rusty memory," Craig said as he pulled onto the main road. "From what I remember there are a bunch of cafés and restaurants downtown. Right?"

"Good memory. I can't guarantee they're exactly what you remember, though. There's been a lot of turnover of small businesses the past few years."

"Hmm, I can imagine. It's always the little guy that gets hit the hardest when change comes."

"Unfortunate and true."

Craig stole a look and caught the pensive expression that drew her tapered brows together. "Anyone you know?" he gently asked.

Jewel considered the question for a moment. She nodded. "Phyllis Heywood. She owned a small boutique with a lot of handmade jewelry and accessories. The rent got so high she couldn't keep place. Then there's the bookstore and the diner that were around since I was a girl." She paused. "They've all been replaced with high-end shops and a real estate office. And those are the ones that I know about."

"Ouch."

"Exactly. And of course there are the businesses that never recovered after Katrina. A lot of people are still living in trailers and are out of work."

Craig nodded. "I know it won't solve all the problems that are going on down here, but this film will definitely bring business and jobs to the community."

"But for how long?"

He wasn't ready to reveal his entire plan. There was no guarantee that it would all pan out. "Let's say we'll take it one day at a time." He reached over and covered her hand with his. An electric charge shot between them.

Jewel's eyes seemed to brighten, and Craig heard her short intake of breath that matched his own. If he was going to get through this business lunch in one piece and not find some hidden corner to ravish her in, he was going to have to keep his hands to himself. He returned both hands to the wheel and concentrated on the winding road.

Once they were in the center of town, Craig suggested that he find a place to park and they walk around until they settled on a place to eat.

They strolled along the streets of downtown New Orleans and shared comments on the many changes that had engulfed the area. Intermittently their arms or fingertips brushed as they sidestepped other walkers and pretended the subtle touches didn't happen. Instinctively, Craig's hand found its way to the center of her lower back as he guided her along the narrow streets. The heat from her body sizzled on his fingertips, and it took all of his concentration to stay on task and not focus on what her skin would feel like next to his. *Talk, don't think*, he reminded himself. *Talk.*

"I know it's been a while since I've been here, but I got to admit, it feels totally different. Nothing like I remembered," he said. "I mean, it kind of looks the same, but the vibe is off."

"I know what you mean. I feel the same way. The only difference is that I've been here to see it happen."

"Hmm." He lifted his chin in the direction of a small bistro up ahead with a sandwich board out front announcing its menu. "Let's check this place out."

They walked up to the sandwich board, scanned the menu, looked at each other and grinned in agreement. Craig held the door open for her, and they stepped inside.

The interior of Appetite Noir took one back to the early days of good old down-home New Orleans eating. The heavy wood beams, picnic-style tables, stained wood floors, zydeco and blues in the background, and the aromas of barbecue and crayfish made a tantalizing combination.

"Table for two?" a young hostess asked.

"Yes, please," Craig responded.

The waitress grabbed two menus and instructed them to follow her. Craig took the opportunity to drop his hand to the small of Jewel's back once again, and the gesture was still as thrilling.

The waitress stopped in front of a small booth-type seating arrangement and placed the menus on table. "Your server will be right with you. Enjoy."

"I didn't even know this place was here," Jewel said as she took a slow look around. She set her purse on the space next to her and lifted her menu. Sitting opposite Craig Lawson would take work on her part. She would have to pretend that his eyes didn't affect her, that they didn't have the power to strip her of her facade. She would have to avoid watching his lips move when he spoke so that she wouldn't fantasize about how they would feel, what he would taste like.

She stared at the menu. The words swirled around in front of her. This was why she should have said no. Stirring up the dead embers of her soul could serve no purpose other than to lead her down a road of momentary fantasy. To even imagine that there could be something between them was silly, childish. Craig Lawson was a man of the world. A womanizing man of the world based on what she'd read on the internet. He was a man that cast his lot into a world of make-believe. He'd left his home, his family, his roots to run after a dream. And there didn't seem to be anyone or anything that had slowed him in that pursuit. But what would it be like to become part of the fantasy—even for a little while?

"Know what you want?"

Jewel blinked. Her gaze landed on his face, and she was certain he could read the salacious thoughts she'd had about him. She swallowed. "Um, no. Everything looks good."

Craig chuckled. "That is true. But I can't remember when I last had some Nawlins crayfish. I want a bucketful."

Jewel laughed. "Me, too, now that I think about it."

Craig slapped his palms on the table and leaned forward. "You gotta be kidding me. You're right here in the mix."

He tipped his head back in disbelief, and Jewel stole a quick look at the tight cords of his neck. She ran her tongue across her lips. "Guilty," she murmured.

Craig's gaze settled on her face. "We 'bout to change that right now, darlin'." His right brow rose to punctuate his declaration just as their waitress approached.

They placed their order for two buckets of crayfish, seasoned fries, coleslaw and a pitcher of beer.

"I'm going to regret this in the morning," Jewel said when the humongous order arrived and was placed in front of them.

"Live for the moment, darlin'. Sometimes we just have to give in to our fantasies."

Jewel's belly clenched. It was as if he'd read her mind or channeled her thoughts. She cleared her throat. "Maybe you're right."

For the next few minutes, the only conversation between them was groans of delight.

"Damn, I missed this," Craig finally said. He wiped his fingers and mouth with the linen napkin and then took a long swallow of beer. The bucket was still half-full.

Jewel wiped her fingers and mouth as well and pushed out a breath. "Whew." She giggled. "I haven't thrown down like that for a while." She put her napkin aside. "So, Mr. Lawson, I hope you don't think that I've forgotten our agreement." She reached for her mug of beer.

"Agreement? The film?"

She pursed her lips in feigned annoyance. "You know perfectly well that's not what I mean."

He tried to look sheepish. "Okay, fine. What do you want to know?"

"If you missed this all so much," she said with an encompassing wave of her hands, "then why did you stay away for so long?"

Craig linked his long fingers together, rocked his jaw and took a sobering breath. "I'm sure you've heard about my family—the famous and the infamous." He chuckled.

"A little—more about your uncle the senator."

Craig nodded. "Well, there is a whole host of us Lawsons. And from birth expectation is high—unreachable for some of us. We had to live up to the long legacy of the name as well as what was deemed to be our role in the ongoing saga of our lives."

"And you clearly decided that you weren't going to toe the family line."

He snorted a laugh. "Something like that. It didn't go over well."

"What was it that you didn't want to do?"

Craig paused, trying to frame the story in his head. "My father, Jake Lawson, is the youngest of the three brothers. My uncle Paul is the eldest, and my uncle Branford the senator. My grandfather Clive runs the family—his sons—like a well-oiled machine. He set down the template for success, and none of his sons ever deviated from it. Gramps's grandparents were slaves. His parents grew up on a plantation." He gaze rose from studying his fingers to land on her face. "Very much like your home." He took another swallow of his beer. "My template was to follow in my father's footsteps. Jake Lawson is probably—at least the last time I checked—the most influential land developer in the country. If it's being bought, sold or imagined, my father more than likely has a hand in it."

"And he wanted you to join the family business."

Craig nodded in agreement. "It wasn't for me."

"Why wouldn't your father want his son to pursue his own destiny?"

His jaw clenched. He glanced away. "He has his reasons," he said, his voice low and gravelly.

Jewel watched the array of emotions flit across Craig's countenance. There was clearly more there than he was telling. But it wasn't her place to pull it out of him. Everyone was entitled to their secrets, her included.

"You have sisters and brothers?" she asked, attempting to lift him out of the pit that he'd lowered himself into.

A soft smile tugged at the corners of his mouth. "Yeah, my brother, Myles, and my sister, Alyse."

"Do they live here?"

"Yeah."

"They must miss you," she said softly. As an only child, she'd never known what it felt like to have a sibling to share a life with, memories, joys and sorrows.

Craig finished off his beer, peeled the shell off a crayfish and popped it in his mouth. He chewed slowly. "You have sisters and brothers?" he asked, changing the subject.

"No. Just me."

They studied each other for a moment.

"What did your parents want for you?"

Her expression softened. "They wanted me to be

happy. My happiness took the form of art, and my dad was behind me a thousand percent."

"What about your mom?"

Her deep sigh was audible. "She died when I was six. Ovarian cancer."

"Oh...man, I'm really sorry."

"It's okay." She swallowed. "My dad...he really stepped up. He was mom, dad and my best friend. He sacrificed a lot so that I could pursue my art. I'll never be able to repay him for all that he did for me." She expelled a breath as a wave of sadness swept though her. She pushed it away. "So what do you do besides create make-believe and date all your leading ladies?"

Craig tossed his head back and let loose a hearty laugh that warmed Jewel all the way down to her toes. It was a feel-good laugh.

"Ah, Ms. Fontaine, you wound me," he said in an exaggerated drawl. He pressed his hand to his chest.

"Well, if it's on the internet, it must be true," she teased.

"Yeah, right. And Kanye will win as president."

"Touché." But she really *did* want him to tell her about the women in his life. Did they matter? Did he remember their names? Would he remember hers?

He leaned back in his seat and angled his head to the side. "The tabloids, TMZ...always blow things out of proportion. They always think they have the inside story on what goes on in people's private lives."

His voice had taken on a hard edge, Jewel realized.

"They don't. They have no clue and what they don't know they make up." He refilled his beer mug from the pitcher.

"Is that what happened to you?" she asked softly.

His dark eyes flashed for a moment, and in that split second she caught the depth of hurt that swam beneath, and then just as quickly it was gone.

Craig shrugged. "It comes with the territory, darlin'." A smile curved his mouth. He lifted his mug and took a short swallow of beer.

"Do you watch your own films?" Jewel asked with a warm smile. She knew that they needed to switch gears, lighten the mood and move away from the murky waters of the past.

Craig grinned. "Only the dailies."

"Dailies?"

"Yeah. The cuts from each day of shooting." He rested his arms on the table and launched into an animated discussion about the behind-the-scenes activities of filmmaking.

Jewel listened, fascinated as much by what she learned about the moviemaking process as what she did about Craig Lawson. He was a passionate man. A dedicated man, a man of conviction. He respected his crew and was loyal to his friends. Like her he was well traveled, and much to her amazement he spoke French and Spanish—just as she did. He told her about some of his many trips around the globe, the people that he'd met, the customs and cultures that he'd encountered. Like his uncle Branford, he was well versed in the political climate of the States as well as abroad. And nowhere in any of the scenarios that he presented was there a significant other in the picture.

"Can I get you two anything else?"

They both looked up at the server that they didn't recognize then took a look around the restaurant. The clientele had shifted from late lunch goers to dinner

guests—they could tell by the briefcases resting beside polished shoes and the relief in the after-work
laughter. They'd been talking for hours.

Craig grinned at Jewel. "Uh, I think we're done.
Can I get the check, please?"

"Sure thing." She slipped the leather carrier out of
her apron pocket and placed it on the table.

The instant she turned away, Jewel and Craig burst
into laughter. Jewel checked her watch. "We've been
here for almost four hours!"

"Time flies when you're in good company," he said
as he gaze settled slowly and completely on her face.

Jewel felt the heat rise to her cheeks. Her stomach
fluttered. "Yes, it does," she said softly.

They strolled slowly back to Craig's vehicle, com-
menting on the shops and people that they passed
along the way.

This felt good, Jewel realized. It had been so long
that she'd been out with a man she'd forgotten how
wonderful it felt to be looked after, admired, to be
in the company of a handsome, sexy man that any
woman would switch places with her to be with. But
this was real life, not some story on the big screen.
She knew in her gut that nothing much could happen
between them. In another couple of months he'd be
gone, on to his next project in some far-flung corner
of the world.

She studied his profile as they walked and talked.
It was as if his features had been carved by a skilled
hand. She wanted to reach out and stroke the curve
of his jaw, the angle of his forehead, run her finger
along the full lips. And then as if he was once again

r ing her thoughts, he took her hand. The jolt of the contact set her heart racing.

His long fingers curved around her hand and held it possessively. She stared at him. He brought her hand to his lips and tenderly kissed it then continued walking, as if they always walked through the streets of downtown New Orleans holding hands.

"Thank you for a lovely afternoon," Craig said with a smoldering smile.

They stood facing each other, inches apart, on her front porch. Jewel's heart thumped. "I'm glad I went."

"Are you?" His brows tightened as he took a step closer, forcing her to look up.

Her throat worked. "Very."

"That's good to know, because I want to do it again."

Jewel swallowed. "Lunch?"

"Dinner...and then breakfast."

The implication was clear. Heat flashed through her limbs. Her head swam.

"How does that sound?"

"It sounds..."

Before she could form the words, he'd slid his arm around her waist and pulled her flush against the hard lines of his body, and the world disappeared as his head came down and those lips that that she had fantasized about kissing covered hers. The kiss was electric, slow and sweet. She couldn't think over the hum that echoed deep in his throat as he deepened their kiss, teasing her mouth with a swipe of his tongue. Her entire body vibrated and felt weak all at once. Her fingers held onto the tight ropes of his arms, and all she could piece together in her head was that she didn't want it to end. But then it did.

Craig looked down into her upturned face. "You let me know when," he said, his voice low and ragged. He traced her bottom lip with the tip of his finger, turned and strode down the walkway to his car, and like waking from a dream he was gone.

But it wasn't a dream. She ran her tongue across her lips and tasted him, shut her eyes and saw him. It was very real.

Chapter 4

Craig was met at the front door of the hotel by the black-jacketed valet that gallantly opened the chrome and glass door and wished him a practiced "Enjoy your stay." Craig strode across the lobby floor and stabbed the up button on the elevator panel. He was more than two hours late for his sit-down with his team. He hadn't intended to be gone as long as he had, and neither had he intended to be so affected by a simple kiss. The entire ride back from Jewel's home to the hotel his thoughts leapfrogged each other, never allowing him a moment to catch them and try to figure out what he was thinking and feeling.

"Well, there you are," Anthony greeted him the moment Craig entered the suite. "Thought you'd forgotten all about us." He eyed Craig for a response.

"Yeah, sorry for the delay. Got caught up." He

avoided Anthony's pointed stare and shrugged out of his lightweight leather jacket and tossed it on a chair. "Where are we with things?"

"Everyone has arrived, and we were working out the shooting schedule. The primary actors, Milan and Hamilton, arrived about an hour ago. They're getting settled in their rooms."

Craig nodded, taking in the information. "Cool. I want to have a sit-down with the primaries in about an hour."

"Sure." He paused. "So...how was lunch?"

"Filling." His cell phone chirped in his pocket. He pulled it out and saw his sister's name on the screen. He blew out a breath. "Gotta take this." He pressed the talk icon. "Hey, sis." He turned away from Anthony and crossed the room to the window. "How are you?" He didn't have to wait long for his sister to read him the riot act.

"Why do I have to read about you being back in town? You couldn't call?"

Craig briefly shut his eyes. He knew his sister. And when she went on a tear, she didn't stop until she was beyond satisfied. "Sorry, sis. I've been crazy busy from the moment we landed."

"Lousy excuse," she groused. "So," she puffed into the phone. "How are you and where are you staying?"

He held back a smile, envisioning his petite sister's dark eyes cinched at the corners and her mouth in a tight, disapproving line. As the youngest of the three and the only girl, Alyse learned early that she had to be just as tough if not tougher than her big brothers and be able to stand toe to toe with their father.

"I'm fine, thanks, sis. And I'm staying at the Marriott in the Quarter."

"Fancy," she teased. "So I'm free this evening. I can meet you at your hotel."

Craig knew that, much like him, the word *no* didn't factor into Alyse's vocabulary. He exhaled slowly. "Sure. How about eight?"

"I'll see you then. Myles is out of town, by the way. But he should be back by the weekend."

"I'll be sure to give him a call."

The elephant sat between them. Their father. Thankfully Alyse didn't bring him up. Craig was not in the mood to discuss their father at the moment, but he knew he wouldn't be able to avoid the conversation later. "Look, sis, I gotta run. I'll see you tonight."

"Fine. Looking forward to seeing you, Craig," she said, her tone finally softening.

"Me, too, sis. Later." He disconnected the call, shook his head and slid the phone back into his pocket. The sound of voices and activity drew his attention to the main room. Milan Chase had arrived, and one would think that his crew had never been in the presence of a movie star with the way they tripped over each other to introduce themselves.

Milan Chase was the epitome of classy, sexy beauty, but more than that she was an incredible actress who knew her worth down to the last penny and who had two Golden Globes and an Oscar nomination to her credit. Not only was she good at what she did on camera, she was an astute businesswoman who was notorious for tough negotiations for all of her contracts. Even her lawyers deferred to her. He'd had brief reservations in casting Milan for the lead role. Not because of her ability, but because of their history.

Craig entered the open living space, and like the parting of the sea, his crew moved aside as he strode toward Milan.

"Glad you got here safe and sound," he said in an intimate tone. He took her hands in his and kissed her right cheek then her left.

"Craig," she said in her patented throaty whisper. "Good to see you again." Her lashes fluttered for an instant.

"You, too. How are your accommodations?"

"Perfect."

"Good." He released her hands. "I was in the midst of planning a meeting in about an hour. You good with that?" He slung his hands into his pockets.

"Absolutely. I'm anxious to get started."

Craig nodded. "You can hang out here or wait in your room until we're ready. Up to you."

"I might as well stay, get familiar with the crew."

"That's fine." He patted her shoulder and started to move away.

"Craig…"

He glanced over his shoulder then turned. "Yeah?"

Milan stepped closer. "Are you free later tonight?"

His eyes widened for an instant. "Tonight? Actually, I have plans."

She lowered her gaze then looked directly at him. "Tomorrow night, then."

He cleared his throat. "I'll, uh, let you know. Is there a problem?"

"Not at all. I thought we could catch up for old times' sake."

He rocked his jaw. The last thing he needed was to rekindle the embers with Milan, but he didn't want her as an adversary, either. "Maybe we can do drinks," he offered to appease her. "How's that?"

"Sure." She flashed her movie star smile. "Drinks sound fine."

"Craig…"

He turned toward the sound of his name. "Duty calls. Check you later." He walked over to Anthony.

"Yeah, what's up?"

"Looked like you needed rescuing," Anthony said under his breath.

"You noticed that, huh? Thanks."

"I let everyone know to be in place for the meeting. The main thing is the shooting schedule for week one. Everything cool with the location?"

"Yes. I have some adjustments to make to the contract and I'll get it signed."

Anthony's right brow rose. "You? Paul or Diane can do that."

"I'd prefer to handle it myself."

"Mmm-hmm."

"Don't, okay? It's not like that."

"Hey, my man. It's your party. All I ask is to keep the fireworks to a minimum."

Craig slapped Anthony's back. "No worries." He caught a glimpse of Milan out of the corner of his eye. He hoped that sentiment would remain true. "Got a call from Alyse."

"You knew that was going to happen."

He snorted a laugh. "Yeah. Meeting her later tonight at the hotel bar."

"Public place. Good move," he teased.

"Very funny."

"Well, you know how Alyse can be."

"That I do," he conceded good-naturedly. He pushed out a breath. "Soon as Hamilton gets here, we can get started."

"In the meantime, let's go over a few things for the shooting schedule and the staffing."

"Sure."

"So what about your pops?" Anthony hedged once they were seated at the round table away from the team.

Craig looked up from the notes on the iPad. "What about him?"

"Guess that answers my question."

"I hope so."

Jewel finished packing up the bakery boxes filled with cupcakes for her client's daughter's sixteenth-birthday party. She tied each box with her signature lavender bow and tucked a business card in each one. She had to admit that over the past few months the requests for her baking services had increased considerably. As it currently stood, she had the space in her kitchen and the time on her hands to efficiently complete her orders. But she wasn't too sure how long that efficiency would last at this rate. The extra income wasn't enough for her to sit back and relax, but it did help. Maybe Minerva was right and this was her next career move, which shifted her thoughts back to her lunch and conversation with Craig. It was exhilarating and simultaneously disheartening to listen to his unwavering passion for his work. She'd had that once. And had anyone asked her five years earlier if she ever saw anything different in her life, she would have responded with a flat-out no.

The past five years had been hard, harder than she often admitted even in the quiet of her own mind. There were those days when she missed the travel, the work, the accolades, the excitement of creating something from nothing, allowing her imagination to become a physical reality.

There were times when she'd questioned her decision to leave that life behind her, to throw in the towel, so to speak. Yet, even after all this time, her fall from grace still stung.

It was a New York showing. The promotion leading up to her gallery opening had been in every art magazine, newspaper and blog and on the lips of every reputable critic in the business. The buzz in the art world was near deafening in anticipation of Jewel Fontaine's new work. Rumor had it that she had taken a departure from her traditional oil painting and classic sculptures to something more avant-garde and edgy. It was a risk. But the artistic visionary in her guided her in a new direction.

She'd always been anxious on opening nights, but this night was different. She was actually scared. Her personal assistant, Mai Ling, had spent the better part of the day convincing her that the fans and the critics would love it.

"You're a brilliant artist, Jewel," Mai said. "You've carved a solid reputation for excellence, and one show is not going to change that. The work is phenomenal, and anyone with a grain of sense will see it. So stop worrying. It's going to be fine." She gave Jewel a reassuring hug. "I put your outfit on the bed. The car will be here to pick us up at six. You have an interview with *Art Digest* and the reviewer from the *Times*. Then it's on to the after-party."

Jewel pushed out a breath. She didn't know what she would do without Mai. *Efficient* wasn't a word that did her justice. "Great. And you have the car to pick up my father from the airport?"

"Of course. I don't want you to worry about anything beyond looking beautiful and talking about your work."

"I'll try. Is Simon coming?" she asked with an edge of doubt in her voice.

Mai's lashes fanned her eyes. "He didn't RSVP," she said softly. "But you know Simon. He never was one to follow protocol."

Jewel knew that Mai was attempting to ease her angst, but the truth was her on-again, off-again relationship with Simon Devareau had been switched to the off mode for weeks. Simon was a writer and arranger for some of the biggest names in the music industry, and his time and talent were always in demand. He was a temperamental musical genius who could go for weeks, sometimes months without seeing or talking to her when he was in the throes of composing new work.

They'd met on the beaches of Rio two years earlier and had hit if off almost instantly. She was magnetically drawn to his brooding good looks and his passion for his work. They shared many things in common, the arts being one and mind-blowing sex the other. They spent endless hours discussing their work, sharing ideas, sparking others. But Simon always maintained an invisible wall, one that she was never able to penetrate. She wanted more. He knew it, and the wall grew thicker and higher. Their times apart became longer, the silences louder. Jewel wanted it to work. She believed that there was room in their lives for each other and the work. Simon didn't say it in so many words, but his actions spoke volumes—his work took priority. Period. And the harder she tried to make him cross the line, the harder he pulled away. She knew it was a mistake to hope that he would be there for her big night, but she couldn't stamp out her need to want him with her.

"I'm going to head over to the Guggenheim and make sure that there are no last-minute glitches, then I'll meet you back here no later than five so that I can get ready."

"Thanks, sweetie. Call me if there are any problems."

Mai gave her an *are you kidding me* look, shook her head and walked out.

When the limo pulled up in front of the Guggenheim Museum, it was a scene right out of Oscar night. The red carpet led from the street up to the front entrance to the museum. Reporters and photographers lined the roped-off entrance, and the instant Jewel stepped from the limo behind Mai, the flash of lights from cameras and cell phones and the shouting of her name rose in a cacophony of light and sound. The reception was overwhelming, and Jewel's stress level skyrocketed. She did her best to keep her smile in place as she walked the carpet, stopping every several feet to take a picture or answer a quick question. Finally they made it inside.

The Ronald O. Perelman Rotunda designed by the iconic Frank Lloyd Wright could hold fourteen hundred people for a reception and three hundred for a sit-down dinner. Even Jewel gasped at the opulence of the space that was strategically lined with her latest work, set off by the polished glass and chrome of the event space and marble floors. Circular linen-topped tables with white votive candles as centerpieces were arranged to the side of the space to accommodate the after-party dinner reception.

"Oh. My. God," Jewel said in a gush of awe.

Mai squeezed Jewel's bare arm. "It's going to be a fabulous night," she whispered in assurance. "Now let's mingle." Mai took Jewel's arm and guided her around the extraordinary space.

If only Mai's prediction had been true. It was apparent within the first hour that the buzz among the patrons and the press was anything but complimentary.

"Terrible."

"Not her style."

"What happened to her?"

"Definitely not what I expected."

"Disappointing."

Jewel tried hard to ignore the demoralizing commentary. But the sit-down dinner where she was surrounded by self-declared connoisseurs of art who worked hard at maintaining polite conversation that pointedly didn't include the exhibit, was the longest night of her life, with the only highlight being that Simon did arrive and was by her side during the interminable meal.

There were points when she wanted to run out and

break down and cry, but she knew she had to keep up the front of confidence.

The silence was so heavy on the ride back to her hotel that it made her head pound. Simon offered to spend the night, and for the first time since they'd been a couple she turned him down. She needed to be alone and didn't want him to be around when she read the reviews in the morning. The fact that her father was a witness to her embarrassment was enough.

She sat opposite Mai the following morning looking at one review after another that eviscerated her work. Every outlet from the venerable *New York Times* to *New York* magazine, *Art and Culture*, *Contemporary Art Review* and every blog and newspaper in between were, uncharacteristically, in agreement— the exhibit was an epic failure. Even the international press had a field day at her expense. One critic went so far as to intimate that Jewel Fontaine's star had finally fallen.

"Jewel… I am so sorry. I don't know what to say."

Jewel lifted the coffee mug to her lips and took a sip. "There's nothing to say. It's all here," she said, pushing the papers aside. She glanced off into the distance.

"You know how critics are. They wouldn't be critics if they didn't have something to disparage. It will pass. All of the great artists were blasted by detractors that didn't understand what the artist was trying to convey."

"Not like this." She huffed. "Some of these reviews are almost personal."

"But you can't take it personally."

"I know you're trying to make me feel better, Mai. You're wasting your time." Jewel pushed away from the table and stood. "I'm going to get dressed, pack my bags, meet my father and go back home."

"The flight is at one."

"Hmm. Thanks."

The trip back home with her father was the second and ultimate blow.

For the prior six months Jewel had been traveling, studying and immersing herself in the production for her show at the Guggenheim. She kept in contact with her father by phone. They spoke at least once per week. The small lapses in the conversation, the long pauses between one idea and the next, and often the disassociation with whatever it was that they were discussing she tossed off as her father, much like herself, being preoccupied. When she saw him for the first time in six months, he physically looked the same, but there was often a vacancy in his eyes and a faraway tone in his voice. This she attributed to the travel, exhaustion and the excitement of the evening. The plane ride, however, was the most devastating experience of her life.

One moment her father seemed perfectly fine. Then he began referring to Jewel by her mother's name—Estelle—and by degrees he became more and more agitated and seemingly disoriented, not understanding why he was on a plane or where he was going. Jewel was terrified, and his agitation grew to a point where the flight attendants had to intervene. Fortunately they were only twenty minutes out of Louisiana and Jewel was able to calm him without him being restrained. By the time they landed, he seemed to be himself again, but exhausted, as if the lapse had been as much physical as mental.

The diagnosis was what every child fears for their parent— early-onset Alzheimer's disease. Whatever idea Jewel might have had about returning to New York or going back to Europe came to a grinding halt. Her father couldn't be left alone, especially in that enormous house. The doctors prescribed the latest in medication that was touted to slow the disease but not stop it. For a while the medication seemed to work, and then it didn't. They tried combination after combination, with the same result—"You should put him a facility where he can be cared for." For Jewel that was not an option.

Augustus Fontaine was her dad. The man who had been her rock for the better part of her life. Now it was her turn to be there for him.

For a while she tried to paint, to sculpt, but her father needed her more and more. Maybe it was some macabre blessing in disguise, she often thought. After the debacle of her showing at the Guggenheim, no one was beating down her door. She'd lost her mojo, and there seemed to be nowhere in her day or in her life for her to reclaim it. Instead, she turned all of her time and attention to caring for her father, until it became too much for her to handle alone. She hired Minerva.

That had been a little more than two years ago. The disease had plateaued and remained at the same stage for quite some time. She supposed that was a good thing, and she'd fully accepted the turn that her life had taken. But the hard reality of her father's care had done major damage to her bank account, and without the income from sales of her work, tours and speaking engagements, there was not much to replenish it with.

And then came Craig Lawson.

"Need any help with those?" Minerva walked into the kitchen and settled on the opposite side of the counter.

"I'm almost done. Thanks. How's Dad?"

"Fine. He had a good day. And might I ask about yours?"

Jewel tucked in a grin and busied herself with stacking the boxes. "Well…it was very nice."

"How nice?" she probed.

Jewel pushed out a breath. "Nice enough that I might do it again…if he asks."

Minerva's light brown eyes widened. She clapped her hands in delight. "Hallelujah, and let the choir say amen!"

Jewel couldn't help but laugh. "Gee whiz, Minerva, it's not that bad."

"Oh, yes, it is. When was the last time you went out…with a man?" There was a long pause. "Exactly. And it don't hurt that he's drop-dead gorgeous and wealthy."

"That's all very true, but you are getting way ahead of what is going on. He lives between London and California. He has the kind of life that I have been out of for quite some time. Even if there was something going on between us—which there isn't—there would be no way to make it work," she added dismissively, even as she replayed the way his mouth felt on hers, the way he tasted and the way she wanted more. "It's just two adults in a business arrangement that some-what enjoy each other's company."

"Hmm," Minerva murmured with a rise in her brow. "If you say so." She started for the archway that led to the dining room. "I have to run into town to pick up a few things. I should be back in an hour or so. Do you need anything?"

"No. I'm good. I'm going to sit with Dad for a while."

"Okay. See you soon."

Jewel plopped down on the stool and gazed off into the distance, trying to paint a portrait of what her life might look like with a man like Craig Lawson in it. But then she looked at the stack of bakery boxes and her eyes lifted to the floor above where her father slept. She pushed back from her seat and stood. This was her life.

Throughout the meeting with his team, Craig struggled with keeping focused on the items at hand. His thoughts continually shifted between topics of discussion and kissing Jewel Fontaine. He was pretty sure that was a bad move on his part. He had a long history of getting involved with people he worked with, Milan Chase being a prime example. He didn't want his somewhat jaded history to repeat itself with Jewel, but the truth of the matter was that, as inappropriate as it might be, he wanted to see her again. He wanted to take her to his bed and strip her naked. He needed to see and feel for himself if her skin was as silken as it looked. Did that lovely scent that drifted around her find its way beneath those gauzy dresses she wore? What would it feel like to be sheathed inside her? The merry-go-round of his questions was endless. He was immensely happy when the meeting came to an end.

"We can start preliminary shooting next week. Exteriors," Diane was saying as Craig pushed back from the table.

"Get the full schedule printed up and sent to everyone's tablets," Craig instructed her and Paul. "Norm, you can get some stills as well for the storyboards."

"No problem, boss," Norm, the technical director, said.

Craig checked his watch. He had time to shower and change before meeting up with his sister. He crossed over to Anthony before he headed to his room. "As soon as the revised contract is ready, let me know. I'll drop it off and get it signed."

Anthony shot him a sidelong look. "Not a problem."

He walked over to the minibar and poured himself a short glass of bourbon. "I'm gonna get ready to meet up with Alyse. I need all the fortitude I can get." He tossed the warm liquid down in one swallow, shut his eyes briefly against the burn then set the glass down. He clapped Anthony on the back. "Thanks for holding it down, man."

"We got this," he said with a grin.

Craig turned away and lifted his hand in salute.

He changed into a black cotton shirt and black slacks, slid his phone, credit card and room key into his pocket, and headed down to the lobby to meet his sister.

He was seated in one of the lounge chairs checking out the day's headlines when Alyse pushed through the revolving door. She didn't see him at first, and it gave Craig the opportunity to take in and appreciate the attractive and self-assured woman his little sister had become. His heart filled with warmth and good memories, which at the same time partnered with sadness that he could have allowed his rift with his father to keep him away from his sister. He stood just as she turned her head in his direction.

Her arms stretched wide, and her dimpled smile beamed as she literally ran to him. Craig swept her up in a hug, pressing her face to his chest. She locked her arms around his waist and craned her neck to look up at him.

"God, it's so good to see you," she said as tears formed in her eyes. She sniffed hard and stroked his strong jaw. "Those pictures are much better looking than you, though," she teased, deadpan.

Craig tossed his head back and laughed. It *would* be his little sister that had no problem giving him a reality check to remind him that he wasn't all that special. He pressed his palm to his chest. "You wound me. No respect for your elders." He grinned down at her. "It's good to see you, too, sis," he said with affection.

"Point me to the drinks and food and let's get this reunion started."

"We can go someplace else if you want," he offered.

"No, why bother? We're already here."

"Sounds good to me." Craig bent his arm and she slid hers through before leading her into the hotel's bar and restaurant.

Alyse had barely taken a breath once they were seated before she launched into her barrage of questions.

"So how long are you in town for and why didn't you tell anyone that you were coming?" She reached for her glass of water.

Craig leaned back in his seat. "About two months if everything goes according to schedule. And I know I should have called you and Myles." He paused. "I'm sorry."

"You should be. We haven't seen you in God knows how long," she groused. She shot him a glare. "I read that Milan is the lead." Her brow arched. "Ulterior motive?"

He pushed out a breath. Alyse was one of the few people other than Anthony who had told him from the start that getting involved with Milan Chase was a mistake. At the time he didn't care. They were hot for each other and they let it burn until there was nothing left but ashes.

"I don't have an ulterior motive, *and*," he qualified, "there is nothing going on now. She happened to be the best person for the role."

"Hmm." She rolled her eyes. "Just be careful, that's all I have to say about it. But speaking about your notorious love life, who are you seeing these days?"

His thought immediately leaped to Jewel. But he couldn't truthfully count her as someone he was seeing. Besides, the minute he let Alyse know that Jewel was the owner of the location where the film was to be shot, he would never hear the end of it. "You'll be happy—or at least surprised—to know that I'm not seeing anyone. I'm totally focused on this film."

"What are you plans when it's completed?" she asked with a hint of hesitation mixed with an unspoken plea.

Craig linked his long fingers together and shrugged slightly. "When it's done I'll head back to LA, to the studio for editing, then home to London. I have a television pilot that I'm contracted to work on in the fall."

Her long lashes lowered over her eyes. "Oh," she said softly.

"But I promise to stay in touch."

The waitress came to take their drink and dinner order. Once she was gone, Alyse continued her inquisition.

"Is it true that the movie is about our family?"

Craig rocked his jaw. "Let's just say that the Lawson legacy is the inspiration for the film."

"Does Dad know?" She stared across at him.

"I have no idea what he knows. I'm sure he doesn't care one way or the other what I do," he snapped, his expression hardening by degrees.

"You don't believe that."

"Why wouldn't I? He made himself very clear, Alyse. And if nothing else, I take Jake Lawson at his word."

The last confrontation with his father still stung all these years later. As the eldest son, it was expected that he would follow in his father's footsteps and one day take over the helm of JL International. Craig had had his sights set elsewhere. Since he was a kid he'd been fascinated by the wonder and magic of film. He would watch his mother prepare for her small film roles, and sometimes she would let him come on set. His mother nurtured his thirst for the arts, his father starved him. Things only grew worse between him and his father after the scandal and his mother's tragic death. When Craig entered college, his goal was to major in film as much for himself as well as homage to his mother. His father went ballistic and refused to cover the cost unless he switched his major to international business, which he claimed to do to satisfy his father. But unknown to Jake, Craig stayed on the film track. Instead of his college graduation being a day of celebration, it was an epic nightmare when Craig's degree was an MFA in film instead of an MBA in international business.

"I don't give a damn what it was you thought you wanted! You spent my money on this piece of crap degree to do what—become famous like your trifling, lying mother!"

"Don't you dare talk about my mother!"

Jake had whirled toward his son, his face twisted in rage. He'd pointed a warning finger at Craig. "I told you—" his voice shook "—this movie shit is nothing but an empty path filled with narcissistic assholes that want gratification from everyone but themselves. It's crap. It's frivolous, and it's not worthy of a Lawson! Didn't you learn anything from what your mother did to me, to us, to this family?"

"I can't live my life for you, Dad. I can't and I won't. This is my life, my dream. You had yours. You *have* to let me have mine."

"I don't have to do a damn thing." He'd snorted a nasty laugh. His dark eyes narrowed as he glared at his son. "This is what you want. Fine." He tossed his hands up in the air as if he'd conceded defeat, but Craig instantly knew better. His father never gave in, but he'd never expected what his father said next.

Jake had pursed his lips and slid his large hands into his pant pockets. "I want you to pack your things—everything. I want you out of my house by morning. I don't want to hear from you. I don't want to see you. Tomorrow I will meet with my attorneys to have your name removed from my will. You want your own life—you got it. Let's see how far you get on your own without everything that I've provided for and this family. Now get out of my sight."

For a moment, Craig had stared at his father in disbelief. Dozens of scenarios and monologues raced through his head, but nothing was remotely up to the level of hurt and disappointment and, yes, uncertainty that twisted inside him. He swallowed. "Fine. If that's what you want." He'd turned to walk away so that his father would not see the burn of tears that hung in his eyes.

"No, it's what you want!" his father tossed at Craig's back. "Live with it."

That had been a little more than ten years ago. And true to his father's demand, Craig had not been back. Unfortunately, his self-imposed exile also affected his relationship with his siblings.

Alyse wrapped one hand around her glass; the other she lay flat on the table and stared at her fingers.

"Look." He reached across the table and covered her hand. "Don't get yourself all mixed up in this beef with me and Dad. It's our ugly mess, not yours."

"But we're family, Craig," she said, her voice cracking with emotion. "You're a part of that family that has been missing for over a decade."

"That's not on me." He shook his head and glanced away.

The waitress returned with their drinks, and before they were on the table, Craig swiped up his and took a deep swallow. He lowered his head then looked across at her. "Let's enjoy the evening. We haven't seen each other in ages. Catch me up on what's going on with you and Myles."

Alyse visibly relaxed and launched into an animated monologue about her latest significant other, hirings and firings at the office and Myles's rise up the corporate ladder. "He's set to head up the new office in Detroit. As wild and crazy as the Motor City is now, real estate is a steal. There is so much potential. In another ten years that city will be unrecognizable and ready to compete with New York and LA."

"I'm sure you're right. It's definitely primed for a turnaround." He was certain that his father had seen that coming from miles away and was ready to pounce the instant that opportunity presented itself.

Their dinner arrived, and while they ate they reminisced about the crazy times they had growing up, with the conversation constantly peppered with *remember when?*

"Wow, it's nearly ten," Alyse said in amazement following her final bite of cheesecake.

"I'll drive you home."

"Don't be silly. I have my car." She grinned. "I'm a big girl now, remember."

"Yeah," he said, his voice warming. "I remember."

The valet brought her midnight-blue Lexus RX around to the front. Craig stood by the driver's door while Alyse slid in.

She glanced up at him. "When will I see you again?"

He braced his hand on the roof. "We'll work something out. Let me know when Myles is back in town and the three of us will hang out." He smiled.

"You plan on seeing Dad?" she asked hopefully.
"No."

"He misses you, you know. He'll never admit it, but I know he does."

He leaned down and kissed her forehead. "Drive safe. Love you." He stepped back and shut the door.

"Love you, too," she said through the open window then drove off.

Craig stood there until her car was out of sight. His father missed him. Hmm. He doubted that very much. It was wishful thinking on Alyse's part and nothing more. Just wishful thinking.

"Fontaine residence," Minerva said into the phone.

"Hello, this is Craig Lawson. I was hoping to speak with Ms. Fontaine."

"One moment."

Minerva put the phone down and went in search of Jewel. She was just coming down from sitting with her father.

"Ms. Jewel, there's a call for you. Mr. Lawson," she added with a twinkle in her eyes.

Jewel's heart beat a little faster, but she kept her expression neutral. "Thanks, Minerva." She came down the last few steps and walked toward the den. "I'll take it in here."

She walked in and closed the door halfway behind her, took a breath and picked up the phone. "I have it, Minerva," she said and waited to ensure that Minerva hung up the extension. "Hello," she said once she heard the telltale click. "How are you?"

"Good. Better now," he said and wished that he hadn't. "I mean, it was a busy morning. I, uh, have the revised contract as well as the shooting schedule, and the check. I wanted to drop it all off later this evening if that's okay."

Jewel grew hot all over. The tips of her ears were on fire. Flashes of their parting kiss on his last visit danced in front of her. *This evening.* Evenings were always difficult for her.

"Umm, sure. How is seven, seven thirty?" She swallowed. Her father was usually settled and calm by then.

"Not a problem. See you then."

"Okay."

"Take my cell number in case...of anything."

"Hang on a sec." She got a piece of paper and a pen from the table and took down the number.

"Feel free to call anytime. See you this evening. Enjoy the rest of your day."

"You, too." She squeezed the phone in her palm for a moment then returned it to the cradle and stared at the number in hand. *Call anytime.* She pushed out a breath and walked out.

"Too busy for an old friend?"

Craig slid his phone into his pants pocket and turned. "Milan." His eyes roved over her. As always, she was photograph perfect. She had the looks and simmering sexuality of a hot young starlet with the edge of maturity rolled in. Whenever Milan walked into a space, bystanders were swept up in the swirl of her aura. The magnetism that she exuded as easily as she breathed was what made her an undeniable star on the big and small screens. This role was made for her, and as much as he didn't want to stir up the coals of their past relationship, he knew that Milan would not make that easy. It was all in her eyes and the teasing flicker at the corners of her mouth. He sat on the edge of the table and folded his arms. "What can I do for you?"

Milan took a step toward him. "I think you have the answer to that."

Craig lowered his head for a moment and shook it slowly from side to side. He looked at her. The corner of his mouth curved into a grin. "Not happenin', baby. We both know that. A friendly drink is as far as it's ever going to go."

She stretched out her manicured finger and ran it along the line of his jaw. "Why? You're not seeing anyone. And we have a history. We're both going to need to unwind at the end of those *long* workdays." Her lashes lowered over her trademark smoldering eyes.

Craig stood. He looked down into her upturned face. "I'm sure you'll find something to satisfy you, but it won't be me. Not again."

Their tumultuous past flared between them.

"How many ways do I have to say I'm sorry," she begged.

"You don't. Just do what you're being paid to do." He started to move past her. She grabbed his arm.

"Craig... I'm sorry. When are you going to forgive me?" She blinked rapidly. "I miss you."

His cold look stripped away the facade. "You *are* good," he said, his tone dripping in sarcasm. "If I didn't know the real you and what you're capable of, I would almost believe the BS you're slinging."

Milan's five-foot-six frame jerked as if she'd been

pushed. Her beguiling expression morphed into one of stunned disbelief then anger. "You don't talk to me like that," she said between her teeth.

"Milan... I'm not going down this road with you. Let's keep it professional. You're here for the movie, and that's it. If you've changed your mind about the role, let me know now and we'll start looking for a replacement." His unflinching gaze held her in place.

She pressed her mouth tightly together, hurled a death stare at him and then spun away.

Craig filled his cheeks with air and pushed out a long breath. Anthony had warned him about signing Milan on to the project. But he wanted the best for the film. And, unfortunately, Milan was the best for the role. They both knew that. But, hell, he'd kick her to the curb in a heartbeat and move on if she couldn't keep the past in the past where it belonged. He never should have agreed to anything even as innocuous as drinks. Leading her on was the last thing he wanted.

"Trouble in paradise?" Anthony asked, sidling up next to Craig.

"Not anymore."

"Good. The last thing we need is diva drama. So... how did it go with Alyse?"

Craig smiled. "Good. Really good. We had dinner, talked, laughed—like old times."

"Glad to hear it. I'd love to see Alyse. It's been a while."

"We plan to get together when Myles is back in town. I'll let you know." They didn't talk about it, but he knew that Anthony carried a torch for Alyse. They both also knew that Alyse, unlike Craig, wouldn't cross her father.

"Sounds good. Listen, Norm wants to meet with us for a few."

Craig nodded in agreement, but his mind was on seeing Jewel later. It was going to be a long day.

"Everything okay?" Minerva asked when Jewel exited the den.

"Yes. Fine." She tried to breeze by Minerva, but she wasn't having any of it.

"Then why do you look like a frightened doe? Did something happen?"

Jewel rubbed her hands together. "Nothing happened. He's going to drop by later to bring the revised contract and the check, that's all."

Minerva studied her. "You aren't reconsidering, are you?"

"No."

"Then what is it?"

She understood that Minerva was concerned for her. In the short time that she'd been part of the family, Minerva had taken on not only the role of caregiver but surrogate mother. A role that Jewel embraced. She'd been without a strong female figure and nurturer in her life since she was six when she'd lost her mother to cancer. Of course her father stepped in and filled as many of the empty spaces as he could, but he could never be the mother that a part of Jewel would always miss. Although tragic circumstances had brought Minerva to them, it was also a blessing. She'd come to lean on Minerva when things became difficult and accepted Minerva's unsolicited wisdom as part of the package.

Jewel walked into the living room and sat down

on the side chair. She crossed her legs at the knee and linked her fingers together. "I know financially it's the right thing to do," she began.

"But?" Minerva sat opposite her on the love seat.

"But…he kissed me…well, we kissed each other."

Minerva's eyes widened. "Really, now. Well, that changes things—or does it?" She leveled her gaze on Jewel.

Jewel glanced away. "I don't know if it does or doesn't. It complicates things, that's for sure."

"Why?"

"You know why. We've talked about this."

"No, *you* talked yourself out of it before there was a this."

Jewel pursed her lips. "Maybe," she mumbled. "But now what? What if it didn't mean anything? He's notorious for being a womanizer. I'm probably one of many. I'm sure he felt he owed it to me for saying yes to the deal," she rambled on, stacking up a litany of excuses.

"Hmm, all that, huh?"

Jewel's gaze jumped to Minerva's reproving expression. "Sounds like you are setting yourself up to be disappointed."

"But it's all true!"

Minerva shrugged. "Says the gossip sites. But you don't know that for yourself. Besides, what's so wrong with grabbing a little sunshine, no matter how fleeting? You deserve it, sweetheart. You're young, beautiful and single, but you've buried yourself in this house and under the weight of your father's illness. Do you really think Augustus would want that

for you? Your father would want you to live your life
and be happy."

Jewel lowered her head. "Easier said than done."

Minerva pushed up from the chair. "It's only
as hard as you make it." She started to walk away,
stopped and turned back. "Oh—" She pressed her
hand to her forehead. "Our church committee is putting together donations for the middle school. It's a
damn shame that the teachers have to go in their own
pockets for supplies and such. Anyway, I was wondering if you wanted to part with any of your things
in the cottage? Things you don't plan to use no more."

Jewel's stomach instantly knotted at the mention
of the cottage. She swallowed. "Um, I'll take a look
and let you know." She forced a smile. She knew what
Minerva was trying to do.

"Whatever you could spare I know would be appreciated."

Jewel watched Minerva walk away and realized
that her heart was racing. She couldn't remember the
last time she'd set foot in the cottage that she'd converted into her home studio. After New York her life
spiraled downward. Her relationship with Simon im-
ploded along with her career, and she couldn't bring
herself to cross the threshold of a place that represented all that she'd lost—especially her confidence.
She'd lost confidence in herself as an artist and as a
woman that a man wanted to commit to.

Minerva was right in some respects. She'd turned
off the lights of her life, and for the first time in longer than she cared to remember, the switch turned on
when she met Craig Lawson. Maybe it was time. She
got up and walked out.

* * *

The cottage was situated behind the main house. Several generations ago it served as home for the servants who lived on and worked the land. She'd modernized it, adding plumbing, insulation and electricity. After a few coats of paint and some personal touches she'd made it her own. When she was in the throes and frenzy of a new project, she would sequester herself in her studio for hours and days at a time until she collapsed from exhaustion. Her father would come to look for her only to find her curled up on the floor with a drop cloth as a quilt. Eventually, she added a cushy couch and stacked sheets and blankets on a shelf for those nights when she couldn't make it the few hundred feet to her bedroom.

Those days were behind her. She knew there was nothing beyond these doors for her, even as she stood motionless in front of the cottage entrance. She swallowed down her reticence then reached into the pocket of her shift and took out the key. Her hand shook ever so slightly as she aimed the key at the lock.

Slowly she turned the key and pushed the door open. She expected to be hit with a blast of dust, cobwebs and stale air. Instead there was a lingering scent of jasmine. She stepped fully into the space and shook her head sharply in disbelief. Everything was just as she remembered it. She walked, trance-like, to her wood and metal worktable and gingerly ran her fingers across her sketchpads and the glass jars where she kept her pencils and brushes. Turning, her gaze scanned the walls that held her paintings— some completed, others mere shadows of ideas—then to the easels and the shelf that held her cameras, the cabinet where she kept her molding clays, tools and wood for her sculptures.

She pressed her nose against the stacked sheets and inhaled their recently washed freshness. That was when she noticed the vase of fresh flowers on the small table by the couch where she often slept.

Her eyes welled, and the tears slid down her cheeks. She sniffed and swiped at her eyes. She planted her hands on the curve of her hips and took another slow turn around her space. "Damn you, Minerva!" she whispered in grudging gratitude.

Jewel was frosting a wedding shower cake when Minerva sauntered into the kitchen. She'd been able to avoid Minerva for the better part of the day, but she knew it couldn't last forever.

"Dad okay?" she asked without looking up.

"He's napping. I want to get started on his dinner." She walked to the refrigerator, sidestepping the elephant in the room.

"How long?"

Minerva glanced over her shoulder. "How long for what?"

"How long have you been taking care of the cottage?"

She removed a package of chicken breasts and shut the refrigerator door. She shrugged. "'Bout six months, I suppose."

Jewel blinked away her disbelief. "Six months?"

"Hmm. About that." She ripped open the package and turned on the water in the sink.

Jewel plopped down in a chair. "Why?"

Minerva turned and faced Jewel. "Because I believe in you even though you've stopped believing in yourself."

Jewel lowered her head. "I guess I have in a way." She pushed out a breath. "I feel like I lost my passion."

"It's still there. Buried under all the other mess that you've let pile up on you."

"Maybe."

"You'll never know unless you give it a try."

Jewel shook her head. "I...don't think I can go back down that road."

"You been tellin' yourself that nonsense for so long you actually believe it." She made a noise with her teeth. "Well, if you ain't gonna use that stuff in there, I'll just pack it up and take it on over to the church to distribute to the school." She opened the overhead cabinets for the seasonings and began humming something Jewel was sure was a spiritual under her breath. She seasoned, and she hummed. She prepared the chicken in the pan, and she hummed. She cut up fresh string beans, and she hummed.

"Fine!" Jewel conceded after ten long minutes of humming, the ghosts of her ancestors having challenged her with every note and a reminder that she had no idea about real hardship.

Minerva looked over her shoulder with a wide-eyed expression of innocence. "I'm sorry. What?"

"I said...fine. I'll keep my things." She took the frosted cake and put it in the secondary refrigerator that she used for her baking clients.

"Well, now, that's a start." She turned back to the stove.

Jewel planted her hand on her hip, slowly shook her head then walked out of the kitchen.

Chapter 5

Jewel stepped out of the shower and rubbed the fogged mirror clear with the edge of the towel. She stared at her reflection. Physically, she hadn't changed much in the past five years.

At thirty-two, her skin was still smooth and even, though not as bright as it once was. A stray strand of gray would pop up in her hair every now and then, which she quickly made disappear. Her eyes, wide and deep brown, haloed with long dark lashes, were reflective of her mother, her father would always say, and her thick, wild curls had been a nightmare to contain when she was growing up. Now she simply let the mass of mayhem do what it wanted. She did manage to exercise on a regular basis and she ate well, so her body maintained its original design, with a bit of extra padding around her hips and the swell of her breasts, which she attributed to age and maturity. Fortunately gravity hadn't gotten its grip on her as of yet.

It wasn't the outside that had changed. Anyone that hadn't seen her in years would surely recognize her. It was beneath the exterior that was different. There was a huge empty space inside her that she tried to fill with the running of the house, taking care of her father and baking for a growing clientele. But when she lay alone in bed every night, the longing in that empty space mushroomed. Even when she'd been lonely or hurt or confused in the past she'd had her art to fall back on. But for the past five years she hadn't even had that to console her.

What would be so wrong in snatching a bit of happiness? Craig's kiss reminded her that she was still a desirable woman, a woman with needs. She turned away from her reflection to get ready for her evening.

It was a little after five when Jewel went to check in on her father. Minerva was removing the dinner dishes when she walked into his bedroom.

Every time she saw her father her heart twisted. She fully understood the meaning behind the phrase *a shell of a man*. Augustus Fontaine was once a robust six-foot one, two-hundred-plus-pound man, muscled from his years of hard physical labor with a spark in his eyes and hearty laugh that was infectious.

Unlike Jewel, anyone who had not seen her father in many years would never recognize him, except perhaps in those moments that were becoming more rare, when the spark of recognition lit up in his eyes and he smiled. Those moments were what she longed for each day.

"Hey, Daddy," she greeted him and pushed a smile across her lips as she walked over to where he sat by the window.

"He's having a good day," Minerva whispered as they passed each other. She patted Jewel's shoulder and walked out.

Jewel sat on the windowsill next to her father's recliner. He was staring at the apple tree outside his window. "Need to pick some of those apples before the frost sets in. Have Estelle make some pies," he said more to himself than to Jewel. "I love her apple pies."

Jewel swallowed and blinked back tears. Her mother, Estelle, had been gone so long that the only memory Jewel had of her was from pictures and the stories her father told her. She reached for her father's thin hand and brought it to her cheek. He looked up at her with muddy brown eyes.

"It's me, Daddy," she said softly. "It's Jewel."

He stared at her for what seemed like forever. He smiled. "Jewel is sho' a pretty name." His forehead tightened and his face tensed as if he was straining to grasp something just out of reach.

She caressed his hand.

"Hey, baby girl," he said clear as day. "You have dinner yet? I just finished. Pretty good today."

Jewel's heart pounded. "Hey, Daddy. No, I haven't eaten yet. I will. Wanted to check on you first."

"Don't wait till late." He shook his head. "I read somewhere that it's not good to eat late." He looked at her and frowned. A cloud dulled his eyes. "Need to get the horses in. Storm's coming." He pulled his hand out of her grip. He turned his head and stared out the window.

Jewel squeezed her eyes shut then leaned down and kissed him tenderly on the forehead. He looked at her with a mixture of confusion and gratitude. "I'll come back and check on you later, Daddy."

"Storm's coming."

She offered a faint smile. "You may be right," she murmured and walked out.

"I'm not too early, am I?" Craig asked when he stepped across the threshold.

"Not at all. I'm getting set up in the kitchen. Have you eaten?" Jewel shut the door behind him.

"Uh, not really."

She threw him a smile over her shoulder. "Follow me." She led the way into the kitchen. "I'm trying out a new recipe."

"If it's anything like your muffins, I'm sure it'll be spectacular."

Jewel laughed. "We shall see. You'll be my taste tester."

His brows rose in mock alarm. "What are you fixing, exactly?" He placed the envelope with the documents on the table.

"Grilled, stuffed red snapper with a mushroom risotto and fresh green beans." She eyed the ingredients on the island table.

"I'd offer to help, but I'm not very handy in the kitchen. More of a grill man."

"Perfect. When I'm done you can slide the snapper in the grill."

"Touché."

"You can pour some wine or something stronger,

if you like. The stronger stuff is in the glass cabinet in the living room. Help yourself."

"What can I fix for you?"

"There's a bottle of white wine in the fridge."

"Got it." He went off to grab the bottle of bourbon then fixed Jewel a glass of wine.

She sipped while preparing the snapper, all the while commanding her fingers to stop shaking and her pulse to slow down. If she didn't get too close to him or allow him to look right into her eyes, she would be fine. Even as she chatted mindlessly—about what, she had no idea—she simultaneously questioned why, in heaven's name, she had invited him to dinner.

"I wanted Norm, my technical director, to come by tomorrow to take some of the exterior shots of the house, the grounds and the rooms on the lower floors," Craig was saying.

Jewel took a swallow of wine. "Tomorrow. Sure." She used baking thread to sew the snapper closed. "So it begins," she said before setting down her glass of wine. She went to the sink and washed her hands. "The grill is the bottom shelf. Already preheated," she said while keeping her back to Craig.

Craig lifted the tray with the snapper and put it in the oven grill with a flourish. "How's that for grilling?" he teased. "Told you I had talent."

Jewel turned, and he was right behind her. Her breath caught in her throat. She could see the reflection of light in his eyes and the way his dark lashes framed the intensity of his gaze.

"Need me to do anything else?"

His question sounded innocent enough, but what lurked around the corners of his mouth said something completely different. God, he smelled good. Her heart thumped. She swallowed, tried to look away but couldn't.

"I haven't stop thinking about the other day," he said. The deep timbre of his voice strummed her insides like a plucked guitar string.

"Oh," she managed. There was no room to escape without their bodies brushing and colliding with each other. That was a no-no.

He reached out and ran his hand slowly down her arm. "It's all I've been thinking about. That's new for me," he confessed. With his other hand, he caressed the curve of her jaw. Her lids fluttered. Her heart raced.

"What about you? Has our kiss crossed your mind at all?"

She should lie. She should pretend that it was nothing. "It has," she admitted.

"Hmm. We should do something about that." His gaze moved slowly over her face.

Jewel felt her body heat, and it had nothing to do with the oven.

And then his mouth was on hers and his arm drew her close; with his other he threaded his fingers through the explosion of her curls and pulled her to him. The tip of his tongue teased her lips, and she felt a shot of current race through her limbs.

She gave in. Gave in to the sensations, the feel of him, the taste of him. Her mouth parted to welcome him, and she felt more than heard the moan that rumbled deep in his throat.

Craig eased back, and Jewel felt bereft, as if she'd been suddenly left alone in the dark and she didn't want to be there. She wanted to step back into the warmth of light that radiated around him. She draped her fingers around his neck and leaned in, confident in her role of aggressor. But not for long.

Craig pressed her back against the sink, the hard lines of his body commanding hers to relent and merge with his. His lips worked hers; his tongue teased and danced in her mouth.

Jewel allowed herself to float on a magical ride of sensual pleasure. Every nerve ending stirred. She felt as if she'd finally been awakened after a long sleep. So what if whatever happened between them was only temporary? She deserved to feel like a woman, a desirable woman whose long-unattended needs would be satisfied.

"Jewel," he murmured against her lips before resting his forehead on hers. He released his hold on her and placed his hands on the curve of her hips. He looked into her eyes. The edges of his mouth flickered with the beginnings of a smile. "We'll never get through dinner at this pace."

His gaze was low and lazy, as if he'd been stirred from a cozy dream, Jewel thought. She pressed the tip of her finger against his bottom lip. "You're probably right." She stepped out of the space he'd cocooned them in and went to sit at the island counter. She reached for her glass of wine. Her hand trembled ever so slightly. She drew in a breath then took a long, much needed swallow.

Craig reached for the wine bottle and refilled her glass. He straddled the chair and rested his forearms across the back.

"Ply me with wine? Is that the plan?" Her fingers wrapped around the stem of the glass.

"I wish I could say I had a plan." He zeroed in on her. "I don't. I hope you understand that."

Jewel lowered her head for a moment then looked at him. "What if *I* did?"

His brow rose in question. "Have a plan?"

She ran her tongue across her bottom lip. "I wouldn't exactly call it a plan, but more like a proposal."

"Now I'm really curious."

She shook a stray curl away from her face and drew in a breath of resolve. "I'm...attracted to you." She swallowed. "And I believe you're attracted to me."

"Very much."

Emboldened by his reply, she continued. "You'll only be here for a couple of months at best. I'm not looking for commitment, or long term, or empty promises. I'm not in a position to ask for what I can't give in return. Once you're done here, you'll go back to your life. I get that. Totally. But...in the time you're here...let's get to know each other, explore whatever this is...until it's time for you to leave."

There, she'd said it, taken a leap of faith. She had absolutely nothing to lose—besides her pride, of course.

"Wow." He shifted in his seat and then studied her for a moment. "Two, three months..."

She nodded.

"And you're good with that?"

She nodded again. Her pulse raced.

"My time is not my own, especially when I'm in

the middle of a project like this. But... I'll make it my business to make as much time for this as I can."

"Fair enough."

He gave her a lopsided grin and reached out and stroked her chin with the tip of his finger. "Best negotiation I've ever been involved in."

Jewel released a laugh of relief. She pushed up from her seat and stood over him. She knew what she was doing was just this side of crazy. But for once she wasn't going to plan something to death—she was going to go with the flow. So far she liked how things were flowing.

"You want to show me the contract?"

He grinned. "I want to show you a lot of things, but we can start with the contract."

Jewel served up their plates and suggested that they eat on the back veranda. Craig carried the plates, and Jewel brought the glasses and the bottle of wine.

"Oh, I forgot the salad," Jewel said. "Be right back." She darted off into the house, which gave Craig a few moments to process what had transpired.

No doubt he was totally attracted to this woman. More than he'd initially realized. But he'd never expected that she was the kind of woman who would be willing to get involved in a relationship that was transient at best. He wasn't sure what he'd expected when he kissed her, or when he made the unnecessary trip to her home. It certainly wasn't her very unorthodox proposal. He didn't know how he felt about that. A part of him, the rogue playboy part, was thrilled. But that other part that secretly longed for something that went beneath the surface wasn't as certain.

Jewel returned with a large salad bowl and placed it on the center of the circular wrought-iron table.

"Everything okay?" she asked and sat down.

"Yeah." He pushed a smile across his face. "Some work stuff I was thinking about." He relaxed in his chair. "I know you can't wait to experience how well I grilled the snapper," he teased.

Jewel giggled. "It's all in the wrist, I'm sure."

"Exactly, exactly." He cut into his fish and put a forkful in his mouth. Slowly he chewed to savor the incredible combination of flavors. "Man…this right here—" he pointed to the fish with his fork "—needs to be on one of those cooking shows or in some book. Wow."

Jewel grinned. "Glad you like it. After all, you did have a hand in the preparation."

He cut into another piece. "You bake, you throw down in the kitchen…what other talents do I need to know about?"

Her buoyant expression deflated by degrees. She focused on the food on her plate. "That's pretty much it."

"I doubt that," he said softly. "You're an artist in every sense of the word."

Jewel sipped her wine.

"That showing in New York was, what, five, seven years ago?"

Her eyes jumped to his face. She swallowed and reached for her glass. "Why?"

Craig angled his head. "You haven't been on the scene since." He'd looked her up, read about her rise in the art world and her monumental fall, the scathing reviews and the follow-up stories about how she was finished and how, almost like a self-fulfilling prophesy, she'd disappeared.

"Your point?"

"Why?"

"It doesn't matter why. That was then. I've moved on. Let's leave it at that."

"The reviews were pretty vicious," he continued, undeterred by her stonewalling. "Was that it?"

Her expression hardened. She set down her fork and looked him in the eyes. "Let's just say it was the perfect storm of events. I made a decision, and I've lived with it. End of story."

"I work with actors every day, some of the best. I can spot a poorly acted scene a mile away. *That* was a poorly acted scene."

"What difference does it make?" Her voice rose. "Why do you care one way or the other?" Her eyes were wide.

He placed his palms down on the table and looked directly at her. "Because if I'm going to get myself involved with a woman that I am crazy attracted to… I want to know who she is." That was only partially true. For the most part, a woman's backstory didn't mean much for him. He rarely cared, but in this case he did. He wanted to know the real Jewel Fontaine.

Jewel bit down on her bottom lip. She turned her head and stared off into the tranquil night. A sparrow landed on the top branch of the tree, and the first splash of stars sprinkled across the sky.

"The reviews were only a part of it," she said quietly. "My artistic sensibilities were another," she said, attempting to sound cavalier.

"As artists we're always going to be scrutinized

and criticized for what we do. It's part of the game. Some critics live for the opportunity to tear an artist apart to satisfy their own lack of ability."

"I know that in a cerebral sense, but here—" she tapped her chest "—here's a different story."

Craig drew in a breath. He knew all too well what it felt like to be torn apart by the press, to have your work trampled on and dismissed. It was deeply personal, like having someone you love hurt. It was difficult enough when it was strangers, people who didn't give a damn about you as person. But when it came from those who professed to care about you, that was a whole different kind of hurt. So yeah, he understood, but he also knew that you had to dust yourself off and keep moving.

"I know me and you are totally different. Everybody deals with their stuff in their own way. All I'm saying is a true artist, a creator never lets that go, because when they do a part of them dies inside. And on that note, I'll leave it alone." He held up his hand. "Promise."

"Thank you," she said softly.

Craig refilled her glass and then his own.

"So, tell me how you wound up selecting my home all the way from London."

He chuckled. "It was actually a pretty long process. We'd been looking for a location for about six months…" While they finished off their meal, he went on to tell her about the myriad of homes and locations his team had gone through in several parts of the country until Paul Frazier finally found hers. "The minute I saw it, I knew this was the place."

"What were you going to do if I'd stuck to my guns and said no?"

The corner of his mouth lifted. "In this business you always have a fallback plan. We had another potential location, but I was determined to convince you to change your mind."

"You're very persuasive."

"One of my many talents."

"Is the list of talents long?"

"And varied."

They laughed at the double entendre.

"I want to show you something," Jewel said, pushing back from the table. She grabbed the bottle of wine and her glass.

"Sure." He followed her off the veranda to the cottage behind the house.

"Hold these a sec." She handed him the bottle and her glass then unlocked the door. She flipped on the light switch.

Craig walked in behind Jewel then stepped past her and into the studio. He reverently touched the completed works and works in progress, the sculptures and the tools of her trade. He turned toward her.

"These are some of the pieces from New York."

"Hmm." She folded her arms. "A testament of sorts."

He continued to examine the works. "You were ahead of your time. It happens with all great artists." He leaned against the wall. "And the others?"

"Some ideas I had that never materialized."

"So you have been keeping up with your art?"

She heaved a sigh. "Actually, I haven't. I stuck these in here ages ago and haven't been back here…

until today. Minerva…the housekeeper, unbeknownst to me, was maintaining the space."

"You had no idea what she was doing?"

"Not a clue." She sputtered a laugh. "She told me today that she was going to donate some of my art supplies to the local school and that I should come here and see what I wanted to keep. This is what I found," she added with a sweep of her hand.

"What did you decide?"

She crossed the room and sat on the cushy love seat. "I decided to keep everything."

"Will you paint again?"

"It's been so long."

"You never lose it, you know. It's like riding a bike. You just have to get back on and start peddling."

"Humph, easier said."

"Why did you bring me here, Jewel?"

She linked her fingers together and looked across at him. "I'm not sure, really."

"I think you know." He came to sit beside her.

"I spent so much time here," she said thoughtfully. "Hours, days on end when I was in the middle of creating a new piece." She smiled. "My dad finally had a bed and couch put in so that he wouldn't find me sleeping on the floor in the morning." She looked around. "This space represents my past."

"It can be your future if you let it." He pursed his lips in contemplation, leaned forward and rested his arms on his thighs. "Look, I'm not in any position to tell you what to do. What I can tell you is that when you're given a gift—and you've been given a gift—it's damn near a sin to misuse it or to keep it for yourself."

"Is that what you told yourself when you walked away from your family?"

He flinched, looked away then back at her. "Yes. It was," he finally said, the day of that decision racing through is mind. "I had a choice to make—my happiness or live in the shadow of someone else's happiness for me."

Jewel looked away. "Are you satisfied with your life based on what you had to give up?"

Craig exhaled and leaned against the back of the couch. "I won't BS you and say that there haven't been moments when I questioned myself. And it's not always easy for me to accept what I left behind in order to move forward. But I do know that if I hadn't done it, I would always second-guess myself. I would be miserable and I would blame...him for my misery."

Jewel angled her body on the couch so that she could face him and then tucked one leg beneath her. She sipped her wine. "Not handing all this over to Minerva's church and the local school, I suppose, is some kind of decision, in a way."

Craig looked at her and chuckled. "Yeah, kinda, sorta. It's a start." He touched his glass to hers. His expression sobered. "To starting something new."

"Something new," she whispered.

Craig put his glass down on the table and turned toward her. He reached out and tucked a curl away from her eye. "You're not like anyone I've known," he said as if realizing that idea for the first time.

"I hope that's a good thing," she said. Her voice quavered ever so slightly.

"I think so." He moved closer and plucked her glass from her hand and set it next to his. "I think that maybe this *exploration* that you mentioned is worth investigating." He leaned closer and cupped her chin, bringing her close to him. "You still good with that?" he asked against her lips.

Jewel's pulse thundered in her veins. There was still time to back out. All she had to do was move away gracefully. "Very good with that," she said instead and welcomed the pillow of his lips.

His strong arms slid around her and pulled her as close as their sitting positions would allow. His fingers stroked the curve of her spine, sending shock waves along her limbs.

Jewel moaned when his thumbs brushed along the undersides of her breasts then down the curve of her waist to her hips.

The burst of flavors from their meal was heightened by the wine as their tongues touched, danced and melded together.

Craig deepened the kiss before easing away to nibble along the column of her neck and in the V of her dress. Jewel's body quivered in response, and her breathing stopped and started.

This was so unlike her. She was always deliberate and thoughtful about getting involved. But Craig Lawson had her thinking and feeling all out of her comfort zone. Her head spun, and her body simmered. All she knew for sure was that she wanted Craig to keep stoking the flames.

Craig groaned deep in his throat. He eased back and stood. He took her hands and pulled her to her feet. "Are you sure you want this?" he rasped before dropping a hot kiss at the base of her throat.

Jewel's body shuddered. A million reasons why she shouldn't zipped through her head, but the one reason why she should beat them all to the finish line: she wanted to be reminded what it felt like to make love to a virile sexy, hot man that she couldn't stop thinking about. She wanted to feel his bare skin. She wanted his hands on her body, his body in hers. She wanted to reclaim her woman power.

"Yes," she whispered.

He looked into her eyes one last time before he possessed her mouth. He gathered her and held her tightly against him.

Jewel gasped at the erotic feel of his erection pressing against her belly a moment before Craig dipped lower and melded them together, pelvis to pelvis, rocking his hips against her in prelude of what was to come. He palmed her derriere and worked her to meet his undulations.

"Baby," he groaned against her mouth. "I want you...now." He eased the straps of her sundress off her shoulders and slid it down her body until the soft fabric pooled at her feet. "Let me look at you." He took a step back, and his dark eyes raked over her from the top of her head to the tips of her toes. He reached out with a single finger and outlined the curve of her breasts that flowed over the lilac lace that held them.

Jewel shivered. Her eyes momentarily fluttered as waves of heat flowed through her. Her inner thighs trembled when he stroked her there.

Craig lowered his head and stroked the valley of her breasts with his tongue. Jewel moaned and gripped his arms to keep on her feet. He reached behind her and unfastened the clasp, stripped her of her bra and tossed it aside. "Hmm," he murmured and took a turgid nipple into his mouth. His mouth suckled, and his tongue laved and teased, sending shock waves through her limbs.

Jewel grabbed the back of his head and held him in place, tossing her head back in ecstasy.

Craig turned them around slowly and backed her up toward the overstuffed full-size bed, nibbling and licking her exposed flesh in the process.

Jewel tumbled back onto the bed and looked up at him. The fierce heat and unrelenting determination in his gaze terrified as much as it thrilled her. There was no turning back now.

Craig tugged his black V-neck sweater over his head and tossed it aside. His soft, faded jeans were next. Jewel swallowed and ran her tongue hungrily across her bottom lip when her gaze landed on the imprint of his erection bulging against his black-and-white-striped shorts. He crossed the short space that separated them and made his way to her lips, beginning with hot kisses on the inside of her ankles, up her legs and behind her knees. He nuzzled her sex, and she squirmed before he dipped his tongue into the indentation in her belly.

His hands, his mouth, his tongue seemed to be everywhere at once. Jewel's thoughts scattered like windblown leaves. All that she was capable of understanding was the incredible sensations that scored her body and ignited the blood in her veins.

Craig eased her panties over her hips and down her legs. His fingers gently stroked and primed her there, and her arousal dampened his fingers. He inched his way up the curves and valleys of her body until he was pillowed between the rise of her breasts. He covered one with his palm, the other he taunted with his tongue until Jewel writhed and moaned beneath him.

She didn't know when or how, but Craig had sheathed himself and positioned his weight above her. He tenderly brushed the riot of curls away from her face and caressed her cheek. He pushed her thighs apart with a sweep of his knee and rose up on his own. The heat of his eyes moved over her face. She'd never wanted anything as much as she wanted him in that moment.

Jewel looped her hands behind his head and bent her knees. Craig pushed forward, finding her wet, open and ready. She sucked in a lungful of air as the pressure of his entry began to fill her. Her heart pounded, and she bit down on her lip to keep from crying out. It didn't work. The symphony of desire sang from the center of her being as he buried himself deep within her, hovering there to allow them both to savor that first moment.

Jewel whimpered. Her body shook as he began to move, slow and deep and steady. Bright lights flashed behind her closed lids. Waves of need raced through her. She found his rhythm and met him stroke for stroke, raising and lowering her hips in time with his thrusts.

Craig was lost on a ride of pure pleasure. Part of him wanted to pound away, take it all now, fast, and satisfy the raging need that fueled his every movement. The other part of him wanted this feeling to last forever. He could stay there forever, cocooned in her wet heat that suckled and milked him every time he moved. But as much as he wanted this to be eternity, he felt the steady building in the heaviness of his sac, the pulsing and thickening of his cock.

A deep groan rumbled in his chest. His jaw clenched.

Jewel saw the bright lights. Currents of electricity shot up the backs of her legs. Her vagina began to clench and unclench. Her breath hitched in her throat. Her fingers pressed into the muscles of his back. Her ankles locked around him. A scream burst from her lips as the first wave of her climax slammed through her and then another and another until she was delirious with pleasure, lost in delight.

Craig slid his arms beneath her hips and held her in place as he rode the final wave to his release and his body slumped against hers.

Their hearts banged and pounded against each other. Their breaths ran and danced and then mingled into one unified breath, one heartbeat.

Craig nestled his head in the sweet curve of her neck. Jewel caressed his back and the tips of his ears.

She had no words for what she was feeling. Incredible, sensational, fulfilled, joyous—nothing would explain it. She closed her eyes and held Craig close. She didn't want to think beyond today, this moment. If nothing ever came of things between her and Craig, she would always have tonight.

"You okay?" he asked in a ragged breath in her ear.

"Fine. You?"

He rose up a bit and looked into her eyes. For a moment he simply stared at her. "Better than fine," he said.

Jewel smiled. She ran a finger along his bottom lip. He reached around him and pulled up the sheet to cover them before rolling off her and resting on his back. He scooped his arm under her head and eased her close. Jewel rested her head against his chest, and the crazy feeling that this was where she belonged suddenly felt more real than she dared to hope. *Crazy*, she thought before she closed her eyes and drifted into a light sleep of satisfaction. *Crazy.*

Craig listened to her steady breathing while he gently played with a strand of her hair between his fingers. He could easily get too caught up with this woman. He'd thought that if he had sex with her then whatever it was that was making him crazy would burn itself out. If anything it had only intensified his longing. And it was far from *just* sex. He'd made love to her the way he'd wanted to truly make love to a woman for longer than he cared to remember—not just with his body but with his soul. That reality left him with an unfamiliar feeling of vulnerability. This woman had opened a door inside him and stepped in. He angled his head and watched her sleep. He kissed the top of her head and closed his eyes. *Be careful what you wish for* was the last thought that floated through his head before he drifted off to sleep.

Jewel felt herself slowly rising from the depths of satiated sleep. A comforting warmth was wrapped around her. It took a moment for her to piece together the odd weight that she felt across her thighs and realize that it was Craig's muscled leg, and that the added heat she felt radiated from him. Her heart leaped. They were so close, chest to breasts. He held her tightly against him, as if in his dreams he was afraid he might lose her if he let go.

That's what she told herself, what she would like to believe, if only for the moment. She'd forgotten what it felt like to be ravished at night and wake up with the man who had delighted in her body in the morning. She'd forgotten how decadently good that sticky feeling between her legs could be, or that subtle ache on the inside of her thighs where they'd been widened and bent to accommodate the man who rode between them.

She didn't want to make more out of what had happened between her and Craig than what it was—two adults who were attracted to each other had had sex. That was it. Her lashes brushed his chest. She inhaled his scent. Her clit twitched. That's all it was. She couldn't expect more. But for now she would make believe that this was forever. She closed her eyes, drew in a long breath of him and drifted back to sleep.

Craig dressed as quietly as he could so as not to wake Jewel. He wanted to stay and say to hell with the demands of his day and just lie with Jewel. If only it was that simple. He buttoned his jeans then pulled his sweater over his head. He stood over her for a moment and watched her sleep. It took all of his willpower not to crawl into bed with her and find his way back between the warmth of her thighs. Usually by this time he would have been long gone with a kiss and a promise to call. He shook his head and stepped into his loafers. This was *temporary*. They both knew and understood that, but a place deep in his soul kept whispering *forever*. He leaned down and placed a gentle kiss on her cheek. She sighed softly and curled tighter into sleep. Craig tiptoed out and shut the door quietly behind him.

Chapter 6

Jewel blinked against the early dawn light that slid between the slats in the vertical blinds. Languidly she stretched and turned on her side, expecting to see Craig. The spot next to her was empty, the sheet already cooling. She pushed herself to a sitting position and pulled the sheet up to her chin, drawing her knees to her chest. Her eyes, accustomed now to the light, moved slowly around the space. The only indication that she hadn't slept alone was the faint scent of Craig that still lingered on her skin.

She blew out a breath. Why should she have expected more? Wine and great sex. There was no reason to think that he thought any more of their encounter than that. No explanation needed, although it would have been nice, the decent thing to do.

For a moment she shut her eyes, and her mind

flooded with the night they'd shared, the way her body had responded to his every touch, the power she felt in what she was able to do to him. Her body still throbbed.

Jewel tossed the sheet aside and swung her feet to the floor. No point in lying there. She had a full day in front of her. She quickly got dressed and attempted to ease back into the main house without running into Minerva. That little maneuver didn't go over very well. Minerva walked into the kitchen as Jewel inched through the front door. She felt like an errant teen coming home after curfew when Minerva's censoring gaze collided with hers.

"Good morning," Minerva said with a quick once-over. "You're up early." Her slippers whispered across the floor with her footfalls. "Breakfast?"

"Um, sure." She followed Minerva into the kitchen and took a seat at the counter.

"Coffee?" Minerva asked over her shoulder.

"Yes, thanks."

Minerva put on the coffeemaker. Jewel rooted around in the fridge for the bag of cinnamon and raisin bagels and put two in the toaster. She had a feeling the inevitable conversation would need more than coffee. She plopped down on the stool at the counter and waited. But she didn't have to wait long.

"I saw Mr. Lawson's car outside last night," she said casually, while keeping her back to Jewel.

"Mmm-hmm, stopped by to drop off the new contract."

"Took a while."

Jewel bit back a smile. "Really?"

"I couldn't sleep, and I noticed the lights on in the

cottage. Had to be after one in the morning. When I got up to get some warm milk about four, the lights were off, but his car was still parked."

The bagels popped up and so did Jewel. She plucked them from the double toaster and put them on plates. "Butter, jelly, cream cheese?" she asked sweetly.

Minerva swung around with her hands planted on her hips. Her eyes narrowed. "Are you going to tell me or are you going to make me beg?"

Jewel sputtered a laugh. "Fine. He spent the night. Happy?"

A slow smile spread across Minerva's mouth. "Well, it's about damned time!"

"Minerva!"

"What? It's true. You're a young woman, and he's a handsome man. And I think he likes you."

Jewel sat up straighter. "Really?"

"Of course. I can tell these kinds of things."

"Well, it's only temporary. He'll go back to London or LA when all of this is done."

"Never heard of long-distance relationship?"

"Minerva. I'm not thinking that far ahead. And I've been down the long-distance-relationship road," she said, thinking of her time with Simon. "I know how difficult it can be, especially when work comes first." She lathered her bagel with cream cheese.

"Make the most of the time you have," she said sagely. "You deserve some happiness in your life. And I like the glow."

"Glow?"

"Yes," she teased, "the glow in your eyes. I haven't seen it in a very long time. It looks good on you."

Jewel lowered her head. She did feel different. Alive. Her body still strummed from her night with Craig. But the reality was, it was just sex, and the fact that he was gone when she awoke spoke volumes.

Craig stepped out of the shower and wrapped a towel around his waist. He padded into his bedroom and went straight for his cell phone. He should have left a note for Jewel. But to be honest, his emotions were scrambled. He hadn't expected to feel the way he did—*connected*. And at first he didn't know how he wanted to handle it. They'd more or less agreed that this was a commitment-free thing. As far as he knew, Jewel still felt the same way. Now, he wasn't so sure that he did. What he did know for sure was that he wanted to see her again.

He picked up his cell phone and searched for her name in his contacts and tapped the dial icon. The phone rang and rang then went to voice mail. He started to hang up. Maybe it was a sign. Maybe she saw his name and decided not to answer. Maybe he should leave a message anyway. He pushed out a breath.

"Good morning. It's Craig. Um, sorry I didn't say anything before I left. Needed to get an early start, and you were sleeping so peacefully. Didn't want to wake you." He paused. "Uh, listen, Norm will be by later this afternoon, but, uh, I was wondering if you weren't busy this evening, maybe we could have dinner." He squeezed his eyes shut. "So, when you get a minute, give me a call and let me know. Enjoy your day. And… I enjoyed last night," he added softly. "Take care." He disconnected the call and tossed the phone on the bed. "What are you doing?" he chastised himself before walking off to get dressed.

After her counseling session with Minerva, Jewel finished her breakfast and cleaned up the kitchen. She had some baking orders to fill. The order details were in her phone. It was then that she realized that she didn't have it. She went to look for it and found it on the table in the hall. She must have left it there when Craig arrived last night.

When she tapped in her pass code, she saw that she had a message. Her pulse quickened. She went to her messages. It was from Craig. Holding her breath she listened to his message once, then again. Her beaming smile could have lit up a dark room. He wanted to see her again—tonight, for dinner. A date.

A wave of giddy delight rushed through her veins, and she practically skipped across the room and plopped down on the couch. Her hand shook ever so slightly as she tapped Return Call on her phone. He picked up on the third ring.

"Jewel," His voice dropped an octave. "Hello."

"Hi." Her stomach fluttered with warmth. "I got your message. Thanks for being so considerate and letting me sleep."

"I watched you for a while," he admitted.

"And?"

"And I started to crawl back in bed with you."

"You could have…"

"I'll remember that for next time."

Next time! She allowed herself to breathe. "Um, about tonight…"

"Yes?"

"What time were you thinking?"

"How's seven?"

"Perfect."

"I'll see you at seven."

"Okay."

"And this time I'll be sure I have a place in mind."

They both laughed.

"See you then," she said.

"See you."

Jewel put the phone down and rested her head back against the cushions of the couch. She closed her eyes, and a smile moved across her mouth. *What are you doing, girl?* Whatever it was, it felt good, and for now, that's all that mattered.

Chapter 7

As promised, Norm, the technical director, along with two other members of the movie crew, arrived at Jewel's home at noon.

"Good to finally meet you, Ms. Fontaine," Norm said. "We promise not to get in your way—or at least as little as possible." He smiled. "The plan is to take a bunch of exterior shots and shots of the first floor and of course the surrounding property. A couple of hours, tops."

"Not a problem. Where do you want to start?"

"Why don't we start inside, so we can get out of your way as soon as possible."

"Sure. I'll show you around." She took them on a quick tour of the main level: living area, den, kitchen, a small bedroom that at one time had been the servants' quarters, bathroom and the back veranda.

Norm took notes as they walked, with his two assistants trailing dutifully behind them. He turned to Jewel. "I know I said the main level, but is it possible to see the rooms upstairs to give us more options?"

Her stomach knotted. The last thing she wanted was for her father to become upset with strangers tramping around the house. His setbacks were becoming more pronounced and prolonged, and she didn't want to do anything to make it worse.

"Well, why don't you get started down here? I have to make some arrangements."

He looked at her curiously.

"My father...isn't well," she said in response to his look.

He held up his hands. "Hey, not a problem. I don't want to cause an issue."

"I'll see what I can do."

"Thanks." He turned to his assistants. "Okay, fellas, let's get started. I want multiple shots of everything on this floor from various angles, full shots to close-ups."

Jewel went in search of Minerva, who was just finishing up her father's bathing. She quietly explained what the crew wanted to do, and Minerva assured her that she would keep Augustus occupied in his room—which was to remain off-limits.

"Hopefully it won't take long," Jewel said.

Minerva clasped her shoulder. "It will be fine."

Jewel crossed the room and went to sit on the side of her father's bed.

"Hey, Daddy," she said softly. She took his hand in hers. "How are you today?"

He blinked and slowly focused on her. He smiled.

"Jewel. My Jewel." He squeezed her fingers. "Beautiful as ever. Just finished my bath," he said in a teasing tone.

Jewel grinned. "I bet you enjoyed it."

"Where's that young girl that works with you? Haven't seen her in a while." He frowned in concentration.

Jewel angled her head. "Mai Ling?"

"Is that her name?"

"Yes, Mai Ling. She doesn't work with me anymore."

"Who?" His gaze grew cloudy. He began to fidget.

Jewel gently patted his hand. "Mai Ling doesn't work with me anymore."

He stared at her. "I'm ready for my lunch."

Jewel sighed. She leaned over and kissed his forehead. "Sure thing, Daddy." She turned to Minerva and hoped the heartbreak that she felt wasn't reflected in her expression. "I'll let you know when they are ready to come up," she said softly. Minerva nodded.

Jewel returned to the main level and advised Norm that when they were ready she would take them upstairs.

She sat quietly on the sidelines, in total fascination, while the team took innumerable pictures. When Norm said, "from every angle," that was exactly what he got. What made the process more real was that before every final shot, a digital image was printed first so that they could be sure of every angle.

It was one thing to live and walk through your space day after day, year after year and basically not pay things much attention beyond cleaning and maybe updating furniture or draperies. It was a completely different experience to see your home through the eyes of a lens, the eyes of others.

The very unique features of her home came to life for the camera—the gleam of the wood floors, the intricacies of the crown molding, the banisters and inlays in the walls, the majesty of the sliding doors, built-in cherrywood cabinets, cathedral ceilings and crystal chandeliers. Over the years Jewel and her father had worked hard at maintaining the original woodwork, nooks and crannies right down to the claw-foot tubs and wall sconces. Of course, all of the internal workings of the house had been upgraded, but on the surface the home was very much a reflection of what it looked like more than one hundred years ago.

This home was her legacy. Allowing the filming, although intrusive, had bought her the time and money that she needed to hold on to that legacy until she could find a way to ensure a steady and substantial flow of capital. Her father and her grandparents and great-grandparents deserved to have what they'd earned maintained.

The photography took a little more than three hours. Norm thanked Jewel for her time and even left her with some of the photographs on his way out.

"You have a fabulous place. A lot of history here," he said and took a final look around.

"Thank you."

"Good to meet you. But I'm sure we'll see each other again."

"I'm sure." She stood on the threshold and watched as the team piled back into their vehicle and drove off. Jewel shut the door with a satisfied feeling. She'd made the right decision, and she was starting to believe that everything would work out.

She checked the time on the antique grandfather clock that resided in the foyer. Three hours before Craig would be there to take her to dinner. A shiver of anticipation fluttered through her, and a flash of their night together shocked her senses. There was no guarantee of how many more nights like that they would share together, but if she had anything to do with it, tonight would be another one.

Craig was on his way out of the production suite en route to his room when Milan stopped him in the hallway.

"Hey, Craig."

"Milan." He stopped in front of her.

"I was on my way to find you."

"Problem?" He shifted his iPad from one hand to the other.

"No. Not at all. Actually, I was hoping that we could make some time before shooting to…talk."

He tapped back the groan that threatened to escape. "I could order something up to the suite. We could chat there," he said, giving Milan a graceful way out—without him saying no—and him the distance that he wanted to maintain.

"Are you afraid to be alone with me?" she asked, taking a step to close the distance between them.

His mouth quirked with a sardonic grin. "Why would I?" His lids lowered over his eyes.

"You tell me. You've done everything short of becoming invisible any time I'm in the vicinity. I want us to be able to work together—to be friends."

"I thought that's what we were doing. I'm always available to listen to what my actors have to say." He stared at her. "Should I order up something to the suite?"

Her full lips drew into a single line. "Some other time."

He gave a slight shrug. "Not a problem." He breezed by her, covered the hall in long strides and entered his room. He was pretty sure the hot spots he felt on his back were daggers Milan was throwing.

More than once he'd questioned the feasibility of casting Milan. But artistry won out over his personal hesitation. However, he had no qualms about replacing her if things turned a wrong corner. Anthony had suggested several other actresses that could step into the role. They didn't have the name and face recognition that Milan had, and he was banking on those things to create hype for the film. With Milan and Hamilton in the lead roles, the film was guaranteed to garner the attention and box office success he knew it deserved. But he wasn't above casting an up-and-coming actress and making a star if Milan made life difficult.

He emptied his pockets on the top of the dresser then decided to send Jewel a text message before getting in the shower. He pulled up her number from his contacts.

I heard that things went well today. Great shots. We can talk about next steps later tonight. Looking forward to seeing you. C.

He hit send. Within moments the phone chirped with her response.

Looking forward to seeing you, too.

Craig grinned, pulled off his clothes and headed into the shower.

Chapter 8

Jewel changed her outfit three times, and she was still unsatisfied. Where were they going, exactly? She should have asked him, she worried while she took off the third dress and tossed it on the bed with the other two. He would be there in a half hour and she was still running around in her underwear. Panic set in. The room suddenly grew hot. She darted across the carpeted floor and adjusted the temp on the air conditioner. She then went to stare at the garments hanging in her closet. Again.

She couldn't recall the last time she'd gone out on a dinner date. How sad was that? After several more moments of indecision, she finally settled on a simple black dress, sleeveless, in a fabric that hinted at curves rather than defined them, with a hem that came just to her knees. Silver studs in her ears and a chunky silver-and-black rope chain for her neck.

Jewel took a step back and examined her full length in the mirror, turning right and left and of course trying to get an over-the-shoulder view. Pleased she fluffed her curls, added one more swipe of her bronzy lip gloss and a fingertip dab of her favorite body oil behind her ears and inside her wrists.

She studied her reflection. What would Craig think? Funny that it should matter. For the past few years two of the last things she thought much about were her appearance and her artistic penchant for needing approval, which had contributed to her downfall. The resurfacing of those emotions left her shaky inside, vulnerable—a place that she didn't want to ever return.

She gave a shake of her head as if to toss off the swirling thoughts and then reminded herself that it was one day, one night at a time. She truly had nothing to prove, and Craig Lawson could take her or leave her. Her gaze explored her reflection, settled on her expression, then the body encased in that dress. She smiled. Who was she kidding? For the time being, she preferred if he took her.

Craig pulled into the Fontaines' winding driveway at exactly five minutes to seven. He would have been there earlier but he didn't want to appear as eager as he felt. He put the car in Park, peeked up at the house through the driver's side window then got out while he slid one hand into his pants pocket and strode forward. He hesitated for a moment before ringing the bell and wondered for the thousandth time why he was overthinking a simple dinner.

In concert with the bell echoing in the house, the

door opened. His stomach coiled, and his heart beat just a bit faster. *Damn.* His eyes ran over her from top to bottom, taking in every delicious inch.

"Hey. Hope I'm not early."

"No. Right on time. Come in for a minute." Jewel stepped aside to let him pass.

He stealthily inhaled the soft scent of her and relished that she smelled that good all over.

"So, where did you decide for dinner?" she asked and turned toward him.

"You look incredible," he said with hunger in his voice. He stepped up to her, slid an arm around her waist and dipped his head until his mouth met hers. Jewel sighed softly. "I've been waiting for that all day," he said against her lips.

"Worth it?"

"Absolutely." His gaze rose and landed on Minerva, who was standing at the top of the stairs.

Jewel followed his line of sight. Her face heated. She stood a step back. "Everything okay?"

"Yes, fine," she said and descended the stairs. "Good evening, Mr. Lawson."

"Good evening."

"I was coming down to fix a snack," she said to Jewel. She gave her a quick once-over. "You two have a nice time." She walked away and into the kitchen.

Jewel wished the floor would open. She slowly shook her head.

Craig turned to Jewel with a twinkle in his eye. "Ready?"

"Very." She picked up her silver-toned shawl and her purse from the table in the foyer and led the way out.

* * *

"I don't think I realized that your housekeeper lived in," Craig said as they pulled out of the driveway and onto the street.

"For about two years now."

Craig took a quick look at her profile that was set and fixed on the road ahead. He got the impression that she didn't want to talk about it. But that didn't stop him from wanting to know what caused that look on her face.

"What happened two years ago?"

Jewel's expression tightened. She tugged on her bottom lip with her teeth. "I'd really rather not. It's a long story and not very pleasant."

"I'm a storyteller. I examine life for a living. There isn't much that you could tell me that would surprise or repulse me," he added with a smile.

"I needed help with my dad," she said and offered nothing further.

When silence hung between them for a beat too long he said, "I get it. You don't have to talk about it if you don't want to."

Her expression visibly relaxed. "Thank you. But what we *can* talk about is your film."

He tugged in a breath and resigned himself to the idea that Jewel wasn't going to spill her guts—at least not yet—and for that matter neither was he. But what she didn't say was almost as important as what she did say. Clearly, there were problems with her father. Serious enough that she needed help to take care of him, which might explain a lot of things.

"Right now we're doing the table reads with the actors. The technical folks are working out logistics and

scheduling, costumes and permits. This is all the behind-the-scenes stuff before the next phase kicks in."

"Which is?"

"First day of shooting."

She nodded slowly. "How much of the film will
take place on the property?"

"On film it will seem like mostly all of it. But the
way we have it worked out in terms of shot selec-
tion and scheduling, we should be finished shooting
on your property in about a week, week and a half,
tops. Unfortunately, in order to do that we start early
and leave late."

"I see. What about what's not shot on the property?"

"There are street scenes and some historic sites,
both of which require permits, and the rest we can
finish up on the lot in LA, if necessary. I'm hoping
that we can do everything here. Cuts down on time
and wear and tear on the actors and won't incur extra
expenses for the budget."

Craig slowed the car, peered up at the sign on the
corner indicating Tchoupitoulas Street then turned.
"That's the place up there," he said with a lift of his
chin.

"Emeril's?" she asked, clearly delighted. The
lighted logo of the world-famous restaurant promised mouthwatering delights.

He glanced at her with a self-satisfied smile. "Hope
you like it."

Jewel laughed. "What is there not to like? In all
the years that I've lived in Louisiana, I may have
been here once—and that was ages ago. All I can remember was that the food was to die for. Since then

he's opened other locations, had his own television show…"

"I have another surprise for you."

She snapped her head in his direction. "What?"

Craig winked. "You'll see."

He parked the car in the lot behind the restaurant, and they walked around to the front. The hostess greeted them.

"Mr. Lawson, welcome to Emeril's. Your table is ready. Please follow me."

Craig placed his hand at the low dip of Jewel's back and guided her across the restaurant to their reserved table. He helped Jewel into her seat.

"Chef Lagasse will be right out." The hostess smiled and walked away.

Jewel leaned across the table. "Wait, what did she just say?"

Craig leaned forward as well. The light of mischief sparkled in his eyes. "She said Chef Lagasse will be right out," he responded and tried to maintain a level of utter seriousness.

"Very funny," she tossed back. "You know him?"

"A little," he hedged, enjoying the delight that he saw on her face. He would do anything to see that kind of happiness radiate from her, and to know that he was a part of it made the watching that much sweeter.

"Fine. Play coy. It doesn't become you." She lifted her chin in a semblance of huff.

Craig chuckled. "How 'bout I tell you the whole story over breakfast?"

Her eyes widened. Her lips parted ever so slightly. "Very presumptuous."

"I'm a risk taker, in every aspect of my life." His gaze held hers steadily.

"Do you consider this—you and me—a risk?" she asked in a near whisper.

"Definitely. But it's a risk I'm willing to take."

Rather than respond she lifted her glass of water and took a sip, as much to have something to do as to extinguish the fire in her belly.

Dinner wasn't simply dinner—it was an event, from meeting Chef Lagasse himself with his larger-than-life personality to being taken into the kitchen to watch the preparation of their meal to the food itself, which defied explanation.

When they left the restaurant three hours later, they were still laughing and attempting to one-up each other with the numerous delights of the evening.

"So you met him through your cousin Rafe?" Jewel said while she strapped herself in.

"Yep. Actually, Emeril's head chef is a good friend of Rafe's. He made the original introductions, and the rest, as they say, is history." He put the car in gear. "So...breakfast?" He snatched a look at her.

Jewel turned to him and smiled. "I like my eggs scrambled."

"I'll see what I can do about that."

Chapter 9

They pulled up in front of the hotel, and the valet hurried over to take the car.

"Nightcap? I'm sure the hotel bar is still open, or I can have them send something up," Craig said while he helped Jewel from the car.

Now that she was here, the reality that she would spend the night with him in his hotel room hit home. "A nightcap sounds good...and your room is fine."

He led her inside and across the wide reception area to the bank of elevators. He took out his card key from his inside jacket pocket.

The doors swished open and they stepped into his penthouse suite—a setup straight out of a movie, from the pale plush carpeting, conversation seating, low-slung tables and enormous television mounted on the wall to a full bar and working kitchen.

"Make yourself comfortable, and I'll order room service," he said. He slipped out of his jacket and tossed it on a vacant chair.

Jewel set down her purse on the glass table and rested her shawl across the thickly padded couch. She crossed the wide expanse of space to the floor-to-ceiling windows that opened onto the terrace. She opened the doors and stepped out into the warm night. The lights of the city spread out before her.

Oh, how she remembered nights like this, living like this, whatever she wanted only a phone call away, traveling, seeing the world. She sighed heavily. It seemed like a lifetime ago.

Warm hands cradled her shoulders. A soft kiss dotted the back of her neck. "I almost forgot how beautiful this city can be," Craig said into her hair.

Jewel drew in a breath and slowly turned around, finding herself surrounded by him. Her gaze rose. "It's had its share of problems. Still struggling and rebuilding, but the history will always remain."

He angled his head to the side. "Sounds like my life."

"Mine, too," she admitted with an uneasy smile.

The pad of his thumb brushed across her cheek. "What parts—the struggle, the rebuilding, the history?"

"All of it. The choices that I made…"

"Do you regret them?"

She lowered her head. A frown knitted her brow. She looked right at him. "Sometimes. And when I do, I feel so…guilty." She spat out the last word.

"But once the decision is made, we have to find a way to live with the aftermath."

"How do you do it?"

"Do what?"

She shook her head. "Never mind. It's not my business." She started to move away.

The doorbell chimed. "Room service," the voice called out.

"Be right back."

Jewel wandered back into the main living space as the waiter set up the cart.

"Will there be anything else, Mr. Lawson?"

"No. Thanks." He walked over to where he'd tossed his jacket, took out his wallet and handed over a sizable tip.

"Thank you, Mr. Lawson. Thank you very much. Enjoy your evening. Ma'am." He nodded at Jewel then quietly let himself out.

Craig lifted the covers on the plates. Fresh fruit was on one platter and an assortment of exotic cheeses and dips and paper-thin crackers on the other.

"Wow, I'm hungry all over again, if that's possible," she said eyeing the fare.

He took the bottle of white wine from the bucket, poured two flutes and handed one to Jewel.

"To making choices we can live with," he said, raising his glass to hers.

Jewel lightly tapped his glass. "To choices." She took a sip. "Hmm," she hummed. "Good stuff."

Craig walked over to the couch and sat down. He extended a hand to Jewel. She came and sat close beside him.

"You asked me how I do it," he said.

"You don't have to—"

"I want to." He looked in her eyes. "I want you to know." He took a swallow of wine, paused reflectively and said, "It's never gotten easier. I thought it would. I thought I'd get to a point where I really didn't give a damn, instead of *acting* like I didn't." The corner of his mouth flickered. He looked away. "I miss my sister and brother, my cousins. I haven't been to a family gathering in years, simply because I don't want to be in the same room with my father. So I've stayed away. I've kept busy. I've done everything that I can to show him how wrong he was about me and the choices that I made by being successful in everything I've undertaken." He snorted a laugh. "None of that matters. Not once even after receiving a Golden Globe, or being on the front page of the papers, even getting my first Oscar, have I heard a word of congratulations from my father. Never."

She reached out and covered her hand with his. Jewel saw the sadness in his eyes and the pain that threaded through his words. Her heart ached for him. She could never imagine her father not being a part of her life and rejoicing in her success. "Have you ever tried to reach out to him?" she asked tentatively.

He looked away, pushed up from the couch and stood. He went to retrieve the bottle of wine and refilled his glass. "I'd been gone and out of touch with him for about three years," he began slowly, reeling in the memories. "I was in Paris when I got the call that I'd been nominated for my first Golden Globe. I just knew that if I told him, he would finally see that I'd made it, ya know."

He heaved a sigh. "So, stupid me, I called. The housekeeper answered the phone, and I told her who I was. She came back to the phone a couple of minutes later only to tell me, 'Mr. Lawson is busy. Do you care to leave a message?' I told her to tell him he could go straight to hell." He snorted a nasty laugh. "That was the last time I called."

"I'm...so sorry."

He waved off her condolence. "Don't be. I'm used to it."

"Are you?"

"More wine?" he replied instead.

She extended her glass. "Sure."

Craig pushed the cart closer to them, loaded a cracker with two kinds of cheeses and popped it in his mouth. He refilled her glass.

Jewel reached for the seedless grapes. "You didn't answer my question. Are you used to it?"

"I'm used to the life I've chosen. I stopped asking myself if I should have done something different or stayed here and followed my father's dream for me. I know that if I'd listened to my father, I would have grown to resent him. I would've been miserable. So... our relationship or lack of one is the price I chose to pay for my decision."

"It's so ironic that both of us made life-altering decisions with our fathers at the center of it," Jewel said.

"But we're on opposite sides of the equation. You've never told me in so many words, but I put the pieces together. You gave up a career for your father, didn't you?"

She hesitated then nodded.

"Maybe you'll tell me the full story...when you're ready." He squeezed her hand. "Me on the other hand, I pursued a career in spite of my father."

She lowered her gaze. "What a pair, huh?"

"Yeah, what a pair...that for all of the crazy seem to fit very well together," Craig said.

Jewel's lashes lowered over her eyes. "I think you're right...about the fit," she said coyly.

Craig chuckled deep in his throat. "Why don't I show you the rest of the suite." It wasn't a question. He stood, pulled her to feet, took their glasses and the rest of the wine, and walked toward his bedroom.

Jewel followed him down a short hallway into the master bedroom. Her heart beat double time with every footfall. The lights were already dimmed, but it was clear that the massive king-size bed was the centerpiece of the space. Even though it was a hotel room, it didn't have that utilitarian feel to it. It was cozy in a way, and it held the sexy scent of him. She stepped out of her shoes. There was a love seat by the window with a white shirt draped across the arm. The closet bared its holdings: an array of shirts, suits, slacks and sweaters. Several pairs of dress shoes, sneakers and work boots lined the bottom.

"The bathroom is through there," he said, lifting his glass in the direction of the partially closed door.

Jewel nodded, suddenly nervous and she didn't know why. This was what she wanted, wasn't it?

"You okay?"

She rubbed her hands up and down her arms. "Yes. Fine." She forced a smile. Her eyes jumped around the room.

Craig walked over to her. He lowered his head to look directly into her eyes. "Tell me what's wrong." He held her shoulders.

"It's silly, really."

"Most of the things that bug us are silly, but that doesn't mean they don't matter. So...what's up?"

She tugged in a breath and took his hands in hers.

"Let's not talk about or worry about the silly stuff… not tonight. I don't want to think about it."

"Whatever you want." He cupped her face in his palms. His eyes roamed over her features. "What is it about you?" he murmured in wonder. His eyes narrowed. "I've told you things I've never told anyone," he confessed.

"Is that a bad thing?"

"I hope not. I don't want it to be."

She studied him for a moment. "It's not only your father that did damage, is it?"

Craig took a step back. "That's definitely a conversation for another time." He turned away and walked toward the lounge chair. He slung a hand into his pocket. Jewel came up beside him and slid her arm around his waist. She rested her head on his shoulder.

"Another time, then," she whispered.

Craig turned. He threaded his fingers through her hair, loosening the curls to flow around her face and neck. He palmed the back of her head and pulled her toward him. No more words, no more hesitation. His mouth covered her lips, and he sucked in the sigh that floated up from her center and ignited his.

His arousal from her nearness kept him on simmer all night, but now that he had her in his arms, had tasted her again, felt the curves of her body melt into him, his response was swift, hard and throbbing.

He pressed against her, wanted her to feel what she had done to him, how crazy she'd made him. He reached behind her and unzipped her dress, peeled it away from her shoulders and down her frame until it fell to her feet. Her black bra was next. He tossed it onto the chair and took a half step back to look at her.

Lowering his head he nuzzled the swell of her breasts. Her body shook, and a soft whimper escaped her lips.

Craig eased down her body, planting light kisses along her exposed skin until he was on his knees. He slid his fingers around the band of her panties and pulled them down to her ankles and then tasted her.

"Ooh!" Jewel gripped his shoulders. Her thighs trembled with each flick and stroke of his tongue.

Craig gripped her hips and held her fast, feasting until her trembling and soft cries were more than he could take. He rose, tugged off his shirt. Jewel unbuckled his belt and slid down his zipper. Craig stepped out of his slacks, toed out of his shoes. Jewel stepped over her dress and panties and backed up toward the bed, pulling Craig along with her.

Jewel scooted up to the top, Craig following until he hovered above her.

He pushed her hair away from her face, kissed her forehead, her cheeks, and her mouth. His hands were everywhere. Jewel writhed beneath him, wanting him, letting him know the depth of her desire with each rotation of her hips.

Craig snatched up the thick pillow and shoved it under her hips. He rose up on his knees and reached over into the nightstand for a condom.

Jewel took it from him, tore it open with her teeth then slowly, erotically rolled the sheath down his length, much to Craig's delight.

He clasped her hips tightly in his hands. Jewel bent her knees. He lowered his head and tenderly kissed her, holding them both in a moment of unbridled anticipation. And then he was inside her.

Air rushed out of her lungs in a gasp. Her eyes

slammed shut. He filled her, and in that moment, their initial coupling was more intense than the first, if that were possible.

In unison they moaned and sighed as pleasure whipped through them and they found their beat, slow and steady, hard and soft, meeting each other stroke for stroke.

Jewel clung to him, gave herself up and over to him. Her body came fully alive, vibrated from the inside out. She could barely think; her breath hitched, her heart pounded. She wanted him, all of him. She wanted him so deep inside her that he touched her heart. So when he lifted her legs and draped them across his shoulders, leaving her wide-open and vulnerable to his every move, tears of *yes, yes, yes*, sprang from her eyes. She buried her face in his neck and held on as the first wave of her climax began at the soles of her feet, shimmied up the backs of her legs, vibrated in her thighs, pooled in her pelvis and exploded with such power that the room spun. Her breathing ceased, and a scream clung in her throat until the next wave hit her with such force that her body stiffened as if electrocuted, and the sound that burst from the center of her being sent Craig up and over the edge of this world and into the next.

His head dropped onto the pillow of her breasts. He muttered a curse of disbelief as the final throes of release pumped through him.

Jewel lay curled against Craig's side with one leg draped across him while he gently caressed her, intermittently kissing her hair. So many thoughts scrambled in her head. She didn't want to get used to this, to need this. But it would be so easy. For as much as Craig Lawson wore the armor of the uncommitted, she sensed that there was a part of him that wanted more, that wanted to be connected. He claimed that he had no desire to forge a relationship with his father, yet everything that he did smacked of his need to have that void in his life filled. Even if he was only temporarily with her. She felt the longing in him every time he pushed into her, moaned her name. It was not only physical. He wanted a connection, to belong to someone.

Or…maybe it was all wishful thinking on her part. Projecting her own wants onto him. She closed her eyes. But even if she could make it true, what could she offer a man like Craig Lawson when she had her own empty places to fill?

They had breakfast in bed and watched the morning news like any other couple before enjoying a joint shower and one more romp for the road under the pulsing water.

Jewel sat on the side of the bed and put on her shoes.

"I really don't want you to go," Craig said and sat down next to her. He caressed her cheek.

Her eyes roamed over his face, wishing that it were true.

"I would drive you back, but duty calls and I'm already late. I have a full day today. I called a car service for you. It should be downstairs in a few." He grabbed a shirt from his closet and slid it on. "If you're not busy…maybe later tonight?" he asked with a note of hesitation as if bracing himself for her to say no.

"Call me." She could not allow herself to fall into the trap of being so readily available, something for him to do while he was in town, even if she wanted to leap into his arms and say yes.

He leaned down and kissed her. "Will do."

She picked up her purse and shawl and met him at the door. "Now for the walk of shame," she joked.

"Baby, you could put the walk of shame to shame any day." He swung her in for a long kiss before inserting his card key into the elevator.

They parted at the taxi with Craig promising to call later. As the car pulled off, Jewel looked behind her, hoping like in the movies that he would be standing there…watching, waving. But he was already gone.

Chapter 10

"Who was that?"

Craig stopped short and turned to his right. Milan was sitting in a club chair by the front door. He drew in a breath of annoyance. Milan pushed up from the chair and walked over to him.

"Long night?"

"Twenty questions. And why does it matter?" He continued toward the elevators with Milan keeping pace at his side.

"It doesn't. I was only asking. She's cute, in an ordinary kind of way. Doesn't seem like your type."

The elevator doors opened. Milan stepped in.

"You wouldn't know anything about my type." He stepped back as the doors began to close. "I'll catch the next one."

The minute the words were out of his mouth, he re-

gretted them. He knew that he needed to keep his cool
and not antagonize Milan. The last thing he wanted
was for her to have one of her diva fits on set because
she was pissed at him. There was no telling how she
would react when she realized that the woman she
saw him with was the owner of the home where the
filming was to take place. Any other time he would
have handled things differently, taken her to dinner
and maybe even to bed. But now… He heaved a sigh,
stabbed the button for the elevator and ran a hand
across the close cut of his hair. Now things were different. He was going to have to find a way to make
nice with Milan. Inwardly he groaned.

Jewel had no reason to feel like an errant child
when the car pulled up onto her property. She was
a grown woman. Hadn't Minerva told her as much?
She'd all but given her seal of approval on Craig Lawson. So why was her heart pounding in anticipation
of Minerva's all-knowing look?

She walked up the three steps to the front door,
turned the knob and peeked her head in before slip-
ping inside. Humming came from the kitchen. She
pulled in a breath and pranced into the kitchen as if
she always walked in the door at 10:00 a.m. with her
evening clothes on.

"Morning," she sang.

Minerva turned from the sink, shook out her wet
hands and reached for a towel. "Well, don't you look
nice for this hour," she teased.

Jewel dropped her purse on the counter and sat
down. "I don't want to care about him," she blurted

out, suddenly needing the wisdom of the older woman. She looked at Minerva with wide eyes.

Minerva sighed. She put the towel down by the sink. "There is nothing wrong with caring about a man other than your father. He's the only man who has been in your life for the past five years. I'm not saying that he shouldn't be, but there needs to be more in your life. Your last adult relationship was with Simon."

Jewel looked away. She knew that part of her hesitation was her fear of being hurt again, after investing so much of herself like she did with Simon. That was part of her rationale for getting involved with Craig. She knew it was temporary—there wasn't the possibility of long term and the problems that went along with it. But somewhere in her grand scheme, someone had flipped the script. She was beginning to feel again, to want something for herself again. And it scared her.

"I'm not sure what I should do, Minerva. From the moment we met, something happened. It was like a switch got turned on. My thoughts are clouded with him. But I can't let this schoolgirl crush screw up my head."

"The heart is going to do what the heart is going to do. No matter how hard you try to fight it." She stretched out her hand and took Jewel's. "Enjoy it for what it is. If it's destined to be more than temporary, then it will be. If not, well—" she gave a short shrug "—it's what you expected anyway."

Jewel blew out a breath, then a slow smile bloomed across her mouth. "Guess where we went last night?" She went on to regale Minerva with the incredible meal and actually meeting Emeril. She took the story as far as arriving at the hotel and left the rest to Minerva's active imagination.

"I hope you used protection," she said, wagging a warning finger.

Jewel's face flamed. She popped up from the chair. "I think this conversation has gone on long enough. I'm going to change and then spend some time with Dad."

Jewel listened to Minerva chuckling as she headed up the stairs to her room.

The day seemed to drag by and the late afternoon shower made it dreary as well. For the first time in quite a while, Jewel felt restless. She wanted to do something. Energy whirled around inside her, filled her head and tingled her fingers. She thought of baking but couldn't drum up the enthusiasm.

She grabbed an umbrella from the stand by the door and headed out to the cottage.

"What the hell did you say or do to Milan?" Anthony asked Craig when the crew broke for lunch. "She's been on a tear all morning. You should have seen her at the table read."

Craig's jaw clenched. "She saw me this morning."

"And?"

"Leaving the hotel with Jewel."

"Aw, hell, man."

Craig's face tightened. "Don't start. I'm not in the mood for a lecture." He dropped the script on the table, crossed the room to the minibar and opened the small fridge. He took out a bottle of beer. "Want one?"

"Naw, I'm good."

He opened the bottle and took a long swallow.

"Look, man, do what you want with whomever you want, but don't leave dust and debris in your wake. Jewel seems like a real lovely woman. She's not like the others. And you've been down the road with Milan. You know what she's like and how she can get, especially when she thinks that someone is taking her shine."

"There's no shine of hers to be taken. Me and her are past tense."

"Doesn't matter with someone like Milan. You know that."

Craig flopped down in the chair and turned the bottle up to his lips. He stretched his long legs out in front of him. "I really got a thing for her, man," he admitted. "First I figured it was just physical, ya know." He shook his head. "It's not. I want to be with her. I enjoy her company, the way she makes me feel. Easy. Not like I have to measure up to some ideal."

"That's cool and I can get with that, but, bruh, you ain't gonna slow down. You sure as hell ain't gonna settle down here, of all places. So how's that gonna work?"

Craig looked away, finished off his beer and stood. "I'll work it out."

"I sure hope so. We got a lot riding on this film. Not just you…all of us."

"Yeah, I know."

Once she got started, the embers of her passion ignited. Shape, color, context all came together in swift, sure strokes. There were times when she thought she'd lost the ability to create this way, but she hadn't, and the realization continued to fuel her. Hours passed, and when she finally sat back and looked at what she had done, her eyes filled with tears of joy.

It was him come alive on canvas. She had managed to capture the resoluteness of his jaw, the wide sweep of his brow, the curve of his lips, the penetrating, almost brooding stare, but most of all she had encapsulated what emanated from him—vulnerability cloaked in power. Beyond the probing gaze was a look of longing, something that was just out of his reach.

The portrait was in charcoal and pencil. It would serve as her base when she replicated the piece in oils.

Exhaustion suddenly overwhelmed her. Giving birth to her first creative work in years had drained her physically and emotionally. Her hands trembled ever so slightly as she returned her instruments to their cases, and her legs threatened to give out when she stood.

She dragged herself over to the couch, flopped down and stared at what she had done, realizing then that the only light came from her lamps. The day was gone, and night had taken its place. How many hours had it been? She should go back to the house. But she wasn't ready. Not yet. She needed to savor this moment of accomplishment. Sit here for a few minutes more. Her fingers still tingled with electric energy. A giddy joy bubbled in her stomach. Her lids fluttered against her will. She stretched and yawned, leaned her head back. She needed to close her eyes. Just for a minute.

Her last thought before she drifted off into a deep sleep, with his lifelike image looking down on her, was that Craig had not called as he'd promised.

Chapter 11

"You want anything else?"

"Maybe another glass of wine," Milan said.

Craig signaled for the waiter, who brought another bottle and filled their glasses.

"Thank you for dinner," she said sweetly. She took a sip from her glass.

"It's the least I could do. I wanted to clear the air between us."

She lowered her fake lashes and puckered her polished lips. "We have a history, Craig, one that I can't easily forget. I know I messed up. I only want you to forgive me and maybe…give us a second chance."

He wrapped his hands around his glass. "Listen, Milan, like I've been telling you, there's nothing to forgive. Really. What happened is in the past, and we've both moved on."

"What if I haven't?"

"That's what I need you to understand, Milan. I didn't ask you to take this role in the hopes of us getting back together. I wanted you for this part because you're the best actor for it and I believe this will be a career changer for you."

"Is it because of her?" she challenged.

Craig pushed out a breath and asked himself yet again why he had bothered. But Anthony kept at him to make peace with Milan before things turned ugly. So he'd asked her to dinner, to talk, to make the peace. Where he really wanted to be was with Jewel. It was nearly eleven. He'd promised he'd call her, and he hadn't. If he were honest with himself, he would admit that part of the reason why he hadn't called was that he felt himself moving into the deep end of the pool with Jewel. He could have taken Milan to lunch. But instead he took her to dinner to make things right between them. Now he regretted his decision.

"Well, is it?" Milan pressed.

Craig snapped back to attention. "Is it what?"

"Is it her? Is she the reason why there can't be an us?" She placed her palms flat down on the table.

"Milan..." He shook his head in frustration and ran a hand across his chin. He leaned forward. "It can't work." He softened his voice. "It can't. And it has nothing to do with her."

Milan lifted her chin and turned her face away. "Fine," she whispered.

"I need things to be cool between us. We have to work together. We have a job to do, and I am depending on you to make this movie a success," he added, playing into her vanity.

"Fine," she said again then turned to face him. "It's getting late." She made moves to get up.

"Look, there's something you need to know before we get to the set."

She stopped. "What?"

"The woman that you saw me with. She's the owner of the house where we'll be filming."

It had been two days and she hadn't heard from Craig. More than once she picked up her phone to call him but decided against it. Maybe it was for the best. She'd felt herself falling, but she'd caught herself before she hit bottom.

At least that's what she told herself until the cavalcade of SUVs and equipment trucks arrived.

Jewel stepped out onto the landing of her house. Her heart raced. Car doors opened and shut. Her pulse thundered in her ears. Her eyes skipped over the moving bodies hoping to see him among them and not wanting to see him at the same time.

It was clear that after everyone had disembarked from the vehicles that Craig was not among them.

"Good morning, Ms. Fontaine," Anthony greeted her, coming up on the landing and extending his hand.

Jewel shook his hand. "Nice to see you again. Well, I guess this is it, huh?" she said, watching the unloading process.

"I promise to make this as painless as possible. Today we're going to get the exterior shots done. Unfortunately, tomorrow we'll have to get started about 7:00 a.m., and we'll be inside shooting most of the day."

"Sure. Craig… Mr. Lawson gave me the schedule."

"Great. As soon as the lighting techs set up, we'll get started."

"I'll let you get to it. If you need anything, I'll be upstairs."

"Thanks. We'll be fine. The equipment trunks are like home away from home. We have everything we need." He turned away and began shouting orders to the crew who were now spread over her property like fire ants.

Disappointment mingled with relief. Jewel went back inside and shut the door behind her. Minerva met her in the foyer.

"What's wrong?"

"Nothing," Jewel murmured. "Too late to second-guess."

"Is he here?"

"Who?" she asked, although she knew exactly who Minerva meant. "No," she conceded.

Minerva squeezed her shoulder. "And when he does show up, which he will, you'll be just fine."

Jewel smiled and continued on upstairs.

His plan was to lag behind so that by the time he arrived on set everything and everyone would be in place and ready. He would have no other choice than to get right to work. Work would consume his focus and all of his energies, and he wouldn't have the time or opportunity to look for or spend time with Jewel. If he had his way, he'd spend all of his time with Jewel. But there was no room for distractions. And she was most definitely a distraction, in the best kind of way.

That was part two of his master plan. Part one was to keep his distance and not contact her. It had been hard as all hell, but he'd managed. He had to be totally focused on the film. The quicker he did his part, the sooner he could open his mind to his "distraction." Two whole days, and it took all of his willpower to stay on task and not pick up the phone and call or get in his car and drive over. But he'd made a decision. There was too much on the line, and the person he needed to keep happy and appeased was Milan—for everyone's sake.

After their dinner the other night when he'd told her who Jewel was, Milan had one of her epic tantrums, causing a major scene in the restaurant.

"You think I'm an idiot!" she'd screamed. "I know you're screwing her. It's what you do! Is this how you punish me—by throwing her in my face day after day!"

Every eye in the restaurant had been glued on them. He could tell by the expressions on some of their faces that they recognized Milan. Cell phones came out. This latest public display would be all over the internet in minutes.

Craig had taken her by the arm and hustled her out of there, trying to keep his head down while blasting Milan out under his breath. By this time she'd dissolved into hysterical tears.

She really was crazy. That was the only thought running through his head as he'd whisked her past the curious onlookers and into the waiting car.

He pushed the nightmarish episode out of his head as he pulled onto the Fontaine property and parked his Suburban behind the line of cars. He, as well as the attorneys, had advised Milan that any further public outbursts would result in her being removed from the project as a breach of the morals clause. Apparently when she'd signed on, she didn't pay attention to the fine print. Knowing what Milan was capable of, Craig had had that little caveat included to protect him and the project.

But he couldn't take chances on pushing any of Milan's many buttons. She was crazy enough not to give a damn just to hurt him. *Artists.*

He hopped out of the car, scanning the grounds for any sight of Jewel. Part relief and part disappointment filled him. He strode toward Anthony. He had work to do, and he couldn't do it with Jewel Fontaine on his mind.

Jewel watched the magic of moviemaking from the safety of her father's bedroom window. Then Craig came into view. Her heart kicked up a beat. She gripped the edge of the window frame, willing him to look up and hoping that he didn't.

She watched him orchestrate the symphony of people and equipment and was mesmerized by the flow of authority that he exuded.

"Who's coming? I hear voices," her father said.

Jewel turned away and went to her father's easy chair that faced the back windows of the property. She knelt down beside him and took his hand.

"It's okay, Daddy, just some folks in the yard. They're making a movie." She smiled at him.

Augustus's cloudy eyes narrowed. "Whatchu mean, movie?"

"Some people thought that our house would look beautiful in a movie about an old Southern family."

He grumbled and began to pat his hand on the arm

of the chair. "Gotta be careful," he hissed suddenly. "Be careful."

"About what?"

He turned to her and blinked slowly. "I think I want toast this morning."

Jewel sighed with a sad smile. She kissed his forehead. "Sure thing, Daddy, just the way you like it. Every day."

"Good morning," Minerva said from the doorway then walked in. She carried Augustus's breakfast tray.

"Morning, Minerva. Let me help you with that." She walked over and took the tray. Under her breath she said, "He seems okay about the hoopla downstairs. Just told me to be careful." She laughed lightly.

"Father knows best, even when he doesn't seem to know a thing," she said in return. She took the tray back from Jewel and went to her charge.

Jewel frowned. She started to ask what she meant but decided that she couldn't deal with two cryptic people and subliminal messages in one setting.

"I'm going down," she announced.

Minerva waved, and Jewel swore she heard her father mumble something about some pretty young girl in his room.

She trotted downstairs and went into the living room. She turned on the television to catch the morning news with the hope of blocking her thoughts from the activity on the other side of her door. She settled on her local news channel just as the entertainment portion came on air. She'd made it a point to steer clear of celebrity news and social media sites after her own debacle on the world stage. But for now it was simply mindless activity. As usual there were the stories and images of celebrities doing what celebrities did. And then Craig's face popped up on the screen in a box behind the newscaster's head.

"Two nights ago, award-winning filmmaker and New Orleans' own prodigal son Craig Lawson was seen up close and personal with his leading lady, Milan Chase, as they left the Brasserie Restaurant after what appeared to be a lovers' spat." The screen flashed images of them hustling out of the restaurant and into a black car, with Craig holding on tightly to Milan's arm. "As many of you know, Lawson and Chase were a big item several years ago when she had a small role in one of his films. Neither of their reps were available for comment. But we can't help but wonder if the explosive couple will be another Brad and Angie."

The woman's voice droned on about the next hot item, but Jewel had stopped listening. She felt sick. Her temples pounded. Two nights ago, he'd promised to call. Two nights ago she'd poured her soul into recreating him on canvas, almost as an homage to what was blooming between them. Two nights ago, he was with *her*. He was no different than Simon. He hung around for as long as it suited him. What she felt didn't matter.

She pressed her fist to her mouth, but it barely held back the sob that escaped. What a fool she'd been. She'd fallen for the voice, the swagger, the looks, the touches, the sex and the aura of mystery. But she shouldn't have. They'd agreed. It was just a temporary thing. Little did she know that to *him* temporary only meant days. He and that woman had a history. They had the kind of life that she'd given up. There was no way that she could compete with that, and she wouldn't.

Jewel wiped her eyes, reached for the remote and turned the television off. *Gotta be careful. Be careful.* Maybe her father knew and understood more than she did.

Chapter 12

He had yet to see her, and as much as he forced himself to stay focused, he couldn't help but wonder where she was. Anthony said he'd spoken with her earlier. Maybe she'd left the property and was waiting for them all to leave before she returned. He wouldn't blame her. His behavior toward her was the kind of shitty conduct he didn't want to be known for. She deserved better. At least Milan was acting like the professional he knew she could be. Her scenes were flawless, and the camera loved her just as he knew the audiences would.

They would lose the optimum light for the daytime scenes in about an hour. Craig wanted to get the last scenes shot quickly and wrap for the day.

"Okay, people," he shouted to get everyone's attention. "We're going to shoot this last scene out of sequence. I want to get the light. Hamilton, Milan, this is your big parting scene. Neither of you are sure if you will ever see each other again. You vow to wait, no matter what. This is emotion filled. I want the audience to feel your pain, your fear and your love for each other. Okay, let's go, people!"

He waited for the crew to reset the scene and for Milan and Hamilton to get their makeup touched up before they got a last look at the script. He took a look at the scene through the viewfinders of the three cameras to ensure they got the angles that he wanted.

"Been a great morning," Anthony said, coming up alongside Craig.

"Feeling real good about this, bro." He turned to his friend and grinned.

Anthony clapped him on the back. "You should. This has awards written all over it. And… I hate to admit it, but you were right about Milan. She's pitch-perfect. Crazy but talented," he added with a chuckle.

"Yeah." Craig laughed as well. "You're right about that. I'm just glad we were able to nip her crazy in the bud."

"So, uh, what about Jewel? You think she's seen any of the pictures or stuff on the news about the other night?"

Craig's jaw clenched. He pushed out a breath. "I'll work it out." He turned his attention to the production. "Okay, let's get this done."

It took almost an hour after shooting the last scene for the crew to pack up the equipment and for the principals, supporting actors and extras to pile into the waiting vehicles and drive off. By then twilight had settled, that in-between time when reality seemed to mix with fantasy.

Jewel dared to open the front door and step outside. She looked around, and it was as if all those people had never been there. It was hard to believe that mere hours earlier the grounds have been covered with lights, people, cameras and cables that ran like snakes across the grass.

She walked over to the swing bench and sat, took her cell phone from the pocket of her shorts and set it beside her. She had successfully avoided contact with Craig all day. Or maybe it was the other way around, because it was Anthony who came to advise her of the progress and when they were leaving. It was him that thanked her for her hospitality and promised to respect her home when they returned in the morning. She pushed up from her seat and returned inside. Maybe a hot shower would wash away her need for Craig Lawson.

Craig lounged in the armchair and stared out the hotel window. He sipped on a glass of bourbon and let his mind wander through the events of the day. No matter how hard he tried to stay focused on the success of a day of filming, his thoughts continued to shift to Jewel. It seemed that the harder he tried to keep her—and them—in the background, the more she continued to sit on the forefront of his mind. The whole staying away agenda was futile. Even though they weren't physically together, she was still with him—deep inside. It would be difficult, that much he was certain of. But somehow he would make it work.

He tossed back the last of his drink and set the

glass down on the side table. Enough of his self-imposed mind game. He wanted Jewel in his life. End of story.

The crew was back the following morning to finish up some of the final scenes. Jewel intentionally stayed out of sight, only peeking out at the unfolding of shooting from the second-floor window. They worked until they lost daylight and finally called it a day.

When all the cars and trucks were gone, Jewel dared to step outside to reclaim her space. A wave of sadness swept through her. She shouldn't have wished that Craig would seek her out to tell her how much he missed her or that Milan meant nothing to him. She was a grown woman and had gone into whatever it was that was happening between them with open eyes. Eyes that, she admitted, had been temporarily clouded by her long-buried desire to be loved again. And she'd foolishly allowed herself to think that it could be Craig.

Deep in her musings and caught in the blur of dimming light, she wasn't sure if it was an image walking across the grass or the movement of shadows until the figure fully formed in front of her. Her breath caught in her lungs. Her stomach knotted.

Craig strode up the short incline and stopped several feet away from the porch landing. "I parked on the street," he offered with a toss of his head behind him, as if it was some kind of explanation. "I wanted to wait until everyone was gone."

"For what?" she asked.

"I wanted to talk to you."

"As I said, for what?"

Craig took a step forward and stopped in anticipation of her telling him to stay put, but she didn't. So he kept walking until he stood on the top step of the landing. He shoved his hands in his pockets. The evening light illuminated for him the emotions that flickered in her eyes—anger and hurt. He'd put that look there, and she didn't deserve it. She deserved his honesty, but he didn't know where to begin.

"Can we go for a walk?"

"No. You can say whatever it is you have to say from right there."

He lowered his head for a moment then looked right into her accusing stare. "I don't know what you've seen or heard about...me and Milan Chase." He saw her nostrils flare for an instant. "But nothing is going on."

"Why should that matter to me? You're a grown man. No strings, remember."

Inwardly he flinched at the chunk of ice she'd tossed at him.

"I don't need your...whatever this is you're doing, your mea culpa. We're both in the business of images. Remember? Pictures tell tales." She snatched up her cell phone from beside her and went through a series of clicks then turned it to face him, swiping from one picture to the next. Images of him and Milan with her hand on his, another with their heads close together, one of her laughing at something he'd said, then the infamous rush from the restaurant and into a waiting vehicle.

She smiled, but there was no joy in it. "As I said,

what do you want? Oh, wait, let me rephrase that. You got what you wanted, so just go." Her voice cracked. She blinked rapidly.

Craig was next to her in a heartbeat. Roughly he pulled her to her feet, wrapped his arms around her and captured her mouth with his. He wanted to embed his feelings into her, burn into her memory that what was going on between them was real, that what he was feeling for her was real, and none of that other crap mattered.

The phone clattered to the floor.

Craig groaned when she melted into him. His arms looped around her to cup her head in his hands and seal his mouth to hers. He felt her heart bang and hammer, his thoughts swirled. There was no turning back now.

They sat shoulder to shoulder on a flat rock over-looking the brook that ran behind the house. A warm breeze blew around them. Craig linked his fingers between Jewel's and slowly and honestly told her about his past relationship with Milan, his reasons for hiring her and what really went on at the restaurant.

"I've been telling her since day one that we were done and that our relationship was strictly professional." He pushed out a breath. "But she kept it in her head that she could change all that. Her performance the other night was the last straw. I had our lawyers contact her agent to remind them that we would invoke the morals clause if she stepped out of line again during filming." He waited a beat. "I need to tell you all of it."

She whipped her head to face him. He held up his

hand. "It's not whatever it is you're thinking. The real reason why she flipped the other night was because of you."

"Me? What are you talking about? I don't know the woman." Her expression twisted in confused outrage.

"She saw me put you in the car when you spent the night at the hotel. She asked me about you and if you were the reason why I refused to be with her."

"And...what did you tell her?"

"That it was none of her business. I also told her that you were the owner of the house. She pretty much lost it after that. Said some pretty ugly things." He lowered his head then looked at her from an angle. "I never meant to hurt you, Jewel. Never. I need you to believe that." He squeezed her fingers. "I know that we don't have a lot of time and I have no idea how things are going to work out when I'm done here, but I want you to believe me when I tell that whatever time I have, I want to spend it with you."

"I do, too," she confessed and felt as if a boulder had been lifted off her chest. A smile beamed across her mouth. "So do I."

Craig leaned in and kissed her so tenderly that she felt as if her heart would break into a million pieces of joy.

Jewel leaned back and stared at him, let her eyes take him in. Yep, she'd done him justice, she concluded. "Come, I want to show you something." She took his hand, and they walked together to the cottage.

She switched on the lights and walked him around to the front of the canvas that took up the center of the floor.

His mouth opened then closed. His eyes registered his amazement.

"This…" He looked at her then back at the portrait of himself. "It's incredible," he managed. He stepped closer. "It seems alive… I seem alive…" He laughed. "I don't know what I mean." He whirled toward her and clasped her shoulders. "Baby, you have a gift." He leaned into her. "A God-given gift, and it's gotta be some kind of mortal sin not to share it with the world. You need to do this. This is you. It's in your soul. You're an artist down to the marrow of your bones."

Jewel pressed her lips together to keep from crying. It had been so long since she even dared to feel that way about herself and longer since someone told her. The feeling was overwhelming.

"It's okay to cry," he said, wiping a tear away with the pad of his thumb. "Tears of happiness, I hope."

She nodded vigorously and sniffed.

Wrapped in his arms she shut her eyes. This could be the real deal with him if she let it happen. And if he did the same.

Chapter 13

Filming continued for the next week with at least another week until completion of the interiors. The schedule was grueling, as it didn't end with cut but continued into the nights, when the dailies were reviewed. But as promised, Craig spent whatever time and energy he had with Jewel. While he worked on set, she worked in her studio, pouring years of pent-up creativity onto canvas. Whether he knew it or not, Craig had given her part of her life back.

They shared dinners at her home, moonlit walks and phone conversations late into the night. It was agreed between them that they would keep their relationship private. The last thing he wanted was for Jewel to become fodder for the tabloids and speculation about his love life. Not to mention that he needed to keep Milan in control. It was a delicate juggling act.

But leave it up to his sister, Alyse, to add her drama to the mix.

"If I had to wait for you to call me, we would never speak," she chastised.

Craig gripped the phone in his hand and inwardly groaned. "Sis, you have to know how busy I've been. We're right in the thick of things right now."

"According to TMZ you certainly are with that... woman. Craig, how could you? You know what she's like. I know she was your rebound after Anastasia, but she's bad news."

"It's not what you think."

"Oh, really? Then what is it? You're back in bed with her, aren't you?"

"No! Christ. Give me a little credit. I'm not involved with Milan Chase. I'm seeing someone else," he blurted out before he could stop himself. *Dammit.*

"Oh, really? Who?"

"Alyse..."

"Tell me, who is it?"

"Her name is Jewel Fontaine."

There was a moment of silence on the line.

"Her name sounds familiar. Wait, *the* Jewel Fontaine? The artist? Wait. Hold up. She owns that house. The one you're filming at! It was in the paper."

Craig didn't respond. He already knew he'd dug a big hole for himself. All he could hope was that he didn't get buried.

"Yes," he said quietly. *"That* Jewel."

"Well, I'll be damned. How'd you pull that off, big brother? Flash her your pearly whites and Lawson charm?"

"Not funny, Alyse."

"Look, do you. Just do it right, okay? You don't have the best track record, if you know what I mean. There are a lot of broken hearts in your wake." She paused. "I want you to be happy, brother of mine. I really do. I know you put up a good front after Ana, but I also know that she hurt you. Bad. I want you to have someone in your life that means something. That's there for you, in your corner. Work can't be everything. Dad is a perfect example of that. He's rich, successful, feared and completely alone. All the success and money in the world can't keep you warm at night or fix the things inside you that are broken."

"Psychology 101," he playfully snarked. Although the imploding of his relationship with Ana had covered all of the tabloids for weeks, that was the tip of the iceberg when it came to the women who had come and gone in his life. The only upside was that the world didn't chronicle all of those details.

"Whatever. But I'm serious." She pushed out a breath. "Anyway, the other reason for my call was to invite you to dinner. Myles is in town for a week, and you promised we would all get together."

"Fine," he conceded. "When?"

"How's tomorrow night."

"It doesn't sound like a question."

"It's not. Brad will be there, and Myles is bringing his new girlfriend—Jessica, I think her name is. You should bring Jewel. I'd love to meet her and talk about her work."

"Aw, I don't know about that."

"Think about it. I swear I'll be on my best behavior."

Craig chuckled. "Highly unlikely, but I'll think about it. I'm not promising anything."

"See you tomorrow. Eight. Love you," she said before he could get a word in.

He placed the phone on the nightstand. It was nearly eleven. He was too tired to drive over to see Jewel, but he wouldn't let the night end without talking with her.

He knew what he felt for her was way beyond what he'd thought it would be. He'd only known her for a matter of weeks, but it felt as if she had always been a part of his life. When they talked it was easy. They laughed, they listened, they shared.

She told him what it was like growing up without a mother and how her father worked so hard to make it up to her and ensure that her dream to become an artist was realized. She went to the best schools, traveled and made a name for herself in the art world, and her father had been with her every step of the way, never asking for anything in return except that she be happy.

The only thing they'd ever bumped heads about, she'd said, was her ex, Simon. Her father had never liked him, didn't trust him, said he was a charmer—and not in a complimentary way. He'd been right, and the breakup took more out of her than she realized; compounded with her father's then escalating illness, she never really recovered. Her father was her reason for everything. She wanted to thank him for all that he had done, so she'd worked tirelessly to make him proud, to pay back the debt of gratitude, and so she barely hesitated when she realized that she would have to give up her career because her father needed her. She hinted at the degree of his illness, only saying that he needed twenty-four-hour care, which was why she'd given up her career, which ultimately led to her dire financial situation. But she said no matter what, she would not have done anything differently.

It was that selfless attitude that he so admired in Jewel. Her depth of caring was like nothing that he had experienced. His father was the polar opposite. To show that you cared was a sign of weakness in Jake Lawson's book, and weakness was unacceptable. But it was more than that. His father's vehement disdain for what Craig chose for a living was totally irrational. He knew that it had something to do with his mother, but he never knew exactly what that was. And if anyone else in the family knew they never told him.

He would make himself crazy going in circles about his father. He reached for the phone and called Jewel. He knew that the sound of her voice would quell the questions and quiet the unending storm within him.

Much to his surprise, he asked and Jewel agreed. Even more surprising was that his baby sis actually kept her promise and behaved.

Dinner was a fun-filled event, with Myles and Alyse vying for the best recounting of their childhood antics. Alyse's new beau was a corporate attorney on the partnership track, and Myles's latest was, of course, a model. He was, of all the Lawson clan, a mirror of their cousin Rafe. Women generally tumbled over themselves to get to Myles, and he'd charm them with his good looks, unavailable demeanor and good old Southern charisma. It was a quality that all of the Lawson men shared. They believed in making a woman feel like a queen.

Alyse and Jewel got on as if they had been friends for years. He got a little jumpy when Alyse whisked Jewel away into the other room, but later found out that Alyse wanted Jewel's opinion on a piece of art that she was thinking of purchasing. Had Alyse asked that question weeks ago, he was sure that Jewel's response would have been quite different. Now that she'd started painting again, her love of the arts had been reignited, and talking about it only fueled her fire. He hoped that in time she would consider showing her work again. But one step at a time.

"I really like your sister and brother," Jewel said as they headed back to her place in Craig's Suburban. "Brad seems like a nice guy, and your brother's girlfriend is stunning, to say the least."

"They liked you, too."

Jewel grinned. "I loved the stories about you guys growing up. I have no idea what it's like to have siblings. You're lucky."

A warmth spread inside him. "Yeah, I guess I am." He turned to her and grinned. "I don't think I realized how much I missed them," he said in a faraway voice. "We were really close."

"You still can be."

"That's pretty hard."

"Only as hard as you make it. You have the means to travel at a moment's notice. You can offer to fly them out to where you are for visits. You can make it a point to come home for holidays."

He pulled onto her street. "You want me to stay?" he asked, smoothly switching topics.

"Of course. But don't think you've gotten away from what we were talking about," she said with a knowing arch of her brow.

"Yes, ma'am." He leaned over and gave her a quick kiss of acquiescence.

A frantic banging on her bedroom door jerked Jewel and Craig out of a deep sleep. Jewel leaped up, disoriented. The banging came again, along with the wailing of her name. She jumped out of bed, grabbed her robe and ran to the door.

She tugged it open with her heart pounding. "Minerva, what is it? What's wrong?"

"Oh, God. Oh, God. I went to check on him and he wasn't in his room! I looked everywhere." She squeezed Jewel's arms.

"What! What are you saying? He has to be here." She shoved her arms into the sleeves of her robe. Waves of hysteria began to build.

"Jewel, what is it?" Craig asked from the shadows of the room.

"My father. He's not in his room." She turned to dart out.

"I'm coming with you." He grabbed his clothes from the floor and quickly got dressed. Minerva was already halfway down the hall.

The trio fanned out in the house, searched every room, every crawl space, but it was Craig who discovered the back door was not locked and partially open.

"You have flashlights?" he asked.

"In the drawer near the sink," Minerva said and hurried to get it.

"Oh, no, if he's gone outside…" Jewel's voice disintegrated into terror.

"We'll find him, and everything is going to be all right. I promise."

Jewel beat back tears with rapid blinks of her eyes. She nodded. "Stay here, Minerva, in case Daddy wanders back," she instructed then followed Craig out onto the back of the property.

Jewel and Craig combed every inch of the property, and more than an hour later they still had not found her father. Jewel was beyond frantic.

Craig held her tight. "Baby, we need to call the police."

She nodded her head against his chest. Together they returned to the house, and Jewel made the call.

While they waited for the arrival of the police, Jewel finally told him the full story of her father's illness.

"He suffers with an aggressive form of Alzheimer's and dementia. Medication worked for a while, until it didn't. We tried everything. Every doctor. Nothing worked." Tears slid down her cheeks. "They told me I would have to put him in an institution so that he could be cared for. My father! I couldn't do that. I wouldn't. After the debacle in New York, he got worse, and I'd lost my confidence. It made sense to put that part of our lives behind us and move to whatever this new one held. I took on caring for him full-time." She swallowed. "Until it got to be too much. That's when I hired Minerva. At first she would come during the day, but after about a year she started staying longer…into the night, until it was twenty-four hours a day." She lowered her head. Craig clutched her hand.

She drew in a shuddering breath. "We were on the verge of losing the house," she whispered. "I'd all but exhausted my earnings, ate into my savings. And then like magic, you came along." She laughed sadly and sniffed back tears. "I thought, *a miracle*. But then I met you, and I looked into your eyes and you turned my world upside down. I didn't want to risk caring about and losing anyone else, even at the thought of losing the house. So I said no. I was scared." Her voice wobbled. "It was Minerva that told me to take a chance on being happy…even if it was only for a little while."

"It doesn't have to be," he blurted out. "I don't want it to be. I'm in love with you. Crazy in love with you."

"You…you love me?"

"With every ounce of my being." He leaned over and kissed her with all of the love that had burst from his soul. "We can make it work," he said against her lips.

"How?" she whispered through her tears.

"We'll find a way."

The lights from the police car lit up the lawn.

"I promise," he said before they ran down to meet the officers and Jewel gave a description of her father.

The trio waited in frightened silence for some word from the police. It was more than an hour later when the officers returned with Augustus in tow. He'd wandered nearly a mile away and had fallen asleep. He was disheveled and totally disoriented, even lashing out at Jewel, which broke her heart into a million pieces. Oddly, it was Craig who was able to soothe him, talk to him in quiet tones and get him cleaned up and back to bed.

By the time Augustus was settled and asleep, they were all beyond exhausted. Daybreak was on the horizon.

"I don't want to leave, but I have to get back. We have an early shoot in town. Will you be okay?"

"Go. I'll be fine." She looked into his eyes. "I can't thank you enough for everything that you did."

"There's no need to thank me for anything. Whatever you need, whenever you need it." He turned to leave.

"Craig…"

He stopped and turned back.

"I love you," she whispered.

He smiled. "I needed that."

She hugged herself and watched him hurry away.

Chapter 14

The filming in town took another two weeks to complete. Craig was beyond busy. As much as he hated it, there was little time to spend with Jewel, but he made it a point to check in with her every day and ask about her father.

The experience that night and seeing the depth of her love for her dad and all that she had sacrificed for him forced him to rethink his relationship with his own father and the importance of family. Even if his father couldn't put his personal issues aside, Craig knew he had to make one last effort, swallow his pride and confront his father.

He was a grown, successful, independent man, but when he pulled up in front of his father's palatial estate—his childhood home—he felt like a child again. He'd thought about calling first, but he knew that if his father wouldn't speak to him, it would be the final break. After debating the wisdom of what he was about to do, he finally got out of his car and went to the front door.

The last person he expected to answer was his father.

"Dad."

The stunned expression on Jake Lawson's face spoke volumes. The ten years since he'd last seen his father showed in the slope of Jake's broad shoulders, the dimming of his once piercing gaze and the firm mouth that had softened.

"Craig…"

Did his voice crack with emotion, or did Craig only imagine it?

"I, uh, was in town… I wanted to see you."

An uncomfortable silence hung between them.

"I suppose you should come in then," he finally said. He opened the door wider and stepped aside.

Craig walked in, took a look around, and the past rushed at him like a speeding train, the good and the ugly. He turned toward his father, who still stood at the door.

Jake extended a hand toward the living area. Craig led the way and took a seat on the couch. He rested his arms on his thighs.

"Drink? Bourbon, if I remember."

"Thanks. Yes."

Jake walked over to the bar, and that's when Craig noticed the slowing of his father's once purposeful step. He was getting old. He had more years behind him than in front of him. The realization shook him.

Jake returned with two glasses and handed one to Craig. He slowly lowered himself into an armchair.

"I saw the write-up about you and this film of yours in the papers."

The corner of Craig's mouth lifted in a smile. "Yeah, we're just about finished."

Jake took a swallow of his drink.

"I understand it's about the family."

"Not entirely. It's based on the family, or a family like ours, the struggle from nothing to prominence and success."

"I suppose you'll be going back to Europe when you're done."

"Not right away."

"Hmm." He took another swallow. "So what brings you here after all this time…to see me?"

Craig hesitated. What he was about to say could go either way. "I've been doing a lot of thinking, a lot of soul searching. I know that you don't think much of what I do. I'll never fully understand it, but I…want my father back. Life is so short. We've spent the past ten years not speaking to each other. Years that we can never get back. I've always respected you and all of your success, and I understand that you only wanted the best for me, for all of us. But I'm not you. I'll never be you. All I've ever wanted was for you to respect *my* dreams. And maybe, just maybe be happy for me, that I've achieved them. It's what you taught me. Go after what I want. That has got to mean something, Dad."

Jake lifted his chin and looked away.

"Just tell me. Now, finally. Why?"

"It was your mother's dream, too," he said slowly,

reaching back in time. "She was good. They said she could be great, and I was her biggest cheerleader."

Craig watched his father's throat work up and down.

"That night...of the accident. She told me she had a last-minute rehearsal and she'd be back late." He pressed his lips together, and Craig could see the pain of the past race across his father's face. "She didn't have a rehearsal. She was with him."

"Him? Who?" His heart began to pound.

"Her leading man." He snorted a laugh. "They'd been having an affair for months. She was going to leave me—us." His voice grew hard. "He was in the car with her that night. He was driving. She was killed on impact. He survived for about three hours."

"But you always told us that Mom was in the car alone," he said, the shock not registering.

"I did it to protect all of you. Back then there wasn't all of his social media bull crap. Your uncle Branford pulled some strings and had the whole thing covered up. We couldn't have that kind of scandal."

Craig felt sick. The vague image that he'd had of his mother was forever tarnished. Now it all made ugly, terrible sense.

"I wanted to keep you as far away from that life as possible, and when you told me that you were going to be a filmmaker, all I could think was that it would take you away the same way it did her. It may not make sense to you. It may never make sense to you, but I didn't want to lose you, too." His voice shook. "But I did anyway. There was nothing I could do to stop you."

"Why didn't you tell me, Dad? All these years."

"I...wanted you to keep the memory that you had of your mother, not the one that I had." He hung his head. His shoulders shook with all the years of grief, and loneliness and loss.

Craig jumped up and went to kneel at his side. He put his arms around his father and held him as he wept.

"Oh, my God, Craig, I'm so sorry," Jewel said as she lay next to him in bed. She stroked his hair. "I can't imagine what your father must have felt."

"He loved her. That I know for sure," he said into the darkness. "I remember when I was little how he used to touch her and light up every time she came into the room, how he'd steal a kiss whenever he thought we weren't looking. And I thought, *I want to have what they have when I grow up.* Humph—it was all a sham."

"I don't believe that. I'm sure your mother loved him. She had three children with him, built a life with him. That has to count for something. Don't dismiss that. Sometimes...things change and cloud our vision for a time, but it doesn't make the past go away."

"I don't know," he said sadly. "Maybe you're right. The worst part is he and I spent all this time being at each other's throats when we could have been each other's ally."

"Now you have the opportunity to work on things between you." She paused. "There is one thing that I want to say, and then I'm going to let it go."

"What's that?"

"Don't shift the animosity that you felt for your father onto your mother. Forgive her. Remember the mother that she was to you. Don't take on a new demon."

He turned fully onto his side to face her and ran his finger down the bridge of her nose. "How did you get so wise?"

"My dad was a great teacher."

"I love you, Jewel Fontaine."

"I totally believe that."

"I gotta run, baby," Craig said the following morning. "Loose ends to tie up."

Jewel sat on the side of the bed and watched him get dressed. "When will you be totally finished?" she asked with trepidation.

He stopped. "Tomorrow."

Her heart sank. "When were you going to tell me?"

"Tonight." He looked sheepish. He came to sit next to her. "I know I should've said something, but the moment I did, it would make it real. I kept thinking I could drag out the inevitable."

She pushed up from the bed and crossed the room. "We both knew you wouldn't be here forever. It had to come to an end at some point." She kept her back to him.

Craig came up behind her. He slid his arms around her waist. "I promised you that we would work it out, that I'd find a way. I meant that."

She didn't respond. He kissed the back of her neck. "We'll talk tonight."

And then he was gone.

Throughout the day Jewel continued to remind herself that she was prepared for this. She'd known the day would come when he would have to go back to his life. She'd wanted to believe that somehow he could make the impossible possible, but if nothing else she was a realist. Their brief idyll was coming to a close. If their love was a script, she wondered how Craig would pen their ending.

Then another reality pressed to the forefront. The money that she'd been paid for the use of the house wouldn't last forever. It would get them through the summer and maybe early fall. Her small baking business, such as it was, wouldn't fill the gap.

She looked around at the canvases in various stages of completion, and an idea hit her. She went for her phone and called Mai Ling. They hadn't spoken in months. Jewel was sure that Mai was tired of trying to convince her to get back to work, to put a small show together. Since the days of working as Jewel's personal assistant, Mai had moved on to running her own publicity office. Mai knew the movers and shakers in the Big Easy and beyond.

Jewel tugged on her bottom lip with her teeth as she listened to the phone ring.

"Mai Ling and Associates. How may I help you?"

"Hello. This is Jewel Fontaine. Is Mai available?"

"Hold one moment."

Jewel had barely sat down when Mai's voice screamed in her ear.

"Jewel! Jewel! Girl. How are you? Oh, my goodness, I was just thinking of you. Are you okay? Dad?"

"Everything is fine. How are you?"

"Crazy busy. But I'd rather be busy with you, as you well know."

"Maybe you will."

"Wait...what are you saying? Don't play."

Jewel giggled. She hadn't realized how much she'd missed her friend. "I'm not. Do you have some time today to stop by the house? There's something I want to show you, then we can talk."

"I'm putting the rest of my day on hold. Be there in a half hour."

"Mai, you are still crazy."

"Yep! See ya soon."

"'Kay."

Jewel disconnected the call, feeling better than she'd felt in hours. A new energy flowed through her veins, an excitement that she hadn't felt in years. She didn't want to get her hopes up. Mai would be brutally honest with her, that much she knew for sure. Then she would decide.

Mai must have taken a jet, because she'd made the thirty-minute trip in record time.

"Oh, Jewel, it's so good to see you," Mai said, hugging her friend. She stepped back and held her at arm's length. She angled her head to the side. "There's something glowing around you. You got a new man?"

Jewel tossed her head back and laughed. "We'll talk over wine and lunch. But first..." She took Mai's hand and led her out of the house and over to the studio. "I need you to be honest," she warned before she opened the door.

"Jewel," she whispered, the reality of what was happening beginning to hit home. "You...you've been working?" Her sloped eyes grew wide.

"Just come inside."

They stepped in, and Jewel came around the back of the canvas to the front. Mai followed.

Her gasps were confirmation. Mai moved reverently from one canvas to the next. "My God, Jewel... these are magnificent." She whirled toward her friend. "Phenomenal." She turned back to the renderings. "They tell a story," she said in awe, studying each one carefully.

"It's the story of *Rendezvous With Destiny* captured on canvas."

Mai frowned. "You mean the film that everyone's been talking about?"

Jewel nodded.

"Yes! Of course, you had a front-row seat."

"These are some of the scenes from the film, but what I wanted to do was to recreate the feeling of the time as well."

"Girl, you did that in spades. These are... I'm at a loss. Tell me you're going to show them."

"That's what I want to talk with you about."

"Consider it done. You know I have my contacts. We won't start off with anything big. Something local, to get the buzz going." Her brows rose to peaks. "They would be perfect publicity for the film! Maybe we could partner with the production company. I'm thinking if you had them filming on your property, you have some kind of connection."

Jewel gave a sly grin. "Something like that."

"Now I need that drink. This could be major. I mean, really major."

Jewel was on a natural high by the time Mai left. Her head was filled with limitless possibility. There was still so much more to do. For a show, even a small one, she would need at least five more pieces. They would need to be sealed and framed.

She felt that she had purpose again. That what she loved about herself wasn't really lost at all. And it took Craig walking into her life…and now walking out for her to find herself again. She supposed that even though there would be a void in her life once Craig returned to Europe, she would still have her art.

This time she believed that she was made of more resilient stuff and could take whatever the critics threw her way without crumbling, plus she had Minerva in her life to help with her father.

She took one last look at the row of renderings. She had her mojo back.

Chapter 15

"So what are you gonna do, man?" Anthony asked over drinks with Craig.

Craig stared into his glass. "Been trying to figure it out." He angled his head toward Anthony. "I can't ask her to run around the world with me. She has her father to think about. And I can't very well stay behind. We have projects lined up for the next two years."

"Yeah, and so where does that leave you?"

"Screwed."

"Listen, plenty of folks have done the long-distance thing. If it's meant to work out, it will. What is she saying?"

"Not much. It was me that told her I'd find a way."

"Humph." Anthony took a swallow of his drink. "Well, then, my brother, I suggest you get to finding a way."

"Thanks," he said sarcastically.

"Hey, I'm really glad to hear about you and your pops, man." He clapped Craig on the back. "I know how much that thing between you ate you up, even if you didn't admit it. Good that y'all made peace. I can't imagine how hard that must have been to hear all that, and even harder for your pop to tell it to you."

"Yeah, it's gonna take some time to get past it. But I'm planning to take Jewel's advice and not shift my animosity from my dad to my mom. It's a no-win situation."

"I hear that. Smart lady."

Craig half grinned. "Yeah."

"You know, if you need to, you can hang back a couple more days. I can take care of the crew and get started on the editing back in LA."

"Thanks, man. I might take you up on that. I'll let you know in the morning." He lifted his cell from the table and checked the time. "I'm going to cut out. Stop by and see Jewel."

"Cool."

They gripped hands and shoulder hugged.

"See you in the morning," Craig said and walked out.

On the drive over to Jewel's place, he went through a dozen scenarios. None of them was going to solve their problem, and he wasn't sure what would. When he rolled up to the front of the property, he called. She answered on the second ring.

"Hey, baby. I'm out front."

"I'm at the cottage."

"Be there in a few."

At least she didn't sound as upset as she'd looked this morning. If anything she sounded happy.

Jewel met him at the door with open arms and a welcoming smile. "Hey," she whispered and stepped into his arms.

"Hey, yourself." He squeezed her close.

"Come on in. How did it go today?"

"Good. It's a wrap," he joked.

"I want to talk to you, and there's something I need to show you."

She led him inside. On the evenings they spent at the cottage, Jewel made it a point to keep the canvases covered, insisting that she never showed anyone her work while it was in progress. It was partly true, but in this case she was more concerned about how Craig would feel about the work. If he felt that the art truly depicted his vision.

They walked around to the front of the canvases, and one by one Jewel removed the cloths that covered them until all four were revealed.

For several moments Craig was completely speechless. Slowly he walked back and forth in front of them. Then he spun toward her. His face looked as if it was lit from within. His eyes actually glowed.

"Jewel, these pictures...they're..."

"Do you like them?"

"Like them? I love them. They're amazing, even more stunning than watching it on film. The way you captured the nuances of their expressions, the body language—they look as if any minute they're going to walk off the canvas and into the room."

He looked at her with awe. "You are incredible. This is what you've been working on and hiding from me?"

She grinned. "Yes. I didn't know how they would turn out or how you would feel about them."

"You don't plan to hide them in here forever, do you? You *are* planning to show them?"

"That's the part I wanted to talk with you about…"

Craig listened intently to what Jewel and her friend Mai had envisioned, and his own mind was on overdrive thinking of the collaborative potential.

"We can do this," he cut in before she'd finished. "I love the idea. We use your art as publicity for the movie and the movie as publicity for your art. It's crazy brilliant, and I know it'll work."

Jewel breathed a deep sigh of relief. "I wasn't sure if you would go for it."

"Whatever can keep us and bring us closer together, then I'm all for it, baby. This may open up the doors to a whole new way of cross advertising, not to mention the business it will bring you."

Jewel plopped down on a chair and looked at him. "I hadn't even thought about that," she said with wonder in her voice.

"Yeah, well, think about it, 'cause I believe that you have taken your art to a whole new level. This is just the beginning."

She leaped up and jumped into his arms, wrapping her legs around his waist. "I love you, love you." She kissed him solidly on the mouth.

"Love you right back, baby. Why don't you let me show you how much?"

"I'm liking the sound of that."

"I was supposed to leave tomorrow, but I can stay on a couple more days," Craig said against Jewel's neck.

She draped a leg across his body. "It's okay. We'll

be okay. I was thinking that maybe I could come out to LA in a few weeks for a long weekend."

"You'd do that?"

"Yes. Of course."

He hugged her tighter. "You just let me know when you're ready and I'll take care of everything."

"No arguments from me," she joked.

"And I'll come to you before I head back to London, and when I get there I'll send for you. You can come and see me work on my next project, maybe get some inspiration," he added and slid his hand down between her legs.

"I'm inspired already," she said against his mouth.

"We're going to make this work, baby," he said, rolling on top of her. "Whatever it takes."

"Show me just how invested you are in our success."

"With pleasure."

"You sure you don't want me to ride with you to the airport?" Jewel asked the following morning.

"No, that's only going to make it harder."

"We'll see each other in two weeks."

Jewel heaved a sigh.

Craig hesitated a moment, but he knew what was on his mind had to be said. "There is one thing that was bugging me about your work."

"What?"

"If we're going to do this together, then you can't have a show of the work this far in advance of the release of the film."

Her body tensed. "Why? It's my work."

"I understand that, but it's based on *my* film."

"So what are you saying? I thought you loved the

concept. You were all for it a minute ago, now it's *your* film."

Craig pushed out a breath. He'd been stung in the past, in his early days of screenwriting, when a woman he was dating took full credit for a project that they'd worked on together based on his idea. He looked at the hurt that masked Jewel's face. That was then—this was now.

"What I mean is if you show it too far in advance, it will dilute their value in relation to the movie and they won't do the movie any good at all. This whole thing has to be timed."

The only thing she'd been focused on was that she'd finished a set of work that she was proud of, work that was gallery ready. Gallery ready meant income—an income that she sorely needed.

Craig walked up to her and held her upper arms. She looked in his eyes.

"If we're going to do this, we need to plan it right, that's all I'm saying. I want this to work. Talk with your friend Mai and see what she says. But as far as I see it, too early is too soon." He pecked her on the lips then hung on for a real kiss. "I'll call you when I land," he said. "Love you." He pecked her lips again, turned and hurried out.

Jewel paced the room. This was her work. She'd come to him with the idea. Sure, the inspiration came from the film, but the work was hers. She'd stayed in the shadows and sat on the sidelines long enough. It was her time again.

"I hadn't thought of that," Mai said thoughtfully as she sat opposite Jewel at the kitchen table. "When is the film being released?"

"At least six months from now. I'm pretty sure he'll take it to film festivals before it's released in theaters."

"That may work." She put down her coffee cup. "Look, this is a stumbling block, not the end of the journey. I know you had it in your head to jump feet-first. But this may be a blessing in disguise." Her eyes lit. She leaned forward. "You will still need at least five to seven more pieces to complete the series."

"Right."

"The film has to do what it has to do in the next few months, but in the meantime, I start building your brand. Leaking information of your comeback. Hinting at a major collaboration that's a game changer for the industry. We get you ready. You get your work ready, and launch the film and your art at the earliest film festival."

Jewel got excited again. "That might work."

"Not might, *will*!"

They lifted their coffee cups in salute.

As promised, the moment Craig landed in LA he called Jewel while he waited for his bags. Although they did the hug and kiss thing and said the *I love you*s, he'd still left not feeling good about things between them. He was thrilled that Jewel had gotten her inspiration back, and having gotten it from the film made the connection between them even tighter. It was like two creative minds thinking as one. That itself was a turn-on. The very idea that she was able to see beyond what he presented and translate that into art blew him away.

If only it was that simple. Two creative minds were bound to clash. They each had their vision, their purpose. That was the crossroads where he and Jewel now stood.

When they'd faced each other in the cottage, he knew the instant the words were out of his mouth that she didn't agree. It wasn't what she wanted. And he understood why, but he also had to consider what he wanted and what would best serve him and the film.

He'd run the concept past Anthony on the plane ride and he was totally on board but agreed that too soon would blow a hole in the entire project.

Somehow they had to come to a compromise.

"Hey, baby," he said when she picked up. "I know it's late."

"I was waiting for your call," she said sleepily. "How was the flight?"

"No problems." He paused, cleared his throat. "Hey, listen, about his whole art meets film. I don't want to get in your way. I know how important your work is to you, just like mine is to me. I can't let what I want stop you. I've lived through that with my father. I know what it did to me, what it did to him, and I would never put that on you. You deserve your moment. So if you want to put a show together, whatever you want to do, I'm behind you."

He didn't know at what point he'd changed his mind. Maybe it was when her heard her voice, or remembered the look in her eyes, or maybe he was finally seeing that to love someone was more than just a feeling—it was doing. Whatever the reason, he was glad that he did.

"That's why I love you," she said softly. "But neither of us has to put our work on hold. Mai and I talked about it today, and we think this will work."

She went on to tell them what they'd discussed and how they would gradually release the work.

"Brilliant! Absolutely brilliant. That'll work. The first showing is the Independent Film Festival, then Sundance in January and Cannes in May. Distribution is key, but I don't see a problem. We can plan on a release after Labor Day but definitely before Christmas to even be considered for a Golden Globe or SAG. I'll have to press my people, but I know we can get the film ready in time."

Jewel breathed a sigh of relief. "I'm so happy."

"I miss you already," he said in response. "Let me know when you want to come out. I'll make all of the arrangements."

"I will." She yawned.

"Get some rest. We'll talk tomorrow."

"Okay." She yawned again.

"I love you," he said.

"I love you, too."

"Good night, baby."

"Night."

Craig slid the phone in his pocket and strode out of the airport baggage area and into the waiting car. Electric energy pumped through his veins. He could see an amazing future spread out in front of him, and Jewel was right at his side.

Chapter 16

The next few months were a whirlwind of activity. Jewel worked every day perfecting her pieces, and bit by bit the collection grew to an astonishing body of work that replicated the film in a way that was surreal. She worked from many of the photographs that Norm had taken and from the sketches she'd done while watching the film unfold on the grounds and in the house.

She was in constant touch with Mai, who dropped in at least once per week to check on Jewel's progress and to update her on her publicity plans, which had begun to roll out. News stations and several key art magazines had been in touch wanting interviews. "We've got them in the bag," Mai had said, "but time is key."

In between Jewel spent as much time as she could

with her father, who seemed to grow more and more frail with each passing day. There were times when she would come into his room and see him sitting by the window and he'd remind her of a broken sparrow, trapped on the ground and unable to fly. The vibrant, robust man of her youth was gone. In his place was the shell of her father.

It was her fear and concern for her father that held her back from taking the trip to London to spend some time with Craig and cut short her visit to New York, where he'd gone to do some of the talk shows. She worried constantly that something would happen and she wouldn't be there for her father. There were nights when she would jerk out of her sleep thinking he'd gotten out of the house again. The idea that she would have to leave him for any length of time grew to be less and less of a possibility each day. But the first showings of the work and the film were happening within a week at the Indie Film Festival, then Cannes and Sundance. She didn't know if she would be at any of them.

"Hey, Daddy," she said softly and crossed the room to where he sat by the window. She took a seat. "How are you today? It's beautiful outside. You want to go for a walk?"

He looked across at her with a faraway expression on his face. He smiled. "You're a pretty little gal."

Jewel's heart knocked. "Come on, let's go outside."

Once outside, Jewel held on tightly to her father's thin arm, and they strolled slowly across the glistening green grass of the backyard.

"I had so much fun running around out here when I was little. Do you remember the time when I climbed that tree, the one right over there?" She pointed to the giant maple that was the centerpiece of the property. "Got halfway up and got scared. Couldn't move. Wouldn't go up and couldn't come down." She chuckled at the memory. "You were the one that coaxed me down." She squeezed his arm and rested her head on his shoulder. "You climbed up and sat with me, talked with me, told me how proud you were because I was so fearless, that I could do anything, and no matter what you would always be there cheering me on." Tears rolled down her cheeks. "You held my hand, and we came down the tree together." She sniffed. "You were always there, like I am now."

"I had my time," he said.

The strength and clarity in his voice brought Jewel up short. She held her breath.

"It's your time, baby girl. Time for you to climb down on your own, spread your wings with that nice fella. I'll cheer you on from the sidelines."

She looked into his face and knew that in that moment, he saw her. Really saw her, and his words weren't some out-of-context ramblings. He was here in the moment with her. Her throat knotted. She wrapped her arms around her father and held on, needing to secure this moment between them just a little while longer. When she finally released him and stepped back to look into his eyes, he was already gone.

The first article on the return of Jewel Fontaine hit the newsstand a month before the Indie Film Festival. And in the following months, she was on the covers of *Art Noir*, *Contemporary Art*, *People*, and *Cosmo*.

She appeared with Craig on the *Today* show and E! to talk about their collaboration without giving too much away. The film and the art worlds were buzzing, and Jewel's phone wouldn't stop ringing.

Craig returned to New Orleans for two weeks and they spent the entire time in bed together to make up for lost time.

"This is all so crazy," Jewel said the morning Craig was preparing to leave for LA. "I never thought I'd be in this place again." She looked at him, and for the first time all the excitement turned to doubt. "All the traveling and reporters and people wanting to know everything about me…you." She sighed and shook her head. "I left all that madness behind and settled for a different kind of life." She looked at him. "I'd gotten used to it. To the normalcy of it. Sure, it was hard financially, and then you came into my life and changed all that, but…"

Craig sat next to her. He lifted a stray curl from her face and tucked it behind her ear. "So what are you saying?"

"I don't know what I'm saying." Her eyes pleaded with him to understand. She lowered her head.

"You've been down this road. You know what it's like under the spotlight."

She shook her head back and forth. "Not like this."

Craig blew out a breath. "All this craziness is the prelim. Once the film hits, the noise will die down and we can go back to being Jewel and Craig." He captured her hand in his. His eyes ran over her face. "I got you," he said. "We're going to do this together. I promise you."

All at once that day in the tree so long ago, when

her dad climbed up to get her and assured her that it was going to be all right, flooded her thoughts and warmed her heart. And all those years later under that very same tree he gave her wings and told her to fly. It was exactly what Craig was doing.

She pressed her head against Craig's chest and shut her eyes. "Thank you, Daddy," she whispered.

Chapter 17

After much prayer and having her arm twisted by Minerva, Jewel set out with Craig to set fire to the industry. Just as Mai predicted, the unveiling of Jewel's first piece at the Indie Film Festival was a phenomenal success, which only upped the ante for the festivals to follow. Jewel and Craig were bombarded by journalists and photographers, all wanting to know every detail of their lives and their collaboration and to capture every moment.

Just as he'd promised, Craig was with Jewel every step of the way. It had been a while since she'd been under the glare of the spotlight, but with Craig by her side she glided instead of stumbled, and before long it was second nature again.

The biggest coup was the early premieres at targeted theaters. At the end the audiences actually stood for a good five minutes, shouting, applauding and stomping their approval. Upon their exit from the theater, the lobby was lined with Jewel's art, which served as the nightcap of the evening and reinforced the audience's theater experience.

The reviews were stellar, one after the other touting the brilliance of the film and the creative genius of the art. The pairing of the two had set the marketing world on its ear. Things only got better when Craig was nominated for a Golden Globe for best picture and best director. And he was informed that Milan Chase received a nomination for best actress.

Jewel leaped up into his arms and squealed with delight the minute he put the phone down.

"Oh, my God. This is so wonderful! Congratulations, baby." She kissed him long and hard. "You deserve this." She caressed his face. "So proud of you."

"We did this. Me and you. Don't ever think otherwise," he said, looking deep into her eyes. "It was your home that set the tone. That meant everything. And your renderings bring it all together. We did this."

She grinned. "If you say so, Mr. Golden Globe nominee."

"I want you there."

"Where?"

"At the Globes."

"Really?"

"Yes, really." He cupped her face in his hand. "Every step of the way...together, me and you."

He hadn't spoken to Milan since they'd completed the final edits months earlier, he thought as he held Jewel close. She'd called and left messages on his cell phone, but he'd never called back. Now with her getting the nomination, they would be thrown back in each other's paths. Not a journey he was looking forward to taking.

"You can't turn down these interviews, man," Anthony admonished. "It's going to hurt your chances and the chances for the film. We open nationwide in a week. You have a major nomination along with your lead actress. People want to see you together."

Craig rocked his jaw and slowly paced the floor of his hotel suite.

"At least do one. *Entertainment Tonight*. They're fair and fun. It'll be easy. Besides, you've been able to keep your distance from Milan so far. You've been in the same cities on the same tours."

"Yeah, but the focus has never just been on me and her. It's not a good look, Tony. There's no telling what Milan may say or do."

"Look, everything is taped. If she does something crazy, we get it cut out before it airs."

He turned to his longtime friend. "All right, tell them I'll do it. But I swear, if this thing goes to hell, I'm blaming you."

"Duly noted."

When Craig and Anthony arrived at the studio, they were swept into the green room, prepped and offered food and drink to bide their time.

"You have about a half hour before they get started. I'm going to check on a few things and I'll be back."

"Cool." He settled on the couch and plucked a grape from the bunch.

There was a knock at the door.

"Come on in."

The door eased open, and Milan stepped into his line of sight. He sat up on the couch. "Milan, what are you doing here?"

She stepped fully into the room and shut the door behind her. "I thought we should talk first."

"Really? About what?"

"About all the mess that has gone down between us." She sighed and folded her hands in front of her. "When we were together, whether you believe it or not, I really cared for you. Really. I knew I wasn't a big star or a famous model, I was just me. I used to pinch myself to be sure that I wasn't dreaming. Me, Milan Chase from Newark, New Jersey, in a relationship with you." She chuckled without humor. "I didn't think you would stay," she said. "I figured it was only a matter of time."

"You didn't have to lie to me, Milan."

She lowered her head. "I know. I know that now. But I thought if I told you that I was pregnant that you would stay with me."

"There never was a baby, Milan! You lied. I did care about you. I could have…maybe cared more. But what you did—" he shook his head "—was unforgivable. To lie and say that you lost it. To pretend to be devastated." He rubbed his face with his hands then looked up at her. "If I hadn't seen the text message from your partner in crime, Delys, I may have never known."

"I've said I'm sorry. It won't change what I did. I accept that, but what I came here to say was thank you."

"For what?"

"For giving me this chance, after all the shit I put you through. I know that you could have picked hundreds of other actors for the part, but you chose me." Her voice wobbled.

"Because regardless of what you think, you are a helluva good actress. I saw that in you. I knew you could do this, and now you've proven to the world that you can. All you have to do now is have the same belief in yourself that I have in you. This is only the beginning, Milan. You have an amazing future ahead of you. But lies and backstabbing—" he shook his head "—will take you down."

She sniffed and smiled while trying not to cry. "They're going to have to redo my makeup."

He got up and crossed the room to stand in front of her. "You're a star. Go get the star treatment."

She leaned up and kissed his cheek. "Thank you." She walked out and straight into Anthony.

A look of panic crossed Anthony's face when he saw her wiping her eyes. "Everything cool?"

"Very," she said and hurried past him.

Anthony came in and shut the door. "What was that about?" he asked, hooking his thumb over his shoulder.

"Finally settling some old business. It's all good." He clapped Anthony on the back. "Let's get this done. I need to go home to my woman."

Chapter 18

The night of the Golden Globe Awards was more spectacular than Jewel ever imagined. It took all of her good home training to keep her jaw from dropping every time she saw another star. And they were all there, from multiple award-winning actors to the newcomers. Not to mention the music royalty that fanned out among the well-heeled guests.

Craig had reserved two tables for the cast and his family. He was happy to see that Milan brought a date, and she seemed truly happy. Everyone was in place except for his father. It was more than he could have expected, but he had to try.

Since his visit, they'd spoken maybe twice. It was almost as if the conversation had never happened. His father had reverted back to his demeanor of indifference. But Craig would not let that steal his moment tonight.

Now that the film had opened and the full array of Jewel's art had been displayed, her phone would not stop ringing. Every producer and director on the East and West Coasts wanted to hire her to do renderings of their films and their actors. She was in such demand that she could pick and choose whom she wanted to work with. Never in a million years would she have thought that her personal passion would take her to this level. She and Craig had created a whole new genre of art. For well into the future she was financially solvent. The worries she'd had barely a year earlier were a thing of the past. And to add to her blessings, Alyse confided that after seeing the film and her art, she'd been looking into landmark designation for Jewel's home. She was getting some very positive feedback from the committee and the cachet of the Lawson name. But she swore Jewel to secrecy. If it came through, Jewel would never have to worry about the house again.

She squeezed Craig's hand. He turned to her. "I love you," she whispered. "No matter what happens tonight. You are *my* winner, and I'll prove it to you later."

"Wicked, wicked woman," he said against her mouth.

The evening's festivities were underway, and one after another presenters and winners took to the podium. The room overflowed with good cheer, laughter and plenty of food and drink. It was one big party.

The first of many wins for *Rendezvous With Destiny* kicked off with Milan Chase's win for best actress in a drama. She was so overcome she could barely get her words out as she looked onto the crowd of her contemporaries standing for her.

"There are so many people to thank, but one person stands out above them all. I must thank Craig Lawson, my director, my mentor, my friend. He believed in me when I didn't believe in myself and gave me an opportunity when I didn't deserve it. I'm standing here tonight because of him. Thank you." She raised her award above her head and was escorted off.

When his name was called for best director, it took several moments for it to register with him. His entire table was on its feet as he pulled himself together and jogged up the steps to the stage.

Jewel was certain she would simply burst with pride and love as she watched him give his acceptance speech, and to see the love from his colleagues overflow and fill the room was overwhelming.

"There are so many people to thank. My entire crew, who work in front of and behind the scenes. The amazing actors who brought this story to life. I can't thank you enough. Hamilton and Milan, this is because of you," he said, lifting the statue. "But the one person that I have to thank and pay homage to is my lady, Jewel Fontaine. Her brilliance inspires me. Her beauty overwhelms me. Her selflessness taught me what it means to truly love another person. Without her I would be half the man I've become. And… if you'll have me, Jewel Fontaine, I want to spend the rest of my life with you working on the other half."

A collective gasp went up from the audience.

Jewel couldn't see for the tears that clouded her

eyes. She stood and blew him kisses, mouthing, "Yes, yes, yes."

Craig grinned like a man finding a million bucks. "Now I'm a real winner. Thank you!"

He was escorted off the stage but held in the wings. The next category was best picture.

She said yes was all he could think about as he stood on the side pacing back and forth. Visions of their life together played out in front of him. If he had to move back to Louisiana, he would. Whatever she wanted. Maybe he could purchase some property and set up a studio. What about kids? He wanted kids, lots of them, and the best part would be making them.

He was so engrossed in the swirl of his thoughts that it wasn't until the escort shook his arm to tell him they were calling his name did it register that he had won.

Craig walked back on stage in a semidaze. The lights, the people, the applause dazzled him. Best picture. It was the pinnacle of an artist's career.

For several moments he stood at the podium to pull himself together. He looked out at the crowd and found his table. The seat that had been empty wasn't any longer. His vision clouded for a moment. His father was there, clapping and nodding his approval. Craig nearly broke down, and it took all of his willpower to keep it together.

He wasn't sure what he said, if he said too little or too much. All he wanted to do was get off the stage and get to his family.

When Craig returned to the table, he was swarmed with hugs and kisses and handshakes. His father stood in front of him. Craig stood a step forward. Jake extended his hand, which Craig took. Jake pulled him into a tight bear hug. "I'm proud of you, son," he whispered. "I always have been." He clapped him heartily on the back then stepped back and gripped his shoulders. "I hear I'm getting a daughter-in-law."

Craig turned toward Jewel, and she stepped into his embrace. "Jewel, this is my dad, Jake Lawson."

"Oh, me and your dad are buddies. Right, Mr. Lawson?"

"When Alyse told me about the house, well… I thought it only right that I take a look from a real estate perspective."

"Your dad's been working with Alyse on the landmark designation," Jewel confessed.

"And, uh, no one was going to tell me?"

"Nope," they all said in unison.

"All this happiness and good news deserves a serious toast," Myles said and began filling glasses.

Jewel turned in to Craig's body so that they were only a breath apart. "I have something else to tell you."

"What?"

"I won't be doing any drinking or traveling for a while, and if you had a date in mind for a wedding… well, we may need to move it up."

He stared into her glowing face then down the curves of her body, hugged in a champagne-toned Vera Wang gown. "Jewel, are you telling me…"

"Twelve weeks. I wanted to wait to be sure. Are you happy?"

"Happy, baby—happy doesn't come close to what I'm feeling." He didn't care that they were in a room full of people and photographers. He pulled Jewel flush against him and kissed her as if they were the only two people in the world.

"I love you, girl," he hummed against her mouth to the applause of onlookers.

"I love you right back."

Epilogue

Jewel set up her easel and lined up the brushes and oils. The light coming in the window was perfect, and she wanted to capture it all.

Her father was in his favorite chair, and the morning sun seemed to put an extra spark in his eyes—or maybe it was holding his first granddaughter.

It didn't seem to matter when he would slip away and talk to Imani as if she was a tiny version of Jewel. When he would tell Imani stories of going into town to buy candy, or the hard days of working at the mill. It seemed perfectly all right. Because Imani needed to know about the past, her past, the history of where she'd come from. Who better to tell her than Grand-dad in his own special way?

Jewel worked quickly, sketching in charcoal to get the lines and angles, and when she was satisfied she began again following her drawing in oil.

* * *

Craig had just returned from working out a deal with his dad to purchase some property to open a production studio in town. He stood in the doorway of Augustus's bedroom watching the scene in front of him, frame by frame, stroke by stroke, generation to generation.

This moment, his family, *this* was a work of art that could never be duplicated. He'd searched for his place in the world. He'd traveled the globe looking to fill the emptiness inside him. And all along everything that he'd ever needed was right in his hometown, where it had been waiting for him all along. He could finally stop running.

Jewel glanced over her shoulder and stared into the eyes of the man she loved.

"Welcome home, baby."

* * * * *

"I'm not sure." He turned. "What do you say, Casey?"

"A minute, sir. No more."

Ryan nodded, said nothing. There was a silence on the bridge, a silence only intensified by the sibilant rushing of the waters, the weird, lonesome pinging of the Asdic. Above, the sky was steadily clearing, and the moon, palely luminous, was struggling to appear through a patch of thinning cloud. Nobody spoke, nobody moved. Mallory was conscious of the great bulk of Andrea beside him, of Miller, Brown and Louki behind. Born in the heart of the country, brought up on the foothills of the Southern Alps, Mallory knew himself as a landsman first and last, an alien to the sea and ships: but he had never felt so much at home in his life, never really known till now what it was to belong. He was more than happy, Mallory thought vaguely to himself, he was content. Andrea and his new friends and the impossible well done—how could a man but be content? They weren't all going home, Andy Stevens wasn't coming with them, but strangely he could feel no sorrow, only a gentle melancholy. . . . Almost as if he had divined what Mallory was thinking, Andrea leaned towards him, towering over him in the darkness.

"He should be here," he murmured. "Andy Stevens should be here. That is what you are thinking, is it not?"

Mallory nodded and smiled, and said nothing.

"It doesn't really matter, does it, my Keith?" No anxiety, no questioning, just a statement of fact. "It doesn't really matter."

"It doesn't matter at all."

Even as he spoke, he looked up quickly. A light, a bright orange flame had lanced out from the sheering wall of the fortress; they had rounded the headland and he hadn't even noticed it. There was a whistling roar—Mallory thought incongruously of an express train emerging from a tunnel—directly overhead, and the great shell had crashed into the sea just beyond them. Mallory compressed his lips, unconsciously tightened his clenched fists. It was easy now to see how the *Sybaris* had died.

He could hear the gunnery officer saying something to the captain, but the words failed to register. They were looking at him and he at them and he did not see them. His mind was strangely detached. Another shell, would that be next? Or would the roar of the gun-fire of that first shell come echoing across the sea? Or perhaps . . . Once again, he was back in that dark magazine entombed in the rocks, only now he could see men down there, doomed, unknowing men, could see the overhead pulleys swinging the great shells and cartridges towards the well of the lift, could see the shell hoist descending slowly, the bared, waiting wires less than half an inch apart, the shining, spring-loaded wheel running smoothly down the gleaming rail, the gentle bump as the hoist . . .

A white pillar of flame streaked up hundreds of feet into the night sky as the tremendous detonation tore the heart out of the great fortress of Navarone. No after-fire of any kind, no dark, billowing clouds of smoke, only that one blinding white column that lit up the entire town for a single instant of time, reached up incredibly till it touched the clouds, vanished as if it had never been. And then, by and by, came the shock waves, the solitary thunderclap of the explosion, staggering even at that distance, and finally the deep-throated rumbling as thousands of tons of rock toppled majestically into the harbour—thousands of tons of rock and then the two great guns of Navarone.

The rumbling was still in their ears, the echoes fading away far out across the Ægean, when the clouds parted and the moon broke through, a full moon silvering the darkly-rippling waters to starboard, shining iridescently through the spun phosphorescence of the *Sirdar's* boiling wake. And dead ahead, bathed in the white moonlight, mysterious, remote, the island of Kheros lay sleeping on the surface of the sea.

DOOR OF DEATH

The short man with the double-barreled Greener pulled both triggers as Gunn plowed past him with the force of a charging bull. The shotgun blasts tore chunks of plaster and wood from the ceiling, raining debris and clouds of dust.

Gunn bounded down the hotel stairs four at a time and streaked across the lobby to the street outside. This was not the time to fight a losing battle on hostile ground.

His ears felt as if someone had driven a rail spike through his skull. The explosions had made him as deaf as a stone. And he waited outside in a soundless world of agony as the long shadows of the afternoon crawled the street and darkened the stares of curious passersby.

"Come on, you bastard," Gunn said softly. "Walk out that door."

BOLT

An Adult Western Series by Cort Martin

#10:	BAWDY HOUSE SHOWDOWN	(1176, $2.25)
#11:	THE LAST BORDELLO	(1224, $2.25)
#12:	THE HANGTOWN HARLOTS	(1274, $2.25)
#13:	MONTANA MISTRESS	(1316, $2.25)
#14:	VIRGINIA CITY VIRGIN	(1360, $2.25)
#15:	BORDELLO BACKSHOOTER	(1411, $2.25)
#16:	HARDCASE HUSSY	(1513, $2.25)
#17:	LONE-STAR STUD	(1632, $2.25)
#18:	QUEEN OF HEARTS	(1726, $2.25)
#19:	PALOMINO STUD	(1815, $2.25)
#20:	SIX-GUNS AND SILK	(1866, $2.25)

BY JORY SHERMAN

TWO EASY PIECES

GUNN

#28

ZEBRA BOOKS
KENSINGTON PUBLISHING CORP.

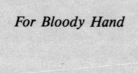

For Bloody Hand

Chapter One

Gunn had an itch in the middle of his back. Square between his shoulder blades. He scratched it, and the itch went somewhere else, to his elbow or to his wrist, along his calf.

There was something goddamned wrong, and it wasn't the itch. It was the cause of the itch.

Fourteen miles of hard riding over rolling hills, up and down slopes of high thick grass and buffalo smell like rancid wool in his nostrils, the wagon behind him creaking like a hundred worn wooden gates, and the quiet so bad under the upturned blue bowl of the sky that he wanted to shout it to thunder and that damned itch making him spook like a gunshy stud.

The quiet. It blared in his ears like a trumpet bell rammed against his skull. It was the quiet in between the groan of the wagon's bed and its wheels straining as they rolled over the rough ground and pounded grass stalks flat with a swish-swash and a sound like the bones and flesh of a man being stretched on a rack in olden times.

Gunn reined up, turned the big Tennessee Walker. "Paxton," he said. "Hold up."

7

"What the hell, Gunn? We ain't been makin' but ten mile a day. We stop now, the muscles on them mules will bunch up."

Ed Paxton's eyes peered out from under woolly eyebrows that were laced with trail sweat. A misshapen felt hat shaded his wind-raw face, threw a shadow across his drooping moustache. He was a short, stocky man with reddish-straw hair that his daughter kept cut so that it fell just to his shoulders, shielding the back of his neck from the sun.

"I want it quiet for a minute," said Gunn, the tall man on the sorrel gelding. His lean form seemed to be all muscle and sinew, with not an ounce of fat. His face was burnished by wind and sun so that his pewter gray eyes seemed chiseled of flint, hard and sharp as a hawk's eyes, colored now, in the daylight, a pale milky blue like a cloud-threaded sky.

"You hear somethin'?" asked Paxton, cocking his head.

"Maybe. Maybe it was something I didn't hear."

A head poked through the canvas tarp behind Paxton, then another. Ed's son, Elias, and his daughter, Marylee. Elias was about 14, Gunn figured. Marylee was a young woman, eighteen, maybe nineteen. He had kept his distance from her ever since they left Fort Laramie, headed for the Gallatin Valley. Her eyes were as blue as cornflowers and no cotton dress could hide her figure, the pert breasts, the slim waist, the flaring womanly hips, the high riding buttocks that bounced saucy when she walked, tantalizing as apples bobbing in a rain barrel.

"Why're we stoppin'?" asked Elias, his freckled face screwed up in puzzlement. A shock of tow hair jutted like straw from under his cap. He had one tooth missing. It was not a baby tooth, so it wouldn't grow back. It wasn't a front tooth, but an incisor, so that he appeared to have a perpetual, lop-sided grin.

"Just restin'," said his father. "You be quiet, son."

Marylee looked at Gunn with inquisitive blue eyes. She was not fooled, he thought. But she said nothing, just looked at him and for a minute he could almost feel her hands on him, touching his waist, moving downward to his loins. She climbed out of the wagon, sat next to her father. She tossed her hair back over her shoulders, stretched, and Gunn thought her breasts would pop the cotton of her blouse. He almost wished they would.

Gunn sat back in his saddle, felt the cantle take up rump weight. He turned his head slowly, first right, then left, until he had listened at every point of a circle. His eyes thinned to slits. The wind rustled the grasses and ebbed so that it was still for a moment. He listened for several moments, as a deer will listen, as the fox will listen, as the plains Indian listens. The three people in the covered wagon looked at him in silence while the pair of mules switched their tails and rumpled their ears to shake off the black flies.

"Damnit, what's wrong, Mr. Gunnison?" asked Ed Paxton. "You see somethin'? You hear somethin'? If you don't, then let's get crackin'."

The man known as Gunn did not say anything. There was really no answer to Paxton's questions. Hunches were private things, not solid enough to be rumors, nor meaty enough to be facts. He didn't even have much of a hunch, just a faint suspicion that something was wrong. Or not quite right.

9

"We'll go on, Paxton, but slow. And you keep the kids quiet and your eyes and ears open." Gunn took off his hat, wiped the sweat band with his finger. He squared the hat back on his head and took the point. Esquire stepped right out, but his ears were cocked forward and he sidled sideways. Gunn straightened him out, but he knew his was not the only mind that harbored suspicion. Esquire, the Tennessee Walker gelding, was as spooky as a cat at a dogfight.

And Gunn's itch was still there, square in the middle of his back.

Maybe, he thought, he should have left the Paxton wagon at Bozeman City, with the others. He had fulfilled his contract, bringing 15 wagons, 155 head of cattle, 8 horses, 10 mules, 20 men, 6 women, 5 children, all the way from Laramie over the old Bozeman Trail. Although the trail had been closed in '68, the forts burned down, the families had wanted to come this way. It was cheaper, shorter, but it was also more dangerous. They had looked at the adobe ruins of Fort C.F. Smith soberly, for a long time, and many in the train had been nervous the rest of the way. Except for that bullheaded Paxton, who paid Gunn extra to take him on to Gallatin City. Paxton knew the country, had been there before. But for some reason, he wanted Gunn's protection. The man was a fair shot himself, and Elias could handle a rifle well enough for a boy.

And Paxton seemed in a hurry, too. While Gunn had actually guided the wagon train, Paxton was the man who knew all the shortcuts. Now, however, he seemed to have thrown caution to the winds. The Gallatin Valley was no place for a lone wagon, an old

10

man, a couple of kids and one outrider, but that's where they were — and it was so damned quiet it was like riding through a graveyard.

Yet Gunn had seen no sign of Indians between the Big Horn and the Yellowstone — no Sioux, no Cheyenne, no Blackfoot. Nor did he sense the presence of hostiles here, along the river as they traveled north to Gallatin City.

He rode far ahead of the lone wagon, seeing signs of settlers, stone cairns along the road, an abandoned sod house, cattle tracks, cow pies, a wagon wheel rotted out and rusted on the iron rim, a grave marker that told of a long ago traveler who didn't make it to the gold fields.

Esquire topped a rise and bristled at sight of the small ranch that nestled on the slope, a meandering creek running through it. A few head of cattle browsed in a corner of a grassy swale and a mule switched its tail in the corral behind the main house. Esquire's ears twitched, twisted, and his nostrils flared, then wrinkled in rubbery folds as he sniffed the air.

Gunn held the horse steady, looked down at the ranch buildings, seeking signs of life. He knew that he had to be in plain view of anyone there. Beyond the house, a stand of timber grew in a grassy ravine, flowed upward to join the stippled spikes of pines, spruce, aspen, cedars and firs that flocked the range of mountains that loomed over the valley, shadowless in the sun.

"What the hell is it now?" bellowed Paxton, rumbling up behind Gunn in the wagon. "You afraid of your own damned shadow?"

11

Gunn didn't have any solid reason for not riding down to the ranch and hailing the people who lived there. This time of day, the hands were likely out working somewhere. Still, it was so quiet, Gunn wondered. Quiet sometimes was noisy as hell and this was one of those times.

"Paxton, I didn't live this long being careless," said Gunn. "This is still Indian country and I'm still your guide."

"Hell, that ranch down there look like it's an Injun camp? Peaceful as a cemetery around here. Likely why those folks built here in the first place. Wasn't here before, when I come through."

"No. It's new. Less than two years old, I'd say."

Elias stuck his head out of the wagon bed and peered intently down at the ranch.

"Where are the Inians?" he said, mispronouncing the word.

"Get back in the wagon and shut up," said Paxton. "Gunn, let's get crackin'. Maybe we can visit with those folks down there, learn a thing or two. You don't seem to know much about this country."

Gunn shrugged and eased Esquire over the rim. The wagon would have tougher going than he and Esquire, but that was Paxton's problem. Gunn had been here before. There was no ranch here, then, and there had been Indians. Cheyenne, Blackfoot, sometimes Sioux. He dreaded the Blackfoot more than any other tribe. They loved to take scalps, especially white men's scalps.

But it wasn't Indians he was worried about now. Not in particular. No, there was something else that wasn't quite right, but he couldn't put a name on it.

12

There's just something wrong, he said to himself.

Gunn cut a wagon trail, beckoned to Paxton to swing the wagon toward him. Paxton acknowledged with a nod and Gunn surveyed the path ahead. Here, the juniper were thick, and there was a lot of scrub pine, balsam, a few spruce, some cedar. It was rough country, rugged as any he'd seen, but someone had cleared the trail, widened it so that a wagon could make it across the slope. That was unusual. Unless someone had built a line cabin somewhere up above the ranch. Or was prospecting. A lot of trouble for a trail that showed little use. And yet it was there, and it made the going easier for Paxton.

Gunn knew a little bit about Edward Paxton. He had lost his wife to the fever when the girl was ten or so. She had helped him raise the boy. Paxton was like a hundred other such men Gunn had met over the years. They came west to seek their fortune, with little thought as to how they would make it, and spent all their money, lost their goods or their families, and then just kept drifting, listening to every scrap of gossip, following every will-o-the-wisp trail.

Men like Paxton were mostly sorry cases. They became gypsies, never settling down, never learning the country. They passed through it and left little trace of their having been there. They were always impatient to get over the next hill, see the next town, dig the next hole, looking for gold or silver. Never mind that most of them didn't make it. Some died of starvation, others of stupidity and foolishness. Gunn had seen men carry loaded rifles in their wagons, shoot themselves to death in the middle of the prairie when the gun went off. They never learned, they never listened. They came and went, all with that same haunted look on their faces. They had left farms and stores back east and had sold off everything to come to a land which didn't want them. Some stuck it out, true, but most went crazy or got killed because they didn't know how to live in country where you could ride for days without seeing another human being.

Paxton was a good enough man. He meant well. He just didn't know what to do with two kids and a wanderlust that was like a thirst to a drunk. He kept going, dragging his kids with him, and he never amounted to a damn. Paxton should have taken up a trade, stayed in one of the settlements, given his kids some schooling. But if the man was bullheaded enough to want to ride over the next hill, and pay Gunn to take him, that was his own doing. Gunn shook his head. He was sorry he had ever laid eyes on Edward Paxton.

Gunn glimpsed the cabin, off in the distance. It was small, stuck up on as shelf just below the main ridge. Another mile, maybe, he figured.

Elias poked his head through the canvas tarp, peered out from inside the wagon. "Can I come out now, Pa?" he asked. "I'm gettin' sick of ridin' back here."

Paxton turned around, grinned crookedly. He winked at Marylee. "Yep, you can come out, now, son. We'll be seein' folks directly. You get that bedding straightened out like I told you?"

"Sure did, Pa."

"Come on, then. Scoot out here. Move over, Sissy."

The boy's sister slid over on the seat, made room

14

for Elias. The boy snugged in between his father and Marylee, braced his feet so that he didn't jounce too much or pitch forward.

The air smelled of pine and balsam, the heady fragrance of cedar, the dry musty aroma of juniper. The team pulled easily on the slight sloping grade. Paxton stopped snapping the traces and gave the mules their heads as they wound through the trees that dotted the slope. Every so often, he glimpsed the ranch below as they passed wide treeless openings.

The mules spooked a lone grouse that had hugged the ground when Gunn passed by. Its markings made it almost invisible until it took flight. It sailed from under a blue spruce, floated gracefully as a kite as it locked its wings and drifted on a current of air toward a grassy sward two hundred yards downslope.

"A beauty, Pa!" exclaimed Elias. "Bet I could shoot him real good."

"Bet you could at that, son." Paxton reached up and tousled the boy's hair, smiled warmly at him. Elias beamed.

"Eli, did you see my bonnet?" asked Marylee. "That sun is hitting me right in the eyes."

"It's back there, some danged where," said the boy. "Hangin' on a hook."

"Watch your mouth, Elias Paxton," said Marylee.

"I only said 'danged.' " The boy grinned wickedly at his sister, snaggle-toothed as an old washerwoman.

Ahead, they glimpsed Gunn's back as he appeared and disappeared at intervals among the scattered trees. Marylee leaned backward, tried to see where she had placed her bonnet. In the dim light of the covered wagon, she could not see much. She stretched

15

farther. One of the wagon wheels struck a rock and she lost her balance, fell halfway into the wagon bed. She uttered a sharp cry and tried vainly to regain her balance. Elias laughed and pushed her the rest of the way inside.

"Stop that!" she exclaimed. Her voice was muffled as she struggled to free herself from the pile of clothing she had tumbled into when Elias pushed her. "Damn you, Eli!"

"Don't swear," said Paxton, giving Elias a conspiratorial wink. "Don't sound good on a lady."

Elias laughed, thumped his knee with the butt of his palm as he had seen his father do many a time. He liked the traveling, seeing the new places. Although he knew his pa had been in this country before, he didn't remember it. He liked seeing the game, the buffalo, antelope, the deer and elk, best of all. And he liked birds. He wished he could fly like them. He wished he had his own horse, like Mr. Gunnison. He liked Gunn. He didn't think his father did, though. Leastways, he never said he did. Marylee liked him, though. He could tell, by the way she looked at him.

Marylee crawled back inside the wagon, finally, panting from her exertions. She sat there in the cool, let her eyes adjust to the dimness. She saw her bonnet, hanging on a hook with another blouse. She reached for it just as Paxton hauled up on the reins, brought the team to a jarring halt. Marylee was thrown against the back of the wagon, striking her head on the backboard. She didn't know it then, but her father had probably saved her life.

The men rode out of the trees, blocked the trail. There seemed to be dozens of them, but three separated from the bunch, rode straight for the wagon.

Paxton jerked the reins, instinctively reached for the hand brake. The wagon lurched to a halt. Elias was pitched backwards, but he regained his balance.

"Hold it right there," said one of the men. All of the riders wore kerchiefs over their faces. Only their eyes showed under the brims of their hats.

Paxton's hand slid toward the pistol tucked in his waistband.

"Mister, you done bought yourself six feet of ground," said the leader. He leveled his rifle across the pommel, cocked the hammer and fired. The .44-40 ball from the Henry smashed into Paxton's chest, flattened against a rib and tore half of his heart to pieces. He grunted and fell sideways.

"No, Pa!" screamed Elias, and his hand reached out for the Greener his pa kept in a boot nailed to the sideboard.

The man next to the leader laughed harshly, drew his pistol. He shot Elias at 20 paces, square between the eyes. The boy collapsed into the seat well, stone dead. Blood trickled from the small hole in the center of his forehead made by the .45 Colt revolver.

"Murderin' sonso'bitches," said the second man. "I reckon that'll take care of them."

"That was just a damned kid," said one of the men in the bunch.

"He was goin' for it," said the man who had killed Elias. He ejected the spent shell, drew a fresh cartridge from his gunbelt. "Come on, let's get out of here. I reckon we got 'em all now."

Inside the wagon, Marylee heard the faint roar of the guns, but the sound was not enough to rouse her

17

from her unconsciousness. The drumming hoofbeats as the men rode away sounded like a distant wind in her dulled ears. But something was wrong. She had heard her brother cry out, or was she only dreaming?

Gunn hailed the cabin, but there was no answer. There were unsaddled horses out back. He rode back of the cabin, noticed that they wore halters, but were not tied. *Strange*, he thought. There was a hitchrail and a lean-to. He dismounted, walked under the lean-to's roof. There was grain in the bins, tack hung on the walls. His right hand settled on his pistol butt. That uneasy feeling came over him again. The hairs on the back of his neck prickled like needles.

Outside, he examined the ground. There were a lot more horse tracks than there were horses. He saw a brassy glint in the sunlight, reached down and picked it up. It was a .44-40 casing from a Henry rifle. He sniffed it. It still stank of exploded black powder. He put the cartridge in his vest pocket, tied Esquire up to the hitchrail. The other horses nickered nervously.

Gunn saw that the back door was open. There were boot tracks going to and from the steps. They, too, looked fresh. Puzzled, he called out softly.

"Anybody in there?"

There was no answer.

He stepped inside. A small room, then a kitchen, not much bigger. A line shack, like he figured. Only something was wrong. The wood stove was still warm, but the fire in the firebox was out. Cold coffee sat in cups on the table. Three cups. Two were full, one hadn't been poured yet. The coffee pot was still

18

on the table. He picked it up, saw that it had left a mark. The pot was cold as stone.

Gunn stalked down the short hall to the big room at the front. And there it was. A feeling of dread came over him. He choked down the bile that threatened to rise in his throat. His stomach boiled, queasy at the sight of the dead men.

There were three of them. None of them wore gunbelts. He saw their rifles leaning against the wall, their guns hanging over their bunks. He knelt down, turned one of the men over on his back, careful not to touch the exit wound, which was as big as Gunn's clenched fist.

He had been shot once, through the heart. Gunn looked at the dead man's face and winced.

This was a boy, no more than 14 or 15. He hadn't had a chance. His eyes were open, staring blankly at Gunn in a look of stark surprise. Gunn closed them with his thumbs and crawled over to the next man.

He had been shot between the eyes. The back of his head was blown away. Blood had sprayed all over one part of the room. Chunks of brain matter lay drying on the floor, all over one of the bunks. This was a man in his thirties, not much older than Gunn himself.

A third man lay near the door. Gunn saw no gunshot wounds. The corpse was lying on its side, curled up with its knees almost touching the chin. The man had died in agony. Gunn eased him over, saw the pool of blood on his shirt. He tore the shirt away, looked at the ugly wound in the man's belly. He turned him over again, saw the small slit in the man's back.

"Christ," croaked Gunn. The man had been stabbed with a long, thin knife. He knew what it was. Most people called it an "Arkansaw toothpick." It was deadly, and this man had found that out. He was in his twenties, and like the others, wore the clothes of a cowhand.

"Why?" said Gunn, as he stood up and tried to reconstruct what had happened.

He opened the front door, looked out. The ranch could not be seen from here, but he wondered what he would find when he rode down there. There were horse tracks out front, too.

So, he reasoned, the men had ridden up here in the darkness before dawn. Some had gone around back, some had come to the front. Probably on foot. Maybe two men had come in first, or three. They had waited. Smelled the coffee. Then, one had knocked on the door. When the young man had come to the door, opened it, he got a foot of cold steel shoved in his gut. The other two had come running out and were shot in their tracks.

Gunn went back inside, the hackles on the back of his neck rippling as though spiders had hatched out in his hair.

He picked up two brass casings from the floor. One was from a .45 Colt, the other a Henry .44-40. Like the one in back. He compared the hammer marks on the primers. The same. But what had the man shot at out back?

Before Gunn could reason it out, he heard the distant crack of a rifle.

He raced out back, just as another shot boomed, echoed off the hills. This one was lower, more like a pistol. He grabbed Esquire's reins, pulled them free. Between the shots, he swore he had heard something else. A cry for help?

Gunn didn't know. He pulled himself up into the saddle, turned Esquire. He heard the rumble of hoofbeats and cursed.

Something had happened back where the wagon was. Trouble.

A fist knotted in Gunn's stomach and the hackles laid back down on his neck, replaced by a cold fury.

He dug spurs deep into Esquire's flanks, but even as the horse lunged underneath him, he knew that he was too late. From the sound of the hoofbeats, so soon after the rifle and pistol fire, Gunn knew that something terrible had happened.

Someone, for sure, had died.

Chapter Two

Gunn rode as though his life depended upon it. He heard the sound of hoofbeats fade in the distance, and cursed himself for having left the wagon so far behind. His own curiosity had gotten the best of him. Now, someone else had paid for his own foolishness.

Where had the men come from? Why had he seen no sign of them? From the sound of the horses, there had to be a bunch of them, a dozen or more. Who were they? He slapped Esquire's rump with the tips of his reins, but the trail was crooked and the horse could go no faster through the scattered clumps of trees.

It seemed an eternity before he reached the wagon. When he reined up, Esquire's tail twitched and his ears batted, curled into cones. The hoofbeats faded away and Gunn saw only a wisp of dust in the sky. He saw the body of Ed Paxton, oddly contorted, hanging over the side of the wagon. A small pool of blood in the dirt below had already started to gather flies.

His heart sank when he didn't see the kids. Then, he saw the tow hair of Elias stirring gently in the wind. He dismounted, climbed up. Gently, he pulled the boy out from under the seat. He choked when he saw the bullet hole in his forehead. His hand felt sticky and when he drew it away from the back of the boy's head, it was clammy with blood. His heart sank even deeper and it was hard to breathe. He laid the boy on the seat, straightened his legs. He dreaded looking inside the wagon.

He heard a low moan as he peered inside.

"Miss Paxton?" he called softly. "Marylee?"

He saw her, then, lying on her side at the back of the wagon. He couldn't see her face. So far, that bunch of riders had left no witnesses. At least five dead, and they got away clean.

Gunn crawled into the wagon. He had heard her moan, so perhaps she was still alive. It was agony, not knowing. He knelt beside her, pushed his hat back on his head. He touched her neck, felt her pulse just back of her ear.

"Marylee," he husked. "You hurt?" He felt her back, turned her over. He could find no wounds. He opened the back flap, looked at her closely as the sunlight filtered inside. "Marylee? Miss Paxton?"

Marylee made a sound in her throat. Her eyelids fluttered. Gunn worked an arm underneath her back, pulled her to a sitting position. What had happened here? She wasn't bleeding, but she was out cold. Had someone struck her? Had a bullet creased her skull? He gingerly felt the top of her head. There were no scratches, no lumps. There was no wound he could detect.

He touched her face with his fingers, turned her over in his arms until he was looking down at her. She seemed to be sleeping peacefully. He rocked with her in his lap, called out her name. Finally, her eyelids fluttered. They opened and shut, opened again and stayed. Her eyes fixed on his face, but there was no recognition there, at first.

"Marylee, are you awake?" he asked quietly.

"Gunn? What are you doing here? Where am I?"

"You're safe, I reckon. Were you hit?"

"Huh?"

"Did a bullet strike you? Did someone hit you with something?"

She shook her head, blinked her eyes again. "I—I, ah, no, I, uh, hit my head when the wagon stopped."

She sat up, startled, stared around her in bewilderment. "We're still stopped," she said. "What happened? Why did Pa do that?"

"Marylee, listen to me. . . ."

"I—I think I heard Eli cry out. I heard noises, but . . . maybe I only imagined them."

"Shush now. You didn't imagine them, Marylee. Some men came up from Lord knows where. They shot your pa and Elias. Can you handle it?"

"What? Pa? Eli?"

"They're both dead. They didn't suffer."

"I don't believe you," she said defiantly.

"I know. Please, this isn't easy. They're both gone. We've got to bury them pretty quick. But I don't want you to see them."

"No. I—I must."

"Let me take care of it."

She struggled to break free. Gunn tried to hold her back, but she scratched him, flailed him with her hands. He fell backward, and before he could stop her, she crawled out the back of the wagon. He heard

24

her running to the front as he tried to scramble to his feet.

Marylee's screams rent the air. The sound blocked out Gunn's senses, made his scalp prickle. He climbed out the back of the wagon, raced around to the front. Marylee had her hands over her ears and was shrieking out her shock and grief like a madwoman. He grabbed her and shook her, but she continued screaming hysterically. Gunn slapped her face, hard, and she started to fight him. He caught her by the wrists and locked her in a bear hug. She broke down, sobbing against his chest.

"Why? Why?" she moaned.

"Easy, girl." He couldn't help thinking that if she hadn't been knocked out, she might be as dead as her pa and brother. He knew the grief she felt now was mixed with anger and fear. She would have to ride it out, but maybe he could give her a shoulder to cry on. He rocked her in his arms, as he stood there, swaying with her trembling body. She wept and screamed, but each time she let out a bellow, her voice grew weaker than the time before.

"Marylee," he said, leading her gently away from the source of her grief, "I'll get them laid out so you can tend to them. Look around, see if you can find a spot you like for the final resting place."

She stopped sobbing, looked at him. She panted, licked her lips. She breathed through her mouth, the lips slack, the jaw crooked from tension. Her blue eyes sparkled with tears, but Gunn saw the light of sanity behind the gleam of hysteria.

"Yes," she sighed. "I — I'll get a washcloth and s-s-some water from the keg."

Gunn took blankets from the wagon, laid them down off the trail, in the shade of a juniper. He lifted Paxton out of the wagon, first, then brought Elias over while Marylee was cleaning up her father. It was bad that she had to look at them like that, Gunn knew, but it could not be avoided. He took the pick and shovel over to a spot that Marylee had picked out, began digging a grave. They'd both have to be buried in the same hole. And what about those men in the line shack? Someone else would have to bury them. If there was anyone around to do it. If not, scavengers would take care of the remains.

Gunn hacked out a trench six feet long and four feet wide. He heard Marylee sobbing as he dug, and he wondered what she would do now that she was all alone in the world. Well, she could decide that later. There was time to talk of those things before they reached Gallatin. Gunn figured they were not far from the Yellowstone now.

He had some harder questions for himself.

Why were the hands in the line shack killed? Who killed them? And who killed Ed and Elias Paxton? And why? Were the two killings connected somehow? Or was there a bunch of madmen riding around killing everyone in sight? Gunn shuddered at the thought. He had some tracking to do before they left the place, some sorting out to do in his mind. Right now, he knew only that five people were dead, killed for no apparent reason, and a dozen men had ridden off toward . . . Gunn paused, looked at the sky, the mountains. If he reckoned right, the men had likely ridden toward Gallatin. And they didn't go along the settled trail, but another way, through the foothills, staying to cover like stalking wolves.

It was too damned bad that Marylee hadn't seen anything. Or heard anything. And he cursed himself for not being closer to the wagon when it happened. Maybe he might have saved both of them. Or he might have lost his life, as well. This was a poor time to be second guessing. What was done, was done, and he couldn't do anything about it.

Her voice startled him. "They're ready," said Marylee and Gunn saw that she had washed her face and swept her hair back, combed it out. "I—I'm going to change. I'll help you if you need me to."

"No, it's about done."

"Gunn," she said. "Thanks."

Gunn choked down the tears, went back to his digging. For a long time the only sound was the clang of the shovel on rock, the swick of the dirt as it landed on the pile. He finished squaring off the shallow grave and went back to get the Paxton men. He saw that Marylee had wrapped them in blankets, covered their faces. He carried them, one at a time, to the grave, putting Elias on the right hand side, Edward on the left. They would lie in their grave with their heads to the east, their feet to the west.

He waited for Marylee, heard her rumbling around in the wagon. He looked down at the dead wrapped in blankets and thought about the men who had done this terrible thing. Were he alone, he could track them. He was badly outnumbered though. The next best thing would be to isolate each man's boot track, check each hoofprint and see if there was anything distinctive about them. He searched his memory, tried to discover some little thing that might give him a clue. There was nothing. Paxton had given no sign, other than a hankering for speed, that there was any trouble ahead in Gallatin or along the way, for that matter. It was a puzzle, and Gunn was determined to figure it out if he could.

Marylee walked up to the grave, carrying a bunch of flowers in her hand.

"We don't have a bible," she said. "Maybe you could say a few words, Gunn."

Gunn swallowed, shifted the weight on his feet. He took off his hat, bowed his head.

"Lord," he said, as Marylee came up beside him, clutched his hand, "take Edward and Elias into your mansion, give them rest. They were good folks. We pray they will find happiness where they're going."

Marylee sobbed, squeezed Gunn's hand hard.

"Goodbye, Pa," she rasped. "Goodbye, Eli."

Gunn's eyes filled with tears. He slipped his hand from Marylee's, grabbed her shoulders. "Go on back to the wagon," he said softly. "I'll be back directly."

She walked away, slowly, as if in a trance. Gunn picked up the shovel, began filling in the grave. The dirt chunked soft on the blankets. He mounded the grave off, set a stone at the head. He took the pick and shovel back to the wagon and slipped them into the loops of rope that held them to the sides and pulled the loops tight, knotted them securely.

"You can go back there while I hitch Esquire to the back of the wagon," Gunn said. "Take all the time you want. I've got a few more things to do here."

Marylee stood there for a long moment, studying Gunn's face. When he offered no explanation, she walked away, headed for the grave. Gunn caught up his horse, unsaddled him, threw the saddle in the back of the wagon. He put a rope and halter on Esquire, tied him to the right rear of the wagon, giving him plenty of slack. He slipped his Winchester '73 out of its scabbard, made a wide circle on foot, using the wagon as a center point.

Above, some distance off the trail, Gunn saw where the men had first ridden up within view of the cabin. Broken branches, fallen twigs, told him where they had tied their horses. Two men had stayed behind to keep the horses quiet. The others had split up into groups of three, encircled the line shack. Gunn followed all of the tracks, making mental notes as he did. He could tell the approximate weight of each man, whether he was carrying a rifle or a pistol or both. The tracks were less than three hours old.

Three men had come down behind the cabin, another three had gone to the front. Three more had taken triangular positions above and to the sides of the shack. These three carried rifles. Gunn verified this from the marks of rifle butts, confirming that his assessment that three men carried both rifles and pistols was correct. There were eleven men who had come here to kill three men.

But why would they kill Ed Paxton and his son? The three men in the line shack had been dead a good two hours before Gunn arrived on the scene. The tracks, he hoped, would continue to tell him their story. He examined each individual track carefully. He knew where the men had stopped and their boot prints showed that one man had whispered to the others. He had shifted his weight, while standing next to another man. Boot up, boot down. He saw where they had crouched and sneaked down to the cabin. At one of the rifle positions, Gunn found something else, too.

The rifleman had crawled under a spruce, then crawled out. In his haste to leave, some of the contents of his shirt pocket had spilled out. There was a bag of Durham, a hotel key, and a small tin badge with the words "Gallatin Vigilance Committee" struck into the metal. The hotel key was attached to a rectangular-shaped piece of wood, and there was a room number, "12" burned into the wood. There was no hotel name on either side. Gunn stuffed these items in his pocket.

He examined every spot where the bushwhackers had approached the line shack. He found a black silk handkerchief with the initials "OJ" embroidered on one corner. This evidently belonged to one of those who had entered by the front door. Gunn found it beside the steps and it had not been there long. It smelled of sweat, but there was no dust on it.

The men had done their killing quickly, efficiently. No questions asked, no trial. Why? What had these men done to deserve such swift deaths? "Vigilantes, my ass," muttered Gunn as he stuffed the kerchief into his pocket with the other materials he had found.

He tried to reconstruct what must have happened and none of the images portrayed reasonable men acting as the law in a lawless land. No, the three cowhands had been gunned down brutally, without warning, without recourse. The verdict was final. Gunn thought about going back inside, but he already knew that the "vigilantes" had not lingered. The tracks showed him that. The killers had done

30

their dirty work, then walked through the cabin to check if any more were inside, and gone right out the back door. That's probably why one of the men didn't find his silk kerchief. The heels of his boots were new, not worn. He put those to the man who had dropped the kerchief because his had been the ones that went up the left side of the steps. He was probably wearing the kerchief like a mask and when he shot to kill, he had pulled it down. It still showed wrinkles where it had been knotted.

A very expensive kerchief, Gunn mused. And, unless he missed his guess, the boots were the best money could buy.

He climbed back up the slope, following the tracks of the men who had come down to surround the cabin. The riflemen's tracks joined theirs. They had gone back to the horses. Gunn rode up, looked down the backtrail where he had come with the Paxtons.

The trail was not visible from that spot. The men had not left right away, however. Again, they had split up, and these tracks were much fresher than the others. One lone horseman had ridden away from the others, while the other two bunches had flanked the backtrail. From the sign, Gunn figured they had waited for more than an hour before leaving that position. They had ridden to the site of the most recent shooting, the place where Ed and Elias Paxton were killed.

Gunn followed the tracks of the lone horseman, running when he could, dropping to his knees when necessary. He already had a hunch where the tracks would lead, but he had to know for sure. He stopped, looked ahead, shielding his eyes from the bright sun.

A rock outcropping loomed above his own backtrail, but more importantly, if his instincts were correct, the rocky lookout would explain why the vigilantes had missed killing both him and Marylee.

Gunn saw that the horseman would have had to circle the rock outcropping and come up from behind. But there, it offered a perfect view of the backtrail where it crested the ridge and began winding through the stippled trees. He found the tracks where he had expected to find them. He found his own tracks, the tracks of the wagon. He compared the two, trying desperately to fix a time in his mind.

He could come close, and to Gunn, it was close enough. He walked rapidly off the trail, circled the rocks. There was a path up the back side of the rocks. He scrambled to the top, found the place where the horseman had waited. He could not see the line shack or the ranch from that position, but he could see the place where the two groups of horsemen waited, flanking the road. And he saw the Paxton wagon.

"Damn!" he said. It was a million to one shot, but that was how it had to have happened. The answer did not please Gunn. Rather, it only gave him more unanswerable questions. Quickly, he raced down from the rock outcropping, kicking up dirt and pebbles in his headlong rush. He loped toward the wagon, trying to get it all straight in his mind. If only he had been more observant, he thought, maybe Ed and Elias would be alive. Or maybe they'd all be dead.

"Let's get the hell out of here," said Gunn, breathless from running. He gripped his side where it ached, heaved to replace the spent oxygen in his lungs.

Marylee's face blanched. She finished buttoning her blouse, tucking in her shirttails. She had changed, Gunn saw, into denim trousers, one of her father's shirts. She had on one of his hats. For a moment, he had mistaken her for her father.

"What's wrong? Is something chasing you?"

"Climb up in the seat. I don't think we're out of this yet."

Gunn held her around the waist, gave her a boost onto the seat. He climbed up behind her, grabbed up the reins, released the handbrake. The mules lurched forward.

"You scared me," she said, as the wagon bounced along, jolting her until she had to brace herself to keep from falling off the seat. "What happened to you?"

"Nothing," he said, "but I've got an idea that those riders didn't shoot down your pa and your brother by accident. I think they were waiting for us."

"You mean, they were looking for us?"

"Maybe. Did your pa write to anyone in Gallatin, telling him he was coming?"

"Yes, I think so. He had business there. He sent a letter out from Fort Laramie a few days before we left. There was an army dispatch rider leaving that particular morning."

Gunn sighed. The ache in his side was going away. His breathing returned to normal. A hundred yards before they reached the line shack, Gunn turned the team, left the trail. He picked it up again, below, where it switched back to avoid the steepness of the slope.

"Gunn, what's all this about?" Marylee asked after Gunn had been silent for several moments.

"I don't know, but someone knew we were coming. Who did your pa know in Gallatin?"

"Why, a number of people. I can't recall any specific one. He talked about getting rich there, about some partner he was going to look up. I didn't pay much attention. Now, I almost wish I had."

"I wish you had, too," said Gunny, wryly.

"Where are we going?" she said. "Wasn't that a cabin back there?"

"We're going to take a look at that ranch down there, see if anyone's there who can shed light on what happened."

Marylee leaned over the side, looked back up the slope.

"Why, that is a cabin up there, and it's right on the trail. Gunn, why didn't you go there?"

"Never mind," he said.

"You'd better tell me. I'll pester you constantly if you don't. I can be very persistent."

Gunn looked at her. With her hair swept under her pa's hat like that, and her shirt open at the throat, she looked beautiful. Her blue eyes crackled with faint lightning and her lips were moist, full, slightly open, as if she was pouting. He had never really looked at her before, he realized. Well, she looked no less womanly in pants and shirt. In fact, even more so. The shirt clung to her breasts, outlined their perfect pear shapes, the jutting nipples so that there was no mistaking her sex.

"There are three men in that cabin," he said tightly.

"All of them shot to death."

Marylee gasped.

"You didn't kill them, did you?"

"They were already dead when I got there. They were killed by the same men who killed your pa and your brother."

"That's awful," she exclaimed.

Gunn's jaw tightened.

"I think they would have killed you and me, too, Marylee if they had known we were there."

Marylee fell silent. She looked over at Gunn, saw the muscle quivering in his jaw. She reached out, put her hand on his. He felt its touch, sighed inwardly.

"Gunn, I'm scared. I don't understand any of this. I'm really scared."

Gunn turned his hand over, squeezed hers with the three fingers that were not holding the reins.

"Don't be frightened," he said. "But I think we'd better get rid of this wagon before we ride into Gallatin. Maybe you had better stay with someone until I get to the bottom of this."

"No," she said defiantly. "I want you to promise me one thing, Gunn. Promise on your mother's heart. As long as you're hunting these men, you'll take me with you."

"I can't promise something like that."

"You'd better," she said. "I won't take no for an answer. I mean it."

He looked at her again. She wasn't pouting now. The woman meant business. She held her head proud and high and there was no fear in her eyes.

"All right," he said. "But you don't know what you're getting into."

"Neither do you, Gunn," she said softly, cryptically.

The team circled another switchback and the trail wound ever closer to the ranch house. Marylee moved closer to him and he smelled her perfume. She gave off the scent of lilacs and honeysuckle and when her body touched his, he felt the heat soak into him, burn through him.

He hoped to hell he could talk some sense into Marylee before they rode into Gallatin. For all he knew, he had a long trail ahead of him, and she would only complicate matters.

The wagon rumbled along the trail, bouncing them together, and finally, Marylee leaned up against him, held onto his leg for support.

He felt her head on his shoulder and when he looked down, her eyes were closed. She looked like a child.

But Gunn was not fooled. Behind that innocent, trusting face, was a woman, fullblown and in season.

Chapter Three

Gunn hailed the ranch house several times as they drove up in the wagon, but no one answered. He drove up to the gate, near a hitch-rail and reined up. He set the brake, stood up. That's when he saw the two dogs on the front steps of the house.

They were both dead. Flies boiled over their eyes, their lolling tongues. He could smell them from where he was.

"Gunn, what's wrong?" asked Marylee.

"You'd better wait here," he said. "You know how to use that Greener of your pa's?"

"I do."

"Check it over, keep it on your lap."

"What's that funny smell?" she said.

Gunn looked up, pointed to the sky. A pair of buzzards circled overhead.

"There's dead here, too," he said softly. "Wait for me."

He jumped down from the wagon, took his Winchester with him. He walked through the open gate, looked at the ground. He had seen these tracks before. One set was made by a man wearing new, expensive boots. The tracks were much older than those at the line shack.

Gunn circled the house, detected no signs of life. There were horses in the corral and stable. They had not been fed or watered this day. He returned to the front of the house, climbed the steps. The front door was unlatched, and he went inside.

A man lay face down in the hallway. He was dead. He had been stabbed in the back and the knife had punctured through to his belly. He didn't die easy. His finger lay in a bloody smear, where he had tried to scrawl a message. All he had managed to do was make a small circle. Gunn stepped over him, checked the bedrooms. A woman lay on one of the beds, her vacant eyes staring up at the ceiling. She had a bloodstain on her abdomen. There was more blood on her neck. Gunn saw that she had been stuck with a knife in both places. A long, thin knife. She never had a chance.

Gunn closed the door to the woman's room, walked to the kitchen. An Indian woman, a servant, or a cook, he surmised, lay under the table. Her mouth was open, her eyes shut. She had brought her hands up to her face, but that hadn't been enough to ward off the lethal knife that had sliced through her neck. Her wound lay open, like the belly of a butchered hog and Gunn winced at the swiftness and brutality of it.

The door to the storeroom was open, but the back door was closed shut. Gunn looked inside the dark, murky storeroom, saw the barrels of flour, tins of beans and other vegetables stacked on shelves. A can of Arbuckle's coffee lay on the floor, unopened.

Curious, Gunn stepped inside. It was quiet as he stood there for a long moment, trying to see in the corners, behind the kegs and wooden bins.

He started to leave when he heard an odd sound. Like a feather scratching on a hollow piece of wood. Like someone breathing. Gunn levered the Winchester, cocked a shell into the chamber. His thumb caressed the scored hammer.

"Mister, you'd better come out with your hands empty," he said softly, his voice without a trace of fear or anger.

Something rattled under the bottom back shelf, and Gunn heard a scraping sound. He stepped into the shadows, away from the doorway's silhouetting light. He raised the rifle to his shoulder, took aim.

"Make it slow," he said, his finger curling around the trigger. "You move too quick and I'll blow you to kingdom come."

"Don't shoot, Mister," said a small voice. A moment later, Gunn saw a face peer up at him from out of the gloom. Gunn lowered his rifle, eased the hammer down to half-cock.

"All right. Come out of there, son. I won't hurt you."

A young boy scrambled from behind the barrels and kegs. He was trembling. The light from the doorway spilled onto his dark hair, illuminated his pasty face. His eyes were small, close-set, glittered like beads. He appeared to be no more than eight or nine. His nose was wide, flattened at the nostrils. Indian boy, Gunn guessed. He bore some resemblance to the dead woman in the kitchen.

"Who are you?" Gunn asked.

"The mister and missus call me Tommy Blue," he said.

"Step outside, so I can get a good look at you."

"You are not going to shoot me, are you?" The boy spoke fair English, but he had a slight accent. He seemed to be pretty bright, Gunn thought.

"No, son. I want you to look at some dead people, tell me who they are."

"I know they're dead," said the boy. "When I didn't hear them for a long time, I went out. I was hiding in here and I got back quick when I heard you come in."

"Is that woman in the kitchen your mother?"

The boy nodded. He fought back tears. But he couldn't control the trembling in his legs and arms. Gunn touched him on the shoulder. The boy was brave, too, he thought.

Gunn gently guided Tommy Blue into the hallway. There was no need to take him through the house. The boy had suffered enough.

"What was your mother's name?" Gunn asked.

"Blue Flower. That's why they called me Tommy Blue. My pa was a white man. He's dead. I never saw him. We been with the Ransoms a long time. They sent me to school. We come out here with 'em last year."

"Those the other people? The Ransoms?"

"Uh huh. They were killed before it was even light out."

"Where were you when all this happened?"

"Ma sent me in the storeroom to get some flour for *tortillas*. I heard the noises and I stayed put."

"How many were there?"

"I only saw one. But I heard a lot of horses

outside. I think only that one come into the house. I think he killed Mister Ransom first, and then my ma. I think Missus Ransom was still asleep. I heard him go into her bedroom and she screamed once. I was plumb scared, Mister."

Gunn's throat constricted.

"Did you say you saw the man who killed them?"

"He come in here, looked right at me. He didn't see me though."

"Did you know him? Had you ever seen him before?"

Tommy shook his head.

"What did he look like?"

"He was real big and he had big whiskers that curled up on the sides. He had on clothes like the banker wears."

"A suit?"

"Yeah, I think so. He had a gun on, but he was carrying a funny-lookin' knife."

"What do you mean by that?" Gunn asked patiently.

"It was real narrow and looked sharp. There was blood on it, but I could see it real plain."

"Yes. Look, Tommy Blue, do you have any kin? In Gallatin, maybe?"

"No, sir. But I know the schoolteacher there. Miss Loomis. Sary Loomis."

"Sarah?"

"Uh huh. Sary."

Gunn smiled. He led the boy out the back door. No need to put him through any more. His mother was dead and she was not a pretty sight.

"I think we'd better take you to Gallatin. We ought

41

to get there before nightfall. I'm not going to bury these people. The marshal in Gallatin might want to take a look around. Do you want us to take your mother with us?"

The boy thought about it. Gunn tightened his grip on the boy's shoulder as he started to weep. They stood on the back porch steps, in the quiet of late morning. Gunn knew what the boy was going through. He had lost a loved one once. His wife, Laurie, had died brutally, too.

"Well?" asked Gunn, when the boy stopped crying, began gasping for breath.

"No, I don't think that would be good," said Tommy. "I—I don't want to think of her dead like that."

"I understand. Best we leave them be. The town marshal will take care of them. We can give your ma a real nice funeral."

"We don't have no money," said the boy.

"How old are you, Tommy?"

Tommy drew himself up. He was still no bigger than a minute, or maybe a half-second. "Fourteen," he said. Gunn was surprised. His small stature was deceptive. Well, fourteen was a hell of an age to lose your mother. Gunn stepped off the porch. "Come on, I want you to meet someone else who just lost her pa and brother. Maybe she could use a little sympathy, too."

"I heard shooting," said Tommy. "I thought the men were coming back. I heard 'em shooting up at the line shack afterwards, too. That's why I didn't come out."

"I understand," said Gunn.

Marylee saw the boy with Gunn, jumped down from the wagon.

"What happened?" she asked. "What have you got there?"

"Marylee," said Gunn. "The folks in there are dead. The boy's mother was one of them. This is Tommy Blue, and he's fourteen."

Marylee broke into tears. She swooped the boy up in her arms, and they both started crying all over again. Gunn stood to one side, looked back at the house. He wondered why a man would sneak in, methodically stab three people to death. If he was a vigilante, what crime had these people committed? No, there was something all wrong about this. Someone had killed a whole lot of people and there had to be a big reason behind it. But for the life of him, Gunn could not come up with any answers. Not a one of those slain had put up any fight. The Ransoms and Tommy's mother were caught completely by surprise. Probably the boys in the line shack, as well.

"Come on, Marylee," Gunn said. "We've got to try and make it to Gallatin before nightfall. This won't keep."

"Yes, yes, I know," she said. "Oh, this poor boy. Whatever will we do?" She dried her eyes, tried to put up a brave front, but no one was fooled. She helped Tommy climb up into the wagon. Gunn got the team moving and saw that Marylee had her arms around the boy. Maybe, he thought, the two of them can help assuage each other's grief for a time.

For Gunn, the senseless killings back there made his flesh crawl. It seemed to him that they were all riding straight out of hell.

They crossed the Yellowstone late that afternoon. Gunn was weary, stiff from sitting on the hard wooden seat. His legs were cramped and his shoulder muscles ached from the strain of handling the team.

"Gunn, me and the boy are plumb tuckered," said Marylee. "Don't you think we ought to stop for the night? How far to Gallatin?"

"Another half day at least," Gunn said. He held three fingers up to the horizon, just below the falling sun. It would set in about a half hour. Each finger represented 15 minutes and there were only 2 of them between the sun and the mountain peaks. "You may be right. We've got water here. The mules could use a rest."

"Me too," said Tommy Blue.

"We'll pull off the trail some," said Gunn. "Wouldn't hurt to keep a lookout. Don't make too much noise."

"All right," said Marylee, relieved. "I think a good night's sleep will do us all good."

Gunn pulled the team well off the trail, but within easy walk to the river. He found a grassy sward, high, with good visibility. They were protected on one side by a jumble of rocks, and he set his own bedroll in a stand of aspen. Beyond, he hobbled Esquire and the mules, in a small meadow where a stream flowed. There were willows thee, plenty of grass. He watched Marylee set up the camp near the wagon, which he had backed up to the rocky outcropping. It was a good enough spot. He walked down to the river, filled his canteen. The setting sun turned the water to a

44

burnished gold. He drank, filled his wooden canteen, took off his boots and socks, dangled his feet in the cool water.

Tommy Blue ambled down a few moments later. He stripped out of his clothes, swam in the shallows. The boy didn't speak until he emerged, dripping and shivering in the late afternoon chill.

"Why are you called Gun?" he asked, as he slipped back into his clothes.

"It's got two ens on the end of it. My name's Gunnison, but I don't use it much."

"Why?"

"Too long," Gunn laughed. "You feeling better, Tommy?"

"No. I feel real bad inside."

"Yeah. I know. You sleep in the wagon tonight, try to put all this out of your mind. You will have to tell your story all over again to the marshal in Gallatin. If they pick up those men, you'll have to testify against them in court."

"What is that?" asked the boy. "Testify."

"Tell a jury, a bunch of people, and a judge, what happened, what the man you saw looked like."

"Yes, I have heard of this."

"Well, don't fret about any of this now. You get a good night's sleep and we can talk about it when you're feeling better."

"O.K." grinned Tommy and he scampered off, up the hill. Gunn sat there for a time, until he smelled beans cooking and his stomach started growling. He put on his socks and boots, walked slowly back to the camp in the thin darkness of dusk.

They ate beef and beans, drank strong coffee.

Marylee wasn't very hungry, but Tommy Blue put away his share. Gunn ate hearty enough, but he knew he was off his feed too. The events of the day crowded in on him and he knew the others felt it too. A sadness crept over them and no one knew what to say.

"It's always worse at night," said Gunn quietly. "Everything bad is, the grippe, a sore toe, grief."

"Yes," sighed Marylee and she looked across the campfire at Gunn.

"I'm sleepy," said Tommy. "Thanks for supper, Marylee."

Marylee took him in her arms, gave him a motherly hug. The boy waved at Gunn and crawled up into the wagon. They listened to him toss and turn for a while and then it was quiet. Marylee stared into the fire and watched the blaze turn to coals.

"More coffee?" she said. "There's plenty left."

"No, I've had enough. Mighty fine meal, Marylee."

"I dread going to sleep without Pa and Eli," she blurted.

"I know."

"Where are you sleeping? I didn't see you bring your bedroll in after you put up your horse."

"Yonder in the trees. I can hear things over there, away from the river."

"I thought you might stay close to the wagon."

"You let out a yell if anything scares you. I'll be here."

"Yes," she said. "That's very comforting." Her tone was flat and Gunn wondered if she was thinking about what happened to her loved ones that day. He looked at her, but she was just staring into the fire.

46

She wasn't weeping, but her face looked wan and tired in the glow and flare of the coals. He sat there, wondering if he should linger, or leave her alone with her thoughts.

"Gunn?"

"Yeah?"

"Why do you think those men killed all those people and my pa and Elias?"

"I don't know, Marylee. It doesn't make much sense when you first look at it."

"But then?"

"Well, if you look at it real close, and from every side, you generally find there was a reason to it. Sometimes it's hard to find a reason, though."

"Do you think you could find one?"

"I don't know. Given time, and some luck, I reckon I could."

"How would you go about it?"

"Well, either there's a connection between those killers and your pa, or between maybe the Ransoms and the killers and your pa just walked into it on an unlucky day. Could be lots of reasons."

"But you don't think it was an accident that my pa was killed, do you?"

"Well, hardly an accident. He might have been in the wrong place at the wrong time, though."

"Do you think that's the way it was, Gunn?"

Gunn looked at her. Marylee wasn't anybody's fool. She had done some thinking, all right.

"No," he said slowly. "I don't think that's the way it happened at all."

She got up, then, threw the last of the coffee into the pile of coals.

"That's what I thought you'd say," she said. "Goodnight, Gunn. And, thanks."

Gunn wanted to say more to her, but he knew it was not the time. She had enough on her mind as it was. If there was a connection between the killers and Paxton, it would not be easy to prove. Marylee didn't know any of her pa's friends in Gallatin, and Gunn didn't know a soul there. He didn't know if there was a vigilante group or not. Maybe only one of the men was a vigilante. Or, maybe he had once been a vigilante and the group had disbanded. At this point, he couldn't jump to any conclusions without landing in the briar patch.

"Goodnight, Marylee," he said. "Sleep tight."

Gunn set some wood on the coals in case they wanted a fire in the morning. He could keep it fed during the night, for that matter. He walked through the gathering darkness, back to where he had set out his bedroll. The night creatures were beginning to stir. A bat sliced the air over the river, scooping up insects, and an owl called from the deep woods.

Gunn unbuckled his gunbelt, rolled it up, put it under his saddle, near where his head would be. He jerked off his boots and set them within reach, sliding them together so nothing dangerous would crawl into them during the night. He loosened his shirt, lay down on his blankets. His coat served as a pillow. He put his hands behind his head and looked up at the dark sky. The first star winked on, and then another. The tiredness seeped out of his muscles. Esquire nickered softly and he heard the mules brushing against the willows, the chomp of their teeth as they munched the gamma grass.

He tried to put the dead people out of his mind. But there was one thought that kept intruding. If the killers were after Paxton, why not take him somewhere else? Further back on the trail, or between the Ransom ranch and Gallatin? That was the question that bothered him most. They had made no attempt to frame Paxton after they killed him, and if they were vigilantes, supposedly acting in the name of justice, why did they kill Ed and just leave him? No, there was a lot more back of this than met the eye. Gunn couldn't figure any of it out at this point and the thinking made him more tired than if he had wrestled bears and longhorns all day.

He closed his eyes, turned over on his side, the weariness of mind and body suddenly dragging him deep into a sound sleep.

Hours later, when the moon was up, he awoke with a start. A sound, something not quite right, had penetrated through his sleep-sogged brain. He reached quickly for the pistol under his saddle.

The Colt wasn't there.

Chapter Four

Gunn froze, peered into the darkness. He listened intently, heard only his own pulse hammering in his ear. He felt again for his pistol, searching under his saddle for the holster and gunbelt. A moment later, he felt a hand on his shoulder.

"Gunn, it's me."

He turned, saw a dark shadow looming over him. Even in the dim light, he saw that she wore only a shawl and a long nightshirt, probably her pa's. The cloth clung to her body as if it was plastered on.

"Marylee, what's the matter?"

"I—I couldn't sleep. I took your pistol so you wouldn't shoot me if you woke up."

Of course, he thought, she knew where I keep my pistol at night. When her pa was alive, she saw him asleep often enough.

"That's a hell of a thing to do."

"Gunn, don't be mad. Here's your gun." She handed him the holster and his pistol. He shoved it under the saddle.

"All right. Now go back to the wagon and try to get some sleep."

She scooted close to him, touched his chest with her hand. Her fingers worked through the hairs, brought warmth to his flesh. She rubbed him there for a long moment, without saying anything.

"I want you," she breathed. "I want you to hold me, touch me."

"Marylee. . . ."

"Please. Every time I closed my eyes, I saw my pa and my brother. Then I thought of you out here, all alone. And me all alone. Gunn, I need you."

He knew it was rough on her. Had to be. Losing her entire family in one day had to be about the meanest thing that had ever happened to her.

"Life's not fair, and I know it's tough for you. But you crawl into my bedroll and neither one of us will get much sleep.

"I don't care," she snapped. "I—I don't have anyone else to turn to, Gunn. Just you."

"You make it hard on a man," he said, without thinking that the phrase had a double meaning. "I mean—to turn you down," he added, lamely.

"Don't turn me down, then," she husked, and her hand slid down inside his shirt, around to his side, then back again. She scooted still closer to him, nestled her head against his. He could smell her faint perfume, felt the softness of her cheek against his, the silk of her hair falling over his ear.

Gunn lay back, and she withdrew her hand from inside his shirt, skated it down to his bulging fly. She leaned over him, kissed him wordlessly. Her hand stroked the bulge, made it swell until it pressed against his trousers at the crotch. She moaned, grazed his face with her burning lips, plucked at him with a fervent urgency that set his blood to boiling.

"All right," he rasped. "You'll have it your way, Marylee. Now you've got me into it and I hope you know what you're getting into. No promises, no hobbles, no corral."

"I know. I know you might not think much of me after . . . after we do it, but you don't know how it's been. Ever since I first saw you, I wanted you. I wanted you to take me in your arms and crush me against you. I wanted you to kiss me with those cold hard lips of yours and look at me with those steel gray eyes, look at me with the lust I felt in my heart for you."

"I had no idea."

"No," she whispered bitterly, as she crawled over his body and lay next to him, "because I hid it. I hid it from my pa and from Eli, even from myself. But I wanted you, Gunn, wanted you so much I couldn't stand it and when I went to bed at night, knowing you were outside, sleeping near, but out of reach, I tossed and turned and wept into my pillow. I burned with a fire I had never felt before and hoped you would notice me and feel what I felt for you."

"I'm sorry you were disappointed," he ventured. "I had a job to tend to, and a man doesn't tamper with his boss's daughter."

"Ha! I'll bet."

"Look, Marylee," he said, "how old are you?"

"Eighteen, almost nineteen."

"Almost half my age."

"Age doesn't mean a darn, Mister Gunn. Feelings mean everything."

She swarmed over him, then, peppering his mouth

with kisses, grabbing at him with desperate fingers. She unbuttoned his shirt, kissed him on the chest, on his own nipples until they stung. Gunn wrestled with her, but she was like a tigress, a wanton that had no shame, only a fierce desire to be taken.

"Have you ever, damnit Marylee, been with a man before?" he groaned.

"None of your business. Gunn, please don't fight me. I'm so hot I can't stand it. I'm burning all over. All over. Inside and out."

"Well, young lady, we're not getting anywhere this way. Let's take off some duds and see if we can't come to some mutual understanding. This is like trying to make love in a hammock with straitjackets on."

"Umm," she breathed, blowing into his ear, "I'd love to take my clothes off with you."

"Marylee, you don't have even a thimbleful of shame, do you?"

"Not with you, I don't," she purred.

He heard the whisper of cloth as she flicked off her shawl, pulled her nightshirt over her head. Gunn struggled out of his shirt and trousers, lay there naked for a moment as she fluffed her hair. Then he reached for her, pulled her down to him.

Her body was warm, fulsome, soft, pliant. She rubbed her breasts against his chest and he felt her nipples go hard. She pressed her hips against his, burrowed between his legs. He felt the bristly patch of hair rub against his manhood and it throbbed with blood, stiffened like a dagger. Her lips touched his and ignited fires between them. He wrapped his arms around her, returned her kiss, jabbed his probing tongue inside her mouth.

"Oooohhh," she moaned and her body writhed against his as if she was trying to crawl inside his skin. He rolled her over onto her back and his hand roamed over her flesh, explored the soft valleys, the delicate and sensuous curves, the rubbery nubbins of her nipples. She moaned and kissed him on the mouth and ears and neck as her own hand kneaded him with desperate, loving fingers.

He kissed her breasts and she arched against him, thrusting her loins up into his, her thighs undulating with desire. "Take me, take me," she crooned.

Gunn rose above her, pried her legs apart with his own, and settled between her thighs. She reached down for him, guided his swollen manhood to her steamy portal. He sank his probe into her, into the warm, moist pudding of her sex, felt her shudder as he slowly slid through the tunnel of her pulsating cave. She was sweet, hot as boiled honey, and she bucked when he touched her maidenhead.

"So," he whispered, "you have not been with a man before."

"No," she said, as if ashamed. "You're the first, Gunn."

"I hope you don't regret it."

"Never," she said passionately, and squeezed him with her arms, thrust her hips upward, impaling herself on his shaft. The thin, leathery membrane of her hymen resisted him and he began to stroke her gently, pushing harder each time, stretching the maidenhead until it weakened, parted like a delicate curtain.

Marylee cried out briefly, and bit her lip until the salty blood stung the exposed underflesh.

"It's good," she sighed. "It feels real good, Gunn."

"I didn't mean to hurt you."

"No, it was a good hurt. Right pleasureable."

He plunged deep into her, then, plundering her flesh with relentless, driving strokes until she bucked with a sudden burst of ecstasy, until her body clung to him, quivering as waves of pleasure rocked her senses, made her quake with electric spasms.

"Ah, ah," she moaned, and Gunn drove deeper, retreated slowly, again and again. Her hands swarmed over his back, clutching, kneading, digging in when the pleasure spasms rippled through her body. Her cauldron seethed, bubbled with sweet lava as the muscles in her legs distended and contracted with every electric tremor of her sheath.

Gunn was surprised at the depth and breadth of her passion. She seemed transformed during those moments when she left her girlhood behind and became a woman. Her face turned savage one moment, soft the next, and when her fingers dug into his back, Gunn felt the power of her unleashed passion, the abandonment with which she gave herself to him.

He exploded deep inside her and his brain filled with lights and flashes of exploded stars. She jolted against him in the final throes of her own climax and held onto him with steely arms, rigid, dug-in, fingers. He spent himself in a blind, thrilling rush, floated off somewhere like a wind-blasted leaf. He lingered in the high places, mindless, his body turning indolent, his manhood softening like melted wax inside her.

"Oh, Gunn," she gasped, "that was so beautiful. I—I never knew it would be like this. So perfect, so sweet. I feel like I've been falling through a whirlwind."

She rose up, grabbed his head in her hands, kissed him hard on the lips. He held her gently in his arms, stayed nestled against her, feeling the warmth of her flow through him like the springs up on the Yellowstone. Later, she lay against him like a purring kitten, and he pulled the blanket over them as she fell asleep. He closed his own eyes, finally, and slept, the contentment in his heart locking out the horror of the day, the questions for tomorrow.

When Gunn awoke, Marylee was gone. Her side of the bedroll reeked with the aroma of their lovemaking and the scent of her perfume lingered in his nostrils like the smell of incense in a quiet room. He stretched, pulled on his trousers, tucked in his shirt and jammed on his boots. He stood up, put on his gunbelt and went to find the mules and Esquire. There was a mist on the river when he took the animals to drink, a coolness on the land that gave a freshness to the morning. He felt good. He was relaxed and rejuvenated and he thought of Marylee, wondered what she thought of him in the harsh light of day.

He led the horse and mules to the wagon, saw that Marylee was awake, bright-eyed, glowing from some inner light.

"Good morning," she said pleasantly. "I feel wonderful."

"I feel pretty good myself."

"I'm glad. You made me very happy, Gunn." Then she blushed and crawled into the wagon to wake up

Tommy Blue. He crawled out, finally, rubbing sleep-clogged eyes and grinned shyly at Gunn.

"Are we going to Gallatin today?" he asked.

"Sure are. Quick as we can get the mules rigged up. Hungry?" Gunn looked at the boy, wondered if sleep had helped erase some of his grief.

"No, not much."

"Marylee?" Gunn asked.

"I'm full of . . . well, no, I'm not very hungry either. Maybe we could stop somewhere or eat in town."

"We ought to be close enough so that we can eat in Gallatin," said Gunn. In a half an hour, they were back on the trail, heading north. They would not pass through Bozeman this way, but strike Gallatin first, from the south. As they drew closer, Tommy became more animated, pointing out landmarks. When they reached the Gallatin River, Gunn let the team drink, got a hatful of water for Esquire. Several trails conjoined with theirs and the road widened. The foothills receded behind them and ahead, they saw the smoke from woodfires hanging in a pall over the town.

They rode in without causing much attention. Gunn took the team to the livery stable, telling the man they'd get their gear after they found sleeping quarters. He arranged for Esquire to have a stall, be grained and watered. The mules could stay in the corral out back. Gunn stripped his saddlebags from in back of the cantle, took his rifle out of its scabbard. He paid four dollars to the man, who gave no name, and ushered his charges to the Gallatin Hotel.

"You can eat here and rest up," he told Marylee and the boy. "I'll get a room, too, and be back later with your things."

"I — I don't know how much money Pa had," said Marylee.

"We'll worry about that later. Keep your eyes on the boy here, and stay put."

"What are you going to do?" she asked.

"After I put these saddlebags and my rifle in my room, I'll see the marshal. He'll want to go out to the Ransom place and put things right with them."

"Gunn," she said. "I'll worry about you."

"Worry about yourself, first, Marylee."

He checked Marylee and the boy into one room, took another for himself. The desk clerk was full of questions, but Gunn didn't answer them. When Marylee started to reply, he gave her a sharp look and shook his head. The boy was quiet, reserved, and he followed meekly as the man took Marylee and Tommy upstairs. Gunn watched them go, looked around at the seedy lobby with its dusty chairs and tables, the old men who sat there looking out the window, working their toothless gums. He climbed the stairs to his own room, alone, a pensive look on his face. He opened the door, went in. He put his saddle bags and rifle in the closet, looked around. It wasn't much of a room. There was a bed, a dresser, a water pitcher, bowl, towel, washcloth, a table, two chairs. He didn't expect to spend much time in it, anyway. It would suit him. He left, locking the door.

The marshal's office was several doors down, across the street from the livery stable. Gunn hadn't noticed it when they arrived because the sign in the window was temporary and hadn't been placed there. The sign said U.S. DEPUTY MARSHAL. And underneath, OPEN NOON TO 4 PM. The blind was drawn to keep out the sun and the door squawked when he opened it. His boots thumped a hollow sound on the wood floor as he walked to the short counter, looked over at the man seated behind a desk.

"You the marshal here?" Gunn asked. The office looked as if its occupant had just moved in. There wasn't much in it, and nothing looked very permanent.

The man was pot-bellied, had a girth on him like summer steer, with bushy eyebrows, a frazzled handlebar moustache, close-set hazel eyes, mutton-chop sideburns that hadn't been trimmed in a month. He wore a leather vest with a star on it set inside a circle. Pot-iron, Gunn figured, but he couldn't read the legend on it.

"Deputy," said the man, his voice a low whiskey growl that rumbled from somewhere in his massive chest. He did not move to get up, but sat there, toad-like, scrutinizing his visitor with a squint that almost erased his eyes. He appeared to be a man in his early forties, and one who had lived every minute of it. "What's on your mind?"

"Marshal around?"

"Well, there's marshals and there's marshals. I'm the only one that counts in Gallatin and I don't recollect seein' your face around here."

"No. I just rode in, but there've been some killings. You might want to look into them."

"Killings? What killings?" The man bristled and his eyes did not squint any more. He didn't get up, but he looked prepared to do so, and to draw his pistol, too, if that was called for.

"People name of Ransom. An Indian cook name of Blue Flower, three cowhands, and a man and boy I came out here with."

"Jesus Christ almighty," said the deputy marshal. "What in the hell's goin' on here? For Christ's sake, man, who in the name of Jehosaphat are you?"

"The name's Gunn. I brought a wagon in from down south. We were jumped by a bunch of men. The Paxton man and his son were shot dead. I found the cowhands in the line shack, and later on, the Ransoms and their cook. They were stabbed to death."

"You just stay right where you are, Mister. Don't you even blink. I want hear this slow and I want to hear it straight. You got that?"

"You don't need to push, Marshal. I came to see you, remember?"

The deputy got up from behind his desk, an effort, and swung 250 pounds of flab in Gunn's direction. He put one pudgy hand on the butt of his Peacemaker Colt and stood two feet behind the counter when he came to a halt that left his overhung belly jiggling under his gunbelt.

"When did all this happen? Did you bury 'em? What in Christ's hell are you doin' in Gallatin? Wha'd you say your damned name was again?"

"Hold on," said Gunn. "You talk like a Gatling gun. Yesterday, no, I come peaceful, and the name's Gunn, short for Gunnison."

"Gunnison, Gunnison, damned if that name don't clap a bell. You wanted anywheres?"

"I don't think so. Not by the law, anyway. I didn't catch your name."

"Merle Lescoulie. I'm deputy territorial marshal here, United States and I'm tellin' you, man, you done forked a bad horse with this talk of the Ransoms and their hands. I don't know fuckfiddle shit about these Paxtons."

"I buried them. The daughter was knocked cold when it happened. The Indian woman's son, Tommy Blue is with her. I brought them both in, put them up at the Gallatin Hotel."

"Shitfire and save sulphur, man, you brought them here? Why don't you put a bullseye over their hearts and open up a shooting gallery?"

"I don't get your drift, Lescoulie."

"We got vigilantes here, law and order assholes, who just might be interested in witnesses. The town marshal quit two months ago and I'm the only law here, almost."

"You think vigilantes killed all those people?"

"I don't know. Maybe you killed 'em. We been missing a lot of people around here lately and never once did anyone come forward to say they was even dead or missing. Maybe you'd better start at the beginning and tell me everything, and I mean every goddamned thing, you know about this. You sit in that chair over there and leave your hardware on the counter. That Mex knife, too."

"Marshal, I don't take this rig off unless I'm sleeping or taking a bath."

Lescoulie's hand tightened on the butt of his pistol. He started to pull it from its holster. Gunn stepped around the counter, strode to the man, and grabbed his wrist with his left hand. With his right, he pulled his own Colt so fast it was just a blinking blur to the marshal's eyes.

"You keep that in your holster," said Gunn firmly, "and I'll put mine back."

"Mister, I'm a deputy—" Lescoulie began.

"I know what you are," said Gunn. "You're a sonofabitch trying to push me. And I don't push. You want a story, fine. Meanwhile, those folks out there are turning ripe and whatever clues are left may get eaten up by the rats."

Lescoulie's fingers relaxed. Gunn loosened his grip, stepped away, holstering his Colt.

"You pull that right fast, Mister. You must know how to use it."

"I haven't used it lately, but I practice a lot."

Lescoulie's attitude changed. He smiled, or gave a wrinkle to his lips that was as close as he could get to smiling and waved Gunn to a chair.

"Hell, let's just jaw about this. I'll listen and if you're still a suspect when you're finished, I'll let you off with a warning."

"A warning?"

"Yeah, Gunn. Because once I know and start rounding up deputies, then everyone will know. And, unless I miss my guess, your life won't be worth the price of a plug mule at a saddle horse auction."

The marshal sat down. Gunn took the chair, sat on its edge warily. Lescoulie ran a sweaty hand through his thinning hair and adjusted his belly behind the desk. Gunn opened his mouth to talk, when they heard a shout outside, and the boom of a pistol shot, so close it rattled the windows.

"That came from the livery," said Lescoulie. "Christ almighty, you ain't even got the dust off your face and here's trouble."

Gunn stood up, looked out the window, across the street. The stableman staggered onto the boardwalk, clutching his chest. Another shot rang out and the frontal bone in his skull blew like a pieplate into the air. A spray of pink froth followed the smash of a bullet through his brain. He pitched forward, dead before he hit the ground.

The marshal was on his feet and out from behind the desk so fast Gunn couldn't believe it. When he had to, the man could move.

"You, watch my back," he said. "Come on. I think that was someone wanting to call on you real bad."

"Me? Who knows I'm in town, besides you?"

"That dumb jasper at the livery stable, for one, and now, whoever put his lamp out."

Gunn paled, felt his knees go weak. For all his bluster, Lescoulie was pretty damned smart.

Chapter Five

Marshal Lescoulie lumbered past the dead stable-man and into the livery, his gun drawn. Gunn was right behind him. The smell of gunpowder still clung to the air, mingling with the scent of horse sweat, manure, feed and liniment. Esquire stomped the floor of his stall, restless. When he saw Gunn, he whinnied, looked at him wall-eyed.

"Easy boy," said Gunn. Wisps of white smoke hung in the air; motes of dust danced in the slanting rays of sunlight that streamed through the open back doors. Lescoulie poked around the stable, pistol drawn.

"That your wagon?" he asked, pointing to the canvas-covered Springfield, just inside the back doors.

"That's Paxton's outfit."

Lescoulie approached it from the rear, raised his pistol to eye-level. "All right," he growled, "come out of there with your hands up." Surprised, Gunn stepped back, his hand poised to draw his own pistol. There was a scuffling sound inside the wagon, then Tommy Blue stuck his head out.

"Don't shoot, Mister," he said.

"Come one out, Tommy," said Gunn. "The marshal won't hurt you."

Tommy slithered over the backboard and dropped to the ground. His face was waxen with fear, his eyes wide. His lower lip trembled.

"Boy, you been here all along?" asked Lescoulie. Tommy nodded.

"Thought I told you to stay put," said Gunn.

"Miss Marylee, she sent me to get some things for her. I didn't do anything, honest."

"I know you didn't, Tommy," said Gunn kindly. "I want you to tell Marshal Lescoulie here all you saw and heard. That stableman was shot and killed."

"I'll ask the questions, Gunn," said the marshal. "Boy, what did you see?"

"Nothin'," he replied. "I was inside the wagon, when this man come in. He asked a lot of questions and I just stayed quiet and hid, like I did at Ransoms."

"What questions?" Lescoulie, Gunn thought, had all the smoothness of a hammer. "Be quick about it, boy."

"His name's Tommy," said Gunn.

Lescoulie shot him a look of profound annoyance. Outside, a crowd gathered around the dead man. Their babble was laced with fear, an undercurrent of anger that a man had been murdered in front of the marshal's office. The marshal ignored it, his eyes boring into Tommy's like a pair of drill punches.

"You go on, Tommy. Tell me what you heard in here."

Tommy looked at Gunn, drew himself up to a manly height. He blinked, screwed up his face as he tried to remember everything he had heard. Gunn noticed he was still a little shaky. The poor kid had seen enough death to last him a long time in the past couple of days.

"Well, the stableman, I guess his name's Barnett 'cause that's what the man called him when he come in here, askin' questions. Barnett wasn't scared or anything. The man wanted to know who belonged to this wagon, and whose horse that was over there. It's Gunn's horse, but Mister Barnett said he didn't know, that he was just working there."

"That all?" persisted Lescoulie.

"No. This man he got real mad. He asked who come in the wagon and Barnett wouldn't tell him. The next thing I know, there was a shot and somebody running. Then I heard another shot over by the door. I was real scared. I thought he was going to shoot me, too."

"And you didn't see him?"

"Not his face, but I saw his back. He ran out those doors there and I took a peek."

"So?" Lescoulie looked as if he was going to eat the boy alive.

"I-It looked like the same man who killed my ma," said Tommy Blue, and tears welled up in his eyes. "He was big and he had on the same clothes."

"Sonofabitch," said Gunn.

"Make that double," said the marshal. "Boy, you get what you want out of that wagon and then hightail it out of here. Don't you say a word of this to anyone, hear?"

"Yes sir." Tommy jumped back up in the wagon, banged around inside, and emerged a few moments

66

later, a large satchel in his hand. He scurried out the front doors and disappeared from sight. Lescoulie walked to the back of the stable, beckoned for Gunn to come close.

"We got something real serious here, Gunn," said the marshal, *sotto voce*. "Worse'n I thought."

"How so?" asked Gunn.

"That man the kid called Barnett. That was his name, all right. Steve Barnett."

"You know him?"

"Know him? I hired him. Man who killed him called him by name. That's what bothers the living hell outta me."

"You said that was his name. Barnett."

"Yeah, but nobody was supposed to know that but me. He went by the name of Harvey Smith here. Been on the job a week. You know, under the covers, so to speak. He was a deputy United States marshal, and by God, I'm going to get to the bottom of this if I have to turn this town upside down."

Gunn let out a low whistle.

"Well, somebody knew who he was," said Gunn. "Any idea how they found out?"

"Easy enough, if someone broke into his room at the boarding house. I got Barnett a job here, trying to get a line on the vigilantes. Didn't want anyone to know who he was. Expect I'll have to go to Mrs. Jennings' boarding place and do some lookin'. You keep this under your Stetson, hear?"

"So there is a vigilante bunch," said Gunn. "You might want to take a look at this." Gunn reached in his pocket, pulled out the badge he had found near the line shack on the Ransom place. He hadn't wanted to show it to anyone until he was sure he could trust that person. Lescoulie, for all his bluster, seemed to be a straight shooter. The man seemed to genuinely want to bring the illegal vigilante committee to justice.

"Where'd you get this?"

"Ever see one before?" Gunn had to know, before he said another word.

"No, but I've been looking until my eyes plumb ached and turned black as two pissholes in the snow. This bunch seems to be better organized than anyone thought."

"How'd you get onto them?"

"Whispers. Whiskey talk. Somebody wrote a letter to a senator, and the senator wrote to the territorial judge and the judge wrote to the territorial marshal and the territorial marshal sent me in here."

"What have you found out?"

"Not much. Some unexplained killings. A lot of froze-up people with lockjaw. Scared. Vigilantes was mentioned a time or two, but no names. That's where I'd like to know how you come by this piece of tin. Might be it belongs to you."

"That's not even close to being funny, Lescoulie," said Gunn. "I found it up at Ransom's line shack, nearby, where somebody lay in ambush for those poor luckless cowhands."

"Find anything else?"

"Maybe. You got some time?"

"Yeah, but let me get some chores done. I got Barnett to take care of, and I'll have to round up a posse, get some wagons out to the Ransom spread. Meet you at Beaman's Saloon in a half hour. We

68

ought to be able to find a quiet corner where we can chew the bull's fat."

"I'll see you there, Lescoulie."

"My friends call me Merle."

"You'll be the first to know, Marshal."

Lescoulie winced, grinned wryly. Gunn stalked from the stables, glanced briefly at the dead man. Bystanders stared at him as he strode through their midst, but he paid them no mind. He had some questions of his own to ask, and he wanted to look at some tracks before they got messed up or wiped out by the gawkers. He walked to the end of the block, circled to come up behind the stables. He saw boot tracks there that he had seen before. The boots, he figured, were new and expensive. They belonged to a killer, the same man who had been at the Ransom place. And now, he was in Gallatin.

The killer had killed again and Gunn wondered who he would kill next.

Beaman's Saloon & Gambling Parlor was a block off Main Street at the corner of Front and Cedar. It was not the only saloon there, but it was the least busy. A mule and a swaybacked mare stood hipshot at the hitchrail. Many of the citizens, Gunn knew, were still in the main part of town, talking about the shooting of Harvey Smith, alias Steve Barnett.

He heard raucous laughter from the saloon across the street, a whiskey emporium called The Silver Diggings, and someone was plunking a guitar at The Nugget, next door to Beaman's. Gunn waded through the batwing doors, stepped to one side, narrowed his

69

eyes to adjust to the shift of light. There were two old coots seated at the bar, five stools apart from each other, and the bartender was playing solitaire down at the far end. The card tables were empty, a player piano stood silent against the back wall. Apparently, Gunn mused, the saloon didn't come alive until nightfall. It was a good spot to talk on a quiet afternoon.

Marshal Lescoulie's massive frame darkened the doorway a few minutes after Gunn ordered a beer and sat down at a table in the far corner, away from windows, prying eyes. Lescoulie strode to the table, gestured to the barkeep. Evidently he was known there, since the man behind the counter brought a pail of beer and a quart jar, set them down in front of the marshal.

"Barnett took lead in the back, and then another ball blew his brains out. The sonsofbitches. I talked to the boarding house lady and she didn't know anything. She was shaking like a dog shittin' peach seeds, so I figure she knew some asshole was ransacking Steve's room. I looked it over and it looked like someone tried to be careful, but his saddlebags looked like a pack rat had been in them. They left everything, his badge, his orders, but they knew who he was all right, the mother-lovin' bastards. I swear, Gunn, there wasn't a better man than Barnett when it came to blending into the background. He had some close squeaks before, but these sonsofbitches had him cold. But that ain't my worry now. Can't bring Steve back, but maybe I can save someone else from getting 'dobe walled like that."

"Who?" asked Gunn, surprised at Lescoulie's long-winded speech. He might as well have been talking to a post, though, since the marshal poured himself a quart of tepid beer and drank it down like water, the liquid gurgling and sloshing down his throat in one noisy rush.

Lescoulie belched loudly, wiped a sleeve across his foamy lips and squinted at Gunn as though he had just noticed he was sitting there.

"What'd you say?"

"You said someone else might get killed."

"You. That's what the killer wanted to find out. Who you were, first off. And he was pretty interested in those kids you brought in, too, the way I figure it. My advice to all three of you is to clear out, go on up to Bozeman or Butte and forget all about this."

"I don't think I can do that, Lescoulie."

"I figured you'd say something like that. I did some checking on you, Gunn. William Gunnison. Captain with the Tennessee Volunteers. Missionary Ridge. And, you been in Montana Territory before. Oh, there's no fly-sheet on you, I reckon, but one of those jaspers outside the livery recognized you, wondered if you'd shot Barnett. He was ready to put the brand to your ass."

"Anybody I know?"

"Man with too much whiskey in his gut. I wouldn't worry about him."

"What's your next move, Lescoulie?"

"I'm packin' out for the Ransom spread. Anything I should look for?"

Gunn told him about the blood that Ransom tried to write in, but didn't tell about the silk handkerchief with a man's initials on it, the bag of Durham or the hotel key. The key didn't match the ones from the Gallatin, so he had some checking to do himself. The hotel had to be big enough to have at least 12 rooms.

"You say the man drew a circle in blood. Big, little?" The marshal poured himself another full quart of beer. His hand wrapped around the glass, made it all but disappear.

"About five inches across."

"Could it have been an initial? The start of a word?"

"Maybe," said Gunn. "Why?"

"Oh, just wonderin'."

Gunn didn't believe him. For all his bluster, he had Lescoulie pegged as a shrewd and canny man. He knew that a U.S. marshal usually had to rely on his wits to stay alive, especially the man who worked on the frontier, often beyond any semblance of law. Lescoulie looked like a man who had ridden a river or two and maybe he looked fat and soft, but when he had to move, he could move.

"Yeah, well, I'll poke around here, see if I can dig up anything that might help solve these murders," said Gunn.

"You're not the law here."

"I know. But there wasn't any law where Paxton and his son were killed. None when the Ransoms and their cook and hired hands got their lamps put out."

"This ain't open prairie, either. Lots of places for a bushwhacker to hide."

"We didn't see them when they hit us, either."

"What's your stake in this?"

"Let's say, Lescoulie, that I think justice is blind as a bat and sometimes I like to help her see."

Lescoulie roared with laughter, took a healthy swig of his beer. Gunn was still nursing his. The only good thing about it was that it was wet.

The marshal's laughter shut off like well water at the spigot. He leaned across the table, a conspiratorial look on his face. Gunn realized, then, just how cagey and sly Lescoulie really was. That laugh was for the patrons, to keep them lulled into a sense that these were just two men who came in for a beer.

"Gunn, listen real close. I don't know when I'll be back. Tomorrow, the day after. I been trackin' this bunch all over the territory. This badge might say 'Gallatin' on it, but I've seen some just like it that say 'Kalispell,' 'Helena,' and 'Butte.' We got an organization here and I think it started in the mining camps or somewhere along Bozeman's Trail."

"Political?" interjected Gunn.

"Maybe. Maybe not. I think just money at this point. Feller comes into a town, stirs people up, but he does it quiet. Then he gets the goods on a man, rigs them ever' whichaway, and next thing, the man is dead, shot or stabbed, and no one lets out a beller."

"Got to be a reason," said Gunn softly.

"Aha! A glimmer of light in that fog-bin you call a brain. Damned right, Gunn. Things look diff'rent, but they all got the same brand on 'em. You got to look under the hide. I looked high and low, but I ain't come up with it."

Gunn leaned back, let out a whoosh of breath. Lescoulie had dumped a handful in his lap. The Ransoms were part of it, maybe Paxton, too. But it wasn't just this one thing or two things. Somebody was putting a remuda together, some secret bunch that might take in the whole territory.

"What could it be?" Gunn asked aloud. "What in hell's that big?"

"I wished to hell I knew," said the marshal. "But you got to figure he's smart. One man. Has big schemes. He wants something and he's figured out a way to get it and hide his tracks. I've sat up many a night puzzlin' over this. Only one thing I can think of and that don't make sense."

"What's that, Lescoulie?"

"Gold. Cattle, maybe."

"You got a list of the dead?" Gunn asked.

"Most. I can't see anything common among 'em."

"Maybe I can."

"Yeah, Gunn. Maybe you can. I'll drop the list off at your hotel. In the meantime, you try and think why this bunch would kill a man and his boy without asking any questions first."

Gunn had thought of that. On one hand, it seemed a deliberate murder, then, after seeing the Ransoms and their help wiped out, it lost all sense whatsoever. Maybe there was no pattern here at all. Maybe there was no connection, or maybe there was. Maybe the killers wanted people to think there was a connection when there really wasn't. It was baffling.

"Maybe these vigilantes murder, then murder again to throw you off the track," ventured Gunn. "Kill one man for a reason, another for no reason at all."

"I thought of that. Jesus you think anyone's that mean and calculatin' and ruthless?"

"Yeah," said Gunn, thinking of Elias Paxton, Tommy Blue's mother, the whole bunch of dead he had left back there beyond the Yellowstone. "I think

74

someone's that bad and that smart."

Lescoulie finished off his pail of beer, stood up. He tossed a pair of cartwheels on the table, hitched his gunbelt. Gunn looked up at him, smiled crookedly.

"You be damned careful, Gunnison. I'll see you when I see you."

"Yeah, Merle. The same."

Merle Lescoulie smiled and lumbered toward the door without a backward glance.

Gunn wondered if he'd ever see the man again.

Chapter Six

Gunn tapped lightly on the door to Marylee's room. The door opened and Tommy Blue's face lit up.

"Come in, Mister Gunn. Marylee's got something to show you."

Gunn saw that the boy's face has been scrubbed, his hair combed. He was still wearing his old clothes, but Gunn could take care of that.

"We had some food, too. Marylee found some money. She took a bath. Me, too."

Gunn laughed, stepped inside the room. He closed the door. Marylee sat on the bed, looking through a stack of papers, odds and ends. She looked up at him, beckoned for him to draw near.

"What's going on?" asked Gunn.

"I've got some things to show you," she said. "Tommy, go read some more."

"Aw, can't I listen to you? I want to see, too."

"Tommy," she said sternly. "Remember your promise."

"Oh, all right," he pouted. "But, shucks. I wish't I was to Missus Loomis's." Neither Gunn nor Marylee paid him any attention.

The boy picked up a reader Marylee had given him and sat in the corner by the window. He looked at Gunn, but the man shook his head. Tommy made sure the chair scraped and that he cleared his throat and that the pages of the book riffled as he opened it. Marylee shot him a dark look.

"Sit on the bed here," she told Gunn, patting a place beside her. "I want to talk to you about my pa and show you some things."

Gunn sat. "All right," he said. "Those his things?"

"Yes." She looked at him lovingly, squeezed his hand. "First of all, let me explain how Pa was. He didn't talk much about what was important to him. He was loud and he liked to order us around. I think he was just trying to hide his true feelings."

"That happens."

"Well, he kept these papers here, in a strong-box. I knew about them because he always kept the box locked and he always hid the key from me. I wanted to snoop in it a long time ago. But I never would have, of course, without his permission."

"Of course," Gunn smiled. Marylee smiled back at him, sighed. She looked lovely with her face freshly washed, her hair combed out, dark and luxuriant. She wore a loose frock, was barefoot. She had a dark red sash around her waist that emphasized its daintiness. If the boy had not been in the room, Gunn wondered how long he would have been able to keep from taking her in his arms and kissing her. Her ears were cute. He had never noticed them; had never been this close to her in daytime. Cute, yes, and her mouth, when she talked, made his blood stir.

"Listen," she said, in mock reproof, "this is serious. I had Tommy bring these things from the wagon. Pa's keys, his strong-box, and everything in it."

"Yes, and you almost got him killed."

"I know. I'm sorry. But Gunn, I opened Pa's private box and I've been reading all these papers. There's a letter here. It tells why he was bringing us to Gallatin. It might even explain why he was killed."

She rummaged through the pile of papers on the bed, and Gunn saw that she was trying hard not to cry. She found what she was looking for and, with trembling hand, gave it to him. "Read this," she said, her voice choking with emotion.

Gunn saw that it was a letter as he took it from her hand. It was written in ink with a fine quill. The words were legible. The stationery wasn't very good, but it had the name of a hotel on the top of it.

FOSTER HOUSE

The address underneath was in Gallatin, on Front Street.

Dear Ed:
   Looks like your grubstake might have paid off, partner. I found us a rich vein. Assays out real good. I had it done up to Billings. Some trouble though. Can't file on it yet. You better come on out quick. Make sure you get here exactly on August 26. I'll meet you in Gallatin at this hotel.

The letter was dated June 2, 1875. It was signed *O.*

"You know who this is? Who wrote this letter?" Gunn asked Marylee.

"Look," she said, "I found something else." She handed Gunn a document. "Pa loaned some man here five thousand dollars. This is the contract. It was notarized and everything. I didn't know Pa had that much money."

Gunn looked at the document. It was duly notarized and called for the party of the first part to lend the sum of $5000.00 to the party of the second part, to wit, one Owen Jamison, in return for one-half of all mining claims, mines, ore, precious metals or other significant minerals that the party of the second part might discover, file on, claim, or otherwise attach for a period of five years from the signing of the document. The notary's lavish signature was scrawled above a line that had his name printed out underneath: Cassius Llewellyn MacGregor. A mouthful, Gunn thought. Edward Paxton's signature was small, tight as his fist must have been, and the other man's signature was larger than any of the others, with the O in Owen very large, and the J in his surname a looping oval almost as big.

"This Owen Jamison. Ever hear his name before?"

"No. But Pa talked about someone he was going to meet here and hinted that there might be a change in our fortunes."

"Well, it looks as if Owen Jamison might have some explaining to do," said Gunn.

"What do you mean?"

"I mean your pa was killed on August 25th, one day before we were to arrive in Gallatin." He did not tell her about the silk handkerchief with those same

79

initials, OJ, embroidered in one corner. The bare threads he held in his hands were starting to connect up, form a pattern, perhaps even evidence.

The Foster Hotel was old, but it had obviously been built to last. It was made of stone and wood, held the dominant location on Front Street, nestled among smaller shops, dry goods stores, saloons, a barber shop, a gunsmith's shop. Gunn approached it slowly, from the opposite side of the street. He wanted to look it over, first, see what kind of clientele it drew. It was not a seedy place, from outside anyway. The boardwalk was swept out front, and there were benches, freshly painted, where some old-timers, dressed in worn, clean suits, sat and talked, as the last rays of the sun drew the shadows down the walls of the false fronts on either side of the hotel building.

There was a sign in one of the windows proclaiming: UNDER NEW MANAGEMENT.

Gunn crossed the street, looked at the horses tied at the hitchrail. He checked the brands, but they were not familiar to him. There were two of them and they had not been there long. One was a bay mare, well-fed, barrel-bellied, and the other, a claybank gelding that looked like a mountain horse, good chest, trim legs, well-shod.

The hotel lobby was spacious, decorated with artificial potted palms, and mounted heads of elk, moose, antelope, buffalo and mule deer. It was a man's hotel. Ashtrays stood on spindly twisted iron legs and the overstuffed chairs were covered in cowhide. More men lounged there, reading, talking, and a pair of men by the wall played a game of dominoes as a third man watched and kibitzed.

The hotel clerk was going over the books, looked up when Gunn leaned over the counter. He was a thin, nervous, ascetic-looking man, bald as a buzzard, wearing pince-néz glasses on his bony, aquiline nose.

"I'd like a room. One night."

"We just do have a vacancy, sir," said the clerk. "It's small and you must vacate by morning. It's called for."

"How come?"

"We generally cater to permanents here. I suggest you try the Gallatin if your stay is to be longer."

"How many rooms have you got?" Gunn asked, playing the dumb stranger.

"Why, we have fourteen rooms on three stories, sir."

"Well, give me number twelve if you have it."

"Ah, no sir, that room is taken."

"Well, what have you got that's not taken?"

"Number four, sir."

"How much?"

"For one night, that would be, ah, let me see, I can let you have it for three dollars and seventy-five cents."

Gunn whistled long and loudly.

"It might possibly be cheaper at another hotel. As I said—"

"That'll be fine. Where could I get a bath and some whiskey this time of day?"

"Bath is six bits, and I can bring a bottle to your

room. Payment in advance for room and services."

Gunn paid for the room and bath, though he wouldn't take it, and said he'd pick up his own bottle. The clerk handed him a key attached to a square piece of wood with a leather thong. The key was skeleton, and the board had FOSTER HOUSE burned into it faintly. Except for the lettering, it matched the key Gunn had found at the lineshack on the Ransom ranch.

"Can you find it all right, ah, let's see, Mister Paxton, is it? Top of the stairs, three doors down on your right. Your bath will be ready at six of the clock. Just come to the desk and I'll take you to the bath room."

"Fine. I can find the sleeping room."

Let that name Paxton raise some eyebrows, Gunn thought, as he took the key, mounted the stairs. He kept on going, to the floor above, careful to step softly and avoid squeaking boards. The stairs and hallways were carpeted, though the threads were worn, and he made no sound as he searched for room number 12.

The room was at the left end of the hall. Builders had blocked off one end, made a concave entrance-way that obviously connected what once had been two rooms. There was no room numbered 13. Some people were superstitious, he mused. There were two doors. One locked, or was bolted, from the inside. He knocked on the other door, heard no answer. He took out the key he had found, put in the lock. He turned it, the lock clattered and the door swung open as he pushed it with the toe of his boot.

There was a short hallway, bare of furniture, a

print hanging lopsided on one wall, an out-of-date calendar on the other. Gunn walked into the front room after closing the door, relocking it. He saw a large divan, two easy chairs, a table around which were five straight-backed chairs. Bottles of whiskey and rye, partially emptied, were clustered at the table's center, surrounded by smudged glasses that reeked of stale liquor. Cigars and cigarettes, ready-mades and roll-your-owns, littered a large ashtray, and there were wadded up scraps of paper on the floor.

He checked the windows, opened them. It was a long drop to the street, but he might have to get out fast. He walked back to the table, picked up three of the clumps of wadded-up paper, unfolded them. They seemed to be maps, or parts of maps. They resembled those scribbles he had seen during the war, makeshift military maps drawn in the field during the heat of battle. He stuffed them in his pocket, moved to the adjoining room through another short hallway littered with socks, undershorts and shirts. A bedroom. He opened the window in there, looked down at a side street. Another long drop.

He looked inside the closet, saw the clothes hanging on a small square-cut beam, studded with hooks. The suits were expensive, well-cut, made to fit a big man. A silk handkerchief stuck out of the lapel pocket. He pulled it free, saw the embroidered initials in the corner. Except for its color, gray, it matched the black one he had found at the Ransom spread. He put the handkerchief back the way he had found it. There were three pairs of highly-polished boots set in a single row on the floor. He picked up two separate pair, looked at the soles, found them to be relatively new. A pile of socks, these of a better quality than those in the hall, lay in a corner. In the opposite corner was a large locked strongbox. He almost missed it. It was covered with a blanket and the blanket was laden with a stack of neatly folded shirts. He tried the heavy lock. It would take a crowbar or a quarter stick of powder to blow it, he thought. The shirts, too, were well-made, with neatly sewn yokes and cuffs. These were not the shirts of a working man, but of a gambler, or a banker. Gunn stepped out of the closet, made his way to the next room.

The third room had cots in the center, and bunks jammed up against the walls. The wallpaper, a dizzy and monotonous design of faded flowers, was peeling in spots, showing old newspapers and wood under- neath. Gunbelts heavy with pistols hung from the posts and a commandeered hall tree. There were rifles, too, and boxes of ammunition, dynamite, mining tools: picks, shovels, fuses, caps, lamps, candles, rope, nails, pulleys, slings and stacks of canvas ore bags. There were work clothes and hobnail boots, dirty caps and dusters lying helter-skelter all over the room, and on a table, more maps, these well- drawn by a draftsman or cartographer.

Gunn leafed through the pile of charts, found one that seemed to be of the Ransom spread, or part of it. He studied it carefully, noting the ridges and simply drawn compass rose that indicated "north" with a single capital "N." Certain spots were marked on the map with initials. He saw an "M" and an "H." The prominent landmarks were spelled out: "ridge," "gully," "hill," "trail," and there were elevation numerals in certain places, distances set down. There were a series of squares labeled RANCH HOUSE, and above it on a ridge, the word SHACK.

Gunn walked to the door, the one that locked from the inside only, and slipped the latch, but left it closed. A precaution. He wanted to examine some of the closed trunks in the room, see if he could find any clues that would give him the identities of the men who bunked here.

He put together a picture in his mind. The head man lived in the other part of the compartmented living quarters. The men who worked for him, or with him, bunked in here — their bedrolls were askew on the bunks and cots. There was a door between the cubicles. He figured three or four men lived in this room, but it could sleep two or three more. It was a headquarters of some sort, the whole shebang. He prowled through the closet, saw more modestly-priced men's clothing hanging on hooks, stacked on shelves. In the big chest-of-drawers, he found kerchiefs, belts, socks, and to his surprise, another pot iron vigilante badge.

"Paydirt," Gunn whispered and picked it up. He drew his knife, a Mexican copy of a Bowie, and made a mark on the backside, a small and barely visible X. He put the badge back where he had found it, closed the drawer.

If he ever ran across it again, he would damned sure know where he first saw it.

There were no letters, no paper of any kind with a man's name written down. He roamed back into the front room, tried to piece together what he had learned, what he might expect. He sniffed the stuffy

85

air, knew that men had been here the night before, but were not here now. Were they coming back? Where had they gone?

They were miners, or prospectors. They also had an arsenal, so they were not strangers to the gun. He didn't like it. He didn't like being here. Snooping around in someone else's things. But he was a man groping through the darkness. He had bits and pieces of things, but nothing solid, nothing he could put together in one lump and call it by a name. Was this Owen Jamison's place? His headquarters? There was a way he might find out. He could ask the desk clerk. There was no reason to hide anymore. Someone knew his name. Someone knew he had brought Marylee and Tommy Blue to town.

Gunn slammed his right fist into his left palm. The anger turned his face hard, flickered in his eyes. The frustration rippled through him like an elusive itch. He couldn't find it, he couldn't scratch it. It was just there. Something important, something in the jumble of things he had seen or heard or felt or touched, and damned if he could figure any of it out. He needed names, he needed proof. He needed, most of all, a witness who would come forward and put these men at the Ransom spread two days ago.

The problem was, all of the witnesses were dead.

Only Tommy Blue and Marylee Paxton were alive, and they hadn't seen anything worth counting on.

Gunn heard the footsteps outside the door, the click of the key in the lock. His blood froze. He backed away, out of the room. He didn't want to jump out a window. He raced on tiptoe to the other room, his senses screaming with alarm.

He was glad now that he had had the foresight to unlatch the other door. The front door opened and he heard voices, low and gravelly, as at least two men walked into the front room.

Gunn wondered if they had closed the door behind them. He stood by the other door and listened. More footsteps. Damn! Maybe the whole bunch was coming.

"Lay off that loudmouth, Hank," said a voice in the next room. "We got time for that later."

"Hell, I just wanted to wash my mouth out with a little rye, Belker. Mind your own damned business."

Gunn held his breath. He had names. Two, anyway. A front and a back. But no faces to go with them. Not yet. The footsteps beyond the door grew louder and Gunn tensed. Maybe he wouldn't be able to get out that way, after all. The footsteps stopped, just outside his door.

For a second, all time stood still.

"Hey, Jim, which glass is mine?" said the man who had been called Hank. Gunn heard two glasses clack together. They sounded like thunder and he nearly jumped out of his skin.

"Hell, how should I know, Parsons. You got hoof and mouth?"

Both names now, Gunn thought, but he was wondering why the man in the hallway hadn't moved. Gunn could hear his own heartbeat pounding in his eardrum like a crashing sea.

He heard a muffled voice, and the two men in the other room stopped their rustling. It was very quiet.

Gunn reached for the door, ready to hurl it open. Then he heard whispers and the pound of footsteps

87

coming toward him from the other room.

"Get him, Jim!" yelled Hank Parsons.

Gunn yanked the door open just as Jim Belker rushed into the room. He heard the cock of the man's pistol, turned for just a moment to catch a glimpse of his face.

In the hallway, just outside the door, stood a short, thick-bodied man. He had a double-barreled shotgun in his hands. The twin snouts, black as the sunken eyes of a snake, pointed straight at Gunn's belly.

The pistol exploded with a roar as Jim Belker fired pointblank at Gunn's head.

Chapter Seven

Gunn pitched forward, head low, neck bowed. He charged like a bull through the door as the bullet from Belker's big .44 Remington ripped into the frame, crushing wood into pulp, sending a shower of splinters flying in all directions. The short man with the double-barreled Greener pulled both triggers as Gunn plowed into him with the force of a charging bull. The man screamed as he was powered off his feet, driven backward five yards before his feet left the floor and he slammed to the carpet, still propelled by Gunn's terrible force.

The shotgun blasts tore chunks of plaster and wood from the ceiling overhead, raining debris and clouds of dust on Jim Belker as he reached the doorway, cocked his converted Remington for another shot at the fleeing Gunn.

"Stop, you redass sonofabitch!" Belker yelled, then choked on the dust, blinked as plaster, blown to powder, flew into his eyes. He fired blindly, heard the bullet thunk into flesh as a man screamed in mortal agony. "I got the bastard," he croaked, his throat full of dust. He staggered through the doorway, his shoulders white with plaster, rubbing his eyes.

Gunn took the corner flying, and hit the stair-rail

without stopping. He bounded down them, four at a time, and he kept running long after the shouts of the men he had left behind faded away. His ears felt as if someone had driven a rail spike through his skull. The explosions so close to him had made him deaf as a stone. He did not even hear the clerk shouting at him as he streaked across the lobby. He was out-gunned and crippled with excruciating pain. This was not the time to fight a losing battle on hostile ground. He halted outside, however, waited in a soundless world of agony as the long shadows of afternoon crawled the street, darkened the stares of curious passersby.

"Come on, you bastards," said Gunn softly. "Walk out that door."

Belker and Parsons looked at the stunted man on the floor. Blood coursed from a rip in his trouser leg, pooled up on the floor.

"Christ, I'm sorry, Mick," said Belker. "I was trying to put lead in that sonofabitch."

Parsons flapped his hands to clear away the smoke. He held a cold pistol in his hand, looked down the hall wild-eyed as a half-broke mustang. "He comes back here, I'll put his lamp out," he said.

The man called Mick winced, struggled to his feet. He drew a blade from a sheath on the back of his belt, reached down and lengthened the slit in his trousers. There was a long furrow on his left leg. The wound was turning blue along the crease. He turned around, saw the hole in the wall.

"I didn't stop the ball," he said tightly, "but I

slowed it down some."

"We'll get him, Mick," said Belker, nervously. "You'd better tend to that."

Mickey Gato withered Belker with a scorching look. He was the product of an Irish mother and an Apache father, born with the blood of bandits in his veins. He had been raised by the Chiricahuas, and men who knew him said he grew up just plain mean.

"You won't get him now," snapped Mick. "Know who that was?"

"A damned thief, that's what," said Hank Parsons. His pale skin contrasted sharply with the swarthy red-bronze flesh of Gato. He was rail-thin, muscular, with an Adam's apple that was sharp as a spear-point, seemed on the verge of breaking through his skin.

"That was Gunn. The one they was a-talkin' about down at the Roost."

"That was *him*?" Belker's mouth froze in surprise. He was a stocky man, unshaven, with hair sprouting from wide flat nostrils. His nose had been broken more than once and looked like a chunk of putty on his blunt hammerhead of a face.

"Damn," uttered Parsons, his Adam's apple rippling underneath the alabaster skin of his throat. "We'd better tell Owen."

Mick fixed him with a look of raw contempt, reached down for his emptied Greener. He picked it up, limped toward the rooms at the end of the hall.

"You do that, Parsons," he said. "You go out that door downstairs, see how long you last."

Parsons scampered after the short dark man. "Whatta ya mean, Mick?"

"Yeah," said Jim Belker, turning to follow, "that Gunn feller's done lit a shuck."

Gato kept moving, favoring his sore leg. "Bet your poke he's a-waitin' outside for you. This ain't the first I heard of Gunn. He raised hell down on the Brazos a while back, and I heard of him up in Bannack, down in Wyoming and Colorado. You ask some of the boys stayin' over at the boardin' house. They been talkin' about him."

"Hey," said Parsons, "is that the jasper what was at Black Mesa?"

"You bet your white ass it is, Parsons," said Gato, as he stepped through the debris in the doorway to the bunkroom. "I know me some Mimbres down south that still think he's bad medicine."

Parsons and Belker looked at each other. Belker swung the cylinder out on his Remington, ejected the hulls, and nervously stuffed two more beans in the wheel. He slammed the cylinder back snug under the barrel, followed after the two men.

"Hank, whatcha think?" he asked. "Reckon we ought to study this a while?"

"Damn right," replied Parsons. "I thought all that jawin' about Gunn was pure deep hogwash."

For a moment, Belker turned almost as pale as Parsons was naturally. The two men stood there as Gato sat on the edge of a bunk and cracked open the double-barreled shotgun. He fished two fresh shells from his pocket and shoved them into the chambers. He snapped the gun shut. The sound made the other two men twitch.

"What you aimin' to do, Mick?" asked Belker.

"Get me some water and some of that salve in my

kit," said the short half-breed. "I'm goin' to sit here a while and wait, in case this Gunn comes back."

"You think he will?" asked Parsons, his voice quavery as he looked back through the open doorway.

"No, but that man's just plumb full of surprises."

There was a silence between the men for several seconds. Then Belker cleared his throat. "If he don't come, then what?" he asked.

Gato looked at Belker as he would look at a beetle under his boot.

"Then I'm goin' to think about killin' him 'fore I go after him real serious, Belker."

"Jesus," said Belker. "I'll fetch you some water and a towel, Gato."

"I'll get your salve," added Parsons.

Neither of them wanted to look at the hate in Gato's eyes just then. They had seen that look before and knew that it meant someone was surely going to die damned soon.

Gunn waited a half hour. The pain in his ears subsided and his hearing returned. He saw lamps flicker on in some of the hotel windows across the street. Men streamed into the saloons, strolled down to the cafe at the end of the street. A man on a mule rode by, slapping its flanks with a worn leather quirt. Two painted women emerged from the hotel, walked into the saloon a few doors down.

Gunn walked back toward the Gallatin, peering into the faces of strangers with his slate-gray eyes. All of them looked away and stepped aside to let him pass. The racing blood that had surged hot through

93

his veins settled down, but the quivering in his gut remained. He had come close to buying a piece of the farm back there. But that wasn't what bothered him. By all rights, the short dark man should have just walked through the open door of the hotel room and gone about his business. But he hadn't. He alone had detected Gunn's presence. He looked like a half-breed Indian. Ute? No, not Arapaho either. Apache, maybe. Black hair, the squat face. Well, either the man had eyes that could look through walls or else he could hear a fly crawl across a wall. The man was uncanny. And dangerous.

Gunn went to his room, lay in the dark, thinking. He ought to check on Marylee and Tommy, but he didn't want to get tied up with them. He now knew the names of two men who might or might not be the killers he was looking for—and he had seen another of their bunch, the halfbreed. He needed to put a name to him as well.

There was a way to find out, if he was careful. In a town full of saloons, one of them had to be a watering hole for that bunch. The trick now was to find out which one and just keep his eyes and ears open.

Gunn arose from the bed, knowing if he stayed there, his weariness would drag him into the depths of sleep. He checked his knife and gunbelt, left the room. At the desk, he spoke to the nervous clerk.

"Anybody been asking for me?"

"Not for you. About you, just about everybody. And the marshal, he left this for you." The clerk reached down behind the counter and grabbed an envelope. He handed it to Gunn. It was light, thin.

Gunn folded it, put it in one of his back pockets.

"Where can a man get a drink and not be asked too many questions?"

"Ah, you might look into a saloon down Main here. Miners Roost, it's called. Pretty rough bunch goes in there, though. If you want quiet . . ."

"I had quiet," said Gunn. "Thanks. Miss Paxton asks for me, tell her I'll see her tomorrow."

"Yes sir," said the clerk, a note of respect in his tone. "Enjoy your evening."

Gunn smiled, flicked the brim of his hat in a farewell salute. He strode through the lobby, conscious of the lounging men whose stares tracked him to the door.

The saloon was the noisiest on the street. The hitchrail out front was packed with saddle horses and mules. The painted false front bore the legend: MINERS ROOST. There was a likeness of a buzzard perched on an ore bucket next to the name. Lamplight poured through the slanted slits in the batwing doors. Laughter and the clink of glasses, the fluttering snick of poker chips and the riffle of waxed cards floated outside on the air that spun out spools of blue smoke and the tangy scents of rye and beer and throat-burning whiskey.

Gunn slipped through the bat-wing doors, angled for the bar at the left side of the room. Men sat at tables, drinking, playing cards, talking, and they stood in clusters, joking, pouring the drinks down, slapping one another on the back. A pall of smoke hung over the main room, drifted up the stairway to the second floor. Lamps, brightly lit, hung on L-shaped trusses, away from the walls, high enough to cast their light downward and be out of the way of lurching drunks. Miners' tools decorated the walls, stuffed birds and animals sat perched on shelves: hawks, pheasants, grouse, prairie chickens, rabbits, a coyote, quail. The floor was littered with sawdust, soaked with spilled whiskey and beer. Glitter gals circulated through the room, sat on laps, cadging drinks, stroked men's whiskers, toyed with watch-chains and moustaches. Gunn took it all in with a single glance, wedged his way to a place at the bar.

Two bartenders were behind the long slab of thick pine, aproned like butchers, with their sleeves rolled up, armbands above the elbows. One of them stopped in the middle of his conversation, stepped up to the bar across from Gunn.

"Name your poison," he said.

"You got any whiskey that doesn't eat holes in a man's stomach?"

"You got the money and I hear it clink on the bar, we got Old Overholt, Gallatin's Straight."

"I'll have the Overholt," said Gunn, "a fresh bottle."

The bartender's eyebrows arched and his eyes narrowed. Gunn threw coin on the bar. The barkeep nodded, brought a glass and a new bottle of Overholt, grabbed up the money. He made a mark on the bottle with a piece chalk. "Two bits to the neck, two bits an inch," he said.

Gunn peeled away the seal, pulled the cork as he looked around. The men were farmers, mostly, a few miners and prospectors, cowhands, a mixed bag. A woman at a far table, dressed in a tight bodice, short, frilled skirt, a velvet band in her blond locks, looked at him, smiled coyly. Gunn stood a head taller than the other men lining the bar.

"Stranger, you look as out of place as a long-tailed cat in a room full o' rockin' chairs," said a voice behind him. Gunn turned, looked into the face of a grizzled old coot who sported a broken lip and a shiner the size of a silver dollar on one eye.

"Looks like you stood up when the man said 'shut up,' " said Gunn amiably.

"Wal, I got me into an argyment day or so ago and t'other feller won when I walked into his fist. Name's Quint, stranger. Gordie Quint, and I ain't seed your face in the Roost 'till just now. You got the look of a man lookin', but I don't see no badge. 'Course I didn't see no badge on that man, Smith, neither 'n I hear tell he was a U.S. marshal."

"I heard that too."

"Saw you at the livery after it happened. Wondered who you was. Feller says your name is Gunn."

"They call me that."

"None of my business."

"Here, pour yourself a drink, Quint. Maybe you're the man I've been looking for." Gunn slid the bottle across to a grateful Quint, watched as he poured with a shaking hand. He drank the shot quickly, never blinked an eye. Gunn drained half of his and saw through blurred eyes as the tears welled up, misted his vision. He told himself he wasn't as used to the hard stuff as Quint. The whiskey was genuine, though. It bit, but it smoothed out once the initial shock was over.

"I hope not, from the talk about you, Gunn."

"Just some questions."

"Mighty dangerous, sometimes, to ask questions in Gallatin."

"I figured that. You a miner?"

"Wished I was. Prospector. Made a poke up in Alder Gulch, keep looking for better ground. Bein' a miner ain't been too healthy lately, though."

"Maybe that's what I wanted to talk about," said Gunn.

"Yep, figgered so. You was up on Grasshopper crick and I heard tell about that, too. You done some good." Quint seemed to be on the square, thought Gunn. He could have been anywhere from 50 to 75, but his blue eyes sparkled with a lust for life and his beard was trimmed, the moustache neatly mantling a pudgy mouth. His skin was dark from being out in weather, the cheekbones rosy from wind and whiskey, the wrinkles deeply etched, peppered with blackheads.

"Have another drink, Quint. Too much bottle for just me."

"Why, thank ye, kindly, Gunn. Yair, we can talk, you keep your voice low and don't look to go-damighty serious about it. I got me some questions, too, but I don't ask after I seed what happened to a pard of mine last month."

"What was that?"

"Poor ol' Lee got robbed and kilt. Over on the Beaverhead. Had him a strike. Silver. Soon as he filed, they come and kilt him."

"Who?" asked Gunn.

"Called themselves vigilantes. Claimed Lee Moore,

98

sweetest guy ever lived, took his pleasure with some settler's woman in the Gallatin Valley. They come and got him, he put up a fight, and they run him through with a pig-sticker."

"Long, thin, knife—what they call an Arkansas toothpick?"

"Yep. They was four or five of 'em. Wore bandannas over their faces."

"You saw all this, Quint?"

"Most of it. Happened right fast."

"What about the mining claim?"

"I come over to Gallatin to check on it and that's why my face looks like someone's been chunkin' rocks at it."

"You'd better have another drink," said Gunn. Quint poured it, but didn't drink down as he had the others. Gunn wondered if Quint knew how helpful he had been. He had given Gunn still another set of details that might connect with those he already had. Here was an eyewitness who could put the vigilantes at a silver mine, connect them with a murder. Maybe the same bunch who killed the Paxton men and the Ransom family and hands. Were all the murders connected? Gunn had a hunch that they were. All he had to do was prove it. Right now he was working on hunches; strong ones, but only hunches nevertheless.

"Anyone know you saw your friend murdered?" Gunn asked as he took another sip of the whiskey. It went down smoother this time.

"Naw. I was in timber, opposite slope, tracking a deer when I heard all the commotion. I saw the men drag Lee out, heard them charge him with a crime. When he tried to get away, this big feller started

99

sticking him with that blade. Time I got down there, Lee was gone."

"You tell the marshal about it?"

"Nope. Couldn't prove nothin'. I buried Lee, come lookin' to see could I file on his claim. I got beat up just fer askin'. Went back to the mine and it was posted."

Gunn's eyes crackled with light, flared blue steel for a moment, then paled to a frosty gray, like polished pewter.

"Any name on the signs or posts?" he asked quickly.

"Gallatin Mining. Nothing new there. I seen them signs all over."

"Who owns it?"

"Near as I can tell, the same man who owns this saloon, and half the saloons and gambling halls in town. Think he owns a hotel, too."

"He got a name, Quint?" Gunn's voice was flat, cold as a chunk of iron.

"Yep. Owen Jamison. Big feller. Wears fancy clothes, boots polished so's you can see your puss in 'em."

Gunn felt the hackles rise on the back of his neck, goosebumps erupt on his arms. There it was again, and this time, a clear connection.

Owen Jamison. This was the man Paxton had grubstaked, taken on as a partner. Maybe this man was Paxton's killer. Now, Gunn thought, he had much more than a hunch.

Chapter Eight

Gunn stared into the bottom of his shot glass, swirled the dark amber liquid around, then drank it straight. He was getting a sinking feeling in the pit of his stomach. The letter to Paxton from Jamison was the most puzzling part of all. Or was it? The man had evidently found traces of silver, but said there was a problem with it. Could this be the same man Quint had told him about? How could a man with nothing, who had to borrow five thousand dollars as a stake, suddenly wind up owning half the saloons in town?

"A penny for your thoughts, Gunn," said Quint. "You seem mighty bound up in 'em."

"I was thinking of this Jamison. You ever see him?"

"He comes in here. I was lookin' for him. Seed him onc't, three, four days ago. Him and his bunch rode out of town 'fore I could stop him. Big feller, fancy duds."

"Which way was he going?"

"South, I reckon. About a dozen men with him."

"One of them a short little halfbreed?"

Quint paled visibly. He took another shot of whiskey. It didn't seem to affect him. He swabbed a paw across his mouth, leaned closer to Gunn. He looked around the room before he spoke.

"They call him Gato. He's one mean bastard. You stay clear of him, hear? He's a Apache er somethin'. Don't make no noise, got ears like a deer. He can slip up on you, blow your head off and that's all you'll hear."

"I know," said Gunn wryly.

"You know him?"

Gunn told him what had happened earlier. Quint shook his head in disbelief. "You were mighty lucky. Hank Parsons, Jim Belker and Gato. Plumb mean, ever' one. I heared tell that Gato kills for the fun of it."

"Why hasn't the law gotten him for murder?" Gunn asked.

"Witnesses. They die."

"I see," said Gunn. "Look, Quint, I want to talk to this Jamison. You think he'll come in here tonight?"

"Might be. He's got him a night woman, a house here in town. But he plays with that kitten over there what's been makin' eyes at you ever since you walked in here."

Gunn turned, and the same glitter gal he'd seen before smiled at him. He nodded to her. If a hand was dealt, he would play it out. As if reading his thoughts, she rose from her chair, patted the man she was with on the cheek, and strolled toward Gunn. He didn't stop looking at her as she wound her way through the tables, lithely avoiding the grasping hands, the pinching fingers.

She looked, Gunn thought, like a queen of Satan,

with her flaring hips, shapely legs, the large breasts tugging at her bodice like melons. Her dazzling smile promised warmth and affection. Her eyes sparkled with wickedness, and her body swayed capriciously, wickedly, provocative as a turned-down bed, inviting as sin itself.

Men turned their heads to watch her as she approached Gunn, and they muttered disconsolately when she passed them by. Quint leaned over so far to look at her, he nearly fell from his barstool and Gunn could feel his hot panting breath on the back of his neck. "Steady, Quint," he said.

"They don't call me 'Dirty Gordy' fer nothin'," he cracked.

The woman sidled up to Gunn, rubbed against his leg. It was unobtrusive to most, but Gunn could feel the heat of her through his trousers. She looked into his eyes, smiled without showing her teeth. She had a mole next to her dimple that seemed to wink at him.

"Hello there," she drawled, and her voice was soft, low-pitched, with a slight husk to it. "I don't believe we've met. I'm Angel. Short for Angelica. Angel Norris. And who might you be?"

"They call me Gunn."

"Sounds familiar. You work for Owen?"

"No. Like to meet the man though."

"Well, maybe you will. Would you like to buy a thirsty gal a drink?"

"You want what's in my bottle?"

"Oh, no. Angel only drinks champagne. Expensive champagne." She rubbed Gunn's leg with hers, seemed to melt against him. When he looked down at her, he could see the dark crease between her breasts.

103

The breasts were like melons, creamy smooth, well-rounded, and seemed on the verge of bursting over the rim of her wired bodice.

"I can stand you a drink or two. Have a seat? You know Gordon Quint here?"

"Dirty Gordy? I should say." She laughed and the laugh was not forced but bright and ribbony, going up and down the scale like melody. Gunn stepped aside, pulled an empty stool up, shoved it next to Quint. He helped her up, surprised at her lightness, the slimness of her waist. She looked to be about twenty-five, no deep wrinkles around her mouth or eyes, a button nose, full lips, slightly uneven teeth that made her no less attractive.

Gunn called the bartender over, ordered. "Champagne for the lady," he said, reaching into his pocket for some paper money. He lay the bills on the counter until the barkeep stopped glaring at him. He turned to Angel.

"You don't appear to be the usual dance hall gal," he said.

"That's what they all say. Gunn. Umm, I like your name. It sounds so—so rugged and manly. No, I don't dance much. I run the place for Owen. He likes me to meet everyone, be nice to the men. Not too nice, just nice enough."

"I didn't mean . . ."

She laughed again and he marveled at the genuineness of it. Gordon couldn't take his eyes off the woman's breasts. He seemed about to pounce on her, gobble them up. Gunn poured himself a half-shot as the bartender served a large glass full of champagne to Angel. He took a dollar bill from the stack and never cracked a smile, even though Gunn smiled politely at him.

"I know what you meant," she said. "I take it as a compliment. Owen doesn't tell me what to do. I staked him about a year ago and he offered me a partnership in this place. I was a widow and lonesome for people, so it's worked out."

"How long ago did you become a partner?" Gunn asked.

"Oh, let's see now. Must be three months."

"Interesting," said Gunn, casually.

"What, me, or my sad story?"

"Both," he laughed.

A man entered the saloon, looked around, saw Angel and beckoned to her. "Excuse me," she said, sliding off the stool. Gunn watched as she walked to the door. Her hips didn't sway this time. She walked in a straight line. The two stepped outside and he could not hear their voices over the din.

"Purty nice filly," said Quint. "But you ought to see the woman Jamison keeps to his home."

"He's not married, then?"

"Nope. But Julie Novack is even purtier'n Angel there. Don't come into town much."

"Where's Jamison's place?"

"Northeast, 'bout two mile out. He's got him some cattle out there, raises some crops I hear. Maybe it ain't his place, come to think of it. Julie Novack's a widder woman. Jamison cuts a wide swath, I hear tell."

"Yeah, I think so," said Gunn.

Angel returned alone, and she was long-faced until she saw Gunn, then she brightened, flashed him a

105

wide smile.

"Bad news?" asked Gunn.

"Not really. Owen sent a message by that he won't be in tonight. Something came up and he'll be gone a few days."

Gunn stiffened slightly. A distant warning bell clanged in his brain. "Sorry," he said. "I was hoping to meet up with him. Anything serious?"

"I don't know," she said, pensively. "Could be. Unlike him to send someone else." She sighed deeply, then brightened. "Hey, we need some music in here. Harry," she said to the barkeep, "get Dave and have him play that pianner. We need some life in here."

Gunn detected an undercurrent of sadness in Angel's tone, a false gaiety about her as she tossed her head, fluffed her blond locks. The smile she pasted on was as phony as a forty-nine cent piece. He wondered at the change in her. Was she in love with Jamison? Probably. But if so, how did she tolerate his living with another woman, a woman he was not married to, who was also beautiful?

Women were often a puzzle to him. Just when he thought he knew one well, she would surprise him. Long ago he had come to realize that women were not easily labeled, like men. There was a lot of good in the bad ones, and a lot of bad in the good ones. When Laurie was alive, he thought all women were pure and sweet and loving. Since her death, he had met all kinds, but he still did not know any more about them now than he did back then. He had long since given up making comparisons. Each woman he met was unlike any other, and he knew he would have to accept or reject each on her own terms.

He offered to buy Angel another champagne, but she'd had enough drink for one night. He was glad when she shook her head as the piano player began pounding out a lively tune. "Not now," she said, sweetly, "but if you come back later, about closing time . . . I have quarters upstairs. I'd like to talk to you—alone. Just the two of us, Gunn. Mmmm, how about it?"

Her voice was so soft he had to strain to hear, but he heard her words and was once again dumbfounded. She emphasized them by gripping his arm, just above the wrist and squeezing him. There was a sensual urgency in the pressure of her hand that made him giddy. She said goodbye to Quint and slipped away to mingle with the crowd. Just before she left, though, she had touched his arm at the elbow and given it a tight squeeze. Gunn felt all hollowed out inside, confused. But the heat of her touch still lingered on his arm.

"Quint, I'll be saying *adios* myself. Been good talking to you. Much obliged for the information."

"I'll be around, Gunn. I'm stayin' at the boarding house, you want me."

"Same place where Barnett, I mean Smith, stayed?"

"That's the place. Missus Jennings' boardin' house."

Gunn paid for the rest of the bottle, left it for Quint. He had a hunch he wanted to follow up. A couple of hunches, in fact. He strode to the batwings, turned once more to look for Angel. She saw him. He nodded, saw her nod slightly as he touched a finger to his hat. A look passed between them and it was like her touch on his arm, slight, but warm and compelling. Angel, for whatever else she was, was a woman, and that, in itself, made her mysterious and desirable.

Be careful, he said to himself as he pushed through the batwings.

Owen Jamison looked at the hotel register the clerk handed him. He didn't recognize the handwriting, but he knew damned well that a dead man couldn't sign his name. He did know Ed Paxton's signature, and this one wasn't even close.

"Saw him run out of here like the devil was after him, Mr. Jamison. Far as I know he never did use his room. Well, you saw it. Nothing in it."

"No. He didn't go there."

The clerk swallowed nervously, continued his account of the incident. "After we heard the shooting upstairs, this man come pounding down the stairs three or four steps at a time. Before I could say 'Jack Robinson,' he was gone. Then I up and went upstairs, talked to Mr. Parsons and Mr. Belker. They told me that this jasper tried to rob them."

"You get a good look at him, Bob?"

"Sure did. When he checked in I saw him real plain. Tall, on the lean side, square-jawed. He had kinda wide shoulders, straight and level. I ain't likely gonna forget his eyes. Real pale and gray, almost, like smoke. He was packin' iron, had a Colt on his hip. Had a fancy knife, too, an eagle's head handle, brass and bone or something inlaid in it. Didn't have no saddlebags er nothin'. I guess he was a robber all right."

"Yeah," said Jamison. "I reckon so. You keep an eye out for him in case he comes back here, will you, Newsome? You see him, anywhere, you come tell me. I want to know straight off."

"I'll do that, Mr. Jamison."

Jamison gave Bob Newsome a five dollar gold piece, walked back up the stairs to his hotel rooms at the end of the hall. He did not hurry, but walked slowly, thinking, mulling over in his mind the things that had happened. After Belker and Parsons had told him about the stranger being in his rooms, he had thought to check with the hotel clerk. It was a stroke of good luck that the man had checked in, paid for a room. But he hadn't brought back his key and he hadn't stayed there. The bed was unmussed, and the water pitcher full, the bowl and chamber pot were both dry, unused. So obviously, he had come just to snoop around.

Signing Paxton's name to the hotel's guest book was downright arrogant. The sonofabitch.

Jamison was a sturdy man, just under six feet tall. He had one leg that was shorter than the other, but few knew this. He had his boots custom-made, one with a sole and heel slightly thicker than the other so he wouldn't walk with a limp. He had a mane of wheat-colored hair that swept back from his broad forehead, curled upward just above his shoulders in back. His eyes were blue as cornflowers, set wide under craggy, bushy brows, straddling a large nose that brooded over thick, slightly pudgy lips.

He extracted a cigar from his inside coat pocket, stuck it in his mouth. He twirled it slowly with his lips, moistened the end, savoring the strong aroma of fresh tobacco in his nostrils. His suit was made of dark worsted wool, tailored to fit his sturdy frame. He wore a nickel-plated .38 made by Smith & Wesson, cross-draw rigged, on his left hip. The coat draped over the pistol, concealed it perfectly.

He knocked on the door of his room. Belker opened it. "Put away that gun, Belker," snapped Jamison. "You don't think the bastard's going to walk in here again, do you?"

Belker sheepishly put his pistol back in its holster.

"No, I reckon not," he said sullenly. He was still smarting that he had missed the stranger, hit Mickey Gato instead.

"Get Parsons and Gato in here. We got to palaver."

"I'll get 'em, Owen."

Jamison sat down on the divan, searched for a match in his vest pockets. He found one, struck it and the acrid smell of sulphur filled the air. He lit his cigar, puffed it to a glow and belched plumes of smoke from his mouth. Gato limped into the room, followed by Parsons and Belker.

"Take a seat," said Jamison. "Jim, pour us all a drink. Rye for me."

Belker poured the drinks. Jamison opened his coat, threw an arm over the back of the divan, drank his rye neat and dragged on his cigar. The others drank. Parsons rolled a smoke. Gato just looked at Jamison with glittering agate eyes.

"Well, we know that bastard called Gunn was here. He knew where to come and he had a damned key. He didn't break in, he just walked in. I want to know how and why."

There was a silence in the room. The silence got thicker and deeper. Then Parsons cleared his throat. Belker tapped a fingernail against his glass. Gato moved his sore leg, dragging his bootheel across the rug.

"Hank?" said Jamison. "You have any idea?"

Hank Parsons tried to find a place to look where he wouldn't have to see Jamison's accusing stare. He tried the ceiling, the wall, the floor. Finally, he cleared his throat again and looked off at the print hanging on the wall just above Jamison's left shoulder.

"Well, sir, near as I can figger, somewhere I lost my damned key. Warn't here when we got back from Ransoms and I looked ever'where for it."

"You dumb bastard. You lose anything else?"

"Uh, well, yeah. My vigilante badge."

"So he's probably got that, too."

Parsons nodded. The two other men looked at him as if he had suddenly grown goat's horns out of his skull. Hank squirmed and fidgeted in the silence that welled up in the room again like a smothering presence.

Jamison dragged hard on the cigar, expelled a plume of smoke in Parson's direction. His eyes seemed to pulse like glowing blue coals as he stared at the man. He looked at Belker and at Gato. All three were good men. He had chosen them carefully. The others in his bunch were not so special. They took orders as long as they were paid, and they had a liking for adventure. That was about all he could say for them. But these three, they were a different matter. Each had a talent he could use and yet, Parsons was the weakest link in the small chain he had forged.

Belker was a man with nerves of iron. He also knew powder and had once worked with a mining engineer. He could blow a hole in the side of a mountain and do a quick assay on the spot that turned out to be pretty accurate. He could swing a pick and lay to with a shovel as good as any man. He was a damned good shot, and he could draw a pistol with blinding speed.

Parsons was more of a thinker, a watcher. He had some background in geology and was good at digging up information. It was he who dug through claims, checked with assay offices, and figured out which mines were richer in ore. He was slightly absentminded, and careless, but was invaluable to Jamison's plans.

Mickey Gato was a tracker, and he could read the earth like a book. He was able to pick out rock formations that were elusive to the others, lead them there over the best ground, the fastest way. He was also a cold-blooded killer and Jamison liked that. Jamison himself had no compunction about killing, in fact, enjoyed it. He liked to do it close up, see the victim's face as he died. His favorite weapon was the knife, and he wore a scabbard that nestled next to his spine. In the scabbard was a long, thin-bladed knife known as an "Arkansas toothpick."

"Well, we know now that Gunn is going to be a chicken bone in our throats if we don't rid of him," said Jamison. "All I've heard of him, and I don't know if any of it's true or not, means he's not going to be easy. I don't want to lose any men. We're just about to get out of the vigilante business and make some big money."

"You got some idea what we're gonna do, Owen?"

112

asked Belker.

"I've been thinking about it. Gunn's in town, and the marshal's probably gone out to the Ransom place. We've got to clear both of those situations up. Hank, you go ahead and file on that claim out there. We'll worry about the legalities later. Meantime we've got the other claims we jumped taken care of, I think.

"Jim, you and Mick, take care of Gunn. I'm going to round up some of the boys and waylay Lescoulie on his way back to Gallatin."

"I want Gunn," said Gato. "I don't need Belker."

"All right, Mick. That O.K. with you, Jim?"

"I almost had him. He was lucky. I'll back Mick if he wants or I'll help you with Lescoulie. I don't have any damned use for either bastard."

Jamison smiled.

"No, I think you'll have to take care of Paxton's kid and that Indian boy."

"Kill 'em?"

"No, that'd stir up too much of a fuss," said Jamison. "You get 'em, hide 'em out until I get back from taking care of Lescoulie. They'll just disappear and it won't raise no stink. Another thing—if Gato can't get Gunn right off, we'll use the kids as aces."

"Sounds smart to me," said Belker.

"Damned smart," added Parsons.

"I won't miss Gunn," said Gato, and his face turned dark as a thundercloud.

Jamison smiled thinly.

He knew Gato. The half-breed was at his best when he was stalking his prey. He made no noise and he almost never missed. Gunn was as good as dead.

"All right. Stay out of the Roost tonight. I'll tell

113

Angel we won't be in. We'll take the rest of the boys on this. They ought to be waiting for us by the time we ride by the boarding house. Gato, I want Gunn out of the way by the time I get back."

"He's wolf meat," said Gato, his voice cold as a tombstone.

Hank Parsons shuddered. Belker's mouth went dry suddenly. Jamison sighed and his eyes shone like blue flames.

Yes, Gunn was as good as dead.

Chapter Nine

Gunn went to the livery stable. There was a new man on, half-asleep. A boot in his side aroused him.

"I want that Tennessee Walker saddled in five minutes. Put the rifle scabbard on, cinch him up tight, but room enough to put your hand between the strap and his belly."

"Yes, sir," said the man, who was in his fifties, at least, slightly bent from a bad back. "Be four bits."

Gunn paid him, strode out, headed for Foster House. He hurried, avoiding the splash of lamp and lantern light, his hat pulled low, the brim shading his face. He took up a position opposite the hotel, stood in the shadowy space between two buildings, motionless.

A man stepped out of the hotel lobby, stood by the front window while he rolled a cigarette. He struck a match and his face lighted up for a moment. Gunn smiled thinly. This was the man who had come to the Miners Roost with the message for Angel. The man threw the burnt match onto the street, walked slowly along the boardwalk, back toward Main Street. Gunn didn't know the man, but he had a hunch that he'd find him at the boarding house later.

A few moments passed before two more men emerged from the hotel. Gunn recognized one of them as the man who had shot at him. Jim Belker. The other was a man he did not know by sight, but his instincts told him that this was Owen Jamison. The two men stood there, silhouetted by the light spilling through the front window. The man with Belker was tall, solidly built, wearing a gray suit, a Stetson hat. Soon they were joined by two more men. Gato, he recognized. He took the other man to be Hank Parsons. He studied his face carefully.

Gato wore a dark duster which flared at one leg. Gunn figured he had his shotgun underneath the duster, hanging from his shoulder by a sling. Parsons and Belker were visibly armed. All but Parsons wore spurs. The four men spoke in low tines. Then Parsons went back inside the hotel while Gato walked to the hitchrail and climbed aboard a small, stocky pony. He rode off toward Front Street.

Belker and the man Gunn believed to be Jamison spoke together a few more moments, then stepped off the boardwalk. Jamison climbed onto the saddle of a tall, maybe 16 hands high, black gelding. Belker went to another horse, but the men appeared to be arguing. They raised their voices so that Gunn could hear them from across the street.

"I damned sure don't trust that breed," said Belker. "I ought to stay here and make sure."

"You'll just get in his hair, Jim. Better come with me. We don't have a hell of a lot of time."

"Aw, Owen, it'll take Jake a whole damn hour to get those boys at the boarding house ready to ride," snapped Belker. "That goddamned breed is gonna need a gun to back him up."

"Let me worry about that. You know what I want. You get those people out of the way, you can see if Gato needs any help. For now, you get on over to the Gallatin and take care of that business."

"Well, I don't like it much, Jamison, but you're the boss."

Gunn had heard enough. Jake, he gathered, was the messenger, and the rest of the bunch was staying at the boarding house. If he didn't brace Jamison now, there'd never be a better time. Besides, he had a sinking feeling that Belker was going to kill Marylee and Tommy. That had to be the only one reason Jamison had ordered him to the Gallatin Hotel.

Gunn started to step out of his hiding place between the two buildings when something made him pause. He looked down the street. A shadow, something moving, had caught his eye. He looked at the place where Gato should have been, still riding his pony, and the man wasn't there. The pony stood in front of a dark storefront, reins dangling.

There was no sign of the halfbreed.

Belker climbed up into the saddle, looked down the street at the same time. "Now, what d'ya suppose happened to Gato?" he said. Jamison turned in his saddle, looked down at the riderless pony.

"Let's get the hell out of here," Owen shouted, clapping spurs to his horse.

"It's got to be Gunn!" yelled Belker, and drew his pistol.

Gunn stepped out onto the boardwalk, drew his pistol.

"Hold on," he said, and went into a fighting crouch. Belker saw him and cracked off a shot. An orange blaze, a puff of white smoke belched from the barrel of his pistol. Then he slid sideways, concealing himself along the horse's neck. Gunn tried to find a target. The two men rode in opposite directions. Belker's bullet notched a corner of the building near Gunn's head.

In a moment, the two men were gone, out of pistol range. Gunn holstered his pistol, started to walk away, when he heard a sound behind him. He turned, looked down the dim tunnel between the two buildings then threw himself headlong onto the boardwalk. Twin explosions rocked the silence, shattered the dark with orange fire. A hail of lead whistled over Gunn's head, rattled on the wood of the buildings across the street. The hotel window shattered with striking shot and panes of glass tinkled like wind chimes as they fell.

Gunn rolled off the boardwalk, clawed for his pistol. He heard the snap of the shotgun as Gato cracked it open. Gunn drew, twisted for a shot. He fired straight down the space between the two buildings, holding belt high on the target he imagined still to be there. The flash from his pistol illuminated the darkness. There was no one there, and he didn't hear the closing snap of the shotgun.

Quickly, Gunn got to his feet. He ran a zigzag pattern to the other side of the street, raced between a saloon and an empty pawn shop, stood just off the boardwalk, waiting. His eyes scanned the other side of the street. His gaze lingered on every opening, every blob of shadow.

Where was Gato? His senses shrieked to pick up any sound, any movement, a footfall, the scrape of a boot on wood or dirt, the creak of leather, the clank of metal. Voices poured from the hotel, voices of men under strain, angry voices full of fear and puzzlement. Gunn edged backward, away from the street. He would lose his perspective, but there had been time for Gato to come at him from another direction. Gato could pin him down here for hours. Innocent bystanders could be in the way.

Somehow, he had to get to the Gallatin before Belker did. A sinking, queasy feeling began to settle in Gunn's stomach. He flattened himself against the sidewall of the barber shop, began to creep toward the back alley. His one chance was to put real estate between him and Gato, get over to the hotel before Belker did any harm.

He was halfway along the wall, when he heard a boot scrape. The ensuing silence screamed in his ears. Where was it? Where in hell was Gato? The sound had seemed to come from the alley. If he went that way, he would be cut off, perhaps killed. If he made a mistake, Gato might be waiting for him on Front Street. There would be no place to run, no place to hide.

The sound could have been anything. Now that it was gone, his mind warped it, twisted it all out of shape so that he could no longer distinguish truth from something made up by his own imagination. Was it a boot scraping in the dirt, or a dog rubbing against the side of a building? A cat rustling through garbage? Something smaller, or bigger.

Gunn looked both ways, listened. He hugged the

wall, made himself as flat as possible. The Apache was good. He moved fast and he had eyes like an eagle. Somehow, he had spotted Gunn from across the street. Uncanny. Unless you knew that a man close to the earth, to nature, could detect sounds, see movement, far more keenly than a man raised in civilized society. Gato, it appeared, was a hunter, closely attuned to his total environment, and he alone had seen Gunn, made his stalk as quiet as a wraith.

Gunn knew that even such a man as Gato could not see in total darkness. He could hear. He could detect movement. He could see better than most men, perhaps, but if a man in darkness held totally still, if he did not move a single muscle, nor twitch an eyelash, then even a man such as Gato could not see him.

Gunn became part of the wall. He became night and shadow and wood. He suppressed his breathing to a slow, even, noiseless inhalation and exhalation. He set his mind apart from his body, frozen to the wall like paint.

Every sound became magnified. He heard the anxious voices issuing from the hotel, footsteps crisscrossing the street a few yards away. He heard the far-off whicker of a horse, the disembodied laughter from a saloon. He strained to hear the in-between sounds, the meaningless shuffle that could mean a stalking man, the random creak or rustle that could signify leather or cloth in secretive motion. No moving man could be completely silent. A man made sound. It was up to his ears to hear, to his senses to define.

He heard *something*.

The faint whick-flap of strained leather in the back alley. The whisper of cloth sliding along wood. The soft tap of a boot toe settling onto the ground. The small crunch of sand underfoot. He heard these disconnected noises and put them together in his mind. When it went completely silent, he held his breath, imagined himself to be stone or wood, an invisible part of the night itself.

He could not see, could not move his head, but Gunn sensed the presence of a man nearby, at the end of the narrow corridor between the two buildings. He could almost hear the man's pulse, his heartbeat, and he knew Gato was there, looking hard, looking straight at him. Gunn held his breath until he feared his lungs would burst, or he would sink into unconsciousness. At any moment, he expected the roar of the shotgun, the flash of exploding flame, then the final darkness as his life was ripped from him with a sudden blasting wind laden with lethal buckshot. He ached to draw and go into a crouch and call the final shot on his terms. He wanted to go down fighting, kill the man who killed him.

The silence stretched to an interminable, unbearable length. And in the silence he saw his own mortality. He saw how vulnerable he was and cursed himself for being so foolish as to think he could trick the stalking killer's eyes, could fool Gato into blindness. His lungs burned with the trapped air, swelled against his shirt until he thought they might explode.

Gunn held on a minute later.

In that terrible moment, he heard the softest shift of weight, the reluctant step of a man backing away, turning, perhaps. The waiting was agony. His brain, starved for oxygen, began to bend reason, to choke up his senses, to blot out thought like a towel smearing inky words, soaking them up into jumbled fragments, wiping them away into meaningless gibberish.

Still, he held on.

Another moment passed, and Gunn felt his knees go weak, felt the strength in his sinew and bone drain away. He fought against giving in, letting his body go limp, expelling the dead hurting air in one blessed rush of relief. There was another sound and his senses sprang to life. He knew there was no one at the end of the corridor anymore. Gato was gone, creeping along the alley, moving faster now, not so quiet as before.

Gunn let his breath out slowly, felt the searing ache in his lungs subside. Still, he hugged the wall, and when he inhaled, he drew the breath in slowly, shallowly. He regained his composure a piece at a time, and when he was sure, he turned his head, so slowly it took several moments, and looked toward the alley, his heart pounding hard, beating a tom-tom at his temples. It was like hearing the deer come in, the panic of waiting for the shot. Buck fever. Only now it was his life on the line. He knew what it was to be hunted, to know that a gun was pointed at him.

The sounds in the alley faded away, and Gunn stepped away from the wall, his back suddenly a mass of throbbing muscles. He had a decision to make. He had no idea how much time had passed. A few seconds, several minutes? More? It had seemed like an eternity to him, standing there, waiting for the last sound he would ever hear. Yet he was calm now. He had passed through that agonizing moment in eternity. It was time to take command, to outwit Gato, kill him if possible, and get out of this nerve-wracking game of hide-and-seek.

Gunn hunched low, crabbed along the wall, back to the street. He looked out, both ways, saw a few gawkers rubbernecking from the hotel. Down the street, Gato's pony still stood there, hipshot. Gunn drew his pistol, cocked it, took careful aim and fired. The bullet spanged the dirt just behind the pony's rear hooves, stinging its legs with a spray of grit. The pony lurched, broke into a run, its reins dangling, mane flying. It galloped to the end of the street and turned left as Gunn sent another shot into the ground behind it.

Gunn raced along the boardwalk, past the hotel, in the opposite direction. He reached the end of the row of buildings on the block, ducked alongside, panting for breath. He quickly ejected the two hulls, shoved two loads into the cylinder. He holstered his weapon and waited. He stuck his head out, looked around the corner.

A small figure in a duster emerged from between two buildings down the street. He heard a savage Apache curse, then Gato disappeared again. Gunn breathed deeply, regained his calm.

He had won this round, but he knew it would not be so easy the next time.

Carefully, Gunn crept alongside the building, crossed the alley, reached the next street. The buildings were dark here, and he took advantage of their cover, as he crossed the street, passed between buildings and slowly edged his way toward the Gallatin Hotel. He gave Gato a quarter hour to a half hour to catch up his runaway horse. Not much time, he knew, but it was the best he could do under the circumstances. He came up behind the Gallatin, entered a hallway where a candle lantern flickered dimly.

He took the stairs two at a time, reached Marylee's room. The door was slightly ajar. Gunn waited outside for a few moments, listening. There were no sounds from inside. He drew his pistol, entered the room cautiously. A single lamp fluttered as its flame burned low. The room was empty. Gunn's stomach churned, boiled with a sickening bile that rose up in his throat.

A chair was overturned, a satchel lay in one corner, its contents strewn in disarray. The bedclothes were roiled. The coverlet was missing. Not much of a struggle, but enough to tell him that Marylee and Tommy had not gone willingly with Belker. He must have threatened them with his pistol to get them to leave. He saw no bloodstains, so perhaps they were not hurt.

He cursed under his breath. Jamison had won this round, and if Gunn didn't find the pair of captives, he would lose the whole match. He looked through the material that had been in the satchel, found a money pouch, the papers she had showed him before. He gathered them up, replaced them inside the carpetbag. He left the pile of clothes where they were, left the room. He walked down the hall to his own room, found the key and unlocked the door. It was dark as he made his way to the lamp. He struck a match, lifted the chimney, turned up the wick. The flame caught and light spilled into the room. It was untouched, as he figured. He dropped the carpetbag at his feet.

He sat in a chair, rubbed his forehead in thought. Belker would take the kids somewhere, he knew. But where? He had some ideas, but none of them seemed likely. He would not go back to Foster House. He might have a hideout somewhere. Belker could be almost anywhere. It seemed to Gunn that he would hole up somewhere to guard them. He would need supplies, someone to guard them. That narrowed down the possibilities considerably.

He arose from his chair, opened the closet. He grabbed up his saddlebags and rifle. He picked up the carpetbag, left the room. He did not lock it. He would not be back. Downstairs, he checked the satchel at the desk, asking the clerk to keep it in the safe. He paid a week's rent on Marylee's room, checked out of his own.

"Did you see Miss Paxton and the boy leave?" he asked the clerk.

"No. I thought they were in their room."

"Have you been here all along?"

"No, I left to run an errand for Mr. Belker."

"Belker? You take orders from him?"

"I do. I understand that they come from Mr. Jamison. I work for Mr. Jamison. He owns this hotel. Partnership."

"Who's the other partner?" asked Gunn.

"Why, the wid—I mean, Mrs. Novack."

"Julie Novack?"

"That's right. Sir, I don't see that any of this is—"

"Mister," said Gunn, "don't say another goddamned word, or I'll crack your jaw wide open."

The clerk gulped, backed away from the desk.

"See that you hold onto that carpetbag," said Gunn. He slung his saddlebags over his shoulder, stalked from the lobby to the street. He headed for the livery stable, boiling mad inside.

He was halfway there when the sound of hoofbeats stopped him in his tracks. He turned, looked down the street. Coming at him full gallop was Gato, astride his pony. As Gunn watched, he slid over the side, Apache-style, and Gunn saw the snout of the Greener come up, take aim.

The pony chewed up the distance, fleet as a deer. Gunn saw the horse and rider grow larger as they pounded toward him. He was caught in the open and there was no time to think.

There was no time even to say a final prayer.

Chapter Ten

Sometimes a man makes a decision in a split-second that alters his fate for eternity. In that temporal, fleeting fraction of a moment in a man's brief life, life sometimes teeters on one edge of the fulcrum, death on the other. And how a man lives often determines how he dies.

Gunn had faced such decisions before. He had faced death, as well. This time, however, he was caught out in the open, without warning, and Gato was shaving the time down to zero. Gunn could almost feel the man's fingers tightening on the triggers of the double-barrel. At this range, the buckshot would spray a pattern of deadly lead five or six feet wide, six feet deep.

Still the man came on, sure of his target, certain of his unwitting prey. Gunn had no time to drop the saddlebags and rifle, draw his pistol and fire. His rifle had no round in the chamber. His Colt was a hundred miles away, buried in the mud of dwindling fractions of seconds. Time was the enemy as much as Gato was. Time had run out and it was either face death bravely or succumb to a final fear that would lock him in his tomb without his having fought valiantly for his own life.

Gunn thought fast, but something snapped in his mind. He remembered in a blinding flash something he had done in the war. It came back to him now as he looked at the onrushing horse and rider, saw the deadly shotgun loom larger and larger. He dropped his rifle and started running as he reached for the saddlebags over his shoulder. He ran straight toward the charging horse, swinging the saddlebags around and around over his head.

He hurled the saddlebags straight at the shotgun, then dove headlong at the charging pony. He hit in a skidding slide and rolled to the right. The shotgun boomed as he heard the *whup* of the leather saddlebags as they slapped the barrels head-on. The pony swerved to avoid him and Gunn clawed for his Colt as he rolled, bounced to a squatting position.

The saddlebags took the full brunt of the shot charge and flew high in the air. Gato, his grip loosened as the horse swerved sideways, struggled to hang on. His Greener tumbled from his grasp, hit the street butt-first, bounced crazily end over end until it slammed into a watering trough next to the board-walk. Gato tugged on his saddlehorn, pulled himself into the saddle.

Gunn cocked his .45, fired off-hand at Gato. The bullet went wild, knocking shingles from an overhung roof. Gato, regaining control over his pony, dug his spurs in, slumped over the saddle, reined the animal into a zigzag motion. Gunn fired again, and the bullet smashed into the cantle, ripping wood and leather to shreds as it ground its way through. The smashed ball smacked into Gato's buttock and he screamed in pain. Blood soaked onto the saddle, but the bullet, half-spent did not break bone nor penetrate deeply.

Gunn rose to his feet, took aim again, but the horse and rider turned the corner and disappeared from sight. Angrily, he flipped open the gate, spun the cylinder of his .45 and worked the ejection rod to kick out the empty hulls. He replaced them with fresh bullets, holstered his pistol. He walked back to his rifle, picked it up, rubbed the dust off the barrel. His saddlebags, riddled with double ought buckshot lay in the center of the street opposite the livery stable. He picked them up, heard the loose shot rattle. The leather thongs that stitched them together were intact. He shouldered them, walked warily over to the fallen shotgun. He picked it up by the barrels and smashed the stock to splinters on the water trough. Then he dropped the Greener into the trough. He strode to the stable, dusting himself off. He saw no further sign of Gato.

The liveryman cowered in a corner, shaking like a wet dog.

"Y—your horse is ready, Mister," he stammered. "I hope like hell you're going to ride him clear out of town."

Gunn laughed.

"I aim to do just that," he said.

The sign said: MRS. JENNINGS' BOARDING HOUSE. It was painted white, with a brown scroll border, letters in black. Gunn rode close to it to make sure he was at the right place, then circled the house to see if it was being watched. It was a large, two-story frame building on the corner, with a field surrounding it. There was a chicken house, a corral, a large stable, tack room, and in a far corner, pigs snorted at his presence. They were penned up in a large enclosure that connected to another, smaller field.

Gunn tied Esquire to a tree a block away, fed him a handful of oats to keep him quiet. He walked carefully to the boarding house. The house was dark except for a single lamp burning in a downstairs window. A picket fence enclosed the front and back yard. A stairway on the side led to the upstairs. He opened the gate, walked up the path to the porch. He tiptoed onto the porch, stood in shadows. He knocked discreetly, stepped aside to wait. He saw the wavering flame of a candle as someone came toward the front door.

"Who is it?" called a female voice.

"The name's Gunn, ma'am. Need to talk to you."

"Just a minute." He heard the latch rattle, the tumblers click on the lock as she inserted the key and twisted it. The door opened a crack. "I have one room, but it's very late."

"I'd like to see it, if you please, ma'am."

He heard a sigh. The door swung open.

"Very well. Please come in."

He stepped inside. She pulled the door shut behind him, locked it. "The boarders enter by the upstairs door. I keep my downstairs doors locked after nine o'clock of an evening," she said. She held the candle up close to his face, scoured him as she examined his features. He felt the warmth on his skin as he looked at her, unable to turn away. She almost took his breath away.

"I'm Lenore Jennings," she said, taking the candle away from his face. She was tall. Even in her bare feet she came to his shoulders. Her eyes were hazel, green and brown and gold. The flecks of color danced in the candlelight, like motes of fine dust swimming in sunlight. Her russet hair swept back from her face revealed high cheekbones, a patrician nose, full, sensuous lips framed by womanly dimples. She appeared to be in her late twenties and the robe she wore over her lacy nightgown did little to conceal the perfect swell of her breasts, the graceful curves of her hips, or the slender legs and trim ankles that flashed below her hem as she walked down the corridor.

She opened a door to a parlor, just off the passageway, walked to a table. She lit a taper from the candle, rattled the chimney of an ornate lamp with a painted glass shade. The lampwick glowed, flared into flame.

"Will you have a chair, Mister . . . Gunn, was it?"

Gunn took off his hat, sat in a spindly chair with a straight back. He felt like a schoolboy called before the teacher for discipline. Mrs. Jennings, if that was she, laughed and beckoned to him.

"I think you'll find this one more comfortable," she said, pointing to a large leather rocker that sat in a corner glistening in the shadows.

"Yes," he said. "Mighty obliged, ma'am."

"You are Mister Gunn, then."

"Yes'm. Just Gunn. And would you be the Mrs. Jennings who owns this place — or her daughter?" He saw the rows of books on the shelves as she turned her back on him. They were leather-bound and looked both expensive and well-read.

Lenore laughed. Her laughter was low and throaty, sensual. She sat in a loveseat next to a small desk, and the lamplight was becoming to her. It glimmered on her soft auburn hair, turning it to rust-gold, and played with the shadows of her lips, giving her a look of infinite mystery. When she crossed her legs, her robe fell open slightly, and Gunn saw the curve of her breasts, the long planes of her legs, the slender, delicate ankles. He wondered that she wore no shoes. The bare feet served to give her a bewildering look of earthiness and sensuality that was overwhelming. He smelled her faint perfume, a hint of lilacs and summer honeysuckle in bloom.

"You flatter me. I'm a widow, have been for a full year, although it seems much longer. I came out here as a miner's wife ten years ago and saw little of my husband. I lived in tents and squalor, in mud and shanties, under pine roofs and tin. I saw men gorge themselves on greed and slake their primal thirsts on painted women. I watched them rob and steal from one another and friend slay friend over a crooked game of cards or a fifth of rotgut whiskey. I've seen it all, Mr. Gunn, and I made my way a long time before Mr. Jennings, rest his soul, died of the croup and lead poisoning over a few ounces of gold and silver buried in a mountain as baffling as the Sphinx of Egypt. But he died long before that, Mr. Gunn, and his place at my table was as empty as his share of my bed for a half dozen years before he gave up his whiskey breath in a final salute to blind folly and the greed that twists

132

men's souls into shapeless icons."

There was no trace of bitterness in her words, but Gunn sensed a rare intelligence in the lilt of her speech, detected a trace of brogue that bespoke a Scotch or Irish heritage.

He wondered, though, why she saw fit to tell him, a complete stranger, all this. She smiled at him enigmatically, and leaned back in the loveseat. Her smile was mocking, self-assured, but maddeningly beautiful. He wondered if she was making fun of him, or merely testing him.

"I—I lied to you, Mrs. Jennings. I'm not looking for a room here."

"I would be very surprised if you were."

"What's that?"

"Mr. Gunn. This modest household has become, and this is not of my doing, of course, an all-male boarding house. There's been little spoken at table without your name coming into the conversation in some way ever since you rode into Gallatin and, though I'm not an eavesdropper, it has been very difficult to avoid hearing your name and accounts of some certain exploits attributed to you. And now I'm curious. I pictured you to either be a man as wee as a weasel or a towering giant with bulging muscles thicker than his brain."

"So am I either?" Gunn asked.

"Why you appear to be a perfect gentleman, albeit a bit dusty, perhaps, in need of a bath and close shave. There is a certain desperate look about you that I find appealing, but I've always had a predilection for taking in stray animals, cats and dogs and the like. My boarding is proof of it. Of late, this household has taken on the character of a kennel. All it lacks is the tang of the veterinarian's apothecary shelf, with its liniments and salves and aromatic bottles."

Gunn laughed, twirled his hat around his knee.

"Well, ma'am, I can see you're a lady who keeps her eyes open and listens well, too."

"You want to ask me some questions. Would you like some tea, or spirits?"

"Tea, maybe. I've had enough spirits tonight."

"Yes, you reek of the demon rum, but I don't hold that against a man as long as he knows his limit and keeps to it. I'll fetch some tea, fresh made. I was reading when you arrived. Jules Verne, a French author. The teapot was whistling and I scarcely heard it. Do you read, Mr. Gunn?"

"Not much. And there's no mister in front of my name. It's just Gunn."

She arose, laughed, and glided from the room. Again, he was struck by her beauty and grace. She was a most handsome woman, and more interesting than many he had met. She had a head on her shoulders and that made her that much more appealing. He stood up, walked to the bookshelf, began looking at the titles. Some were in French, some in English. There was Shakespeare and Tolstoi, Thomas Hardy's "Far From The Madding Crowd," which appeared to be new, Lewis Carroll's "Through the Looking Glass," Disraeli's "Lothair," Mark Twain's "The Innocents Abroad," and Bret Harte's "The Outcasts of Poker Flat," along with Louisa May Alcott's "Little Women."

The book titles began to blur and he stepped away

from the shelf, aware of footsteps in the hall. Lenore appeared carrying a tray laden with cups and saucers, a steaming porcelain teapot, napkins, and what appeared to be pastries sprinkled with brown sugar. Gunn's stomach rumbled. She set the tray on a small table, began to pour tea into the cups. "I have no milk nor lemon," she said.

"Straight'll be fine," said Gunn and they both laughed. He took the cup she offered him and a napkin.

"Perhaps you'll have a crumpet," she said, passing the plate of pastries toward him. "Not the best, not even crumpets, but I call them that. If you have a sweet tooth, that is."

"I'll try one," he said.

She perched on her chair, her legs crossed, bared from foot to knee and it took an effort for Gunn to keep his eyes fixed on his tea and crumpets. Lenore smiled knowingly at him and ate and drank daintily.

"Now, what is it you wish to know, Mist — Gunn?" she asked.

"Do you know Owen Jamison?"

"I've met him. I detest him."

"But you board some of his cronies. A man who lived here, a marshal, was killed today."

"I know. Poor Mr. Smith. Or Barnett. Marshal Lescoulie came by earlier, looked at his room. Yes, I know there are ruffians under my roof. Coming and going at all hours. They keep to themselves, and pay their board, and as long as they behave in this household, they are welcome. From all accounts, you are not without sin yourself, Gunn."

"Do you know a man named Jim Belker?"

"Yes. I do not like the man."

"Have you seen him tonight?"

"No. But Mr. Jamison rode by and I overheard him tell two of his men to meet Mr. Belker at the Gallatin Hotel with two saddle horses."

"Belker kidnapped two kids tonight. Took them from the hotel. Marylee Paxton, whose pa and brother were murdered the other day, and Tommy Blue, whose mother worked for the Ransom family. She also was murdered."

Lenore's face drained of blood. "No," she exclaimed. "I'm so terribly sorry to hear such a thing."

"You wouldn't have any idea where Belker would have taken them?"

"Most certainly not or I would have gone to the authorities. As it is, in fact, I do not know very much about your involvement. I was hoping you might enlighten me. Indeed, the stories at table the past day concerned you, in the main, and I wonder if there is any truth to them. I heard one man say that you once had a family, a wife, who was killed and raped by a dozen men and that you hunted them down and killed every last man of them."

"True," he said.

"Is it not burdensome to you that you took a human life, several?"

"I did not like what I had to do, Mrs. Jennings."

"Lenore, please. But you killed them. Without judge or jury, without legal trial?"

"I did. They were trying to kill me."

"Still . . ."

"There was no law in Jefferson Territory then. Not on the Poudre."

136

"How does it feel to kill a man?" she asked, her voice dropping to a rasp as she leaned forward in her chair. "A human life, after all, is a precious, God-given thing."

He looked into her hazel eyes, saw the wedges of gold and green against the nut-brown glimmer. She was hypnotic and she took him out of time and place, back to the time when he hunted the men who had ravished his wife, Laurie, left her for dead and then tried to put the blame on him.

The first man killed by the gun. A terrible, awesome power flowing through him, an unstoppable force that pulled the trigger. Then, the ground falling from beneath him, falling away and pulling him down as the bullets thudded into flesh and tore out muscle, bone, sinew, and blood. The man's eyes clouding over and the sting of burnt powder in his nostrils. The man going down, dropping like a lifeless rag doll into the dirt. The tight bands across his chest, and the swirling emptiness in his belly, a smothering, a giddiness like the effects of drinking a strong, forbidden wine, the dark cloud of regret rising up in the mind like a thunderhead billowing over a mountain peak, a breathlessness as if a wind blew hard against his face, emptied his lungs and sealed them up with a tremendous pressure. Just for that moment, Gunn had felt his own life mingling with the dead man's, his own spirit flying from his body into the atmosphere, to the heavens, or downward, into hell.

"I can't explain these things, Lenore," he said, and dropped his head like a man gone suddenly weary from the weight of his guilt. "It is," he said quietly, "a hell of a thing to kill a man. Even if he deserves it."

She came to him, then, sliding her cup and saucer back onto the tray, and embraced him. His cup and saucer fell to the carpeted floor and he felt the dampness of the warm tea soak through his trouser leg. She held onto him tightly and Gunn smelled the clean freshness of her hair, the delicate fragrance that wafted from her skin. He was startled at her reaction, felt his gut swarm with moths, beating tiny wings in a dark void as they flapped toward the glow of light somewhere beyond the depths, his loins seethed with an unbidden heat as if a candle suddenly flamed between his legs.

"Gunn, I know what you must have felt. I saw my husband shot down in cold blood by men whose faces I could not see. I saw him die in agony and in that terrible span of moments that seemed like an eternity, I wanted to kill the men who took his life. I wanted to shoot them and cut them, and explode them into millions of pieces."

She smothered his face with kisses then, and he took her into his arms and held her tight to him as he ravaged her neck and her earlobes, savaged her mouth with blunt, hungry lips as she squirmed and writhed against him, her robe spreading until he could feel the silk of her gown, the softness of the flesh beneath, pressing against him with a yearning urgency that rattled his senses.

"Lenore," he breathed.

"Come," she said. "I will shave you and bathe you and give you comfort in my bed. Do you want me, Gunn? Do you truly want me? Or am I imagining all this and just a wanton who has been too long without a man?"

"No," he husked. "I want you, Lenore. I want you more than I've ever wanted any woman."

He surprised himself by saying it, but it was true. There was something in Lenore that answered an ancient call in his heart. She pulled something out of him, out of the deepest part of him, that he thought he had long since buried.

"Gunn," she sobbed, burrowing her head into his chest, "I want you too, so desperately I am ashamed."

He lifted her in his arms and stood up. He carried her from the room and the light bronzed them with an ancient glaze for an instant, a soft glow that bathed only secret lovers in its light.

Chapter Eleven

The big wooden tub sat in a cubicle off the kitchen. It was half-filled with hot water that had turned warm. A pot-bellied stove in the room heated another large bucket of water. Steam plumes rose in the air, billowed as Gunn set Lenore down. She hugged him, began unbuttoning his shirt.

"You were serious, weren't you?" he said.

"I had been intending to take a warm bath tonight," she replied. "Now, I have someone very special to share it with and this is something I would not offer to any man but you, Gunn."

"You flatter a man."

"Hush while I get you out of your clothes. I want a look at this strong body of yours."

She tugged his shirt free of his trousers and peeled it off. She unbuckled his gun belt, wrapped it and set it on a chair. "Sit," she said, pushing him to another chair. He sat down and she knelt, pulled off his boots and socks. "I'll wash those," she said, "before you arise in the morning."

She unbuttoned his trousers, slid them down his legs. She jerked them away until he stood totally naked before her. She stepped back and raked him up and down with an admiring glance. Gunn felt self-conscious for only a moment as she let her robe fall to the floor. The silk gown clung to her body like a second skin, flowing over delicate curves, sweet roundnesses and graceful valleys. She took his breath away with her beauty as she slipped the gown up over her comely shoulders, and over her head. Her russet hair fell to her shoulders, glistened in the light of the lantern that burned overhead.

"Now, into the tub with you," she said curtly, "or I shan't be able to control myself. You truly stir a woman's deepest desires, Gunn. You bring out the wickedness in me just looking at you." She touched his chest, let out a long sighing breath. "Hop in, now."

He hesitated for a moment, drinking in her beauty. She stood so statuesque, so perfect in every line, that he wanted to pinch himself to see if she was real. She had the body of a much younger woman, lithe and smooth as alabaster, and her breasts jutted pertly from her chest, the dark nipples like tiny thumbs in the center of symmetrical aureoles. He let out his breath and climbed into the tub, her hand caressing his back as he slid into the warm water.

Lenore grabbed the heated pail of water, poured it slowly into the tub. "Warm enough?" she asked.

"Perfect," said Gunn.

She set the empty pail down and climbed in, her body even more beautiful when she moved. Like a nymph, she flowed into the water, sat opposite Gunn in the large oaken vat. She giggled, put her hands together and squirted water onto his chest. He laughed, and slapped his hand across the surface, sending a sheet of water cascading over her breasts.

"Oh, I like this," she said. "This is actually fun."

"Haven't done this since the swimming hole on Osage Creek," said Gunn.

"Where's that?" she asked, scrooching down into the water so that her breasts sank beneath the surface.

"A long time back, in Arkansas. Near a place called Fairview."

"Born there?"

"Uh huh."

"My folks moved to Kansas, from Kentucky. Scotch-Irish. The dreaded Scotch-Irish."

They both laughed. Gunn knew some of the history of her people. They were the history of his own, as well, somewhere far back in time. The British treated them like curs, shipped them off to the New World to get rid of them. They turned out to be the boldest pioneers of all, moving ever westward, illegally, like Joe Walker and his kin, and taming a hard land that broke men and women of lesser stamina. She was a proud woman, he could see, forged of that same pioneer stock, tempered on the frontier and now part of the big land that he loved so well, the mountains and prairies, the rivers and streams that swallowed a man up and held him dear and fast, close to the earth and sky.

Lenore stood up, reached toward a shelf. She grabbed a washcloth, a bar of soap off a dish. Gunn watched her lithe movements, stunned once again by her graceful form. When she sat back down, she began lathering the washcloth as he floated in the warmth, watching her in rapt fascination.

"Move closer," she said, "and I'll scrub your body. Then, if you like, you can do the same for me."

He scooted toward her. She put an arm around his neck and began to rub the lathered cloth over his shoulders and chest. She reached around behind him and scrubbed his back. She circled him, laving his skin with a delicate touch, soaping him between the legs, laughing as he squirmed. Her attentions were sensuous and he wallowed with her as she washed his legs and feet, tickling him between his toes and on the soles.

She pressed the cloth into his left hand, the soap in the other. As soon as Gunn tried to grasp the bar of soap, it squirted out of his hands, banged against the wall of the tub and sank beneath the island of suds. He drove a hand downward to retrieve it. He touched it, and the soap slithered away, toward Lenore. She giggled as his hand ventured up her leg, chasing the elusive bar.

"That tickles," she said. "Oh, I do hope you don't find it soon." He splashed toward her, his hand fumbling in the water for the soap. He touched her between the legs and his hand lingered, fondling her sex until she melted onto him. She reached for him, and grabbed his stalk. They swirled around in the tub like playful dolphins, kissing and stroking each other as the soap skidded under their buttocks and bobbed out of reach each time Gunn grabbed for it. He laughed and she kissed him. She laughed as he lost his balance and slid underwater. He came up spluttering and she held out the bar of soap in her hand. He reached for it and she squeezed it. It flew through the air, landed in the water with a *splat*. Gunn dove for it and missed, once again immersing himself.

"Oh, dear me," teased Lenore, "I do believe we've lost our soap again. Gunn, it seems to me that you have no intentions of keeping up your part of the bargain. I scrubbed you and now it's very definitely your turn to scrub me."

"You're a devil," he grinned, and tracked the soap down until he trapped it in the washcloth. He lathered it good and pulled Lenore to him, nestling her in his naked lap. "Now, I've got you," he said, "and I'm going to scrub you within an inch of your life."

"My, I do believe you intend to touch my most private parts."

"I do intend."

He washed her, then, lovingly, gently, slowly, as she squirmed in his arms, teasing him with her sinuous body. She scrooched her buttocks against him, entwined her legs around his waist, and swam over his back, her breasts grazing his flesh with a maddening softness. He washed her breasts when she came around again, first with the cloth, then with his bare hand as she nuzzled his toes with her own. He played with her, toe to toe, and they separated, rested their backs against the tub and looked across at each other with electric glances.

"Lenore," he said, "you're some woman."

"And you're some man, Gunn. I wonder if you're the lover I imagine you are."

"Only time will tell," he grinned.

"If you are, I won't tell," she laughed.

She swam to him again, embraced him and slid up his body until their faces met. She kissed him warm and lovingly, locking her arms around his neck tighter and tighter until he thought she would never let go. And, he didn't care if she didn't. Her tongue was a darting creature inside his mouth, and her lips swarmed over his hungrily as she mashed her breasts against his chest. He could feel the thick nubbins of her nipples pressing into him and when he slid his hand around her waist and drew her to him, her legs parted and she settled on his lap, facing him, rocking up and down until the tub sloshed with waves and splashed their faces and hair, soaked them with foamy lather.

Lenore broke the long, lingering kiss.

"I—I think it's time we—we dried off," she said. "I'll fetch us some towels. We—we can dry each other; 'twill be fun."

"Yes," he croaked, giddy from her kiss, his skin tingling from the exertion.

They rose out of the water together, and Gunn helped her over the side before he climbed out, dripping. She took towels from the stacked linens on the shelf and tossed him one. He started to dry off, but she reached out, grabbed his wrist.

"No," she rasped, "I'll do you. You do me."

"I don't know if I can stand it," he said. He smiled wryly and she sighed as she came close to him. She looked into his eyes and began rubbing her towel over him, never breaking her gaze. Gunn put his towel over her shoulders, like a mantle, and slowly began to rub her there. He slid the towel down her back and around her waist. They were like dancers in slow motion, like lovers creating their own dance. The dance was very old, like something made around a fire in a cave. They sensed this moment as something special between them and looked at their shadows cast on the wall by the lantern light.

Two forms, male and female, rose and fell and circled each other and the towels became sashes or scarves and they made graceful, gliding motions with them, fascinated by the shadow pictures cast on the wall. They were the dancers and they danced only for themselves and to make the shadows move with their wills. The shadows were images they could watch and marvel at from a distance, a distance that stretched through eternity, back, far back, into the primordial past, and on, into an infinite future that was beyond understanding.

Gunn felt as if he had been transported backward into time, into a place near Eden where there was only the two of them, meeting for the first time. He held her to him and she embraced him. They danced in small circles and broke away, watching their shadows do the same. She began to bend and bow and beckoned him to do the same, until their shadows seemed to have a life of their own. Her hair made ephemeral smears on the wall as she twirled in a pirouette, her back arched, her thighs thrust toward him. Then she would disappear behind the mass of his torso's shadow and her shadow would reappear again, on tiptoes, looking like a nymph sent down to earth by the gods.

Their dance slowed and their shadows melded together as she fell into his arms, lay her head against his chest. The silence grew in the room as they held each other and let their heartbeats slow. He felt her fingers dig fleetingly into his back and somehow tug nvitingly at his loins. She slid a hand down to his buttocks and pushed him into her and there, suddenly, was the heat of her in the coils of her thatch as she pressed hard against him, making the hardness come.

"I can hear your heartbeat," she whispered, her ear clasped to his breastbone. "It's strong and steady, like Indian drums, like the throb of the sea against the shore. It's a very comforting sound, Gunn, to a lonely woman."

"Lenore, you . . . you can't be lonely." His voice sounded far away to him, almost like another's voice, because he was bewildered by her, dazed by the magic she seemed to possess. She had transported him, somehow, beyond himself, beyond all worldly cares, beyond his past, beyond the present, into a sorceror's kingdom where the ordinary became transformed into almost mythical occurrences.

He stroked her hair. "No, you can't be lonely," he said again, dumbly, like a man in shock.

"Pull the lantern down," she said. "Extinguish it and take me to bed before I scream in frustration and spoil it all. I am lonely, Gunn. I have been lonely a long time."

He pulled the lamp down, blew out the flame and the darkness engulfed them. But she kept talking as she guided him to her room, their naked footsteps making soft padding sounds on the hardwood floor.

"When you walked through that door, I knew something had struck me, something wonderful and uncommon. No, even before that, I think. When I heard the men talking about you as if you were a legend. They fear you, Gunn, as I feared you, although not for the same reasons. These men, they talked about you with anger and with awe, and the more they talked, the bigger you loomed in my mind and theirs. They are afraid of you. Yes, and so am I."

They entered her bedroom and he saw the open book by the lamp on her desk. There was a quill and ink, paper, and he knew, without asking, that she had been writing before he arrived. The paper was foolscap and the sheet she had been writing on was curled from the heat of the lamp, glowed yellow in the light.

The bed was a lavish four-poster, with a canopy and brass fixtures. "It's very soft and plush," she said quietly, as she turned down the covers and pressed her hands on the mattress. "I bought it when I opened this place, knowing it would be my only comfort during the long, empty nights."

Gunn felt as if she had squeezed his heart with her hand. Her words tore at him, flayed him, although he knew she didn't intend them to prick him that way. She was just being honest, he knew, and even that made him feel a twinge of guilt, as if her loneliness was his fault because he had not found her all these empty years since his Laurie had died. And he did feel loss, if not shame for not finding her before this time.

"Lenore," he said, his voice a gravelly rasp. "I'm sorry you've been alone."

She turned, opened her arms. "Gunn, that's the nicest thing anyone ever said to me."

He went to her, took her in his arms, too choked up to speak. Her arms snaked around his back and squeezed him to her. "Take me to bed," she whispered. "Let me look at you under my canopy, sweet

148

prince, as I lie beneath you in surrender."

She slid away from him, onto the bed, and he followed her, like a desperate man, afraid she would disappear or change her mind. No, he knew she would not do that. There was no end to her. She was deep and exciting and full of startling surprises. He had known a lot of women, but he had never met one like Lenore. Yet he couldn't explain her, even to himself. He couldn't explain her allure, her fascination, even her beauty. That was what was so mind-boggling about her. Lenore was like no other creature on earth. She was a woman, but she was more than a woman. She was beautiful, but it was not beauty that could be painted or captured in words or song. She was like all of the best of the women he had ever known, yet she was unlike any of them. She was the siren of sailors' tales and bards' lyrical poetry, and the goddess of Grecian stories, but she was also warm and real and sensuous, deep as the mightiest of oceans, and more mysterious than the great Sphinx of Egypt or the endless dark heaven with its millions of winking stars.

The lamplight softened her features, chiseled them in comely relief as he lay next to her, caressing her. He kissed her earlobe and she stretched like a cat, nestled closer to him. He kissed her mouth, and she crooned a sigh into his ear.

"Fuck me, Gunn," she breathed, and he fell head-long into the web of her unfolding mystery. She grasped his manhood in her hand and pulled it out full length, held it until it turned rigid as bone. "Fuck me gentle, sweet prince, and teach me how you love."

She wriggled beneath him and he rose above her

149

like some majestic god rising from the ancient conjurer's loam and the light danced in her hazel eyes like sprinkled fairy dust.

"Yes, yes," she gasped, as he entered her, glided smooth into her warm deep sheath. "Teach me everything."

"You *are* everything," he said. "Right now, you are all I know; all I want to know."

She bucked with a sudden spasm, then, as he slid to the core of her, raked his back with gentle talons as her back arched and her thighs shook with the pleasure of him.

She closed her eyes and he looked away for a moment, sensing movement.

There, on the wall, were their shadows, flickering like cave paintings come to life in the heat of the explorer's torch.

Chapter Twelve

Gunn awoke to the smell of sausage cooking. Feeble sunlight filtered through the heavy drapes covering the windows. He looked up at the pink canopy above him, brought his waking brain into alignment with his surroundings. He remembered leaving her during the night to bring Esquire into her stable. She was still waiting for him when he returned. Now, he felt clean and refreshed, even after having had little sleep. He rubbed the sleep from his eyes, shook his head to clear out the last of the cobwebs. He heard the far-off clank of a pan; then, footsteps padding softly down the hall.

Lenore appeared in the doorway, wearing a tan skirt, a soft blouse of linsey-woolsey, carrying a load of towels, his clothing and steaming pan of hot water. She carried shaving soap and a straight razor in her hand.

"Ah, my giant young prince, you have awakened," she said in that lilting half-brogue of hers. "Don't move. I am going to give you a wonderful shave and then we'll break our fast with biscuits and gravy and sausage and fresh eggs."

"I wondered, when I saw that razor, if you were coming to shave me or cut my throat."

She laughed, set the things down on a small table, carried it to the side of the bed. "Oh, now, you would not deserve that, lover. You made a lonesome widow very happy last night. You were magnificent. I didn't know there was a man on this green earth with such stamina."

"There you go with your flattery. It'll work too."

"Oh?"

"Yes, Lenore. I want you again. I will always want you again."

He wasn't sure, but he thought she blushed. "Hush," she said, "and scoot over here close."

"Gladly," he said, and wriggled out from under the covers. She looked at his nakedness and sighed.

"Are you always that way when you wake up?" she asked.

"Damned near always."

"I'm tempted, but you did say you had things to do. Find those children."

"You're right," he said. He lay back, his manhood subsiding, let her soak his face with hot water, then lather it. She was expert with the razor, sliding it over his stubble as well as any barber. She talked as he lay there, soothed by her voice, floating in a lassitude of peacefulness that was rare in his life.

She told him of her life in the mining camps, of her girlhood and the hardships she faced with her late husband, Stewart Jennings.

"Bye the bye," she said, reaching under one of the towels. "I found this on the floor in the room where we bathed. I believe it fell out of your pocket." She handed the folded envelope to Gunn. She gave his face one last swipe with a damp towel, dried the chin and cheeks while he opened the envelope.

"I had forgotten all about this," he said. "Lescoulie left it at the hotel for me yesterday."

"What is it?"

"A list of people the marshal believes were murdered, perhaps by a bunch of vigilantes."

Lenore shuddered. "I loathe the very word 'vigilantes'," she said. " 'Cowards' is more to the point. Men who proclaim self-righteousness, then kill in the name of justice. Hiding their faces behind hoods or kerchiefs."

"Your husband's name is on the list," Gunn said quietly.

Lenore looked at him for a long moment. She snorted and her face screwed up into a look of contempt. She gave him a mocking, wry smile, dabbed around his eyes. "Vigilantes, indeed. Murderers!"

Gunn pushed away his plate, patted his full belly. He took a last sip of his coffee, looked across the table. "Lenore, I've got to go."

"I know," she said, putting her hand atop his.

"I'd like to think I can come back."

"Gunn, you don't have to ask."

"I don't want to take more than is offered."

She started to sniffle, smiled. "Get on with you, now. I've packed you some food to take in those rather tattered saddlebags of yours. I boiled you some eggs, wrapped some fresh chicken, and there's hardtack." He looked over her shoulder at his saddlebags on the counter. He hadn't noticed them before.

"There's two quarts of grain in there, for your horse. He's really a fine horse."

"You put out grain for him too," he said.

"Of course," she laughed.

"You know how to take care of a man."

"Gunn, off with you, this minute, or you'll not leave the house until another dawn passes."

There were words between them left unspoken. He rose from his chair, took her into his arms. He held her a long time, felt the quiet strength in her back and shoulders, the warm softness of her breasts. He tilted her head upwards, kissed her long and lingering on the mouth.

"I'll be back," he husked.

"I'll be waiting for you," she whispered.

The U.S. Government Land Office was buried in a jumble of falsefronts on a back street, on Alder, near the corner of 3rd. Gunn tied Esquire to the hitchrail, adjusted his brim to shield his eyes from the mid-morning sun and stepped over the broken boardwalk, and opened the creaking door to the office.

He stepped up to the broad counter, pulled the list of names Lescoulie had left him from his pocket. He spread it open, ironed out the creases with his palm. A woman seated at a desk, blowsy in a fluffy dress, a trace of rouge rubbed crookedly over her lips, looked up at him. A small, wizened man wearing a striped shirt, dark suspenders and black trousers, finished quilling in something in a ledger.

"Sir?" asked the woman. "Do you wish to file a claim?"

The small man looked up, saw Gunn standing there, and cleared his throat. He wore overly large horn-rimmed spectacles which gave his pinched face the look of an enormous fly. Strips of hair plastered to his balding dome testified to his vanity.

"I want to check some claims," he said.

"Check some claims?" asked the little man. "What do you mean, sir?"

"I have a list of names here, and I want to see who has filed claim on these properties."

The woman opened her mouth, but the small man waved her to silence. "I'll attend to this gentleman, Martha," he said. He scraped his chair back, rose to his feet. He was not much taller when he stood up than he had been when seated.

He put his hands flat on the counter, as if establishing that he was in charge and Gunn would have to go through him to look into any of his precious ledgers.

"I'm Mortimer Coolidge, the clerk here," he said, his voice one tone below a squeak. "Perhaps you might clarify the purpose of your visit. Are you a government official?"

"No," said Gunn, already annoyed with the little bureaucrat.

"What is it you have there, sir?"

"A list of names. Given to me by Marshal Lescoulie."

"Oh, that's different, then. Are you a deputy, then?"

Gunn fixed Coolidge with a look. The man cleared his throat. Gunn shoved the list at him. The clerk picked it up, glanced at it intently. The paper shook in his tiny skeletal hands.

"Why, these persons are all dead, I believe," he said.

"Anything else they have in common?" asked Gunn dryly.

The woman, Martha, pretended not to eavesdrop as she scratched her quill pen on foolscap documents, rattled papers noisily. She was listening to every word.

"Maybe. Might be. I—I see one name here, no two, and here's another, that are now owned by a local company."

"Would that be Gallatin Mining?"

"Why, ah yes, I believe so."

"And is Gallatin Mining owned by one Owen Jamison?"

The woman's face turned ashen.

"Ah, well, ah, yes, I believe so," stammered Coolidge.

"Tell me more about this one, Coolidge," said Gunn, jabbing a finger into the name of Ransom, which was the last name on the list. Gunn had added it himself before leaving Lenore's home that morning.

"Mr. Parsons filed on that property an hour ago," said Helen curtly.

"That will be fine, Mrs. Fowler," said Coolidge, annoyed at her intrusion.

"Any mention of a mining claim on the Ransom property?"

"There were documents pertaining to that," said the government clerk.

"Who owns the property, then?"

"Mr. Parsons filed bills of sale, a deed of trust."

"Do you verify all such documents?" asked Gunn.

"Naturally," said Coolidge impatiently. "Signatures, too. I assure you, sir, all of the documents filed by Mr. Parsons on behalf of Gallatin Mining are properly notarized and all land claims are thoroughly verified by the U.S. Attorney in Billings."

"Who is the notary on these documents?" asked Gunn.

"Mr. MacGregor," replied Coolidge.

Gunn smiled wryly. "Cassius Llewellyn MacGregor," he said cryptically.

Coolidge said nothing.

"I wonder," said Gunn, "if Mr. MacGregor is not also an officer in the Gallatin Mining Company."

"Yes, he is," said Martha Fowler. Coolidge withered her with a look, and she went back to her books, pouting. Gunn wanted to hug her at that moment.

"Mr. Coolidge," he said, "I'm going to leave this list of names with you. I'd like you to check your records and see if Gallatin Mining now owns property originally deeded to these men."

"I don't see—"

"Just do it. Marshal Lescoulie will be very interested in your results. And," added Gunn, "so will I. Take a close look at both the Jennings' claim and one that was once owned by Lee Moore."

"A Mister Gordon Quint was in this morning, asking about that very same property. As for Jennings, I told his widow that he never filed a proper claim in the first place."

"But you didn't check real close, did you, Coolidge?"

Coolidge drew himself up, opened his mouth, but Gunn turned on his heel and walked from the office. He did not miss the look of smug satisfaction on

Martha Fowler's lumpy face, the grin marred by the crooked streak of rouge on her lips.

He blew her a kiss as he closed the door.

Gunn found that MacGregor's notary public office was on the second floor, above Montana Hardware, on Poplar and First. MacGregor's office was closed and a man named Wheeler, who owned the hardware store said he was in earlier, but left over an hour before. "Likely, you'll find him at the Roost this time of day," said Wheeler.

It was nearly noon by the Waterbury clock in the hardware store. Gunn had one more person to see in town before he rode out to the Novack place, but decided it could wait until after he saw MacGregor. Besides, he had some questions he wanted to ask Angel, as well. He left Esquire on a side street, paid a boy to watch him while he was gone.

"If anyone even looks hard at that horse, you let me know," said Gunn, giving the lad a cartwheel.

"Yes, sir." The young man was typical of those Gunn had seen in cowtowns and settlements across the country. He was a loafer, at that awkward age between boyhood and manhood, uncertain of what to do, with very little schooling, if any. Such men loitered on the streets, picking up a dollar here, a two-bit piece there. Sometimes they swamped the saloons or stores, or washed dishes, or ran errands.

"What's your name, son?" Gunn asked, after he gave the boy the dollar.

"Jack. Jack Whitehead."

"You ever go to school?"

"Some. Miz Sary, she taught me some readin'."

"You know a boy named Tommy? Tommy Blue?"

"I seen him some."

"Where does Miss Loomis have her school?"

"You know Missus Loomis?"

"No."

"Well, she got her a school right outside of town. White painted, got it a steeple bell. Used to be a church, but the parson he got run out of town fer foolin' with the married ladies."

"North, south, east, west?" Gunn asked.

"Why, thataway," said Whitehead, uncertain of his directions.

"West, then," said Gunn. "Obliged. Jack, you mind your Ps and Qs and there'll be another dollar for you when I get back. Keep him in the shade."

"Yes, sir. I'll watch him real good."

Gunn walked around the corner, glancing at the men and women strolling across the street and on the boardwalks. It was shortly past noon. He saw the Miners Roost across the street, down the block, and from the number of horses and mules tied outside to the hitch rail, it was doing a booming business for lunch. He started to cross the street when someone hailed him in a whispered voice.

"Psst, Gunn, over here."

He turned, saw the man standing in the shade between two buildings. It was Gordon Quint, and he looked nervous. Gunn strode over to him. Quint retreated from the street, beckoning to him.

"Quint," said Gunn.

"You headin' fer the Roost?"

"I am."

159

"Better not," said Quint. "I just come from there and I don't like it none."

"I wanted to talk to a man named MacGregor."

"He's in there. So is Hank Parsons. And Belker."

"Belker?"

"And a couple of others. They ain't any of 'em sittin' together, neither. And they're all watchin' the batwings to see who comes through 'em."

"What do you make of that, Quint?"

"I heard your name mentioned a time or two. They was all sittin' together and then they split up, scattered. They're all packin' iron. McGregor's sittin' at the center table, pouring whiskey down like rainwater. Besides Jim Belker and Parsons, they's two other of Jamison's men; a fourflusher called Whitney, got a lightnin' scar down one cheek, and feller name of Patterson, has a busted left hand and hair like a tangle of white wire. He's the biggest guy in the room."

"What about Gato?"

"Not there, but I seen him this morning when I come out of the land office. I could swear he tracked me here. I went into the gun shop over on Laramie Street, where most buys their ammunition and feller there said Gato bought himself an old Morse twelve gauge shotgun. He had young Shearman saw off the barrel to about fifteen, sixteen inches."

"So, Gato's only got one barrel now. Enough, if he knows where to point it." Gunn knew the weapon. It was Muzzy-made for Morse, had better than a fifty inch barrel out of the carton. Sawed-off, it could lay down a wide spread, cut a man in two at close range.

"Something's going on, Gunn," said Quint, "and

it's real bad. Those men are in an ugly frame of mind, you ask me."

"What about MacGregor? He armed?"

"I think he has a hide-out in his kip."

"All right. So we have five men in there. Maybe they want to call me out."

"I figger that."

"Angel?" asked Gunn.

"She—she's in there, acting real quiet."

"She didn't try and talk them out of stirring up trouble in her place?"

"Nope," said Quint. "Fact is, kind of think she was disappointed you didn't come back last night. She and me jawed some before those other fellers come in. I seen Belker talkin' to her—he come in first— then he looked mad as a striped-ass hornet."

Gunn considered his options. He could just go away—he had other business elsewhere. Or he could wait, take them one at a time whenever they showed on the street. He could walk inside and open the ball. He could come in the back way and call out Belker first. If he got one, the others might back down. He laughed to himself. He didn't believe any of them would back down. It appeared to him that Belker had something in his craw, all right. And where was Gato? The man was armed. He was in town. Somewhere.

No, he didn't stand a chance going into the Roost alone. But the longer he let this particular sore fester, the worse it was going to get. He wondered which side Angel was on. Maybe they had expected to take him out last night. She had invited him to her rooms. It was a thought. An ugly thought, at that.

"What do you aim to do, Gunn?"

161

Quint's question jolted Gunn out of his brief reverie.

"Quint, I learned a long time ago not to fight the enemy on his own ground if you can help it. The way I see it, the Roost is the place Belker and his bunch picked for a showdown. Gato is the scout. He's out here somewhere, roaming like a guerrilla. He turns me up, he drives me here, into their guns. Or he shoots me dead. The odds are all in the enemy's favor at this point."

"You got that hand down pat," said Quint. "So, you light a shuck and hole up somewheres until they scatter or forget about you."

"I could do that," Gunn admitted. "But a bunch like that just tends to get meaner and stronger if someone doesn't start putting lamps out."

"That's a damned fact. So now what?"

"You mentioning hornets gave me an idea. So now, I throw some smoke," said Gunn, "and see who wants me bad enough to come after me."

"I don't get your drift, Gunn."

"You will, Quint. Just stay out of the way and if you see Gato, you let out a holler."

Gunn's jaw tightened and a muscle quivered in the lower bone. Quint looked into the tall man's cold steel-gray eyes and shivered as if a cold wind had arisen out of nowhere.

Chapter Thirteen

Gunn told Quint what he was going to do. He also asked him a favor. It was the hardest thing he ever had to do in his life.

"You could die real quick," he said.

"Hell, Gunn, I wouldn't miss backin' you for all the gold in Montana."

"All right. The timing has to be right. A half hour from now, you go in the back way and wait for my move. Your hands steady?"

"As a rock," said Quint, grinning. It was a horrible grin and Gunn couldn't look at it. He fished his pocket wallet out, counted out several bills, gave them to Quint.

"Get the best," he told Quint. "Now, tell me again where each of those men is sitting. I particularly want to know where the big white-haired gent is squatted." Quint told him. "All right, we're set. Get going after that shotgun and I'll see you in one half hour. I've got some shopping to do myself."

"I'll be there," said Quint. "I can't wait to see the looks on those no-account faces."

"Just make sure you do exactly what I told you,"

said Gunn.

The two men parted company. Gunn stalked down the street to the Gallatin Dry Goods Company. He walked past flats stacked high with blankets, rolls of cloth, shirts, work duds, shoes, trousers. He passed the racks of dresses, went to the counter. A man and a woman looked up at him. A lone customer finished receiving her change, left the store.

"Yes sir, did you wish to make a purchase?" asked the man.

"I want a cavalry hat, a duster, two pillows, a pair of overalls, a red bandanna, and a cigar," said Gunn.

"Mister, I can sell you everything but the cigar, but my wife Chelsea here can run to the tobacconists while you're trying things on."

"Fine," said Gunn. "I want a big cigar that makes lots of smoke and smells like a tar factory. And I want a place to change clothes. I've got no more than ten minutes."

"Be pleased to accommodate you sir," as Gunn laid a hundred dollar bill on the counter. "Chelsea, quick. Buy this man a cigar. Buy him two."

The woman opened the cash drawer, took out a bill and scurried from the store. In her wake, motes of lint danced in the sunlight that beamed through the front window. The merchant began rifling the shelves, looking at sizes. He threw a hat on the counter and Gunn tried it on. "Too small," he said, although it fit perfectly. He sailed it to the man, who threw him a larger size. This one slid down Gunn's skull until it rested on his ears.

"Perfect," he grinned.

"Right this way, sir," said the storekeeper, not a

trace of puzzlement in his voice. He acted as if this sort of thing happened every day. He showed Gunn to a wardrobe which served as a changing closet. "I'll find you two pillows. We have the down, chicken feathers, or excelsior."

"The biggest you've got, and these overalls need to be oversized, too."

"Will you carry the pillows, sir?" asked the man.

"No, I'll wear those, too. Better get me a big shirt, too. One that would fit a big grizzly."

"I have just the thing."

Gunn pulled the curtain on the cubicle, took off his boots, stripped out of his clothes. He stood in his underwear waiting for the clerk. When he returned, Gunn put on the shirt and overalls, stuffed the pillows inside. He arranged them so that it appeared he had a huge belly. He put on the duster and the hat. Satisfied, he pulled on his boots, strapped his gunbelt back on and rolled up his own clothes. He transferred his wallet to the overall's pocket, left the rest of his papers and keys in his trousers. He stepped out, saw the startled look on the shopkeeper's face.

"Hold these for me until I get back," said Gunn.

"Be most happy to," said the merchant. "I must say, sir, you look, ah, quite different."

Gunn grinned. He followed the man back to the front. Chelsea was there, with two large cigars. Gunn bit the end off one, stuck the other in his overalls pocket.

"Have a match?" he asked.

Chelsea wrinkled her nose up, but her husband gave her a reproving look. She rummaged in a drawer, found a box of sulphur matches. Gunn took them from her and struck one on the heel of his boot. He lit the end of the cigar, blew a plume of smoke into the air.

"Now, mister, if you'll figure up my bill. The hundred's on the counter."

Quint went into Shearman's Rocky Mountain Trading Post and Gun Shop. He was out of breath, panting as he heaved himself up to the back counter.

"Back so soon, Gordy?" said young Keith Shearman. "Nobody's bought any guns since Gato came in here."

"I want a double-barreled breechloader," gasped Quint.

The young man, his blond hair cropped close, grinned wide. "You aiming to shoot someone, Quint?"

"Maybe some birds. You got a breechloader?"

"Expensive."

"How expensive?"

"A hundred."

"Let me see it."

"I made it myself, Gordy."

"Let's have a look. And make it quick, Keith. I got me an apperntment."

Shearman disappeared into the rear of the store, returned a few moments later, carrying a shotgun on a piece of oilcloth. He set it on the counter, rubbed the smudges left by his hands on the barrel.

"This is a twenty gauge, breechloading double-barreled rifle," said Shearman. "I modified a Whitney, improved the breech-locking, made brass cartridges for it. It won't fail you."

"I need a box of double-ought buck."

"One hundred twenty-five with a dozen cartridges, Quint."

"Sold. Clean it out for me, will you? I'm in a hell of a hurry."

"I'll give it a good swab," said Shearman.

Quint paid the gunsmith, hefted the rifle. It was lighter than he had expected. Most of the shotguns he'd seen were imported from Europe, muzzle-loaders, and they weighed more than a rifle. This one was light, with a minimum of iron furniture, twenty-inch barrels, a bead front sight, blued finish.

"You ever want to sell it back, I'll give you a fair price, Gordy."

"I'll keep that in mind, Keith. Be seein' 'ya."

Quint loaded the breech with two shells, stuffed the rest in his pocket. He stuck the shotgun in his belt, walked stiff-legged from the shop. He knew there was not much time.

Gunn got his change, waited in the dry goods store at the front window. At an angle, he could see the front of the Miners Roost Saloon down the street. A half dozen men entered, none came out. It was as if those inside expected a show that afternoon.

When it was time to leave, Gunn walked through the door without looking back at the shopkeepers. He could feel their eyes on him as he waddled across the street, to the sunny side, stepped onto the boardwalk.

He went over his movements in his mind. Everything depended on split second timing. He knew what he had to do and he had to do it quick. If he hesitated, or if he took too much time, he would be cut down. He knew he couldn't count on Quint for much. He was there for insurance, mostly, and Gunn still had reservations about that.

He stopped just before he came to the entrance of the saloon, puffed hard on his cigar. The tip glowed. Satisfied, he tugged the bandanna up over his face, stuck the cigar in his mouth. The kerchief draped over either side of the cigar. He stepped to the batwings. Just before he entered, he pulled on the cigar. He stepped through the batwings, blew out the smoke as he came inside. His face was wreathed with smoke.

His eyes scanned the room, looking for the biggest man in it.

Patterson was a big Swede. His thick shock of hair was prematurely silver, matted and tangled curls of it sprouted from his skull, cascaded down to his shoulders. He sat right where Quint had said he would be, near the door, to Gunn's right. Belker sat in the far right corner. There was a well-dressed man sitting at the center table, all alone. To his left, nearly hidden from view, Whitney sat in the corner, playing solitaire. Parsons was at the bar, one foot on the brass rail, facing the door.

Gunn looked like a buffoon as he strode straight to Patterson's table. He looked beyond, though, at another man and Patterson sensed no trouble. Out of the corner of his eye, he saw Quint at the far end of the bar, holding tight to his coat. Angel sat at a back table, staring at the fat man who entered the saloon wearing that big cavalry hat, with his ears sticking out like pot holders.

As Gunn came alongside Patterson's table, he drew his Colt. It was so fast, his hand was a blur. He rammed the barrel in the Swede's mouth, cocked the hammer.

"Get up, you sonofabitch," Gunn said softly, "or I'll blow your brains to mush." He extracted the barrel and set it on a point square between Patterson's eyes.

"By the Christ!" snarled the Swede. He looked up, saw the pair of cold pewter eyes above the bandanna and rose slowly to his feet.

"Now walk out that front door. You even twitch and I'll put holes all through you."

Every eye in the place was fixed on Gunn now. He prodded Patterson in the back, shoved him toward the batwings. Whitney's jaw dropped open, and he dropped the cards in his hand. Belker stood up from his table to see what was going on as murmurs filled the room. Angel craned her neck, but a man stood up in front of her and blocked her view. Parsons had a drink halfway to his mouth and he froze in disbelief.

"Where you goin', Pat?" asked Whitney, starting to rise from his chair.

Gunn jerked his cigar out of his mouth with his left hand, threw it straight at the gambler. Whitney's hand streaked for his pistol. Gunn shoved Patterson through the swinging doors, and took quick aim at Whitney. He fired and Whitney doubled over, crashed backward into the wall. The big exit wound in his back left a smear of blood as he slid down to the floor, his heart smashed with the force of the .45

169

caliber lead ball.

Parsons threw his glass down, stepped away from the bar, his hand slashing downward to his sidearm. Gunn turned, crouched and thumbed back the hammer, fired, before Parsons finished his move. The man screamed as the ball tore into his gut just above the belt buckle. He pitched forward in mortal agony, thunked into sawdust that began to run red with his blood.

"They're all yours, Quint," said Gunn as he whirled and crashed through the batwing doors. The Swede was still in shock, stood there with his back to Gunn, his hands lifted high in the air.

Gunn stepped up to him, removed the pistol in the man's holster, jammed it in the back pocket of his overalls. It was a big Remington .44, converted from percussion to centerfire.

"Who the hell are you, Mister?" asked Patterson.

"I'm the sonofabitch you've been waiting for," said Gunn, with a smile.

Quint pulled the shotgun out of his coat, cocked both hammers.

"Hold it right there, Belker," he said. "All of you, stay put."

Belker, trying to untangle his legs from his chair, froze. His right hand was already wrapped around the butt of his pistol.

Quint walked a few paces from the bar. He waved the other patrons toward the front. "You, too," he told the bartender. "No one will get hurt if you just do what I say."

Angel looked at Quint in stark surprise. Then she looked at Belker, saw the murderous look in his eyes.

"Better not draw that, Jim," she said. "Dirty Gordy will shoot you full of holes."

"Settle down," said Quint, a new tone of authority in his voice. "I'm real nervous and it won't take much to set me off."

When the room quieted down, he spoke again.

" 'Case you're wonderin', that was Gunn who took the Swede out, killed Parsons and Whitney. He could have killed you, too, Belker. And Mr. MacGregor, he's lookin' for you real hard."

MacGregor paled, swallowed.

"What do you want, Quint?" snapped Belker.

"I just got a message to deliver," said Quint evenly. "You toss me that hardware, butt first."

Belker, reluctantly, lifted the pistol from his holster with two fingers, tossed it toward Quint. It skidded across the sawdust-strewn floor, came to rest under the footrail. Parsons twitched one last time and then was still.

"Mac," said Quint, "you get on home and stay there. Gunn will talk to you, later. Belker, Gunn says to tell you that he'll meet you and Gato tomorrow morning at the stockyards, back of the stables. Nine of the clock, exactly. Got it?"

"I got it, you bastard," growled Belker.

"And another thing, Belker. If you've hurt those kids, you'll die real slow, he says."

"I don't know about no kids," said Belker. "They just plumb disappeared."

There was something about Belker's tone that smacked of the truth. Quint didn't understand everything Gunn had told him, but this seemed important.

"You don't have the kids?" Quint asked.

"Never saw 'em, I swear."

"Well, Gunn will see you tomorrow. Gato, too, if he lives that long."

"I won't forget this, Quint," said Belker.

Gordon Quint reached down, picked up Belker's pistol. He stuck it in his belt, started edging toward the back.

"No," said Quint, just before he turned to run out the back door, "I don't reckon you will."

Pandemonium exploded after Quint ran out. Belker started yelling, asking for a gun, and MacGregor slipped out the front door in a crowd of men who couldn't wait to get some fresh air. Men shouted, ordered drinks, rose up to study the dead men in morbid fascination.

Angel came up to Belker, smiled at him.

"Jim, calm down. If you do get a pistol, you probably won't live until morning."

"What's that mean, Angel?"

"I mean, if you go out the back way, Quint's liable to be waiting. If you go out the front, Gunn might shoot you. Why don't you just have a drink and collect your thoughts."

"Aw, shit, Angel. What the hell do you know?"

She smiled at him.

"I know that Gunn is a hell of a man. Lordie, but did he look funny in that clown outfit? I thought he looked familiar, but with all that padding, I didn't know it was him."

"You don't like that sonofabitch, do you?"

"Belker," she said, turning away, "that's none of your business."

"No, but it might be Owen's," he cracked.

Angel watched as four men dragged Parsons toward the front door. She stepped up to the bar, spoke to her bartender.

"Jerry," she said, "pour me a drink."

"Champagne?"

"No, whiskey. I'll drink this one for Gunn."

"Hey, who is this Gunn anyway?" He had not been on the evening shift the night before, but had heard all the talk that day.

"Gunn? He's the man that got away."

She drank the whiskey slow and neat, but it didn't help a damned bit.

Chapter Fourteen

Gunn slipped the bandanna from his face, let it hang from his neck and prodded Patterson toward the hitchrail in front of the saloon. "Pick out your horse," he said.

"The black at the end."

"Untie him and lead him around the corner. I'll show you where."

"You can't get away with this, Mister."

"I'd just as soon drop you where you stand, Patterson. You want to argue, I'll do just that. So what'll it be? Yes or no?"

"Goddamn you."

"I'll take that as a 'yes.' Now, get to it."

Gunn kept the Colt jammed hard against the edge of Patterson's left shoulder blade. The Swede untied his black horse, led him in the direction Gunn pointed him. The two men and the horse rounded the corner, met up with Jack, who had Esquire tethered in the shade. Gunn gave him another cartwheel. "I've got another one of these for you, Jack. You run down the street to the dry goods store. Tell them, I sent you for my clothes. I'll meet you out back in three minutes."

"Yes, sir."

Gunn removed the pillows from underneath his shirt, tossed them against a building. He mounted his horse before Patterson could make a move. He shoved the man's Remington into his saddlebags, rode around to the side of the black, jerked the Sharps carbine from the scabbard. "Now you mount that horse real slow, Patterson."

"Where we goin'?"

"You'd be surprised," said Gunn.

Jack was waiting for them in the alley in back of the dry goods store, holding the bundle of Gunn's clothes. Gunn paid him another dollar, stuffed his clothes in his saddlebags.

"What's goin' on over to the saloon?" Jack asked.

"Anyone asks, you haven't seen us, savvy?"

"Yes, sir. Thank you sir."

"So long, Jack."

Quint was waiting for him when Gunn rode up the alley behind the saloon. He climbed up behind Gunn, sat back of the cantle. "My horse is on the side street," said Quint. "We better hurry." No one had emerged from the back of the Roost, thus far, and they rode away without anyone chasing them.

"Quint, you're a sonofabitch, too," said Patterson.

"I sure am," said Quint, but he kept the shotgun trained on the Swede's back.

They reached Quint's horse. He dismounted, climbed up into his saddle. He was riding a clayback mare, 9 years old. "What now?" he asked Gunn.

"Have you got a place where we can hide this bastard out? I want you to keep the Swede for the night. He gives you any trouble, shoot him."

"Where you goin'?" asked Quint.

"After I drop off Patterson, I've got to see a couple of people. I'll be by before morning."

"That's good enough for me. I got a little shack I borried just out of town. Be perfect to hide this rascal out till you get back."

"Let's take the back alleys, and keep your eyes peeled for Gato."

"Gato?"

"Yeah, he hasn't turned up yet," said Gunn, the worry lines deepening in his face.

The three men rode west of town, passing the schoolhouse. Gunn said nothing to Quint, but he noticed that someone pulled down a shade as they passed by. Quint turned off on a trail, led them through low, rocky hills until all signs of civilization disappeared. Tucked back in the rocks, a shack teetered on a flat spot at the top of a low rise.

"This'll do," said Gunn. "We'll tie Patterson up, and you keep your eye on the trail up here. Those rocks in back should keep anyone from getting in behind you."

Quint dismounted, held the shotgun on Patterson while Gunn climbed out of the saddle. "All right, Patterson. End of the line," he said. Patterson dropped his weight from the black. For a minute, he looked as if he might want to make a fight of it, but

Quint cocked the hammers on the converted Whitney, and he changed his mind.

Gunn got his clothes from his saddle bag, ordered Patterson inside the shack. He set down the Sharps, leaning against the porch, drew his Colt, rammed the barrel up against the big man's shoulder blade while Quint took his claybank and the Swede's black behind the shack.

"Just pick a corner, Patterson, get out of those duds."

"Huh?"

"Strip out of those clothes and be quick about it."

Gunn, for emphasis, cocked the Colt's hammer. Patterson unbuckled his empty gunbelt, began to take off his clothes. Quint entered the room to see the big Swede standing there in his undershorts, glowering at Gunn.

"You hold him while I get out of this oversized outfit," said Gunn. He changed into his old clothes, tossed the new ones to Patterson. "See if those fit," he said.

"What you got in mind, Gunn?" asked Quint as Patterson got into the shirt and overalls.

"A little insurance," said Gunn, squaring his hat. "Now, get some rope, and we'll tie this bird up. He won't need the duster until morning, but keep it handy."

The oversized clothes fit Patterson and he didn't need any padding. The trouser legs were a little short. The cavalry hat fit perfectly. Quint returned a few moments later with some heavy cord. Together, he and Gunn tied Swede's hands and feet. Gunn ran a loop around Patterson's neck, from behind. "If you try to work out of that rope," said Gunn, "you'll choke to death."

"Looks like I'm set," said Quint. "I got grub here, water. Everything I need."

"I'll see you before morning," said Gunn.

Patterson lay in the corner, trussed like a bull-dogged steer. Wild-eyed, he looked at Gunn with pleading eyes.

"Remember what I said, Quint. This one gives you any trouble, shoot him."

"Nothing would give me more pleasure," said Quint, his eyes twinkling like crazed stars.

He watched Gunn ride down the hill and wondered if he'd ever see him again. Gato was still in town, after all. He had a new shotgun and he was hunting Gunn.

"I'll say one thing for you, Gunn," he muttered. "You got brass."

Quint settled in a chair by the window, the shotgun across his lap.

I hope brass is enough, he thought, as he began the long wait until morning.

Gunn circled the schoolhouse, rode in from the rear. It was very quiet. There was no sign of any children. A buggy and horse stood on the east side of the building, the animal switching its tail. It snorted at him when he rode up, swung out of the saddle.

He climbed the steps to the back door, knocked loudly. The hollow boom echoed through the building. He heard scurrying feet, whispers. He tried the door handle. It was locked.

"Who's there?" a voice called through the door.

"Gunn." He didn't recognize the speaker.

"J-just a minute."

More whispers and footsteps. Finally, the door opened a crack. A woman's face appeared in the narrow opening. She was in her late forties, thin, with frowsy hair done up in buns on both sides. She wore a long, print dress decorated with faded flowers. A brooch hung around her veined neck. She wore tortoise-shell spectacles over a bony nose. "Are you alone?" she whispered.

"Yes, ma'am. Just wanted to ask you a couple of questions."

"Come in. Quickly."

He slipped through the door, surprised at her furtiveness. "Are you Sarah Loomis?" he asked, knowing it was likely she was.

She slammed the door, pulled down the crossbar to lock it from the inside. She tripped the latch, as well. "Yes, come with me."

She led him to a storeroom, tapped lightly on the closed door.

The door opened. There, cowering in the corner on stacks of books, Marylee and Tommy looked at them with wide, frightened eyes. Marylee jumped up first, ran to Gunn and embraced him. She shivered when he put his arms around her. Tommy joined her and grabbed his hand, began shaking it up and down.

"Oh, I'm so glad you're here," said Marylee. "We've been frightened to death."

"You can come out now," said Sarah Loomis. "I think you're both safe for the moment."

The four went down the hall to a small kitchen and office where Mrs. Loomis kept her papers and textbooks. Marylee and Tommy hung onto Gunn's arms, gripping them tightly.

"I thought Belker had kidnapped you both," said Gunn. "I've been looking for you."

"Is that his name?" asked Marylee. "We saw him. He—he broke into our room. We were down the hall, and he didn't see us. We knocked on your door, but you weren't there."

"We ran away and two more men tried to catch us," said Tommy. "But we excaped," he added, mispronouncing the word.

"Yes, and Tommy said we should find Mrs. Loomis. We ran out here and climbed in a window. She just found us this morning."

"Yes, poor dears. They told me what happened. Why, I can scarcely believe such a thing."

"It's true," said Gunn. "I'm glad you're both safe. But it's not over yet. If Belker or any of the others find you . . . well, we can't let that happen."

"I dismissed classes today," said Mrs. Loomis. "But we can't stay here. It's cold and damp at night. I did fix Marylee and Tommy some breakfast. I was trying to decide what to do when three men rode by a while ago."

"I was one of them," said Gunn. Then, turning to Mrs. Loomis, "do you have a place for them to stay? Tonight and tomorrow, maybe?"

"Why, they can stay at my home, of course," the

180

schoolmarm replied, "but I live in town. Someone would surely see us drive in."

"Maybe," said Gunn. He pondered the problem for a moment, stalked to the east window, looked out at the town. "I've got some business to do tonight and tomorrow morning, but first we've got to see that all three of you are safe." He scratched his chin with his thumb.

"Do you have any big boxes here? Cartons big enough for Marylee and Tommy to hide in?"

"Yes, I—I think so."

"Good. We'll load them in the boxes, lash them to your buggy. Tell me where you live and I'll stop by to see if you arrived safely. I don't want to follow you too close."

"That might work," said Mrs. Loomis. Gunn thought she seemed a practical woman. "Come, let's look in the storeroom."

They found two cartons. Gunn told Sarah to bring the rig up to the back porch. While she was gone, he and Tommy lugged the cartons to the porch. Gunn put one on the front seat, for Marylee. He took his lariat from his saddle, lashed the smaller one to the back of the buggy. "Climb in," he told Tommy. He helped the boy inside. "Keep down and hand on," said Gunn.

Marylee got inside the other carton while Mrs. Loomis locked up the schoolhouse.

"I live at the end of Ash Street, north," said Mrs. Loomis. "A small frame house painted brown, with a brown picket fence around it."

"I'll find it," said Gunn. "Now drive slow and if

181

you're bothered by anyone, you scream real loud, Mrs. Loomis."

She looked at Gunn over the top of her glasses. "The children spoke very highly of you, Gunn. I don't understand what's going on, but my heart goes out to them for their tragic loss."

"I won't be far away," said Gunn. "I won't stop in, but if I see your buggy at your gate, I'll know you got home safely."

"Where will you be?" asked Mrs. Loomis.

"Busy," he said.

After riding by the Loomis home, and seeing the buggy parked at the front gate, Gunn continued north, circled the town until he hit the main road to Bozeman. He stopped, some distance off the trail, where he could see and not be seen, and ate the lunch Lenore had packed for him, drank thirstily from his canteen. He watched as the sun fell toward the western hills, fed Esqure some grain, rolled a smoke. There was little traffic on the road. A man and boy rode by on horseback, leading three mules. A loaded wagon, a tarp concealing its contents, drove by from the north, heading into town. Gunn finished his cigarette, spat out the slivers of tobacco that had stuck to his tongue. The tobacco left a rancid taste in his mouth. He checked his pistol, spun the cylinder. He waited for the sun to go down, suddenly weary, sleepy from the sound of buzzing flies and the silence of that empty place.

Later, when the land cooled in the darkness, Gunn

mounted Esquire and rode back to pick up the trail to Julie Novack's place. He didn't notice the man a half mile back riding an unshod Indian pony. The man was carrying a new shotgun across his saddle.

Gato, a patient man, had sat on a hill all day, above the town, watching every movement. When he saw Gunn ride out, he knew where he was headed. It was his luck that the man he hunted had stopped, waited for dark.

Gato worked much better in the dark.

Chapter Fifteen

A road trailed off east of the main road, wagon-rutted, weathered, washed-out in spots. Gunn turned Esquire up, hoping he was on the right track. He had come better than a mile and a half, and if Quint's directions were accurate, the ranch house ought to be over the next hill.

The sky was sprinkled with stars, the moon still set, when Gunn topped the rise, saw the valley spread out before him, dusted with a faint light. Cattle grazed behind elaborate split-rail fences, and he saw the lights of the house a little over a quarter of a mile away. A lantern glowed on the front porch, and a pair of windows on the side, one in front, shimmered bronze in the early evening.

The fences curved outward from the road before he reached the house, and he made a wide circle, coming up behind. He rode to the stables, checked the stock. The corral held four horses, another half dozen grazed in a small pasture, and he heard whinnies from the stables. A bunkhouse was dark, situated some 200 yards from the house, and a barn atop a small knoll reeked of hay and grain. It was quiet, when Gunn stood up in the stirrups and swung his leg over the saddle. He tied Esquire at the bunkhouse hitchrail and walked slowly around the dark side of the house. He stopped several times to listen, heard the squeal of bats working the air overhead, the lowing of cattle, and, underneath, so soft he almost missed it, another sound.

He cornered the house, lay flat in the dark shadows beyond the reach of the lantern. He put his ear to the ground, held his breath. *Well, I'll be a sonofabitch*, he thought. He looked up the road and saw the faint silhouette of the rider. He had heard the unmistakable sound of unshod hoofbeats on the road. Gato, he thought, didn't miss a trick. That pony had been shod before, but the halfbreed had taken the shoes off.

He heard sounds from inside the house: a tapping, boards creaking, a woman humming to herself. Gunn smiled, bent over and took off his boots. He lay them flat, snugged down in the dirt to wait. He watched as the silhouette drew closer, became larger.

Gato did not approach the house head on, but rode up the sidehill to the fence. There, Gunn saw him dismount, tie the pony to a rail. Shadows. The shadow that was Gato separated from the fenceline and the horse, crept slowly down the hillside. Now there was no sound to mark his movement. He was a good 500 yards from the house, and circling, as Gunn had, to come up from behind.

Gunn waited until the shadow disappeared at the opposite side of the house, then stood up, and crouching low, walked softly to the back of the house.

There, he drew his pistol, held it straight down at his side.

A few moments later, he picked up the shadow again, and watched as the halfbreed stalked a silent path to come up behind the corrals and stable. Then Gato disappeared for a long time and Gunn's eyes burned from trying to see movement in the darkness.

When next Gunn saw the halfbreed Apache, Gato was standing next to Esquire. He stood there for several moments. Gunn strained to decipher in his own mind what Gato might be thinking at that moment. The man was smart. He would wonder why the Tennessee Walker was hitched so far from the house. He would wonder if Gunn had gone inside, or was out there in the dark waiting for him.

Then Gato did something that surprised Gunn. He unhitched Esquire, began leading him toward the back of the house. He stood on the opposite side, using the horse for protection. Gunn cursed silently. The halfbreed was taking no chances. Gunn could see only the horse's dark bulk and blur of legs. Gato was as good as invisible. Yet Gunn knew he could see everything in his path.

Gunn knew he would be caught out in the open, without a chance for a shot, if he stayed where he was. Yet he dared not move too quickly, or Gato would see that movement, too. Yet he had to find cover or the halfbreed would spray him with lead without his being able to get off a shot.

He inched around the corner of the house, not touching it, his bare feet making no sound. He moved so slowly, he might have been a shadow crawling around the corner of the house. In the east, the low hills glowed silver, and Gunn knew the moon would rise soon. If it did before he had found cover, he was as good as dead.

His foot touched a sharp stone when he put his weight down, and he almost yelped, but stifled the impulse, gritted his teeth against the pain. He picked another spot, moved like glue toward the back porch. Step, stop, step, stop, Gunn backed toward the porch, measuring his progress in fractions of inches. And still Esquire came on, slowly, hiding the killer with the shotgun behind his 1200 pound, sixteen hands high frame.

Gunn reached the porch, ducked under it, stayed within its shadows until, once again, Gato and Esquire disappeared. Then it came to him, how he would do it.

Once, when he was a kid, his pa had told him if he ever got into a gunfight with a man, "you either stand on top of a hill and shoot down, or stay at the bottom and shoot up. Don't get caught in the middle."

There was no high or low ground here, it was level, but the principle was the same. Gunn emerged from under the porch and stalked to the corner of the house he had recently deserted and took up his position. He would give Gato the high ground. But only long enough so that Gunn could kill him.

When he saw Esquire, Gunn drew breath into his lungs, lifted his pistol up, aimed just behind the horse's hind legs. Then he let out a bellowing yell that ripped the night to shreds.

"Eeeeeeeeoooooouhhhhhoooooooooo! Esquire!" He cocked the hammer of his Colt, fired into the dirt behind his horse.

Esquire's muscles bunched, and he jerked away from Gato, tossing his head to free the reins from the breed's grip. The gelding galloped straight toward the right fenceline. Gato whirled.

Gunn dropped to the ground, cocking his pistol as he fell. He kept his aim steady. Gato hesitated, and Gunn heard the hammers cocking as he fired. The Indian was silhouetted perfectly against the western sky, on high ground, and Gunn heard the bullet thunk into flesh.

Then both barrels of the shotgun went off with a flaming roar. Orange flame and hot lead spewed from the smoothbores and shot rattled against the side of the house over Gunn's head. A window shattered, blowing shards of glass inside the house.

Gunn rolled, fired again at the crouching figure. He heard the bullet smack flesh. Gato grunted in pain, pitched backward. Gunn jumped to his feet, padded over to the fallen man, pistol cocked. Gato, tough as a boot, even when he was dying, tried to bring the shotgun up. Gunn snatched it from his hands.

"It's all over, Gato," he said. "You lost."

He saw the bare gleam of white in Gato's eyes. Gunn held up a stockinged foot, waggled it in the man's face.

"I didn't hear you," Gato said. Then his throat rattled like pebbles down a rainpipe and he quivered one last time. Glassy, frosty eyes glared up at the star-specked sky as the moon rose over the eastern hill, the biggest god the breed would ever see in this life.

Gunn left the dead man where he lay, whistled for Esquire, and walked to where he had left his boots.

He ejected the empty shells from the cylinder of his Colt and stuffed fresh bullets in the empty holes. He holstered the pistol, pulled his boots on. Esquire halted, reins trailing and stood near the fence. Gunn knew he would not go far. The horse began grazing before Gunn reached the porch.

He climbed the steps, stood to one side of the door and knocked.

"Who is it?" called a woman's voice. "I've got a rifle."

"Ma'am, put it away. I mean you no harm."

"Who are you? What was that shooting about?"

"Open the door and I'll explain," Gunn said.

"No. Go away or I'll shoot."

"You make it hard. I aim to talk to you, if I have to shoot my way in."

It was quiet for several moments. Then he heard a thud, the soft pad of feet coming toward the door.

"Tell me your name before I open this," she said.

"The name's Gunn."

The door opened and the woman stood there, looking at him. She wore a flimsy, diaphanous nightgown, and a blue robe of soft shiny velvet. The robe was open and the nightgown clung to her curves, hugged the dark thatch between her legs. She had dark, wavy hair, cut short, green eyes, an oval face. When she smiled, a pair of dimples appeared at opposite corners of her full, rubied lips. Her nose was straight and slightly hooked at the end.

"Well, Gunn," she said breathily, "I've been wondering if you would come out here. Who were you shooting at? And who was shooting at you?"

"His name was Gato."

Her face lightened in an expression of surprise.

"Did you kill him?"

"He's dead."

Julie Novack let out a sigh of relief. She gestured for him to come inside. "I never did feel comfortable around that man," she said.

"Yes'm," said Gunn.

She closed the door. Gunn saw the rifle leaning against the wall, a small carbine. He didn't look around the room because Julie drew all his attention.

"Come," she said. "There's someone here you'll want to see."

Puzzled, Gunn followed the woman across the room and down the hall. She turned into a bedroom on the dark side of the house. She walked to a table, struck a match and lit a taper. She touched the taper to a candlewick. The room bristled with the flickering light.

"What happened to her?" Gunn asked. There on the bed, lay Angel, and she was battered almost beyond recognition. Her eyes were closed. She looked dead, but he saw her breasts rise and fall.

"She came here shortly after noon, her horse near to foundering, all lathered up. She—she was badly beaten by Jim Belker. I cleaned her up. No broken bones, but I fear she is bleeding inside. I gave her some whiskey and garlic. She told me all about you, what happened today at the Roost."

"Belker did that to her?"

"And Owen, I'm afraid."

"Jamison is back in town?"

"That's what she said. She took that beating for you, Gunn."

"How do you feel about it?" He looked her square in the eye.

"Any man that would do that to a woman, isn't a man at all."

"But Jamison. He's your—your . . ."

"Lover? Is that what you're trying to say?"

"I reckon."

Julie blew out the candle. She and Gunn walked into the front room. It was a feminine room, with its lace doilies on the stuffed furniture, the knicknacks on the knotty pine walls, the delicate fixtures, but it was also manly, with the gun racks, rifles, pistols and original paintings of elk and deer standing on high mountain slopes.

"I'll pour you a whiskey, if you like. I want one myself. Poor Angel. She didn't deserve that. I guess we were all taken in by Owen Jamison, weren't we?"

"I wouldn't know," said Gunn tightly.

"A drink, then?"

"I'll drink with you, ma'am, if you'll explain how you and this Jamison hook up together."

She said nothing, but went to a polished cabinet, opened it. A tray full of bottles and glasses slid out. She poured two stiff jiggers of whiskey, gave one to Gunn, took one for herself. He sat on the divan at one end, Julie on the other.

She took a sip of her whiskey. Gunn tasted it, let it slide down his throat. It was smooth, of high quality. His eyes didn't water and his throat didn't burn.

"Well, Gunn, you deserve an explanation, and you shall have it."

"I'd be obliged," he said.

"I don't know how the story got around that

Jamison and I were lovers. Probably he wanted it that way. He certainly did not want anyone to know we were related, and I was somewhat relieved myself."

"Related?"

"Owen Jamison is my half-brother. We share the same mother. He was kicked out of the household when he was very young. We lost track of him for years, and one day he turned up here on my doorstep. My husband, Kurt, had died not long before that, and he was a shoulder to cry on. He said he needed a small stake to buy a valuable silver property. I loaned him the money and he repaid me soon after, with interest. Then he told me of other investments. Within a space of about six months, he informed me that we were about to become rich. I was gullible, at first, then I became suspicious. Upon my urging, we bought some properties in town, all perfectly legal, but the money came in too fast. A month ago, I went to see Mr. MacGregor and began to question him about our holdings. He was very evasive. When I spoke to Owen about it, he told me to stop snooping around. I wanted to throw him out, but I held my tongue. Perhaps that was a mistake."

Gunn showed her the handkerchief he had with the initials OJ on the corner, and the scraps of maps he had found in Jamison's room.

"Did he ever mention the Ransom property to you?" he asked.

"Indeed. He said there was the richest vein of silver he'd ever seen on it. He told me he was going to buy the property."

"He bought it in blood," Gunn said, then told her the whole story of the Paxtons and the hired hands,

Little Blue Flower and the Ransoms.

By the time he was finished, Julie Novack was in tears. "I knew it," she sobbed. "That is one of Owen's kerchiefs. He buys them in Bozeman. Oh, I just knew it."

"Well, it's about over now. If Jamison is back, then he must have killed the deputy marshal, too."

"Oh, no," said Julie. "Marshal Lescoulie is very much alive. He and his deputies, suspecting an ambush, had a gunfight with Owen and his men. Owen was the only one to come back. I expect Mr. Lescoulie will have arrived by now."

"Then I've got to see him, ma'am," he said, finishing off his drink.

"Yes, I can see that. Be careful. Owen is a very dangerous and devious man."

"I'm beginning to see that. Will you have any trouble over this?"

"Tell Marshal Lescoulie, I will be most willing to divulge all of my dealings with my half-brother and testify against him if he comes to trial."

Gunn believed her. He rose from the divan, realizing that he hadn't even been polite enough to remove his hat.

Julie got up, took his hand in hers.

"I'm glad you came," she said. "My mind has been in a torment ever since Angel . . ."

They both heard the scream. Julie froze, but Gunn raced to the hall, dashed to the bedroom. Julie came in a few seconds later.

Angel choked off her scream, stiffened, then pitched sideways. Blood gushed from her mouth. Gunn held her to keep her from falling off the bed.

There was a lot of blood, and it kept coming. Angel's face turned blue then, and she shuddered as her eyes went wide in fear. She slumped over in death and the blood stopped pumping from her slack, blue-lipped mouth.

"Oh my God!" sobbed Julie, as Gunn lay Angel out flat on her back, dabbed at her mouth with Jamison's initialed kerchief.

"Goddamn them," he said. "I'll kill them if it's the last thing I do."

"Yes," whispered Julie, dazed, still staring at Angel's waxen face. "Kill them, Gunn. Kill them for Angel." She paused, drew in a quick breath. "And for me."

Gunn did not say goodbye.

Chapter Sixteen

Gunn caught up the halfbreed's pony, rode it to the place where Gato lay dead. He threw the body over the saddle, lashed it down tight. He shoved the shotgun into the scabbard, walked the horse and its load to the place where Esquire was grazing. He didn't want to leave carrion like Gato for Julie Novack to clean up.

He thought of Angel lying in there, a young, beautiful woman, beaten to death by men of greed. The anger in him boiled, then turned cold as a swordmaker's steel. Men like Jamison were born poison. They infected everyone they touched, from the most ignorant hardcase to their closest kin.

Gunn had seen such men come to the West before, and they left a stain on the land, a taint on the wind, a festering cancer that fed on innocent people. These were the men who ignored the law or forged it to suit their own purposes. These were the men who killed the game and left it to spoil. They raped the land and pillaged it, without thought of the morrow or the consequences.

But Gunn believed that for every bad man, there were a thousand good and as long as he drew breath he would use his gun to protect those thousand and the thousands more who would settle the land and kill the weeds, bring the earth to bountiful harvest. The Gatos and the Jamisons were aberrations, misfits, who plundered and ravaged until the people's outrage was so great that they had to run from justice or meet it at the gallows tree or at the business end of a gun.

A man challenged Gunn at the edge of town, said he was deputized by Lescoulie. He looked at the body of Gato, let Gunn pass.

Gunn rode up to the U.S. Marshal's office, saw the lamp burning in the window. The shade was pulled, but Lescoulie's horse stood hitched outside. The street was quiet, almost deserted at that hour. The faint tinkle of a saloon piano drifted the sound to his ears as he dismounted, tied his horse and Gato's pony to the hitchrail. His boots thunked on the boardwalk as he walked to the door, tried it. Locked. He rapped soundly.

"Lescoulie," he called. "Gunn here."

Gunn heard the floorboards groan inside the office. The door opened and the marshal stood there, ponderous and weary, his grimed face yellowed on one side with lamplight.

"Been wonderin' when you would show up. What you got out there?" Lescoulie squinted into the darkness of the street.

"Gato."

Lescoulie let out a long whistle. "Come in, Gunn.

We got some talkin' to do."

The marshal's desk was strewn with papers, forms. He lumbered to his chair. Gunn sat down. He built a smoke, offered it to Lescoulie, who shook his head. Gunn fished for a lucifer. The marshal picked up one on his desk, struck it and leaned forward. Gunn's cigarette caught and he sucked in the harsh smoke.

"It was a mess over at the Ransoms," Lescoulie said. "We buried 'em. I kept scouts goin' and comin', got word that Jamison was on his way. We set up, caught them in an ambush. He got away. But I don't need a warrant for that sidewindin' sonofabitch. I've got men combin' the town, holding the roads out."

"I know," said Gunn. He dug out the initialed kerchief, the scraps of paper he had found in Jamison's hotel rooms. "The kerchief I found at the Ransoms. It's Jamison's. That's Angel's blood on it. The drawings were in his diggings at Foster House. There's more up there."

Lescoulie pointed to a feedsack on the floor. "I got 'em all," he said. "He ain't there. He ain't anywhere."

"He's somewhere," said Gunn. "Come dawn, he'll show. They'll all show, and if you keep your deputies out of the way, we'll get the whole bunch."

"The Roost is closed down."

"Angel's dead. Jamison and Belker beat her to death."

"Christ."

Gunn told him all that had happened. Lescoulie made no comment, but listened intently until Gunn was finished.

"You think your plan will work?"

"I do."

"Why?"

"Because, Merle, Jamison is a desperate man. Belker wants to notch me on his gun. I figure there'll be a couple more we missed who will be at the stockyards. They'll be vigilantes when they come after me, hiding behind masks. You checked Jamison once, but you're on his ground now. He'll come."

"I'll keep the men I deputized on the prowl."

"Just keep them away from the stables and the stockyards," said Gunn.

"Agreed. We'll meet then, in the morning. Where?"

"In front of the schoolhouse. We'll make a wide loop, come in from the southeast with the sun at our backs. Patterson will go in alone, we'll be on his flanks."

"What about Quint?" asked Lescoulie.

"Quint will want to be in on it."

"I hope it works, Gunn. I'm getting damned tired of buryin' good people."

"We'll make it work." Gunn rose from the chair, started toward the door.

"Gunn," said Lescoulie. "What do you get out of all this?"

"If you knew me, Merle, you wouldn't have to ask."

Gunn unlocked the door, let himself out.

There were men patrolling the street around the boarding house. They let Gunn pass through after he identified himself. He put Esquire up in the stables, knocked on the front door. Lenore opened it, rushed into his arms.

"I'm so glad to see you," she whispered and he felt her damp face against his.

"Angel's dead," he told her, and they went inside, sat together on the divan.

"I saw Gato this morning, after you left. I was worried."

"Gato's dead, too," he said.

"Lescoulie came by, told me what happened." She laughed. "I don't have any more boarders, it appears."

"You have one. For a while. I have to leave early in the morning."

"Jamison?"

"And Belker and the rest."

She shuddered in his arms. "It's customary," she said slowly, "in times of war, or trouble, for the women to take their men to their bosoms the night before they go into battle."

"It's a good custom," said Gunn, stroking her soft hair.

"Come, then," she husked. "Let us attend to custom before the nightbirds fly away and the dawn takes you from my heart."

She took his hand, and they walked to the bedroom, like lovers meeting for the first time, and perhaps, for the last.

Lescoulie looked at the giant, wire-haired man on the black horse. Night still clung to the land, but there was light in the east, a weak glow that flickered on the horizon.

"What the hell is he dressed like that for?" he asked.

"When I switch horses with him," said Gunn, "I'm hoping Belker will remember how I looked in that same outfit yesterday."

"You're a dead sumbitch, Gunn," said Patterson.

"Quint," said Gunn, "gag him before we send him in."

"My everlasting pleasure," said Quint.

Gunn unwound the rope on Patterson's saddlehorn, made him dismount. He put the man up on Esquire, tied his feet to the stirrups, his hands to the saddlerings on either side of the pommel.

"I'm hungry," growled the Swede.

The others laughed.

"We'd better get to it," said Gunn. "We've got a ride to get that light behind us."

Leather creaked and groaned as the men set out, making a wide loop south of the town, heading east. The glow on the horizon lingered for a long time, then the sky broke open. A cream slash rent the night, turned the shadows to ashes. A coyote yipped, then howled melodiously as the nightbirds fled the morning light.

Patterson, a gag in his mouth, the cavalry hat tamped down tight on his head, a kerchief over his face, the white duster flapping bright in the morning breeze, rode straight for the stockyard corrals. His face was red, his nostrils flared with rage.

Flanking him, on foot, Lescoulie and Gunn kept parallel to Esquire, crouched as they moved forward, staying to cover. Quint was moving in from the west, would take up a position behind the stables.

The silence seemed to expand to an unbearable enormity before it cracked with a deadly thunder.

Three men wearing bandannas over their faces rode out of the stables. They rode in perfect formation, heading straight for Patterson. On their vests, they wore vigilante badges, polished to a high gleam. They rode past the stock corrals, into the open. They separated then, spurred their horses to a gallop. Their horses picked up speed. In perfect battle formation, they rode toward the man Belker swore was Gunn. He recognized the horse, the same outfit he had worn yesterday when he killed Parsons and Whitney. Jamison, as the leader, rode in the middle. Flanking him was a dullwitted man called Cap, an errand boy who thought he would be in on an easy kill.

"He's alone," yelled Belker. "Get him."

The three men closed on Patterson. They levered their rifles, shooting fresh rounds into the chambers. Still the horse Esquire came on. Jamison brought his rifle to his shoulder, fired. Dust rose off the front of Patterson's overalls, and he twitched with pain. Two more rifles cracked as Belker and Cap fired at once. Patterson tried to scream, but the gag in his mouth held fast.

Esquire stopped. Patterson sagged, fell over to his side, but the belly cinch was tight and the saddle didn't slip.

201

"What's wrong with that bastard?" yelled Jamison. "Why doesn't he go down?"

"Shoot him, shoot him," screamed Belker. The three men rode toward the stricken figure, bloodlust singing in their veins. Too late, they saw Quint riding fast behind them, coming from the stables. It was enough distraction. Gunn and Lescoulie stood up slowly, the sun a brilliant ball of flame at their backs.

"Goddamn you, Belker, that's not Gunn," said Jamison as he rode close to Esquire.

"Shit," said Belker, "it's Patterson. That dumb Swede."

Jamison reined up his horse. Cap and Belker did the same. They all turned in circles.

"Drop your guns," yelled Lescoulie. "You're all under arrest."

Jamison swung at the sound of the voice, but Cap saw Lescoulie first. He brought his rifle to shoot. Merle shot him out of the saddle as if he'd been jerked by a taut rope. He hit the ground with a thud, as Jamison took a bead on Lescoulie.

"Jamison," said Gunn. "I just wanted you and Belker to know that Angel died last night. This is for her."

Jamison looked at Gunn in surprise, swung his rifle away from Lescoulie. Gunn drew his pistol. His hand streaked upward, the thumb cocking as the pistol rose. He fired and Jamison dropped his rifle, grabbed for his throat. He pitched headlong out of the saddle.

"Gunn, you bastard," snarled Belker, just before squeezing the trigger of his rifle. Gunn looked at him

202

straight in the eyes and fired his Colt. The gun bucked in his hand. Belker twitched as the ball took him square in the center of his chest.

Quint rode up, then, out of breath, brandishing his shotgun.

"Leave any meat for me, boys?" he laughed.

Gunn walked over to Jamison. He was still alive, gagging on blood.

"Jamison I hope you can hear me," said Gunn. "I saw Julie last night. She asked me to do this."

"What's that?" asked Lescoulie, wadddling up, puffing from his exertions. His belly looked as if it would topple him onto his face if it sagged another half inch.

Gunn leveled his Colt at Jamison's forehead.

"This," said Gunn, squeezing the trigger. Quint swallowed a lump in his throat. Lescoulie flinched as Jamison's head bounced under the impact of the bullet as it exploded his brain. The dark hole in the middle of his forehead was clean and bloodless.

"Christ," said Lescoulie. "Give a man some warning, will ya?"

"He didn't give Ed Paxton any warning, nor Elias, either," said Gunn as a coil of white smoke spooled from the barrel of his pistol. He holstered the Colt, walked over to Esquire. Patterson was dead. Gunn took out his knife, slashed the bonds. The Swede fell to the ground with a thundering thump. Gunn looked at the legend on the blade of his knife. It was in Spanish, read *No me saques sin razon, ni me guardes sin honor.*

Do not draw me without reason, nor keep me

without honor.

He shoved the knife back in its sheath, mounted Esquire.

"So long, Quint, Merle," he said, touching two fingers to the brim of his hat.

"Where you goin'?" asked Quint.

"To see a lady," Gunn replied. "Merle, will you take care of Marylee Paxton and Tommy Blue? They're at the schoolmarm's house, Sarah Loomis'."

"I will."

"Quint, you stay out of trouble. I'll be seeing you."

"Wait a minute, Gunn. You ain't gonna take up with Julie Novack, are you?"

"Oh, didn't I tell you? She's Jamison's half-sister. She'll help you straighten this mess out. MacGregor—"

Lescoulie interrupted Gunn. "MacGregor hanged himself last night, after you left. We went to his office to look at his records, found him there. He left a note, explaining everything. That's all we need."

"Well, what about Julie Novack?" persisted Quint. "You sweet on her?"

"It wouldn't be hard," said Gunn. "But no, she's not the one."

"Well, dang it all, Gunn, who the hell is it? It ain't Angel, 'cause she's—and it if it ain't Marylee Paxton, who I hear tell is of age—and if it ain't her, then . . ."

Gunn smiled, rode off toward the east, the rising sun of a new day.

"Damnit, marshal, where's he a-goin'?"

Lescoulie twisted around, squinted as he looked at Gunn riding off into the sun. "Quint, don't you know what a man looks like when he's been smitten?"

"Yeah. Kind of befuddled. Takes leave of his senses."

"Well, that's the way I see Gunn right now."

"I know he's going to see a lady, but who is she? He never mentioned nobody to me. Angel, he could have jumped in her bed at the drop of a hairpin. Could be he's goin' back to see Julie Novack. I hear tell she's a beauty."

Lescoulie laughed.

"Do you know somethin', marshal? I'm plumb dying of curiosity."

"I'd say he's smitten all right," said the marshal. "And I'd bet hard coin that it's with a lady named Lenore."

"Lenore? Who the hell's Lenore?"

"That's the one who appears to have carved her initials in that tall man's heart. And from the looks of him, I'll bet another fifty cents, he doesn't even know it yet."

"Lenore, Lenore," muttered Quint. "Do I know any Lenore? Who the hell is Lenore?"

Quint looked up, then, hoping Gunn was within earshot, but the sun was up full, blazing into his face, blinding him. He shaded his eyes with his hand, and squinted one eye.

But Gunn had disappeared, ridden behind a rise, or angled so, that he was already in town.

"Lenore," Quint said again. "Now that's some name. If'n only I could put a face to it."

Lescoulie sighed, reached into his coat for a pair of gloves. He slipped them on, clapped Quint on the back.

"Come on, Quint, let's get to work. We got some horses to catch, some draggin' to do."

"What about this Lenore? That mean Gunn's agonna stay in Gallatin?"

Lescoulie shrugged.

"It's not for me to say," he said. "Only Gunn knows what he's got inside that big old heart of his."

SHELTER
by Paul Ledd

#3: CHAIN GANG KILL		(1184, $2.25)
#13: COMANCHERO BLOOD		(1208, $2.25)
#15: SAVAGE NIGHT		(1272, $2.25)
#16: WICHITA GUNMAN		(1299, $2.25)
#18: TABOO TERRITORY		(1379, $2.25)
#19: THE HARD MEN		(1428, $2.25)
#20: SADDLE TRAMP		(1465, $2.25)
#21: SHOTGUN SUGAR		(1547, $2.25)
#22: FAST-DRAW FILLY		(1612, $2.25)
#23: WANTED WOMAN		(1680, $2.25)
#24: TONGUE-TIED TEXAN		(1794, $2.25)
#25: THE SLAVE QUEEN		(1869, $2.25)
#26: TREASURE CHEST		(1955, $2.25)

WHITE SQUAW
Zebra's Adult Western Series
by E.J. Hunter

#1: SIOUX WILDFIRE   (1205, $2.50)

#2: BOOMTOWN BUST   (1286, $2.50)

#3: VIRGIN TERRITORY   (1314, $2.50)

#4: HOT TEXAS TAIL   (1359, $2.50)

#5: BUCKSKIN BOMBSHELL   (1410, $2.50)

#6: DAKOTA SQUEEZE   (1479, $2.50)

#7: ABILENE TIGHT SPOT   (1562, $2.50)

#8: HORN OF PLENTY   (1649, $2.50)

#9: TWIN PEAKS — OR BUST   (1746, $2.50)

#10: SOLID AS A ROCK   (1831, $2.50)

Available wherever paperbacks are sold, or order direct from the Publisher. Send cover price plus 50¢ per copy for mailing and handling to Zebra Books, Dept. 2047, 475 Park Avenue South, New York, N.Y. 10016. Residents of New York, New Jersey and Pennsylvania must include sales tax. DO NOT SEND CASH.